Gordon groped fo  to the bedroom floor. He leaned over the bed, sweeping his hand across the carpet until he found it. Pressing the off switch did nothing to silence the piercing tones. He blinked, bringing the glowing red numerals into focus. Four-seventeen? What the—?

The noise finally resolved itself into the ringtone he reserved for Dispatch. He hoisted himself onto the bed and fumbled for his cell phone. Flopping onto his back, he thumbed the answer button. "Hepler."

"Chief, you need to get to Vintage Duds." Country music played in the background.

Irv. The night dispatcher. Gordon closed his eyes and swallowed the curse on the tip of his tongue. "Can't someone tell Betty Bedford there's no such thing as ghosts? I already did a full walk-through with her at ten. And eleven. Where's—who's on duty? Vicki. She's good with Mrs. Bedford. Let her handle it."

"No, Chief. You need to get over there. Now. She's dead."

He jerked upright and hit the lights, squinting against the sudden brightness. "What? And shut off that music." He shielded his eyes with his free hand. His heart pounded at a rapid clip, but his brain hadn't caught up yet. "Dead? Vicky's dead? What? How?" He jumped up and headed for the bathroom.

"No, not Vicky—she's already on scene, along with half the force."

"You're telling me Mrs. Bedford is dead? In her shop?" One handed, he grabbed toothbrush and paste, trying to uncap the tube. Damn cell phones were too small to tuck between chin and shoulder.

"Yes, Chief."

"On my way."

Also by Terry Odell

To close out my love letter, I wish for more sequels to see Penny grow and become a manager, and to meet more customers with unique stories that will warm many hearts yet again.

So that, in the end, she can finally hear Dallergut approve: "Now you have worked here long enough to understand how it's done."

With love,
Sandy Joosun Lee

To Allyson

DEADLY SECRETS

A Mapleton Mystery

Terry Odell

Welcome to Mapleton

Terry Odell

Cover design by Dave Fymbo.
Jacket design by Jessica Odell

For the real Gordon Hepler, who isn't a Police Chief, but wanted to play one in a book.

DEADLY SECRETS

A Mapleton Mystery

Prologue

"**You** have a visitor. A gentleman. Would you like to meet in the sunroom?"

The old man shook his head. "No," he said, perhaps a little too harshly. He gave a mental shrug. What did it matter? If nothing else, being old and dying excused all sorts of rudeness. "Here is fine." He managed a weak smile.

This nurse's aide was nice, not like the regular nursing staff—fat old battleaxes who acted like you should be grateful they bothered to check on you at all. Or pinched old biddies who seemed barely able to carry a food tray. The young ones were sweet, but they burned out fast. A wave of pain snaked through him, and he wondered if he'd be gone before she quit.

She plumped his pillow and raised his bed. "I'll be back in a jiffy."

She returned a moment later, escorting his guest. After pulling a chair closer to the bed, she flashed a sunshine-bright smile. "Ring if you need anything."

His visitor waited until she left, then closed the door behind her. He introduced himself, handed over a business card. The old man couldn't read the card without his glasses, but he knew the name that would be printed there. And the voice.

Reversing the chair, his visitor straddled it and folded his arms across the vinyl back. "Good news. I found him."

The old man whirred his bed up straighter. After three years of searching, could it be possible? His heart fluttered. "You're certain?"

He studied his visitor. They'd never met face to face. The man appeared older than he'd sounded on the phone. Craggy face, broad nose. A fringe of gray hair circled a freckled pate. The odor of stale tobacco hung like an invisible cloak. The old man inhaled the long-denied pleasure of a smoke.

The visitor nodded. "I've got the address right here." He patted the chest of his baggy tweed sport jacket. "You have the money?"

"You'll get it. But—no offense. I'd like to see some ID."

The visitor shrugged. "No problem." He hoisted a hip and dug a wallet from his pocket.

The old man fumbled through his bedside table clutter for his glasses. Tucking them over his ears, he squinted at the driver's license the man held. "Very good. If you wouldn't mind, there's some stationery in the desk drawer."

His visitor brought the paper, with an envelope and pen as well. Without asking, he sat in the chair in front of the television and picked up the remote.

The old man moved the bed table and tilted it to a comfortable writing angle. He'd written the missive countless times in his head, but had never committed it to paper. Too many snooping eyes.

Frustrated that his hand shook, he concentrated on keeping the writing legible. Twice, he tore the paper into small bits and started again. To the annoying background noise of channel surfing, the old man managed to finish his letter. He folded it in thirds, slid it into the envelope and licked the seal. After taking a sip of water to wash the glue taste from his mouth, he tapped the envelope on the table to get his visitor's attention.

"I need the address," the old man said.

"The money?"

"Like I said, you'll get it." He tore a clean sheet of paper in half, wrote a note, folded it in two, and scrawled a name and address on the reverse. Handing it to the man, he said, "Give this to Phil. He'll get you the cash."

2

The visitor frowned, but they'd already discussed it. This damn nursing home demanded all his monetary assets. He'd managed to stash some cash before he'd moved in—for personal emergencies.

His visitor took a paper from inside his jacket. "Here it is. Took some doing, I tell you. Mapleton, Colorado is a one-horse town."

Hands trembling from more than infirmity, the old man addressed the envelope. Should he call? An ache that had nothing to do with the cancer filled him. What could he possibly say?

"There are stamps in the desk."

The visitor took the envelope and stuck a stamp on it. "Nice doing business with you."

"Wait. One more thing. When you get the cash, Phil will give you a small package. Mail it to the address you found for me. There will be enough money to cover your fee and the postage."

"Guess I can do that."

"You'll mail the letter right away?"

"Of course." The visitor slipped it into his jacket, tossed the remote onto the bed, and left.

The old man, filmed in a cold, clammy sweat, heart pounding, sank against the pillows. He thought about ringing the call button. No, not now. The nurse would come in with more drugs. He needed to think.

Chapter One

Five years later

Gordon Hepler yawned and rubbed his eyes. Next time, he swore he'd send Vicky McDermott out to deal with Betty Bedford and her ghosts. Vicky was a damn good officer, and Betty might listen to her—one of those woman-to-woman things. He'd told Betty to put in surveillance cameras, but she swore the ghosts in her shop wouldn't show up on tape. *Yeah, but the customers who pick something up and put it back somewhere else would.*

Then again, dealing with the woman was a break from his normal routine as Mapleton's Chief of Police. Budgets and paperwork. Damn, at thirty-six, he was too young to be riding a desk. He stared at the spreadsheet on his monitor. At this rate, he'd be blind before his contract was up for renewal. Would he accept it?

A promise was a promise, he reminded himself. Even if the person you made it to wasn't around anymore.

Shaking away the ever-recurring doubts about why Dix had insisted he take the job, Gordon grabbed his eye drops from his desk drawer, tilted his head, and dripped the fluid into each eye. Blinking, he waited for his vision to clear, then picked up the first night report. Car blocking a fire hydrant on Ash Street. Nice fine for that one. The Mapleton town council would be pleased.

He continued through the stack. Mostly citizen

complaints. Barking dogs, rowdy teens. He stopped at an altercation at Finnegan's Pub. Triggered, apparently, by an article in the *Mapleton Weekly*.

Gordon found his copy of the paper and turned to the article in question. *Holocaust: Fact or Fiction?* Great. Another one of Buzz Turner's articles, trying to parlay his job into one at a big-city press. Tabloid was more likely.

Drug use caught his eye on the next report and he read more carefully. His town didn't need drug problems. Officer smelled marijuana, but didn't find any hard evidence. Gordon checked the name. Willard Johnson. Not one he recognized. Address was Flo and Lyla Richardsons' B&B. Not a local, then. Table that one for now, until he talked to the officer.

He shoved his chair away from his desk and grabbed his jacket. He stopped at Laurie's desk. "Anything urgent?"

"No," she said. "Except your direct line's made it onto the telemarketer's list again. I've had a few calls." She waved some message slips.

"Save them. I'll handle it later. Meanwhile, if you need me, I'll be—"

"At Daily Bread."

He stopped and glared at his admin's grinning face. "I could be going out on a call, you know."

"Of course, Chief. The cinnamon buns should still be warm. Bring me one."

"One day I'll have a prune Danish just to prove you wrong."

"Change of routine might do you good."

"You saying I'm predictable?"

Laurie gave him an eye roll. "Who, me?"

Gordon grumbled to himself as he ambled along the three short blocks to Mapleton's most popular café. Ten o'clock was a perfectly normal time to take a break. And nobody in town would dispute the quality of the coffee and cinnamon buns at Daily Bread. En route, he checked the parking meters along the street, picking up his pace as he strode past Vintage Duds, Betty Bedford's shop. He'd deal with her another time.

At the door to Daily Bread, he paused, schooling his features into a casual expression. He adjusted his jacket and pushed open the door.

Angie smiled his way, her blue eyes twinkling. "Hey, Chief." She poured a cup of coffee, placed a cinnamon bun on a plate, and set them in front of an empty seat at the counter.

Gordon sat. "I want a Danish this morning. Prune."

"Need more fiber in your diet, Chief?"

Heat rose on his neck. "Forget it. It's a joke." He tugged a hunk off the warm pastry and popped it into his mouth.

Angie spent more time than necessary wiping the counter around Gordon's place. He recognized her look.

"Out with it, Angie. What's bothering you?"

"Nothing." She glanced around the room. "Can you keep a secret?"

Better than she could. "As long as it doesn't involve breaking the law."

Her eyebrows winged upward. "You know me better than that, Chief." She lowered her voice and made a show of wiping the counter some more. "Megan Wyatt's coming into town later today. To surprise the Kretzers. But you can't tell her I told you. And don't breathe a word to them."

The squawk of his radio cut the conversation short.

~ ~ ~ ~ ~

Megan Wyatt ribboned the silver Chevy rental out of the Denver airport, finally leaving the interstate traffic for the tree-lined road to Mapleton. To Rose and Sam. Foothills soon gave way to serious mountain terrain, and long-unused driving reflexes surfaced. Slow when entering a turn, accelerate through it.

After navigating a series of switchbacks, a blue car appeared in front of her, seemingly out of nowhere.

And watch out for idiots admiring the scenery.

Megan hit the brakes, avoiding both a collision and swerving off the side of the mountain. Resigned to following someone who had to be a card-carrying member of the ten-miles-under-the-speed-limit club, she settled in behind the sedan. Florida plates. A flatlander. Probably scared to death at altitudes more than twenty feet above sea level. *Geez.* And trying to use a cell phone? Here in the land of no bars? If he wasn't careful, he'd take the shortcut down the mountain. Straight down.

Tamping back her impatience, she eased off the accelerator, aware she had another twenty minutes before she'd be able to pass. She inhaled deeply and relaxed. Sunlight dappled the road.

How long had it been since she'd visited? Guilt filled her. Three years? Rose's seventieth birthday. A quick recalculation dumped another bucket of guilt. It couldn't have been seven years. How easy had it become to make excuses not to visit? In retrospect, they sounded so flimsy, but Sam and Rose had never complained.

We know how important your job is, sweetie. We're so proud of you.

And if Angie hadn't called, Megan might have kept putting off the visit until a funeral demanded it. No job should be that important. The phone conversation echoed in her head.

"You've got to get back here," Angie had said. "For Rose and Sam."

Her heart had skittered into her throat. "Are they all right?"

"Please come, Megan. It's been too long. Something bad's going to happen, I can feel it."

Although Angie's obsession with hyperbole hadn't diminished since grade school, Megan couldn't deny her friend's concern had been genuine. And, she admitted to herself, if she waited until things slowed down at work, it would be another seven years. Or seventeen. Things *never* slowed down at Peerless Event Planners. There was always one event running, one waiting, and one in recap.

Ahead, the blue car's emergency flashers went on. Was there a problem? She watched as the car slowed and pulled onto the shoulder. Should she try to help? Call 911? As if she'd get a signal here.

The driver opened his door, glanced her way, and adjusted a pair of sunglasses. As she approached, he waved her on. Glad to have clear road ahead of her, she passed, keeping an eye on him in her rearview mirror.

He rounded his car, walking into the forest. What could he be doing in the middle of nowhere?

Answering nature's call, idiot. She drove on, trying not to imagine what would have happened if she'd approached him. She could picture it. "Hi. Need any help?" She shook the image away.

Half an hour later, she pulled onto the main drag of Mapleton, where time seemed to stand still. The grassy park with its red brick paths filled the center of town, framed by the stately Methodist and Episcopalian churches on one end, the modest synagogue on the other. Government center and official businesses to the east, shops and eateries on the west. The same cracked sidewalks, the same planters filled with juniper and potentilla.

Nostalgia drew her around the square, slowing at what had been Sam's bookstore. When he'd retired—was it five years ago already?—the new owner hadn't lasted a year, unable to compete with the big chains and the Internet, not to mention the digital book revolution. Now, Vintage Duds, a second-hand clothing shop, stood where Sam had once fulfilled his dream. A rack of dresses sat on the walk outside the window.

She shook off the reminiscing—and a little more guilt at not being with Sam and Rose to celebrate his retirement.

She'd better let Angie know she'd arrived safely. Her

friend was expecting her; Rose and Sam weren't. Megan parked in the city lot and headed for Daily Bread. As soon as she pushed open the door to the coffee shop, she was engulfed by the familiar aroma of Angie's famous—and all too filling—cinnamon buns. Knowing Rose would insist on feeding her, Megan settled for a deep inhale.

Angie had her back to the entrance as she stocked the display case. Megan took a seat at the counter. Smiling, she rapped the salt shaker against the Formica. "Hey, what does it take to get some service around here?"

Angie whirled, a brief scowl replaced by a huge grin. "Megan! You made it." She rushed around the counter and threw her arms around Megan.

After returning the embrace, Megan inspected her friend. Other than her blonde hair cropped short instead of the ponytail Megan remembered, Angie hadn't changed any more than Mapleton had. Still a petite bundle of energy.

"Safe and sound," Megan said. "Wanted to let you know. You didn't tell Rose and Sam, did you?"

"Of course not. I can keep a secret."

For five seconds.

"Cinnamon buns are warm," Angie said. "Want one? On the house."

"Another time. I need to get over to Rose and Sam's. There's a law you have to arrive hungry, you know."

Angie laughed. "Rose is probably my biggest competition, and she's not even in the business. Coffee?" Angie didn't wait for an answer, merely poured a cup of the steaming aromatic brew into a thick, white mug. "How's everything in the world of event planning?"

Megan took a minute to enjoy the first sips. "Crazy. But Peerless will have to do without me for two weeks. I warned them I was going to be away from e-mail and Internet connections."

Angie pointed to the "Free WiFi" sign. "Got hooked up here four years ago."

"Last time I was here, you couldn't even get a decent cell signal."

"Still hit and miss."

"So, how's business? Place looks busy."

"Yeah, we're getting the hunters, fishermen and nature photographers." Angie winked. "And the word seems to be out that our baked goods are worth the detour. Keeps me busy."

"That's great." Megan glanced around. The other diners were engrossed in their food or their newspapers. She lowered her voice. "I'm here. Tell me the truth. Were you exaggerating, or is there anything concrete you can tell me? About Rose and Sam."

Angie's smile faded. "Not really. But they seem so ... draggy. Right after Justin showed up."

"Justin?" Rose and Sam's grandson. "He's in town? How long?"

"He's been here close to two weeks." Angie leaned forward. "I don't know. I have a ... feeling. And you know my feelings."

Yeah, Megan did. Angie had a minimum of five a week. Eventually, the law of averages said one of them would be true, which, of course, merely reinforced Angie's belief in all the rest.

"And you think Justin could be up to something? You're talking about Jumbo Justin? Justin the Jerk? Get real. He's a lump. Never gave a damn about anything. But he wouldn't harm Rose or Sam. He wasn't that kind of kid. Appeared, sat around, went home."

"Well, he's not sitting around now. You should see all the repairs he's convinced them to make on their house."

"Repairs? Then of course they'd be draggy. Living with contractors is exhausting. Especially if you're Rose and feel obligated to feed them."

Angie wiped the counter. "Maybe I overreacted."

Yeah, just a little. "No matter. Thanks for lighting the fire under me. It's been too long since I've been home. If there's a problem, I'll get to the bottom of it."

Megan waved off a coffee refill and gathered her jacket and purse. "I'll be in touch."

As she rounded the corner to the parking lot, the *whoop-whoop* of a siren filled the air. She stopped as an ambulance sped down the street.

When she realized the ambulance was headed in the direction of Rose and Sam's, she ran the rest of the way to her car. Coincidence? There were plenty of other homes out that way.

She tossed her jacket and purse into the car and peeled out of the lot.

~ ~ ~ ~ ~

Justin Nadell gripped his grandfather's bony shoulder. "They'll be here soon, Opa. Don't worry."

His grandmother tutted from the sofa. "I don't know why you insist on making such a fuss. I slipped, that's all."

"Rosie, you were unconscious," his grandfather said. "You didn't slip, you fainted."

"I don't faint, Sam. I got a little lightheaded. From the paint fumes."

Justin sat and slipped his arm around his grandmother. "Oma, I told you and Opa to leave until the work was done. A nice Florida vacation."

"I've been to Florida. It was hot. Full of mosquitoes and old retired fuddy-duddys."

The wail of the siren grew louder. Justin dashed to the front door, flung it open and peered down the street. Lights flashed through the aspen-lined avenue. The white-and-orange ambulance appeared, the siren shutting down as it neared the house. Justin waved to the driver and went inside.

He sat beside Oma, taking her hand. "They're here. Everything will be fine."

She glowered. "Everything *is* fine. What a waste of time. I'm sure there are people out there who truly need help."

"Rosie, it shouldn't hurt they take a look at you," his grandfather said.

She struggled to rise, pushing Justin away.

"Where do you think you're going?" Justin said. "Sit down." He motioned to the paramedics, then jumped to clear a path through the obstacle course of furniture in Oma's living room. Two men, one a stocky African-American, the other a tall, lanky blond, pushed a gurney into the entryway.

"Such nonsense," Oma said. She crossed her arms across her narrow chest. "Davey Gilman, you can take that contraption back out to your fancy ambulance."

The African-American man crouched at her feet. "Long as we're here, Mrs. Kretzer, might as well let us check you out."

"Listen to them, Rosie," Opa said. "The sooner they check you out, the sooner they'll leave."

She tsked, but unfolded her arms. "Oh, very well. Justin, why don't you bring some lemonade and the platter of cookies from the kitchen. Might as well give these nice boys something for their troubles."

The paramedic Oma had called Davey spread his lips in a wide grin, his white teeth gleaming against his dark skin. "They wouldn't be gingersnaps now, would they?"

"What else with lemonade?" Opa said. "And she baked them this morning."

Davey's grin widened even further. "Here we go." He wrapped Oma's arm in a blood pressure cuff and stuck the earpieces of his stethoscope into his ears.

"I guess that's my cue," Justin said, heading for the kitchen.

The second paramedic intercepted him, a gentle hand on his shoulder. "She's in good hands," he said. "She's known Davey since he was a baby. He loves her like family."

Justin stared into the cool blue eyes of the paramedic.

"To me, she *is* family." He shrugged away.

Justin arranged glasses and the pitcher of lemonade on one of Oma's serving trays. As he peeled the plastic off the platter of cookies, he heard the paramedic's radio squawk. He stopped what he was doing and rushed to the living room. Davey and his partner were fitting everything into their kit, concerned expressions on their faces.

"What's wrong with her?" Justin asked.

"Nothing," Davey said. "BP is normal, pulse is strong, respirations good, lungs clear."

Oma gave her head an indignant shake. "As I told you."

"It's another call," the partner said. "We've got to go."

"You and Tommy can't stay long enough for a nosh?" Oma asked. "Or Sam can put them in a bag for you."

"Sorry," Davey said. "Emergency."

"Is she all right?" Justin asked. "Shouldn't you take her to the hospital?"

"I don't think that's necessary." Davey patted Oma's hand, but shifted his gaze to Justin's grandfather. "Mr. Kretzer, make sure she calls her doctor."

"I'll do it myself," Opa shot a no-nonsense glare at Oma and levered himself from the couch.

Justin followed the paramedics out the door, gripping the porch rail while they loaded the ambulance and sped away, lights flashing and sirens blaring. He stood there a long moment, taking slow, deep breaths. He released the wooden rail, giving it a solid whack before turning for the house.

He spun at the sound of an approaching car. A silver Chevy Cobalt peeled into the driveway, stirring up a whirlwind of leaves and dirt. The door opened and a frantic woman raced up the porch. She rushed into the house as if he didn't exist. "Rose! Sam!"

"Excuse me? Ma'am!" He hurried after her.

Still ignoring him, she beelined to the sofa where Oma sat. "Oh, Rose. Where's Sam?" Her head swiveled as she searched the room. "The ambulance. Is it Sam?"

Did everyone in this damn town know his grandparents? Stupid question. Not only knew them, but cared about them. The slightest incident seemed to bring them out of the woodwork. But how had this woman gotten here so fast? He cleared his throat and strode across the room.

"Excuse me? Ma'am?" he repeated. "They're fine. Now, would you mind telling me who you are, and what you're doing here?"

For the first time, she seemed aware of his presence. "I could say the same of you," she said. She took a seat on the sofa and drew Oma into an embrace, apparently back to ignoring him.

~ ~ ~ ~ ~

Megan inhaled Rose's citrus scent, the familiar 47-11 perfume engulfing her in comfort. "You're okay? Sam, too?" Feeling Rose tense beneath her arms, she eased up on the bear hug.

Rose pushed away, squinting at her. "Meggie? Is that you?" She twisted toward the kitchen. "Sam! Come out here. Little Meggie's home." She returned her gaze to Megan. "Have you eaten?"

Megan smiled at the familiar greeting. Usually uttered before "Hello."

Sam shuffled through the doorway, adjusting his glasses. "*Mein Gott*, Meggie doll. It *is* you."

Tears sprang to Megan's eyes and she blinked them away. When had Sam gotten so *old*? Where was the spring in his step? Rose, too. When she'd hugged her, Megan had been afraid she might crack one of Rose's ribs. Guilt washed over her. No job was worth abandoning the ones you loved. She jumped up and rushed over to hug Sam. "I wanted to surprise you." No need to mention it had taken a call from Angie to get her here.

"This calls for a celebration," Rose said. "Meggie and

Justin. Both home together."

Megan studied the man in the room. If he was Justin, Rose and Sam weren't the only ones who'd changed.

She hoped her incredulity didn't show on her face. Or her wariness, as Angie's concerns threaded through her thoughts. She stood. Smiled politely. "Justin. Hi. Good to see you again."

She looked more closely. No more thick glasses, just clear mocha-brown eyes. A strong jaw line instead of a pudgy face. Sun streaks lightening his brown hair. And a broad-shouldered, muscular torso tapering to narrow hips. But muscles notwithstanding, if he was out to hurt Sam and Rose, she'd strangle him barehanded.

"Megan. It's been awhile. Hi," Justin replied with the same lack of enthusiasm.

Rose got to her feet. Sam moved to her side with a speed that took Megan aback.

"Rosie, you stay put. Doctor Evans will see you tomorrow, and he said to take it easy until then. I am completely capable of carrying some cookies and lemonade."

"I'll help," Megan said. She gave Justin a polite nod and followed Sam into the kitchen.

"The good glasses," Rose shouted after them. "And real plates. And not the everyday ones. And there's some *apfel kuchen*. Maybe some vanilla ice cream. Check the freezer."

"I know, Rosie, I know," Sam called. "As if after all these years I wouldn't know," he muttered. He took glasses from a tray on the counter, put them in the cabinet, and went to the dining room, returning with four cut-crystal tumblers.

"Let me, Sam," Megan said, setting the tumblers on the tray. She took his hands. "What happened? Why the ambulance?"

"Rose got dizzy. Passed out for a couple of seconds. Said it was the fumes from the painters. Justin insisted we call the ambulance—they checked her out before they left on another call."

Megan sniffed. "I don't smell any paint."

"Yesterday, they finished painting the trim. For almost two weeks, people in and out. Pounding and painting. Repaired the roof, the porch, the laundry room. Painted the whole outside." He shook his head and lowered his voice. "I think Justin was smart to call the ambulance. Rose, she'll never admit to any weakness. Always an excuse, a logical reason. Doctor Evans will see her tomorrow."

"I'll come too." Pangs of worry wrestled their way through her system. Could Angie have been seeing signs of Rose's failing health? Or Sam's? But why assume Justin had anything to do with it, deliberate or otherwise?

"She hates being fussed over." Sam's protest was half-hearted.

"Too bad. I'm here, and I'm going to fuss. She can take some of her own medicine."

Sam chuckled. "That would be a sight to see. Now, we'd better get the food out."

Megan went to the hutch and pulled out four dainty floral-patterned china plates, setting them on the polished cherry wood of the dining room table, then brought the cut-crystal pitcher that matched the tumblers to the kitchen. "You think we can get away with leaving the cookies on the everyday platter?" she asked, smiling. "Saves dirtying another dish." When Sam raised his eyebrows, she stood on tiptoe and planted a kiss on his bald head. "Yeah, right."

Once Megan was satisfied they'd met Rose's hospitality requirements, she carried everything to the dining room. Justin held onto Rose's elbow, escorting her to the table. He even held Rose's chair for her. However, he avoided Rose's apple cake with ice cream, and took only one gingersnap. She caught Rose's frown. He'd lose points for that one.

She gazed across the table. "So, Justin. What brings you to Mapleton?"

Chapter Two

Justin finished his cookie and accepted a second glass of lemonade. "Vacation," he said to buy time as he pondered the best answer to Megan's question.

"There's something wrong with my gingersnaps?" Rose's interruption was welcome. "You don't like my *apfel kuchen?*"

"Of course, Oma." Justin patted his stomach. "I'm still stuffed from breakfast."

"I remember when you were a boy, when you would come to visit," she said. "Such a good eater you were then. A joy to feed."

Justin managed a smile. He hadn't eaten for joy in those days. But at least one of them had been happy.

A loud rap on the door rescued him. "I'll get it."

He opened the door to a tall, broad man in a leather jacket over jeans. Blue work shirt, open at the neck. Black tee underneath. Hiking boots on his feet. And a gun at his hip.

"Gordon Hepler." He seemed to notice Justin's gaze fix on the gun, and indicated the badge clipped to his belt. "Mapleton Police. I came by to check on Rose and Sam."

"The paramedics didn't find anything, but she's going to see her doctor tomorrow," Justin said. "There doesn't seem to be any cause for alarm."

"Good to know." Gordon peered around Justin into the room. "Hey, Megan. Heard you were in town. Welcome home."

Good lord, did everybody know everything about

everyone?

"Gordon, come in," Rose said. "Have you eaten? We have *kuchen* and gingersnaps."

Or maybe the man wanted a snack. God knows, nobody ever left Oma's hungry.

"Actually," he said, "I'd like to talk to Megan for a minute."

Wouldn't anyone? The years had refined her looks. Thick, curly, dark brown hair. No more pigtails. Lush lips, spontaneous smile. Braces gone. Same hazel eyes, bright and intelligent. Maybe not quite so mischievous.

He was blood kin to the Kretzers, but she was their ward, who'd lived with them after her parents died when she was five. He was just someone who'd shown up during vacations.

Then, Megan had welcomed his arrivals with less than open arms, constantly devising ways to get under his skin, encouraging her playmates to follow suit. Eventually, she treated him with sisterly tolerance, but he'd never doubted she couldn't wait for him to leave.

Justin backed away. "I'll tell her."

"Wait a minute." Opa came into the room, pushing him forward. "Gordon, do you remember our grandson, Justin Nadell? I don't know if the two of you ever met."

"I wasn't here much," Justin said. "Only visited. Summers, mostly."

Gordon extended his hand. "My folks usually shipped me off to summer camp. Nice to meet you."

"Likewise." Justin returned the handshake.

"Hey, Gordon." Megan joined the group.

The cop gave Megan a quick, clearly appreciative once-over. "You have a minute? I thought we might walk and talk."

Megan turned toward Sam, her eyebrows lifted in question.

"Go," Sam said.

Gordon held the door for her, guided her with a hand at

the small of her back, and then the door closed.

Justin's cell vibrated in his pocket. He pulled it out, checked the display. *Shit. Not now.* Staring at the closed door in front of him, he frowned and let the call roll to voicemail.

~ ~ ~ ~ ~

Megan searched her brain for a mental file on Gordon. According to Angie's gossip updates, Gordon and his wife had split three years ago. Which spared Megan the awkward small-talk *faux pas* of starting a conversation with, "So, how are you and—" what was her name? Cindy?— "doing? Any kids?"

Instead, she kept her mouth shut.

"Let's walk," Gordon said, heading away from the house. Rose and Sam's house sat on a three-acre plot, most of which they left in its natural state. The air smelled of damp earth and what she always thought of as "green." Seven years of city living evaporated.

"I hear you're Chief of Police now," she said. "Congratulations."

He shrugged. "Small town. Small force. Mostly I do paperwork."

"But it's an accomplishment to be proud of."

"I don't know. When Dix—the last chief—got sick, he told the city fathers he wanted me to have his job. The council went along with Dix's recommendation, over the mayor's objections. Dix died about eight months ago, so we'll see what they do when my contract comes up for renewal."

"I'm sure you're proving yourself more than worthy."

He shrugged and cast his eyes downward. "How's life in the big city, being an event planner? You organize weddings, parties, stuff like that?"

"No, I switched to conventions about four years ago. Fewer hissy fits. Less stress. And I get to travel."

"Nice that you found time for a visit. I'm sure Rose and

Sam are glad to see you."

Was he implying she'd been neglecting them? She bit back a response and followed him along a path into the trees, concentrating on the quiet sounds of rustling trees and gentle birdsong.

"Okay, Gordon," she said once they were out of sight and earshot of anyone. "You didn't invite me out for a walk in the woods. What's going on?" Had Angie blabbed about her 'feelings' that there was more than renovations going on at the Kretzers'?

"You were on the highway about an hour ago, I assume," he said. "Drove in from the Denver airport?"

"Wha—what?" That flew in from left field.

"The highway. Into town. You were on it."

"Of course. It's not like there are many options. Mapleton's not exactly a major hub of civilization."

"Did you notice a blue Toyota Camry, Florida plates?"

She stopped midstride. "Yes. I guess so. I can't tell one car from another, but I followed a jerk in a blue car with Florida plates. He drove like a snail, and there's no way to pass along that stretch. He finally pulled over to—you know—relieve himself. At least, that's what I assumed. No gun, no camera. Why do you ask?"

Gordon pinched the bridge of his nose. "There was an ... accident."

She couldn't help but note the hesitation. "I assume it involved the blue car?"

"Yes." She noticed the furrows in his brow and the concern in his eyes. Somewhere between blue and green, the color of Aspen Lake after it rained. Creases etched their corners now, giving him a more seasoned look than the high school jock she remembered. She lowered herself to the log.

"Bad?" she asked.

He nodded. "Fatal."

She got up and paced again, searching her memory. "I noticed him at the switchbacks—the ones after the turnoff to

Aspen Meadows. He might have come from there—I don't remember seeing him before. I rounded a curve, and there he was. I almost hit him, he was going so slow."

"How was he driving? Any signs that he might be under the influence?"

"You mean weaving? A little. I figured he was looking at the scenery. Or not used to mountain driving. Especially if he was from Florida." She thought some more. "Oh, and he was talking on his cell phone, or trying to. Which could explain why he was weaving. Unless he was drunk or on drugs. But can't you tell that with medical tests nowadays?"

"Yes, but not as fast as they do on television." He gave a wry grin. "Besides, it's not our jurisdiction. State troopers handle accidents. We're strictly local. Catch red light runners, write parking tickets."

"And keep everyone safe," she said. "I remember the things the police did when we were growing up. Talk to the kids at school about drugs. Sponsor after school sports. Show them that cops are the good guys."

His grin widened. "You left out making sure no ghosts attack Mrs. Bedford."

"What? Ghosts? Who's Mrs. Bedford?"

"She's the owner of Vintage Duds."

"She sees ghosts?"

"Calls in no less than once a week. Says the clothes hold the spirits of their former owners, and she's convinced they're messing with her shop."

"See. Your job *is* important. You're protecting the citizenry from an entire other dimension."

He chuckled. "I'll keep that in mind. But let's focus on the accident."

"If it's not in your jurisdiction, why is it bothering you?"

"I've got some things at the office I'd like you to look at."

"Now? I just got here. I want to make sure Rose and Sam are okay." Should she mention Angie's harebrained idea that Justin had some ulterior motive for his visit? No. Angie'd undoubtedly blown everything out of proportion. She'd get a feel for things herself first. "Can't it wait until tomorrow? It doesn't seem fair to Rose and Sam to show up and dash out."

"It won't take long. I have to turn everything over to the troopers, but I want to show you first."

He was already standing.

Right. He was a cop. People did what he said. She quickened her pace to match his longer stride as they returned to the house.

"Let me tell Rose and Sam I'm going," she said.

"Tell them you have to take care of something in town. Not that you're coming with me."

"What? Why?"

"I'll meet you at my office. Ten minutes."

~ ~ ~ ~ ~

Justin heard a car door close. From his second-story window, he watched the cop car drive away. Seconds later, he heard Oma saying, "Thanks, doll," and Megan got into her car and drove off.

Justin pulled his cell phone from its case on his belt, pressed the voicemail button. Before the call went through, he mashed the button to cancel the transmission. Better not to know. He had no answers yet.

All Megan had said while they were eating was that she had some vacation and she wanted to visit. And she'd be staying here, of course.

His grandfather poked his head into the room, carrying Oma's plastic caddy of cleaning supplies and an armload of towels. "Your grandmother wants we should fix up Megan's bedroom."

"Of course," Justin said. As if the bedroom wasn't always ready, in case anyone needed a place to stay.

"And these go into the bathroom." Opa dropped the towels on Justin's bed.

"I'd better do some cleaning if we're going to share." Justin took the caddy. "Why don't you make sure Oma's being sensible."

"Rose has an extra mouth to feed. She's in the kitchen. In heaven."

"All the more reason to make sure she doesn't overexert before she sees the doctor." He pretended to examine the contents of the caddy. "So, where's Megan off to?"

"She said she forgot something, had to pick it up in town. I figured it was one of those female items. And Rose needed some things from the market."

Justin laughed. "As if she couldn't feed half the town with what she has here."

"I learned long, long ago never to contradict your grandmother when it comes to food."

"Go. I've got it all under control."

He waited until he heard his grandparents arguing about what Oma should and shouldn't be doing.

All under control. Like hell.

He crossed into the bathroom that connected his bedroom to Megan's. They'd never had issues sharing when he'd visited before, even in their teens. Somehow, now, sharing the bath felt disturbingly … intimate. But first, he needed to inspect Megan's bedroom.

He hadn't given Megan's bedroom more than a cursory check since he'd arrived. It was a generic guestroom, with a few dolls and stuffed animals proclaiming Megan had lived here. He moved to the window, struggling with the sash before the swollen frame groaned and moved upward in the track. He stepped away, feeling the fresh breeze waft into the room. Chilly, but it would get rid of the stuffiness.

Birds scattered from the oak tree outside. Memories of Megan's unsuccessful attempts to get him to climb out one night brought a rueful smile to his face. God, he'd been a mess. Fat, insecure. A coward.

And you're still a coward.

He checked the bookcase. A dictionary, a thesaurus, and some basic reference books suitable for middle and high school were probably Megan's. The rest were from Opa's extensive collection.

The shelves of books reminded him of why he was here, and a quiver of fear snaked along his spine. This might be his only chance. He checked the time, trying to guess how long Megan would be gone. He figured an hour on the outside—better shoot for half that. Using Oma's sprays and polishes to cover his snooping, he set to work.

Chapter Three

Each tick of the old schoolhouse clock on his office wall heightened Gordon's anxiety. Megan should have been here by now. The Colorado State Patrol would investigate the accident, but he didn't want to turn over what he'd found before he'd talked to her.

He buried the tingle of guilt. He wasn't withholding evidence. Merely ... rerouting it. Briefly. And, technically, it wasn't evidence. Simply something ... interesting ... in an accident victim's car.

When the accident call came in, Mapleton had been first responders. Dave Gilman and Tom Reynolds in the ambulance, and Ed Solomon in a cruiser. Technically the CSP was in charge of traffic accidents, but they were spread thin. Gordon liked to think of himself as a team player, and the troopers had never objected to the help. Gilman had inadvertently left an envelope belonging to the victim in the Mapleton ambulance and had turned it over to Gordon for safekeeping.

Tires crunched on gravel. He swiveled his chair toward the window and caught the silver gleam of Megan's car pulling into the lot. It took conscious effort to even his breathing. He slid the envelope into his desk drawer and sorted through Solomon's photos of the accident scene one more time.

"He's expecting me." Megan's voice preceded her sneakered footfalls down the corridor. Laurie's heads up call coincided with a tap on his office door.

"Thanks," he said into the phone. He hung up, took a breath. "Come on in."

"All right, Gordon, I'm here." Megan rested her hands on the back of the wooden visitor chair across from Gordon's desk. "What's so important?"

"You know anyone named Karl Franklin?" He blurted it out, no preliminaries. No way for her to anticipate the question, prepare herself. Unless she expected it.

Her expression was guileless. Her body language agreed. "No. Where should I know him from?"

He pushed a photo across the desk. "This the guy you saw?"

Bracing her hands on the edge of the desk, she leaned forward. And jerked away with a gasp. She sank into the chair.

"You recognize him?" Gordon asked.

She shook her head. "No. I didn't expect something quite so ... graphic."

She'd paled. Gordon rolled his chair back and hurried to her side. "Shit, Megan. I should have prepared you first. I need to find out what you know before the troopers show up, and I blanked out the part where you're not a cop and used to this. I didn't think. You want some water?"

"No, I'm okay. It took me by surprise." She closed her eyes, took a breath, and gathered her composure before opening them. "It's not much worse than the crime scene TV shows. I think what got me is it's real, not makeup. That I might have seen this guy alive. Is this Karl Franklin?"

"According to the troopers, yes."

"Let me see it again."

"You sure?" Had her reaction been to the bloody picture? The body was fresh, nothing grossly mangled. Blood covered the man's face, and the eyes had the glassy stare of death, but as accident photos went, this one was on the tame side.

Or did she know the victim and was reacting on a more

personal level?

She sucked in a noisy breath. "If it's important, I can do it."

"Keep thinking of it as a television show." In school, she'd had a reputation for being open, saying what was on her mind. Now, he saw nothing shifty, nothing deceptive. No red flags. He ignored the twinge of remorse for upsetting her with the picture. But it brought her emotional responses closer to the surface, where he needed them.

"I never got a good look at his face." She held the picture as if she were afraid to touch it.

"Look again, please," he said. "See if any details about the man you saw come to mind."

She nibbled at her lip. "All I saw was the back of his head. Bald on top. He got out of the car, looked my way, then went into the woods. He was wearing sunglasses. And I'm not sure I'd recognize him from this picture anyway. All the blood."

"Don't think about that for now. You said you'd followed him for some time. Close your eyes. Think about it. What did you notice? Was he alone in the car?"

She took a deep breath, as if she were preparing to jump into the swimming hole outside of town. With her eyes closed, she worried her lower lip again before speaking. "I'd say, yes, he was alone. He never seemed to be talking to someone else. I remember noticing the Florida plates, assumed he was a retiree. Maybe because he was bald, but that's silly. Guys can go bald at almost any age."

Gordon rubbed the top of his head, thankful he wasn't one of them. "True enough. But those kinds of impressions might be based on more than lack of hair. The way he stood, walked, might have played a part."

She picked up the picture, squinting at it as if she could see the living man under the corpse.

"I don't know, Gordon." Her eyes widened. "Please, don't tell me I have to identify the body."

"That won't be necessary." He smiled at the relief on her face. "But there is one more question." Trying to read her, he set the real reason he'd insisted on seeing her on the desk. "Any idea why he had these?"

~ ~ ~ ~ ~

Megan cast a slow, scrutinizing look at Gordon. His features seemed rigid, almost expressionless. He was being a cop, she realized. A recently promoted police chief, no less. Not the old friend who had walked with her in the woods a short time ago. He caught her gaze. Held it. Pushed the papers a little closer. She picked up the first one. People. Mostly faces. Blurred and grainy. She looked more closely.

Her stomach churned. This wasn't a gory crime scene picture, but she swallowed, concentrating on keeping Rose's cookies and apple cake where they belonged.

"You found this on the dead man?" She dropped the page as if it were on fire.

"In an envelope in the car. That's a copy."

The faces belonged to her. *All* the pictures were of her.

She shoved the page aside and looked at the second sheet. No pictures on this one, but in neat, block letters— Rose and Sam's address and phone number. And below that, some handwriting, barely legible. Gingerly, she picked up the paper and tried to decipher the faint scrawl.

Use the kid. They'll talk.

Realizing her hands were shaking, she let the page float to the desk. "What does it mean?"

"I was hoping you could tell me."

"Have you asked Rose and Sam? Maybe there's a simple explanation."

"I wanted to ask you first."

"Well, you asked. I don't know who the dead guy is, who Karl Franklin is, or why he would have these pictures."

"Any idea where he got them?"

Reluctantly, she studied the pictures again, trying to ignore the creep factor. The quality was low, but recognition hit. "They're from the company website. A quick trip through Google, click 'Print' and there they are." She squinted. "It might be easier to tell on the original, but it looks like these were actually cut and pasted—with scissors and glue—onto a page, and then photocopied."

Gordon raised his eyebrows. She caught a glimmer of surprise and appreciation in his eyes. He opened a desk drawer and pulled out a large manila envelope. Propping it open, he peered inside, then extracted a clear plastic sleeve. He placed it on the desk. After repositioning his desk lamp, he dipped into another drawer and pulled out a large magnifying glass.

"You really use that? It's not a Sherlock Holmes thing?"

Some of the friend showed through as he gave her an amused grin. "We're a *little* more advanced here, but sometimes the basics work just fine." Holding the glass to his eye, he scrutinized the pictures. "I think you're right."

"Which doesn't answer the question of what the paper means." She tried to think of some innocent reason, but failed. No matter how she tried to spin it, it read like a threat. And judging from the sweat trickling from her neck down her spine, her brain gave it the same interpretation. "You think the *they* in 'They'll talk' is Rose and Sam. Someone wants to find out something they know."

He nodded.

"And it's not Rose's apple cake recipe. I think she'd share that without being threatened."

"Agreed."

"So," she said, "what are you doing to protect them?"

The expression on his face turned the sweat to ice. "I've already assigned increased patrol in their neighborhood. However, at the moment, I'm more concerned about you."

"Me? Why?"

"*Use the kid.*" He pointed to the words.

"I'm the kid? You think that's me?" Of course he did. But she hoped he'd have an alternative suggestion. One her brain couldn't come up with now.

He lifted his eyebrows. "Who else?"

"Nobody, I guess, since there aren't any other pictures. But what does it mean?"

"I see a couple of possibilities." Gordon's expression was all cop.

"What do you mean?"

Megan resisted the urge to squirm as Gordon leaned forward and fixed those not-blue, not-green, not-gray eyes on her. Was she a suspect? How could he possibly think she was involved?

"Let's start with the basics." He raised his thumb. "One. We have someone, ostensibly headed for Rose and Sam's address."

She couldn't find fault with that logic. "Okay."

"Two." He lifted a forefinger. "He's got pictures of you, and apparently has connected you to Rose and Sam."

"Agreed."

"So, the question is, why?"

Well, duh. "And the answer is?"

"He's either already made contact with you—"

"Which he hasn't."

"I only have your word for that."

"Gordon, you're kidding. Why would I lie?"

"Megan, I'm thinking like a cop here, not someone who knows you. This is what any cop would do—will do, once they see these papers." He paused, as if searching for the best way to continue. "Or, they might think he was on his way to meet you. That you're working together. I was hoping you'd give me something I could use to point them in the right direction."

The clouds in her brain parted, and she understood the concern in Gordon's expression. "You mean ... you mean they might suspect *me*?" The words squeaked out. She took a breath. "I'll tell them the truth. I never heard of this guy, nor has anyone tried to coerce me into getting Rose and Sam to say or do anything. I love Rose and Sam. They love me."

"People will do a lot to protect loved ones. There's also the possibility the guy was searching for you."

"Here? How could he know I'd be coming here?"

"When did you plan the trip? Who knew you'd be here?"

Lord, he was dead serious about this. She tried to remember. "I bought my tickets five days ago. I gave my cell number to my boss and my team. And I told Angie."

He jotted notes. "Thanks."

"You can't think one of them is involved."

"I doubt it. If it was you he wanted, why not intercept you at the airport? Why drive from Florida?"

Megan leaned forward. "What if you hadn't seen those papers? Would I be sitting here getting the third degree?"

He shook his head. "Without them, the whole thing looks like a simple, unfortunate traffic accident."

"And you're not going to ... misplace ... those pieces of paper, are you?" As soon as she spoke the words, she regretted the way they'd come out. "I didn't mean to imply that you'd circumvent the law. I mean, I know you would never—"

He pulled his fingertips down the length of his nose. "I won't say I didn't think of it." He put the originals in the envelope, then sealed it and wrote his name across the flap. "But I can't pretend they don't exist. The accident might not be in my jurisdiction, but Rose and Sam are. I'm going to check into it. As a matter of fact, maybe you could convince them to take a nice vacation with you until I get a handle on this."

"They'd never agree. You know that. And it could be nothing. Meanwhile, I could help."

He shook his head. "Not a good idea. Giving you access to an investigation, especially one where you're involved, will make things look bad."

"But what if you didn't realize the pictures were me? I mean, it has been a long time."

He shook his head again.

Of course. She had no right to ask him to do anything that might impugn his integrity as a cop, especially a probationary chief of police. But she could do some checking on her own.

~ ~ ~ ~ ~

The aroma of Oma's brisket floated through the room. Justin's stomach growled. He clenched his jaw and went on with his searching. He'd have to run miles before dinner. And, as the sound of Oma's heavy-duty mixer joined the clattering of pots and pans, he figured maybe even more miles after. With Megan visiting, Oma would pull out all the stops.

He slid the next of Opa's books off the shelf, fanned the pages and shook them upside down. And, as with the others, got nothing but dust for his efforts.

He swore under his breath.

He'd almost finished the shelf when a car pulled into the drive. Damn. So soon? He checked the window. Definitely Megan's car.

She disappeared behind the open trunk, emerging with two of Oma's canvas shopping totes. He swiped the dust from the front of the shelf and brought the caddy to the bathroom. Maybe tomorrow, while everyone was at the doctor's, he'd finally have time to finish searching Megan's bedroom.

He squirted toilet cleaner into the bowl, let it soak while he scoured the sink and rearranged his meager array of toiletries into a cluster in the corner of the counter. Megan could have the rest of the space for whatever female paraphernalia she'd brought. He sprayed something foamy into the tub and wiped it down.

He flushed the toilet, grabbed the toilet brush and

swished it around the bowl as it emptied, then filled.

"Cleaning the toilet for me, Justin? Still can't aim?"

He jumped, spinning around. "Megan. Hi."

She smiled. "I can't remember you ever cleaning a toilet when we were kids."

"We're not kids. I've picked up a few civilized skills. Besides, you know Oma. If I wasn't doing it, she would be, or she'd have Opa doing it. Bad enough she cooks twenty-four seven. She doesn't need extra housework."

Megan scrunched her face and fisted her hands at her hips. He smiled at the familiar gesture.

"You think I'm going to wear her down? Give me a break, Justin. I'm here because I care about them." She shot him a look, almost tangible in its vehemence.

"Hey, hey." He raised his hands in submission, getting rewarded with cold water dripping down his arm. He returned the brush to its holder next to the toilet. "We're on the same side here."

"Sorry."

Her expression made him wonder. Even as she backed into her room, he had the creepy feeling she'd given him the once over, like an alpha dog checking a newcomer to the neighborhood.

He retreated to his room, closing the bathroom door on his side. He grabbed a pair of running shorts from the dresser. Maybe the endorphins would clear his brain. If nothing else, he'd counteract some of Oma's cooking.

Downstairs, Opa's snoring told him his grandfather was napping in his study. Justin checked the kitchen. "Smells great, Oma."

Dabbing her forehead with her apron, she turned from the stove and beamed at him. "Come. Let me know how it is."

He sighed. "Everything you make is delicious."

"But maybe it needs more salt. Come. Taste."

He strode across the uneven floor planks. Was there a crawl space underneath? "You know, Oma, it wouldn't take that long to get a new floor in here. I'd hate for you to trip and fall. They have some great new stuff—looks like wood but it won't warp. And you'd never have to polish it."

She waved her wooden spoon at him. "I've been walking on this floor for forty-two years and haven't fallen yet. It's a perfectly good floor. No need to waste the money." She eyed him, then the pot on the stove, waiting.

He picked up a spoon, dipped it into the simmering soup, and slurped the hot liquid into his mouth. "Delicious."

She nodded in agreement. "You won't be late now. Dinner will be at six. Sharp."

"I'm going around the pond. Shouldn't be more than an hour." He kissed her cheek, then unexpected feelings surfaced from deep inside and he enveloped her in an embrace. "I love you, Oma."

She accepted his hug, then gazed at him, a quizzical glint in her eyes. She waved him away. "And I love you. Now go do your running, and let me cook."

On the porch, he stopped to warm up. He twisted his torso, did some quad and calf stretches, enjoyed the warmth of the afternoon sun. He'd hoisted one leg onto the rail and bent forward in an easy stretch when he sensed Megan's presence behind him. Her scent, a mixture of flowers and spice, drifted through the air, mingling pleasantly with the kitchen aromas and clean smells of the newly repaired porch.

Her voice followed her scent. "Cleaning toilets. Exercising. My, my. This isn't the Justin I remember."

Thank God.

He continued stretching, trying to ignore the neatly manicured, slender fingers stroking the porch rail inches from his calf.

"Looks good," she said.

He angled his head toward her. Her long, sleek, bare leg appeared next to his. Her shiny brown hair cascaded in front of her face as she leaned forward. He stole a glance, only somewhat relieved to find she wore a jersey warmup jacket over—over what? He shoved away some of the fantasies he'd had when he was thirteen. Like the time she'd forgotten to close her door to the bathroom before she pulled her nightgown over her delightfully developing breasts.

Had she been teasing him then? Because she damn well was teasing him now. Why?

"The porch, I mean," she said. "I hear you're responsible for all the repairs."

He switched legs. "The house needed it. Rose and Sam don't notice the way things are falling apart. I ... nudged a little."

"Sam says you were in the thick of things, wielding tools, stroking paint. I'll bet you're a wizard with a cordless drill."

Her tone was low, slow, and sultry. He grabbed his ankle, kept his face hidden against his knee, and held the stretch. "Part of what I do."

She stood up, unzipped her jacket, and arched her back, revealing a form-fitting top. Those breasts had done an excellent job of developing.

"Rose said you were going for a run," she said. "Mind if I tag along? You can fill me in on exactly what it is you do. I thought you'd have done the follow-the-parent's-footsteps thing. Become a doctor or a lawyer."

She didn't know? Rose and Sam certainly hadn't kept *her* accomplishments from him, bragging about the way she was moving up, how she was thinking about starting her own consulting business. Were they ashamed that he'd chosen a different path?

"You run?" he asked. He took in her loose-fitting, knee-length knit shorts and everyday sneakers.

Tossing her head, spreading another wave of flowers and spice, she put her other leg on the rail. "Treadmill mostly. I need to work out the kinks. The drive from the airport got me all stiff. You know how that goes."

He was *not* following that thought. "You sure?"

"Are you implying I won't be able to keep up?"

"Frankly, yes. You're not adjusted to the altitude yet. I figured on doing about three miles—easy jog down to the pond to warm up, run a lap, then walk home to cool down. Until you start cranking out those red cells, it's not smart to push yourself."

She planted both feet on the porch floor and cocked her head at him. "*You* run?"

"I'm not Jumbo Justin anymore, Megan, in case you haven't noticed."

She had the decency to blush, and was uncharacteristically quiet.

"Oh, don't tell me you thought I didn't know what everyone called me."

"I never called you that," she said softly.

"To my face anyway." He trotted down the steps. "I have to go. I promised to be back in plenty of time for dinner. Maybe you should stay and help Oma in the kitchen."

"Kitchen?" She fisted her hands at her hips again. "Is that all you think I'm good for?"

"No, of course not. But now, it's probably the wiser choice."

He jogged away, ignoring her shout for him to wait.

Chapter Four

Years of training told Gordon he should simply confront Rose and Sam. Ask them why Karl Franklin from Florida was looking for them. They'd laugh, say, "Good old Karl. Always—" And that's where it fell apart. Always what? If they'd been expecting a long-lost anyone from Florida, it wouldn't be a secret. He should have asked Megan if the Kretzers had any ties to Florida. If so, maybe Franklin was connected. He jotted a note.

More years of relying on his gut told him he should do this quietly first. Find out more about who Karl Franklin was. Laurie's call announcing the arrival of a Trooper Patterson interrupted his ruminations.

"Send him in." He set the envelope on his desk and pulled out the evidence log sheet Solomon had started.

"Chief Helper?" A young trooper, his blond hair cut high in military fashion stepped into the room. "Pete Patterson."

Gordon stood, rounded the desk. "It's Hepler."

"Sorry, sir."

"No sweat. Everyone gets it inside out. In this line of work, I think I'd prefer Helper."

"Yes, sir. I'm supposed to pick up some of the accident victim's personal effects."

"Here you go." Gordon handed a pen to Patterson, who scrawled his name on the log. "Cause of the accident?"

"Vehicle versus tree."

"Trees usually win those. Especially along that stretch of

highway. Did you respond to the scene?"

"Yes, sir."

"Ugly?"

"Saw a lot worse in Iraq, sir."

Where the kid had probably learned not to volunteer information. He'd make a good cop. Keeping one's mouth shut usually got you more information than barrages of questions. The kid waited. To be dismissed, or because he had something to say after all?

"Any clues to cause of death?" Gordon prodded.

"Can't say, sir. I was there, but they had me controlling access. Clipboard duty."

Gordon caught the hint of frustration. "I guess that got boring. Not many rubberneckers along that part of the road. Maybe next time you'll get to chase away the media hounds." He grinned. "Or even a police chief."

The hint of a smile crossed Patterson's face. "I did get to deny access to a pushy reporter, sir. And I heard some talk about shell casings."

Gordon's heart did a quick hop. "Someone shot the victim?"

"I don't know. They'll probably know once they go over the car. And do the autopsy." He shifted his weight, almost imperceptibly. "Sir, I need to get back."

"Of course."

Patterson pivoted and marched from the room. Mind swirling, Gordon shut the door. Gilman hadn't mentioned a gunshot wound. He and Reynolds wouldn't have missed that. Or would they? How much attention would they give to a dead body? He called Dispatch, left a message for them to get in touch. He'd just hung up when his internal line rang.

"Yes, Laurie?"

"The mayor called. Said to remind you there's a budget meeting at four-thirty."

Damn.

"Thanks, Laurie. I'll be there." He sank into his chair and

pressed the heels of his hands into his eyes. Being Chief of Police wasn't being a cop.

Karl Franklin was dead. If he had been after Rose and Sam, they were safe enough. He pulled up the spreadsheet on his computer. What did the mayor want to cut now? Spare tires on their patrol cars? Kevlar vests? Kibble for Buster, their part-time K-9?

Why me, Dix? I was a good cop. Wasn't I?

~ ~ ~ ~ ~

Megan fastened her hair into a ponytail and trotted down the steps after Justin. She'd probably laid it on a little thick. More like a lot thick—like the frosting on one of Angie's cinnamon buns—but she wanted to find out what he knew. Her chat with Gordon had shaken her. Even more when she considered he'd probably stepped over some ethical boundaries when he'd shown her those papers.

She shivered at the memory of those pictures. And Rose and Sam's address.

Justin was moving farther away. She rushed to the street, turned and hurried to catch up. Her heart pounded. This was nothing like her brisk walks on the treadmill at the gym. He jogged on, seemingly without effort. The distance between them increased. She pushed her pace.

"Justin. Wait. Up." The words seemed to consume any remaining oxygen. Lights twinkled in front of her eyes. He must have heard her, because he turned and jogged in place. Thank goodness. She slowed a fraction, and after what seemed like ten miles later, gasping for breath, reached his side.

His hand grabbed her elbow. "Shit, Megan, what are you doing? I told you not to do anything strenuous until you get used to the altitude. We're at six thousand feet here."

"Didn't. Seem. Bother. You." She bent double, hands on her knees, sucking what oxygen-deficient air she could.

"First, I live at four thousand feet, not sea level. You've been gone for years. You have to acclimate. I've been here over a week. And I'm used to exercise."

"Fine. But as long as I'm here, can we talk?"

"Can you walk? We can go slow, but I'd rather keep moving."

Right now she wasn't convinced she could crawl. She gave Justin a brave smile. "Lead on."

"So, what do you want to talk about?" He'd released her arm, but was watching her as if he thought she'd collapse. Which she might, if she actually had to carry on a conversation and walk at the same time.

"What are you doing here?" she managed to wheeze out.

"Visiting. Same as you. And fixing up the house."

"Tell me … about that. You said—"

He'd slowed to a leisurely stroll, and she took deep breaths. The lightheadedness passed.

"What do you really want to know, Megan?"

"It's not like you visited a lot. A few weeks in summer, and not every year. If you cared about Rose and Sam, why didn't you show up more often?"

"Geez. We were kids. It's not like I could pick up and go where I wanted. I went where my parents sent me. Sometimes a vacation included a visit here. Sometimes it didn't. What, you missed me?"

She swallowed her guilt. No, she hadn't. She tolerated Justin's visits because Rose and Sam expected it. Most of the time, she preferred not having to include him in all the things the kids did. He was clumsy, didn't like to swim, and forget swinging into the pond from the rope on the elm tree. Rose always made them take turns choosing what to do, and Justin usually said, "I don't care." Which meant Rose picked things she thought were more suited to his city-living style. Museums. Children's theater, with lunch in a fussy tea room afterward. Or the movies. The most adventurous activity Rose ever chose was a picnic. Not that any of her choices were *bad*, but they isolated Megan from her friends.

Face it. You were afraid they'd think you were like him. A doofus.

She took a few more deep breaths. As kids, she'd been the active one. Now, she was lucky to hit the treadmill a few times a week. "What happened to your allergies? You hated going outside."

"Five years of shots."

"Contacts?" She pushed an imaginary pair of glasses up her nose.

"LASIK." His stride lengthened. "You want my life history? Mom and Dad were totally career oriented. They barely had time for each other, much less me. One thing I knew was that I didn't want a job so demanding it would become my life."

Justin was still walking, but she had to hurry to keep up. As long as she didn't try to talk, she thought she'd manage. She waited, hoping Justin would continue without prompting. After an annoying few minutes where all she heard was her own labored breathing, and all she saw was Justin's back as the distance between them lengthened, he turned his head.

She tried to catch her breath. The light surrounding him sparkled. Must be sunlight reflecting from the pond. Tiny black dots swarmed in front of her face. She swatted at them.

Justin appeared at her side. But he was far away at the same time.

"You okay?" he asked.

His voice seemed to echo. And then he had her elbow again, and he was dragging her off the road into the shade of the trees. "Sit." He pushed her onto the curb, forcing her head to her knees despite her feeble attempts to push his hand away.

"Shit, Megan, you almost passed out. I've already called the paramedics once today. Breathe," he demanded. "Slow. Deep."

She tried. "You know CPR?"

"If you can talk, you don't need it. But yes."

Another surprise. She tried to stand, but Justin held her down.

"You always were stubborn," he said. "When you feel up to it, I'll walk you home. I can still get a run in."

She shook her head. "No, Rose will smother me. I'll wait."

"I don't think that's a good idea."

She raised her head, got her bearings. "We're almost at the pond trail. There's plenty of shade, and there used to be a bench or two."

He nodded. "Still there."

"Then that's where I'll be waiting. Go on. I'll rest."

He shook his head, but she knew he'd cave. He always had.

"Crap, Megan, don't give me that look."

"What look?"

"The one you perfected when you were eight, I think. The one that says, "I'm right, and even if I'm not, I'm not giving in."

She smiled. "That bad?"

He returned a grin. "There never was any point in arguing with you."

"It's served me well in my job. Which reminds me, you haven't told me what you do."

"I teach." He didn't stop moving. Did he want to keep his muscles warm, or was he afraid to stop for a serious conversation?

"What?"

He swung his arms, twisted his torso, did some quad stretches. "I guess you'd say it's what they called shop class when we were in middle school. Officially, all-purpose handyman stuff." He stopped, stared at her as if daring her to put him down for not being a doctor or a lawyer like his parents.

Her heart had stopped drumming in her ears, and she

stood. He watched, the defiance switching to wariness.

"So, why are you here and not teaching?"

"Spring Break," he said. "I guess I'm not the only one who thought it was a good idea to see my grandparents."

"I agree. They're not getting any younger."

"You sure you want to do this?" he asked.

"I'm okay," she said. "Let's walk." He stayed close enough to catch her if she stumbled.

They strolled in silence, reaching the point where the road formed a T at the path to the pond, then continued toward the trail that ran along its circumference. "So you're teaching middle school shop?" she asked as they approached the benches in the clearing. "That explains what you've been doing at Rose and Sam's."

He gave a quiet grunt. "Not exactly middle school. More like Last Chance Before Jail U. Alternative school. Or, if you want to use the out of date, down and dirty term, reform school."

She'd never have thought of that one. "Um ... you like it?"

"Yeah, I do."

"Well ... that's good then." Justin the Jerk, who couldn't stand his ground, now dealing with what had to be acres of attitude?

He'd gone tense, as if he sensed her disapproval. She realized her tone hadn't been exactly ... positive. "Hey, I didn't mean—"

"Forget it. It's what I do. Period." He paused by the bench. "Sit. Rest."

She sank to the wooden seat. "I'll be here."

He paused, eyeing her.

"Go. What could happen?"

He nodded, then took off, his pace increasing as he moved farther away. He disappeared around the first curve. She leaned against the wooden slats of the bench, enjoying the fresh air. Her eyelids drooped. She swung her legs onto the bench. She drifted.

Slowly, she surfaced to the sound of rustling in the leaves. A deer? She propped herself on her elbows, hoping to catch a glimpse of the animal. They were gorgeous creatures, with their big eyes and delicate legs.

With the image of a deer fixated in her mind, when the man emerged from the trees, it didn't register. Not until he raced to her side, clapped his hand over her mouth and knocked her to the ground did she realize that one, it wasn't a deer, and two, she was in deep trouble.

~ ~ ~ ~ ~

Justin checked over his shoulder. They'd only come a few blocks, and Megan had already caught her breath. He let go of any remaining concern and kicked up the pace to make up for the leisurely way his workout had started. And to get his mind off the two nagging questions. One, would he be able to keep his grandparents' names out of the mess he was trying to prevent? Two, what was Megan doing here, showing up unannounced? And the logical progression. Were the two related?

He pushed himself faster, striving for the mental disconnect where there was nothing but the run. Breathing. Feet hitting the ground. Sweat dripping from his hair, down his face, off the end of his nose. Down his arms, off the tips of his fingers. Washing away stress. Cleansing. Nothing but the run.

No thoughts of the way Megan had looked at him when he told her what he did. Disbelief. Disappointment. The same undercurrents he got from his parents. "As long as you're happy," they'd say. But he could see it in their eyes, hear it in their tone. Working with *those* kinds of people. No status, no prestige. Teaching was honorable, but why not a university professor?

Even Oma, who'd always tried to make him feel special, kept implying this was temporary. That one day he'd see the light and get a high-paying job. But, since she and Opa had lived through the depression, Justin understood the value they put on money.

But it was helping *those* kind of people that made a difference. Like Eldon, who'd found a better use for his hands than pummeling someone into a pulp, and was putting food on his mom's table three times a day. Justin had no delusions about saving them all, but the ones he reached made it worthwhile. His father prided himself on putting punks into jail. Screw that. Justin preferred keeping them out of jail in the first place.

He realized his pace had reached a flat-out run and eased off a bit. Laughter and splashes filled the air as he rounded the curve along the swimming area. A group of kids having some afternoon fun, getting in a quick swim before dinner.

Maybe he'd invite Megan for a swim tomorrow, if for nothing more than to watch her eyes pop and jaw drop again. He hadn't missed the double-take when she'd actually recognized him. Did she even know why he'd never wanted to go swimming?

Probably not.

He tried to recapture the rhythm of the run. His shoes thudded against the packed dirt. Left, right. Left, right. He concentrated on breathing. In. Out. In. Out.

Halfway around the pond, he'd shaken the memories, only to have them replaced by anxiety, which was rapidly escalating to fear. The sleazeball had given him two weeks, and the first one had yielded a big, fat zero. On the other hand, he had fewer places to search. But with Megan here, it would be a lot harder to explore.

If he told her, would she help? Or would she go straight to Oma and Opa? Or Gordon, the cop?

The path veered away from the pond on an upgrade, and he focused on the extra effort he needed to maintain his pace. His mind clear at last, he settled into the run for the remainder of the distance.

As he approached the spot where he'd left Megan, he slowed to a jog. He could make out a second figure sitting on the bench. Had someone joined her? And so what if someone had? Dozens of homes used that clearing as pond access, and Megan knew half the people in town. Of course she'd chat with anyone who stopped.

From here, all he could tell was that the second person on the bench was definitely male. And had his arm around her. A turn in the path blocked his view. When they came into sight again, they were kissing, not chatting. And not the friendly, "Welcome home, good to see you" kind of kiss. More like tonsil hockey. He fought the urge to rush to her side. Her life, her business. And maybe she'd spend time with whoever he was and be out of the house.

Head down, he walked the last twenty yards, making enough noise so he wouldn't surprise them. They didn't seem to notice. Small wonder, engrossed as they seemed to be. Ten feet from them, he cleared his throat. They jerked apart, and two pairs of startled eyes met his. Eyes he'd never seen before.

"Um ... hello," the female said. Aside from her general coloring, she bore no resemblance to Megan. And these were kids, probably high-school.

"Hi," Justin said. "I ... um ... a friend was meeting me here."

"We got here about ten, fifteen minutes ago," the boy said. "Haven't seen anyone." He and the girl exchanged guilty glances. She blushed and dropped her gaze.

"Guess she got tired of waiting," Justin said. "I'll be on my way, then."

"Bye," the girl said.

Justin didn't look back. Megan wouldn't have tried to catch up while he was running, would she? No. Stubborn maybe, but she wasn't stupid. He jogged toward Oma's, keeping an eye out for Megan, half-afraid he'd find her collapsed by the side of the road. He trotted up Oma's front steps. As usual, despite his admonitions, the door was unlocked. Opa glanced up from the television. "You have a nice run?"

"Pretty good."

Opa looked past him. "So where's Meggie? Rose said she went with you."

Chapter Five

Gordon stifled a yawn as the mayor droned on about decreases in parking ticket revenue, raising the fines for speeders, the need for more school crossing guards, and something about coleslaw. Gordon blinked. Coleslaw? Once he realized the mayor was rambling about the Fourth of July picnic plans, which would probably change six ways from Sunday between now and the event, three months away, Gordon let his mind sift through the facts in the Karl Franklin case.

Case? He suppressed a snort. He had an accident victim, not even in his jurisdiction. The only facts he had were that the guy's name was Karl Franklin and he was from Florida. But those pictures of Megan Wyatt. They definitely had his cop sense tingling. Another tingling came from his belt, where his cell phone buzzed. The mayor looked up from his papers and glowered.

"Sorry," Gordon said. He glanced at the display, then arranged his face into what he hoped was a solemn expression. "Police business. I've got to take it."

Good old Laurie, calling right on time. He wondered if anyone on the town council had figured out that he got called away from a lot of meetings. So what if they had. He nodded around the table and beat a hasty retreat for the hallway. Once out of the meeting room, he sauntered toward the exit.

"Thanks, Laurie," he said. "You're a life-saver, as always. I thought I'd go crazy—"

"This one's for real, Chief."

Gordon stopped mid-stride. "What?"

"Another ambulance call to the Kretzers'. And Officer Solomon's rolling."

Gordon remembered the call earlier in the day, but that had been a straight paramedic issue. Why Solomon this time? "Rose or Sam?"

"No. Something about Megan Wyatt. Since she was in here before, I thought you might want to know."

"Details?"

"I heard the tail end of the radio traffic. They sent Solomon out code two, not three, so I figured it wasn't too bad. You want me to find out?"

"Don't bother. I'm on my way to the Kretzers'. Be there in ten." He lengthened his stride, making his way out of the building and across the parking lot to his cruiser. Code two. More than a parking violation, but not urgent enough for lights and sirens. Then again, police code threes were few and far between in Mapleton. He hadn't heard the ambulance siren, so his concerns eased a bit further. He climbed into the SUV and flipped on the radio. "Connie, what's going on at the Kretzers'?"

Connie's voice came over the radio, clear and calm. Gordon would have relaxed at her tone, but he knew Connie could handle an armed robbery, a bomb scare, and a shootout, all at the same time and never sound any more excited than the weatherman predicting a mild and sunny day. At least he assumed she could, should anything like that ever happen in Mapleton. She'd been chief dispatcher longer than Gordon could remember, and he'd never heard her lose her cool.

"Solomon's not on scene yet. Caller reported an injury, possible mugging."

"Anyone else involved?"

"No others injured. The incident didn't happen at the Kretzers'," Connie said. "Solomon didn't request backup."

Gordon thanked her and lead-footed it toward the Kretzer place. He started to switch on the lights, but didn't bother. Traffic was light, and everyone in town knew to get out of his way when they saw the official police SUV. Sometimes it was good to be the chief, he thought. Except for the damn budget meetings.

He switched to the Nextel. "Solomon," he barked.

"Yes, Chief."

"Report."

"Just arriving. Ambulance is on scene."

"I'm about five away."

He arrived in three. The ambulance sat in the driveway. Good sign. If it had been a scoop and scoot, they'd be racing away, sirens wailing. Or did they have a body? Fighting the adrenaline rush, he parked on the street, loped across the lawn and bounded up the stairs. The front door stood open. He tapped once, then stepped inside.

Megan lay propped up on a gurney in the middle of the living room. Dave Gilman and Tom Reynolds hovered over her, Reynolds on the radio and Gilman starting an IV. They worked methodically, and Gordon didn't get a sense of urgency. Relieved, he moved closer. Bruises were already apparent on her face. Her eyes were closed. Plastic tubing hooked over her ears and into her nostrils.

He resisted approaching her while the medics did their thing. Ed Solomon was offering reassurances to Rose and Sam, while the grandson—Justin, was it?—leaned against the wall, clenching and unclenching his fists. He wore running shorts and an oversized sweatshirt, sweat-darkened triangles at the chest and armpits. Matted hair, damp. But breathing easy.

Gordon slid his gaze to the gurney. Megan wore a pair of loose cotton shorts. A warmup jacket hung over the arm of a nearby chair and a pair of sneakers sat on the floor below. Had she been running with Justin? He nodded in Solomon's direction, then edged across the room to Justin's side.

"How is she?" Gordon asked.

Justin stared into space, as if he were trapped in another dimension. A muscle in his jaw twitched rhythmically. He seemed agitated, which was understandable, but it seemed to be more than concern for Megan.

"Justin?" Gordon said. "Are you okay?"

The man blinked and clawed his fingers through his hair. "What?" He shook his head, as if to clear it. "Oh, yeah. No problem."

"Can you tell me what happened?"

Robot-like, Justin stepped to an end table. Picked up a water bottle. Unscrewed the cap, took a long drink. He wiped his mouth with the back of his hand. "I wish I knew. I was out for a run. Around the pond. Megan wanted to tag along, but she's not adjusted to the altitude yet. She got as far as that open space down the road"—he swept a hand in the general direction— "before she realized she'd never make it. She wasn't there when I finished my run. I thought she'd gotten tired of waiting and left. But when I got here, she hadn't shown up."

Gordon pulled out his notepad and pen. "Go on. When did all this happen?"

Justin drained the rest of the water. "It was about four, maybe a little after, when we left the house. Maybe twenty minutes to get to the pond?" The water bottle crackled as he squeezed it, accompanying his speech like a background percussionist. "I don't know. Megan was having trouble keeping up, so we went slow. Stopped a couple of times. I can usually do the pond trail in about thirty minutes. I'd say less this time."

"So, you finished somewhere around five?" Gordon glanced at his watch. It was quarter to six.

"That sounds reasonable," Justin said. "I wasn't too worried—figured Megan had stopped to chat, or had decided to walk along one of the pond trails while I was running." His mouth twisted up in a half-smile. "You know, to prove that she wasn't a wimp."

Gordon nodded. "Guess she hasn't changed."

A sharp hiss came from the gurney. Then a yelp.

~ ~ ~ ~ ~

Justin snapped his head around. The cop spun on his heel and got to her side seconds ahead of him.

"What's wrong?" the cop asked.

"Tweaked her wrist," Dave said. He bent over Megan. "I'm going to immobilize it. I don't think it's broken, but they'll x-ray it at the clinic."

"Can you get this tubing off me?" she asked, rocking her head back and forth on the pillow.

"Sorry, no can do," Tom said.

"You can use the extra oxygen," Justin said.

She frowned. "Yeah, yeah. Sea level to six thousand feet. I got it. But it's annoying."

Justin moved forward, took her good hand, careful to avoid the IV. "What happened?" Please say she did something stupid, like trip and fall on the trail. That she made her way home before collapsing on the porch. As if she hadn't heard his question, she stared at him. Or past him. She blinked, and her eyes cleared.

"Rose and Sam?" Megan asked. "Are they—?"

Oma and Opa appeared on the other side of the gurney. "We're here. You do what Davey and Tommy say," Oma said.

Justin smiled, not bothering to remind her how she'd refused to listen to them a few hours ago. He exchanged a quick glance with Sam, who returned the smile.

"We want to get her to the med center," Davey said.

"Hang on one second," Gordon said. "I'd like to ask her a few questions."

"No can do, Chief," Davey said. "She's bruised and passed out. There's a lump on her forehead, and her wrist should be x-rayed. Docs want to see her."

"Did someone do this to you, Megan?" Gordon asked, ignoring Davey. The scrapes on her forehead and cheeks stood out in bright contrast against the pallor of her skin.

"I ... I don't know. It's fuzzy." Megan said.

"Can you give a painkiller?" Justin asked the paramedics.

"Not until the ER folks check her out," Tommy said.

Justin stepped away to give them room. "Can I come along?"

"Not in the rig," Davey said. "But you can follow us to the ER."

"We'll come too," Sam said. "I'll call Doctor Evans, let him know what happened."

"Of course," Justin said. "Give me a minute to change."

The cop who'd been talking to Oma and Opa nodded Gordon over. Justin was torn between wanting to eavesdrop and getting to the medical center. Oma's insistence that he get his *tuchis* moving made the choice obvious.

"Ten minutes, Oma. We'll be there in plenty of time."

An hour later, they were still in the small waiting room of the Mapleton medical clinic. Oma paced, Sam grumbled. Justin tried to stay calm. He'd grabbed Megan's purse and dealt with getting the insurance ball rolling. She'd had all the requisite cards, and he'd used the opportunity to search for evidence that hinted at any ulterior motive for her visit, but aside from typical female handbag clutter, he had zilch. Maybe they'd keep her overnight and he could search her room *and* her luggage.

The double doors opened. The antiseptic hospital smell intensified. It took a moment to recognize the two paramedics, now in street clothes. They smiled, and Justin stood. "Any news?" he asked.

Davey extended his hand. "Dave Gilman. My partner, Tom Reynolds."

Justin shook each of their hands in turn. "Justin Nadell."

They nodded, then shifted their attention to Oma and Opa. "Nothing to worry about," Tom said.

"*Gott sei Dank,*" Oma said. "Thank God. When can we take her home?"

"You can go see her now," Dave said. "The paperwork will probably take longer than the treatment. The doctor has to release her, but it shouldn't be long."

"Did she say what happened?" Justin asked, lowering his voice.

"You'll have to talk to the doc," Tom said, glancing in Oma's direction. He lowered his voice to match Justin's tone. "Once they're out of the rig and into ER, we're done."

Did that mean they knew something they couldn't tell him?

~ ~ ~ ~ ~

Megan's head throbbed. The bright light in the exam room stabbed behind her eyes like javelins.

"Meggie, doll."

She squinted, bringing her arm up to shield her eyes and grimaced at the sharp twinge in her wrist. Rose and Sam hovered over her, fear and concern etched in their faces.

"I'm fine." Her voice quavered, which made Rose and Sam seem even more worried.

"Is this true?" Rose said, looking at Doctor Evans.

"I see no reason to keep her here," he said. "She needs rest. She'll get more at home in her own bed than in the hospital." He gave Rose a stern glare over the top of his glasses. "But light meals for twenty-four hours."

Rose nodded solemnly. "I have chicken soup."

The doctor smiled. "Perfect. The workup was negative. She's got some contusions, a mild sprain to her wrist. She's probably going to feel sore for a day or two."

"She's right here," Megan said. "And she definitely feels sore." Like her entire body was one big bruise.

"Oh, sweetie. What happened to you?" Rose brushed Megan's hair from her forehead.

Megan furrowed her brow, trying to remember what she'd already said. All she got for her effort was more throbbing. "It's fuzzy." She focused on Doctor Evans. "I remember going to the pond with Justin." She noticed him in the doorway. He gave her a smile and a finger-wave. "And then I was here. Nothing in between. Oh, except I think I remember being in the ambulance. Do I have amnesia?"

The doctor shook his head. "A little short-term memory loss of the events surrounding the trauma are normal. I predict your memory will return in no time."

A plump, gray-haired woman came in with a clipboard. "I'll need your signature, Miss Wyatt. I've called for a wheelchair, and you're good to go."

"I'll bring the car around," Justin said.

Megan reached for the pen. "Um … can't say it'll be legible." She held up her wrist, encased in a thick elastic bandage.

"I'll sign," Sam said. The woman handed him the clipboard, he scrawled his signature, and Rose insisted on pushing the wheelchair. The orderly didn't argue.

It felt like Justin hit every pothole and bump in the road on the drive home, but at last they arrived. She allowed Rose to cluck and fuss, not bothering to protest. Had it been only this morning when she'd left San Diego?

Megan accepted Rose's help changing from her dirty clothes into a clean nightshirt, and crawled into bed. Rose closed the curtains, kissed Megan on the forehead, and tiptoed toward the door. "I'm going to leave the door open a bit so we can hear you if you need anything. You rest, and I'll fix you a bite to eat."

"Thanks." Megan leaned against the pillows Rose had propped up behind her and sighed. God, what should she do? The pain pill the doctor had given her had turned her brain to cotton candy. She closed her eyes.

She opened them a short time later at a tap on the door. Light from the hall silhouetted a figure in the doorway.

"Hey, girlfriend. Heard you had a little mishap." Angie strode into the room carrying a tray. Balancing it, she flipped the switch for the overhead light with her elbow.

Megan squirmed up to a sitting position, grimacing. "Apparently."

Angie set the tray on Megan's lap, then closed the bedroom and bathroom doors. She dragged the desk chair over beside the bed and perched on the edge. "I dropped off some cinnamon buns and Rose told me you'd had to go to the ER." Her eyes shimmered with a mixture of concern and curiosity. "So, spill."

Megan considered the tray. A mug of broth, a small bowl of Jell-O and some applesauce. Rose must have taken Doctor Evans' words to heart. Not a cookie or pastry in sight. She cupped the mug with both hands, inhaling the rich, steamy broth. "I take it you're not referring to the soup."

Angie rolled her eyes. "I told you I had a feeling something bad was going to happen."

"As I recall, you said it was going to happen to Rose and Sam. If this was related to your *feeling*, then I'm glad it was me and not them."

"So, what did happen?"

Megan's head throbbed. "It's all blurry. The doctor said it might take awhile for the memory to return."

"Wow. You've got amnesia?"

"Calm down. It's normal, he said. And short term."

"You don't think you fell, though. Someone did this."

Without warning, the man's voice, his cigarette breath punctuating his threats, were there, although she couldn't see his face. Her hands trembled, and Angie took the mug from her grasp. "Careful."

Megan composed her features. She wasn't ready to deal with Angie's prying. "I told you, I don't remember."

Angie cast a not-so-furtive glance toward the bathroom door. "So do you remember this? Where was Justin while everything was going on?"

"You think ... you think it was Justin? No way." Justin didn't smoke.

Angie hunched a shoulder. "Probably not. Although think about it. He's out running. He could have grabbed you and left you lying somewhere, then come back and played the worry card to ward off suspicion." Angie seemed disappointed. "Or what if there's a serial killer on the loose? And you overpowered him and escaped?"

"You're reading too many thrillers, or watching too much television, Angie. It doesn't make any sense."

The room seemed to blink out. Angie leaned forward, in full mother hen mode. "Oh, I'm sorry. This is real and I'm making stupid jokes. Was it terrible?"

Megan shook her head. "Not really. It's over. Drop it."

"Okay. Can you eat with your wrist bandaged? I could feed you."

"Not necessary." She worked on the soup, easily holding the mug in her left hand. "God, I've missed Rose's chicken soup. I've tried to make it, but it's never the same."

Angie waited until Megan finished the soup, then leaned forward. "What do you think of Justin? He changed, didn't he?"

"And I notice you didn't bother to prepare me."

Angie grinned. "Didn't want to spoil the surprise. He's hot." She glanced at the bathroom door. "And sleeps next door."

"A minute ago you wanted me to believe he could have hurt me. Now you're playing matchmaker?"

"Oh, I was teasing."

"About the mugging or the matchmaking?"

"Shut up and finish eating or Rose will shove it down your throat."

Now *that* threat wasn't so far-fetched. Megan lifted the dish of applesauce close to her mouth and scooped it in. When she'd done the same with the Jell-O, Angie gathered the tray and went to the door. "I have to get going. Call if you need me." She glanced over her shoulder. "Or if you remember the details."

"I'll be fine. And thanks for stopping by."

"What are friends for?"

After Angie left, Megan decided she couldn't put off a trip to the bathroom any longer. When she opened the door, she heard Justin in the next room, talking to someone. He sounded irritated. Maybe a few notches above irritated. She crept across the room and put her ear to the door.

Chapter Six

"What do we have, Ed?" Gordon approached the bench on the path where Justin said he'd left Megan.

Ed Solomon snapped a few more pictures, then ran his fingers through his hair. "Not a whole lot. No decent footprints. No trace I can find beyond a couple of fresh-looking cigarette butts, which I bagged. One with lipstick. Might have belonged to the kids. According to Justin, he finished his run and interrupted a couple of kids engaging in some minor hanky-panky. He said he didn't see any cars parked nearby, so they probably live within walking distance."

"I don't suppose he got their names."

"No, but he did describe them—although you know how unreliable eyewitness descriptions can be. From a distance, he thought she was Megan. Same general coloring. The guy was about five-ten, skinny. When I finish here, I'll go knocking and see if I can round them up. Maybe I can stimulate their memories."

Gordon gazed around the gravel and pine needle strewn clearing. "How many people use this access point, you think?"

"In summer, a lot," Ed said. "Now, not so many. But it's warming up, and runners like to start here, because it's level. A dozen today wouldn't be unreasonable."

"So, we're looking at a window of what? About forty-five minutes between the time Justin Nadell left her and the lovebirds showed up. Any number of people could have passed through."

Solomon nodded in agreement. "Hasn't rained in weeks. No decent shoe prints."

"If this is where Megan was grabbed, you think it was opportunistic, or someone wanted her specifically?"

"Hell, if we knew that, we'd be in the office solving the damn thing."

Gordon walked outward from the bench in an expanding spiral, shining his flashlight on the ground. "I don't see any signs of a struggle. You think maybe the whole incident was an accident? She went jogging, slipped, fell, bumped her head? She just got into town—could have been lightheaded from the altitude. And the Megan I remember wouldn't admit to being stupid."

"You think she's feigning memory loss?"

Gordon shrugged. "At the moment, that hypothesis is about as good as being mugged. We've got no proof of either."

"Better for the citizenry if it's not a mugger. They'll drive us bonkers, calling every time the trees creak in the wind or a cat runs across their yard."

"Call me if you find our lovebirds. Maybe they'll have remembered something. Do your 'I'm a cop, you have to talk to me' thing. I'm going to grab some dinner."

"It's good to be the Chief," Ed muttered.

~ ~ ~ ~ ~

Gordon stood inside the door of Daily Bread, wondering why it felt different. It took a second to realize he hadn't heard Angie's usual cheerful greeting. He checked the counter, where Ozzie, whose broad girth and extra chins attested to enjoying his own cooking, picked up a coffee pot and mug, and paused, clearly waiting to see where Gordon would sit.

Scanning the room for Dave Gilman and Tom Reynolds, Gordon gestured to the booth at the rear where the paramedics waited. Reynolds made room on his side of the vinyl-covered bench, and Gordon sat. Simultaneously, Ozzie plunked a mug in front of him and filled it with hot, black coffee, a shade or two darker than his skin. He wiped his hands on his apron. "Meatloaf tonight, Chief." Ozzie retreated to the kitchen.

Not even a question. Lord, was he in a rut. Was that why he was picking at the accident case? To break the monotony of paperwork and budgets? Or to prove he still had the cop chops? That Dix hadn't recommended him for the job of chief because he thought he wasn't good enough for street work?

He shoved those doubts aside. "Busy day."

"Definitely not the usual routine," Tom said. "What did you want to ask us?"

"The accident earlier today. Trooper on scene said he thinks they were searching for shell casings. You find any gunshot wounds on your victim?"

The medics exchanged surprised glances. "No. No way," they said, in unison.

Gordon nodded. "Didn't think you'd have missed it."

"Well," Dave said, stirring his coffee. "Even if we did, the M.E. wouldn't have found it until after we got him to the morgue. I'm thinking the troopers would have been long gone by the time that happened."

"I'll ask, but I'm sure you're right." Gordon lifted his mug and inhaled deeply before taking a sip.

"You know," Tom said. "We could rig an IV to get the caffeine directly into your bloodstream."

"You saying I drink too much coffee?" Gordon asked.

"Afraid I'll have to vote with Tom on that one." Angie's voice carried across the room. "Ready for a refill?" She was already ambling across the diner, coffee pot in hand.

"Maybe top it off," he said. Dave and Tom slid their mugs closer. Angie filled each in turn, no wasted motion, no wasted coffee. Very little about her was wasted, he thought. Short blonde hair, no makeup other than some light gloss on her lips. No polish on her trimmed nails. She wore jeans and a Daily Bread t-shirt. Her scent was her own—she didn't wear perfume because she didn't want it to clash with the food she served.

And why was he noticing her scent? Or wondering if her hair looked the same when she woke up in the morning. He realized he'd held her gaze longer than necessary. Breaking the connection, he nudged the filled mugs to the medics.

"Sorry I wasn't here when you got in, guys," she said, apparently oblivious to his ogling. "Ozzie take your orders?"

The three men nodded. "They should be coming up, then. I'll check." She half turned, then swiveled and leaned over the table. "Can you tell me what happened to Megan? I was over there, and she says she can't remember."

"Not unusual," Tom said. "Her injuries weren't bad, but she might be suppressing the event itself. Temporary memory loss happens quite often."

"You saw her?" Gordon asked. "So she's home?"

"Yes. Rose has her tucked into bed, snug as a bug." She turned her pale blue eyes to Gordon. "You're going to find out what happened, aren't you?"

"That I am. Ed Solomon's checking out the scene. And as soon as I finish here, I'll go talk to Megan. Her memory might be clearer after she's had a little rest."

"I'll go light a fire under Ozzie and get you on your way." She pivoted and took off across the diner at a brisk pace, her retreating hips providing a pleasant view.

"When you going to ask her out?" Dave said.

"Huh? What? Me? Angie?" Gordon shook his head. "Not my type."

Dave grinned at Tom. "My money says they'll be an item by the Fourth of July picnic."

"Three months? I'm thinking Memorial Day, tops," Tom said.

"Shut up, the two of you. This is a small town, and I don't need you spreading rumors. I've got a position to uphold here. Besides, Angie's dating what's-his-name. The mechanic from Conifer."

"Over and done three months ago," Tom said. "I thought the cops knew what was going on with all the good citizens of Mapleton. You know, serve and protect." The two men laughed.

Gordon swung his legs around and levered himself up from the bench. "Enough." He strode to the register and dropped some bills on the counter. "Angie, I'll take my dinner to go."

Like living in a goddamn fish bowl.

~ ~ ~ ~ ~

Justin flopped onto the edge of the bed, clenching his cell phone at his ear.

"I told you, I don't know," he said. "And things are complicated. You have to give me time."

"There's not a lot of time left." His tormentor's voice was calm. Refined. But the threat beneath the even tones came through loud and clear.

"Maybe I don't care," Justin said. "It's not as if it's going to affect *my* life."

"Don't pull that," the man said. "And even if you don't give a shit about your own life, what about your grand-parents? The only reason I haven't dealt with it myself is as a favor to you. A favor with an expiration date."

Justin felt like someone was twisting his gut with a pipe wrench. "Are you absolutely positive it's here? I've already torn the place half apart."

"My sources say yes."

"But if it's not? Or if it's never found? Everyone could get on with their lives."

"That's not acceptable. It's there somewhere. Find it."

"I have until Sunday night," Justin said. "I'm counting on you to honor our agreement until then."

Without waiting for a response, he ended the call.

Water ran in the bathroom. Had Megan overheard? He held his breath, waiting until the water stopped, expecting her to knock on his door. He remembered the way she used to knock twice before swooping in anyway, and he grabbed his discarded running shirt from the floor and wiped the cold sweat from his face. He took a deep breath, held it for five counts, exhaled slowly, and hoped he could divert any questions she might ask.

Maybe the years had planed away some of her rougher edges. The way she'd barge in and speak her piece, demanding answers, never thinking she was prying into areas outside the bounds of privacy. He recalled she never seemed to draw lines between family, close friends, or casual acquaintances. What was in her head spilled out of her mouth.

He waited a full minute, listening. The far door closed. He dragged his fingers through his hair. Off the hook. For the time being.

Footfalls ascending the stairs, too quick and heavy for either of his grandparents, destroyed any sense of his calm. He tensed as they slowed, approaching his room. But the knock didn't come. Instead, it was at Megan's door.

"Come in," she said.

The door opened, then closed.

"How are you feeling?" The cop's voice. "Up to a few questions?"

Justin wasn't above a little eavesdropping himself. He sidled to the bathroom door and eased it open. He didn't hear Megan answer, but a chair dragged across the floor, creaking a little as the cop sat in it.

After a brief interval of unintelligible whispers, Megan called out, "Come on in, Justin."

So much for stealth.

Megan sat in bed, propped up in a nest of pillows. Too pale, he thought. And when she blinked, it seemed to be in slow motion.

"Is this a good time?" Justin addressed Gordon. "I think she needs to rest."

"And I need to ask some questions."

~ ~ ~ ~ ~

Megan took a sip of water from the glass beside her bed, the cool liquid soothing the dryness in her throat.

"How's the memory?" Gordon asked.

"Blurry," she said, avoiding his eyes. Why did he have to show up here? The stranger had said he'd be watching. Without thinking, she cast a quick glance toward the window. Seeing the closed curtains, she relaxed.

But if the man was watching, and saw Gordon's car, would he think she'd called them? Another thought chilled her. Could the man have bugged her room while everyone was at the hospital?

She trusted Gordon, wanted to tell him everything, but not now. Not here, with Rose and Sam in the house. Why hadn't she told him to go away? Had to be the pain meds slowing her brain functions. She had to think it through. For now, she'd be content that she'd made him promise not to tell Rose and Sam about the papers in the dead man's car.

The pills dulled the pain, but not the fear. She'd do as the stranger demanded and keep her mouth shut about what he'd said until she could figure out what it was he wanted. The doctor had said memory loss was normal, so Gordon would believe her. She hoped.

Gordon muttered something, then reached for his belt. Unclipping his phone, he checked the display. He gave her an apologetic grin and lifted the phone to his ear. "Hepler."

Maybe he'd be called away. She wanted to signal Justin to keep his mouth shut, but Gordon kept his gaze on her as he listened to whoever was on the phone.

"Who's on duty?" he said. After a pause, he continued.

"Tell her Vicky's on her way, that I'll be there later. Then have Vicky call me with an update." He flipped his phone closed and slipped it into its holder. "Mrs. Bedford's on another ghost watch."

Megan smiled. "Do you need to go? We'll understand." *Please.*

"Ghosts?" Justin said.

Gordon sighed. "Not yet. But she's insisting tonight's the night—again—and wants me there."

"Ghosts?" Justin repeated. "Where?"

"I'll explain later," Megan said, winking at Justin, then wincing at the stab of pain in her forehead.

Gordon's expression shifted from exasperated to serious cop. "So, Megan. What can you remember?"

She convinced herself to relax. "I remember running. Falling. Like I'm dreaming. I remember thinking how I had to get to the house, and then I was on the porch, and then the paramedics were poking around."

Gordon wrote in a little notebook. "But you don't remember where it started?"

She glanced at Justin. "We were going to run. I got as far as the Maple Street access and waited on the bench."

"You remember seeing a couple of kids?" Gordon asked.

She shifted her gaze to Gordon. "No. Definitely not. I didn't see anything."

"I told the officer what I saw," Justin said. "But the kids said no one else was around. At the time, I didn't think there was a problem, or I'd have asked more questions. Although the way they were tangled up, I don't think they'd have noticed if an elk walked by."

"No problem," Gordon said. "My officer is out tracking them down." To Megan, he said, "I have a couple more questions if you're up to it."

Of course he'd have more questions. But she needed to steer him away from asking about what had happened to her. "Did you find out anything else about the car accident?"

"What car accident?" Justin looked at Megan, eyes wide, reflecting concern. Or fear? "Were you in an accident?" He gripped her forearm.

She gave his hand a pat, then pried his fingers loose. "No, no. Not me. Nothing like that. I saw the car—before the accident happened. Gordon thought I might have been a witness. But I wasn't."

"Which reminds me," Gordon said. "Justin? Do you know of any ties Rose and Sam have to Florida? Or someone named Karl Franklin?"

After a few seconds of apparent thought, Justin said, "No to both."

"Thanks. I'll ask them," Gordon said.

"Ask what?" Rose bustled in. "Whatever it is, it should wait. Meggie needs her rest. There's coffee downstairs." She scuttled to the bedside and kissed Megan's forehead. "Some herbal tea for you, and I'll bring it up. You two" —she made a shooing motion as if the two large men in her path were nothing but pesky kittens— "out."

"One minute, Rose," Megan said. "I need to ask Gordon one question."

Rose inched her glasses down her nose and glared at Gordon. "Make it quick."

"Yes, ma'am," he said.

Megan waited until Rose was likely out of earshot. "Gordon, remember. Please don't bother them tonight. They've had enough excitement for one day. Bringing up the accident will cause unnecessary worry."

"Is anyone going to tell me what's going on?" Justin asked. "Like maybe how some traffic accident involving someone from Florida could possibly involve my grand-parents?"

"Let's go downstairs," Gordon said. "I'll see you tomorrow, Megan." Gordon motioned Justin toward the door, and the two of them thudded down the stairs.

She threw aside the covers and swung her legs over the

side of the bed. Ignoring the shakiness in her knees and the throbbing in her wrist and head, she scuffled to the closet for her robe. How dare they leave her here, like some invalid.

Chapter Seven

Gordon groped for the alarm, sending the clock crashing to the bedroom floor. He leaned over the bed, sweeping his hand across the carpet until he found it. Pressing the off switch did nothing to silence the piercing tones. He blinked, bringing the glowing red numerals into focus. Four-seventeen? What the—?

The noise finally resolved itself into the ringtone he reserved for Dispatch. He hoisted himself onto the bed and fumbled for his cell phone. Flopping onto his back, he thumbed the answer button. "Hepler."

"Chief, you need to get to Vintage Duds." Country music played in the background.

Irv. The night dispatcher. Gordon closed his eyes and swallowed the curse on the tip of his tongue. "Can't someone tell Betty Bedford there's no such thing as ghosts? I already did a full walk-through with her at ten. And eleven. Where's—who's on duty? Vicki. She's good with Mrs. Bedford. Let her handle it."

"No, Chief. You need to get over there. Now. She's dead."

He jerked upright and hit the lights, squinting against the sudden brightness. "What? And shut off that music." He shielded his eyes with his free hand. His heart pounded at a rapid clip, but his brain hadn't caught up yet. "Dead? Vicky's dead? What? How?" He jumped up and headed for the bathroom.

"No, not Vicky—she's already on scene, along with half

the force."

"You're telling me Mrs. Bedford is dead? In her shop?" One handed, he grabbed toothbrush and paste, trying to uncap the tube. Damn cell phones were too small to tuck between chin and shoulder.

"Yes, Chief."

"On my way."

~ ~ ~ ~ ~

Most of the time, Gordon enjoyed living above the lake on the outskirts of town. Gave him a little distance between work and his personal life—what there was of it. Tonight, the twenty-five-minute drive seemed endless.

Earlier, he'd asked the Kretzers about Karl Franklin. He'd been subtle. Casual. He recalled the way Megan had kept her eyes fixed on him, ready to intervene if he crossed whatever limits she'd set. But he'd simply mentioned it in passing. One of those small talk throwaway lines. "Oh, I understand you've been to Florida. We had a traffic accident earlier involving a Floridian. Maybe you knew him. Karl Franklin."

Sam had laughed out loud. "You've lived in Mapleton too long, Gordon. Even here, you don't know everyone by name and face. Florida's a big state."

Gordon had played the sheepish bumpkin. Megan had smiled. Justin hadn't reacted to the name. So Karl Franklin was a dead stranger. Maybe the quest for whatever he wanted from Rose and Sam had died with him.

From there, he'd gone to Vintage Duds where Betty Bedford had pointed out every damn piece of merchandise that was half an inch out of place. Her definition of place. With all the bric-a-brac scattered all over the shop— "It gives such *ambience,* don't you agree?" she'd said—how the hell could anyone tell if something had been moved? But he'd smiled and agreed. Told her he'd have Vicky—Officer

McDermott—check that nothing unusual was going on.

She'd looked disappointed. "You mean you won't be handling this personally?"

He'd fed her some bull about how Vicky was tuned in to the other side more than he was. Told her to go home and get some sleep.

But Mrs. Bedford had called at ten and insisted on talking to him. She'd seen shadows outside. She'd brought an old cushion from a patio lounge chair, some blankets and a pillow, and was determined to spend the night in the store and catch the ghosts in the act.

"Mrs. Bedford—"

"Please, I've told you. Call me Betty."

"Betty. Aren't you afraid the ghosts will stay away if you're here?"

"I'm going to be in my office. They won't find me."

He hadn't bothered to dispute her logic. He'd walked the perimeter of the shop, inside and out, with her tagging along behind him like an eager puppy. He'd convinced her it was probably a stray dog, or someone taking a shortcut from Finnegan's. Reluctantly, she'd let him leave, but had refused to go home.

At eleven, she'd called again. This time she'd heard noises. Another trip downtown. He'd run through the routine again, telling her that Officer McDermott would handle any more calls. He'd already assigned her to check the Kretzers' place regularly. And to do it without letting them know, since he'd promised Megan not to worry them.

Damn, no ghost had killed Mrs. Bedford. But who had? And why?

Slow down. All he knew was that she was dead. She could have imagined a ghost and scared herself into a heart attack. Or tripped over a mannequin, or any of the myriad obstacles in her shop and broken her neck. Why assume murder? Six months off the street and he'd lost his open-minded objectivity. Or was he so fed up with paperwork and budget line items that he was actually thinking someone being killed was a positive thing?

He ignored the stop signs and two blinking red traffic lights as he sped through town, heading for the flashing cruiser and ambulance lights outside of Vintage Duds. Why the ambulance? Had Betty been alive when the call came in? Was someone else hurt?

He angled his SUV beside Vicky's cruiser and jumped out. Dave Gilman and Tom Reynolds leaned against the fender of their rig, sipping coffee from Styrofoam cups. "Chief," Gilman said. Reynolds bobbed his head.

"What do you have?"

"DRT," Gilman said. "Flat line."

Dead Right There. Although the medics weren't officially permitted to call a death, he trusted Gilman and Reynolds to know the difference between someone who might be resuscitated and someone long gone.

"So why are you here?" Gordon asked.

"Thought we'd stick around until someone releases the body. We might be needed for transport."

"I'll go see what's up," Gordon said. He did a quick turn, scanning the area. "Coffee?"

Reynolds pointed to his left. "Angie brought an urn."

Gordon spotted the white Daily Bread van. Angie waved and approached with a steaming Styrofoam cup. Why was he the last one here?

"Coffee, Chief?" Angie asked.

She looked reasonably fresh. Smelled good, too, above the coffee aroma. Thinking about it, he figured being up this early was normal for her. "Who's baking?"

"Me. Soon. Solomon was grabbing coffee when he got the call. It sounded like my services might be appreciated."

"And they are." He took the cup, had a few sips and handed it back. "Thanks. I've got to check out the scene." He marched up the sidewalk to the storefront, where Vicky waited, clipboard in hand.

"Here you go, Chief. Solomon's got the alley door. Doc Evans is with the body now."

"Glad someone got around to calling me," Gordon grumbled as he signed his name. "Let me look around, but I'm going to want a full report."

He ducked under the tape, stepped into the store and came to an immediate halt. This wasn't the work of ghosts.

~ ~ ~ ~ ~

Justin fanned open the slats of the blinds and peered out his bedroom window. The cops had been checking all night. A plain blue sedan drove by. Did an unmarked car mean things were better or worse? The regular cop car parked out front had left about an hour ago.

Guess we've been demoted from stakeout to drive-by surveillance.

Rubbing his eyes, he climbed into bed. Hands folded under his head, he lay on his back and stared at the ceiling. How had he ended up in the middle of this mess?

Easy answer. To spare his grandparents.

From the other room, he heard the rustling of sheets, a faint whimper. Megan tossing and turning. Again. Was she in pain? Having nightmares? Should he do something? The old feelings of inadequacy, of insecurity, of being a failure, threatened to displace any confidence he'd built over the years. He quashed a fleeting desire to pull the covers over his head. He was an adult now, and beyond those childhood anxieties. Now he had full-fledged grownup anxieties.

The whimpering grew louder. Almost a cry. Justin ripped back the covers and crossed to the bathroom. At Megan's closed door, he paused. He tapped his knuckles against the wood. "Megan?" No answer. Pressing his ear to the door, he heard muffled weeping.

He eased the door open. "Megan?" he whispered into the darkness. "What's wrong?"

She sniffled. "Go away."

He flipped the bathroom light on. "No, I'm coming in." He left the door ajar behind him, providing enough light to see.

She sat up, hugging the covers to her chest. "Just a dream."

Justin crossed the room and sat at the foot of the bed. "Talk to me, Megan."

"I ... I can't." She wouldn't meet his gaze.

"You remembered, didn't you?"

"No. It's ... I can't sleep is all."

"You want anything? Herbal tea? Hot chocolate? Another pain pill?"

She paused, as if he'd posed the question of the ages. She flexed her wrist, then inhaled sharply. "Maybe a pill."

The vial sat on her bedside table, beside a glass of water. He opened the container and tipped out a tablet. She took it from his palm, popped it in her mouth, and he handed her the water.

"I haven't been able to sleep either," he said after she swallowed the pill. "How about we talk until it starts working?"

Handing him the empty glass, she cocked her head. "Another surprise. We hardly ever talked as kids."

"Yeah. I was a loner. Not that you tried to change that."

"The first time you visited—when I lived here—I was six. You were eight."

"I remember. You were a bossy little squirt." He gave her leg a playful punch.

"We were kids. I was insecure. I was afraid of you."

"Afraid?" That hit him like a two-by-four. Megan the Fearless? Afraid of *him*? "Of me? Whatever for?"

She fussed with the sheet. "It hadn't been that long since my parents died. I was a late-in life-baby, and my parents were probably closer in age to Rose and Sam than to parents of other kids my age. Rose and Sam were like family.

"Then, all of a sudden, they *were* family. Deep down, I

worried that they might go away forever, or send me away. Rose used to go help Sam in the bookstore, but I'd panic if she left me with someone, or had someone come stay with me after school."

"That's understandable. You'd had a traumatic loss."

"When you showed up, I thought Rose and Sam might like you more than me. And you didn't like to play with us kids, so you spent a lot of time with Sam in his store. I was afraid they wouldn't have room for both of us, and since you were a real relation, you'd be the one they chose."

He didn't respond immediately, trying to think like a frightened six-year-old who'd lost her parents less than a year before. All the mischief she'd wrought, blaming it on him. It made sense now.

"Maybe we didn't talk enough then," he said. "But my parents, and Oma and Opa, should have explained. I think kids understand a lot more than adults give them credit for. All my folks said that year was that Oma and Opa had a little girl living with them, and that I'd have someone to play with. I didn't have many friends at home, so I thought it might be fun." He grinned. "Even if you were a girl."

"But I wasn't what you'd expected."

"No, you weren't. You didn't like to read. Or do jigsaw puzzles. Everything you did involved running, or included some kind of ball. I was a klutz. And then there was the frog incident."

She ducked her head. "I'm sorry about that one. I still owe you for not telling Rose I put it in your bed."

"I think I checked for nighttime guests for six months—even after I went home."

"I remember being glad when you went home. Like I'd won. You stayed what—three weeks that first time? It seemed endless."

He huffed. "Yeah, on that we can agree. And too bad, because that visit set the tone for all the rest."

"If I could go back, I'd try to be more understanding. You

think we can put it behind us? Start over?" She extended her good hand. "Friends?"

He accepted the handshake. "Friends." Her hand was dry and warm in his. Smooth. In the dim light, he couldn't read her eyes, but she didn't let go. And then he wondered, if they'd grown up close, would he consider her more a sister than a woman? Because he was definitely thinking woman. So what? Sister or woman, it didn't matter. What it meant was he now had one more person to protect.

Or could he trust her with the truth?

Chapter Eight

Gordon stood inside the doorway, taking in the scene, finding the detachment needed to keep from smashing his fist through the wall.

Betty Bedford was secured to her wooden desk chair. Her ankles were crossed in front of her, bound with duct tape. Another wide belt of tape went around her torso. Her arms, taped at the wrists, were behind the chair.

A nuisance, a pest, a thorn in his side she might have been, but she was a vital woman, barely into her sixties. She should have been pestering him for years to come. Her bright, eager eyes, now filmed with death, stared into nothingness.

He took three deep breaths, counted to ten, and called out to Doc Evans, who doubled as the city coroner.

Doc straightened from his crouch next to the body. "She's been murdered."

Yeah, that was a fairly easy call. The slit throat was a dead giveaway. Kind of hard to do yourself when you were tied up. Or tie yourself up afterward. And her shop was in ruins. Heaps of clothing in the center of the room, all her quirky *ambience* pieces broken and strewn helter-skelter. Cardboard boxes, contents spewed, lay upended amidst the debris.

"You going to call the Sheriff's Office in on this one?" Doc said.

"Ya' think?" Gordon scrubbed his hands over his face.

"While we're waiting, what can you tell me?"

"I'm no medical examiner, but I'm willing to go out on a limb and say cause of death was exsanguination." He pointed to the pool of blood at the base of the chair. "She died in this chair, judging from the blood. And from the way the blood's dried, I'd say she's been dead several hours. The ME will be able to tell you more after an autopsy."

"Thanks. Hang tight." A homicide in Mapleton. There'd been one close call, a couple of thugs thinking they could lie low in Mapleton after robbing a Denver jewelry store about fifteen years ago. His father had been in the thick of things, and if not for the quick thinking of Dix, Betty Bedford might have been Mapleton's second homicide victim instead of the first in fifty-some-odd years. Gordon took a moment to collect his thoughts, giving another silent thanks to Dix.

He pulled out his radio, then changed his mind and used his cell to call Dispatch. Buzz would be monitoring the radio, and he wasn't ready to cope with a reporter. Buzz meant well, but his normal stories were gossip, although he called them human interest. This kind of a story would have him salivating, there'd be a special edition of the weekly paper, and he'd no doubt call in every media contact in Colorado. Hell, he'd probably call CNN.

Gordon wasn't surprised when Connie answered his call instead of Irv. Even Angie had shown up at the scene.

"Hey, Chief. Irv called me. Said he felt a little out of his element, so I came in early."

Irv, retired from another small town force, worked three nights a week as a dispatcher. Gordon thought he'd applied for the job as a way to live with his insomnia.

"Thanks. I need you to call the County Sheriff's Office. Get them to roll their Crime Scene Response Team to Vintage Duds."

"Already done."

"Why do I get the feeling I was left out of the loop on this one?"

She lowered her voice. "Chief, I dropped the ball. I assumed Irv had already called you. I should have asked."

He couldn't bring himself to fault Connie. "It's over. Good to know the department runs even when I'm not around. What else has gone down that I should know about? Recap, please."

"Vicky McDermott called it in. Irv rolled the medics and another car. Then he called me. From what he said, I figured we were going to need all the help we could get."

"You thought right. Get me three fresh uniforms to maintain the perimeter."

"On it."

"And if anyone but me calls, your vocabulary has been cut to two words. 'No comment.' Pass the word to the rest of the staff."

"Roger."

"Good work." He hung up and backed out the door. Vicky McDermott stood sentry with her clipboard. She looked pale. He thought of Mrs. Bedford in the chair and figured he was probably a few shades lighter than normal too.

"Someone get pictures?" he asked her.

"Solomon, sir. He brought the good camera. All I have is that dinky point and shoot."

"No problem. The county guys will bring all the fancy gear. I'm going to check around. Then I'll need your report. Say, my office in half an hour?"

"Yes, sir." She hesitated, like she wanted to say more.

"What is it?"

"I keep wondering if I could have done something to prevent this. Or been here in time to see the bad guy."

"I'm sure you did everything according to procedure. I shouldn't have given you two addresses to cover on top of your normal patrol duties." He pulled his ball cap out of his pocket and tugged it on. "For what it's worth, I'm kicking myself too. But hindsight isn't going to help us now. We have to pull together and find the creep who did this."

"Yes, sir. I'll have my report ready."

Her stride was steady as she walked to her car. Buzz, appeared from behind Angie's van, dropping his cigarette into his coffee cup as he trotted up. "Chief! Chief!" He had a pen and notebook at the ready. "Can I get a quote? What happened?" Buzz stood on tiptoe and craned his neck, trying to peer into the shop.

"Buzz, you know we're going to have to notify next of kin before you can run with any story. We don't need your sensationalism."

"What do you mean, sensationalism. I write in-depth studies."

"For starters, your Holocaust article was uncalled for. Mapleton's got a sizeable Jewish population. "

Buzz flapped a hand. "Hey, that was only the first article. I'm thinking my series will be picked up by the national papers."

"Think about the consequences next time you print a one-sided article. You don't want to alienate your readers, or they won't read the next installment."

"Hey. Not my fault they cut the bit where I explained I've got a whole series planned, showing all sides of the picture. I've got a hot lead on some new information. I'm lining up interviews with people from town. I've got a publisher interested in a book deal." He shifted his gaze toward the shop. "But this is more immediate. I promise not to print anything until you give me the word. You've got to give me something, Chief. This is big."

"What do you know?"

"Officer McDermott found Mrs. Bedford's body. And her throat was cut. Do you have any suspects?"

Damn. That was already too much information.

"You know as much as I do, Buzz. And I'm counting on you to keep your word. If I see a special edition of the *Weekly*, you're going to be so far out of the loop, you won't know who won third prize for the best canned beets at the County Fair."

Buzz glowered, then stomped toward his battered old RAV4. "Just doing my job," he muttered, smacking his fists against his thighs.

Gordon waited until Buzz drove off, then found Ed Solomon, camera around his neck, leaning against the wall in the alley behind the store, but away from the door to Vintage Duds. Keeping the scene uncontaminated, Gordon thought, allowing himself a quick glow of pride that his officers knew their jobs.

Solomon had been on duty all day, and the security light above the door emphasized the shadows under his eyes. He snapped upright at Gordon's approach. "Chief."

Gordon nodded. "Didn't expect to see you, but thanks for coming."

Solomon's lip twisted upward in a half-smile. "Hey, pass up a chance to be part of the only homicide in Mapleton history since—well, since before my time, anyway."

"Mine, too. What did you find?"

Solomon pulled out his Maglite, flicked it on and pointed the beam at the Vintage Duds door. "No sign of forced entry. If our guy came in this way, either the door was unlocked, or Mrs. Bedford let him in."

Gordon cursed under his breath. She'd probably heard more noises, thought she was catching her ghost, and opened the door to confront it. But it wasn't a ghost.

Solomon swung the light along the gravel-covered alley. "No prints I could find, nothing unusual, but we don't have any snazzy toys to find the less-than-obvious stuff. No cigarette butts, no candy wrappers. Not like the alley behind Finnegan's."

"Yeah, Mrs. Bedford had everything spic and span tonight."

"I heard the radio traffic. Another ghost watch." Solomon made a clucking sound. "A ghost wouldn't leave prints, or need to open the door."

"You saw inside?"

Solomon sobered at Gordon's tone. "Definitely not a ghost."

"Any flesh and blood individuals show up?"

"Couple of lookie-loos, but I convinced them they should be elsewhere. And Buzz, of course, as expected. I sent him on his way, too."

"Of course. The man must have a scanner on twenty-four seven. The other merchants know?"

"Nobody's come by."

He made a note to touch base with them. Maybe the rumor mill had stopped grinding and they hadn't heard. If they had, they'd have been here. "Crime Scene Response Team is on its way. I've got a couple of things to check at the station, but I'll be back. Until then, grab some tape, block off the alley, let's say one store in either direction. Same thing out front. Might as well show the locals we're putting their tax dollars to good use."

"Will do." He started off.

"Hang on," Gordon said. "Give me the memory chip. I can copy the files and start investigating."

Solomon slipped the camera from his neck and extracted the chip, placing it in an evidence envelope he pulled from his jacket pocket. Gordon signed for it, then waited until Solomon returned with the yellow tape. After helping set the perimeter, Gordon stormed to the station to deal with the communication snafu.

Calmly. Professionally. With great finesse and understanding. Or so he told himself as he resisted the urge to peel rubber as he left the scene.

~ ~ ~ ~ ~

Megan drifted along with the swirling fog of the pain medication.

"Megan?"

She squinted, finding Justin's silhouette at the foot of her bed. Right. They'd been talking. "Hmm."

"Pill taking effect? You think you can sleep now?"

"Maybe." She scooted down in the bed, closed her eyes, and sank into the mattress.

Shapes and shadows danced in her head. Dreamy, ethereal. An abstract ballet. Something lurked at the edge of the shadowy figures. With a rush, it stormed into the midst of the dance. Sharp, jerky motions. A male form. Thick, blocky. He wove in and out among the dancers, tripping them, knocking them down, destroying the graceful patterns of their movements.

She strained to see him more clearly. Discern his features. He had none. A mask? Heart pounding, she reached for his face, frantic to pull away the covering. He grabbed her arm.

"Megan. Wake up."

She struggled to free herself.

"Megan. It's me. Justin. You're having a nightmare. Wake up."

Soothing tones, repeated over and over. *You're safe. Wake up.*

She shot to the surface, gasping, as if it were from the depths of the ocean. "Justin?"

"Welcome back."

She raked her hand through wet, tangled hair. "Whoa. That was some pill."

"Maybe next time half will be enough."

"I think I prefer the pain. How long was I like that?"

"Not too long. Ten, maybe fifteen minutes."

She looked at the clock. It was after six. "You were here the whole time?"

"No, you crashed about five minutes after you took the pill. I went to bed, but I couldn't sleep. I came in when I heard you."

"Heard me? Was I talking in my sleep?" Her mind had cleared enough to know she wasn't supposed to be talking, although she wasn't clear on the details yet. She clenched her good hand into a fist, trying to make order of the muddle in her head.

"Nothing intelligible," he said. "Mostly groans."

It didn't matter. It wasn't whether she talked, but whether the man thought she'd talked. She shuddered, and the shudders grew into uncontrollable shivers. Her throat tightened.

Justin snaked his arm behind her and she clung to him. Just for a minute. Just until she got centered. Heat radiated from his body. She absorbed it like sunshine on a winter day. She buried her face in his chest, concentrating on his steady heartbeat, trying to slow her own to match.

"Oh, God, Megan. Easy. You're safe."

"Just hold me for a second."

"I've got you. Nothing is going to happen to you. I promise."

If only. But now, he was here, he was strong, and she did feel safe. She wasn't shivering anymore. Enough. This was *Justin*. He was practically family. She took one last deep inhale, soaking up his scent before pulling away.

"Thanks," she said, avoiding his gaze.

"Any time." He brushed his fingers along her jaw. Rough, calloused fingers, but oh, so gentle.

Water gurgled through the pipes. "It's nearly six," she said. "Rose and Sam will be up."

"If you want to sleep in, they'll understand."

And invite the nightmares? "No, I'll get up. I have to scrounge a plastic bag for my wrist so I can wash."

"Need any help?" He grinned.

"In your dreams."

"I meant scrounging the plastic bag."

She ignored the feigned innocence in his expression. "Right. Please."

"No problem. Back in a jiff."

"Justin?"

He turned. "Something else you need?"

A way out of this mess. She shook her head. "Thanks."

He dipped his head, then went into his bedroom, closing the door on his side of the bathroom. She lay in bed, staring at the ceiling. Her eyes followed the cracks as if they were a roadmap that would lead her to answers.

When no illuminated route appeared, she sighed and got out of bed. Steadier on her feet than she'd been last night, she padded into the bathroom to check the damages. The swelling on her forehead had gone down, but there was a nice collage of purple and yellow surrounding the red lines where the scrapes had scabbed over. Makeup wasn't going to help. Deciding a bath would be easier than a shower for keeping her bandage dry, she turned on the taps.

And was immediately doused with cold water. Some idiot hadn't flipped the diverter from shower to tub. "Justin!" she squealed.

The door flew open. Justin appeared, plastic bag in hand, panic in his eyes. "What happened?"

He stood there, his eyes widening. His gaze wandered across her body, and she realized her cotton nightshirt bore the results of her impromptu shower. She grabbed for a towel.

"Damn it, Justin, don't you know enough to set the water for the tub after you shower?"

His mouth curved into a grin. "I don't take baths."

She snatched the bag from him. "Out. Out, out, out."

Downstairs, the doorbell rang.

Chapter Nine

Gordon smelled the coffee as soon as he stepped out of his SUV at the Kretzers'. Seeing lights and movement in the kitchen, he strolled to the door and rang the bell. Sam, hair disheveled, wearing a flannel robe and leather slippers, peered out, then opened the door.

"Gordon? Is something wrong?"

"No. Sorry to come by so early. I wanted to check on Megan. Has she remembered anything more?"

"She's taking a bath, I believe. If you'd like to wait, the coffee's ready. You can ask her yourself."

Good as Rose's coffee was, Gordon couldn't linger. He almost mentioned what had happened at Vintage Duds, but decided these folks didn't need any more excitement. They'd find out soon enough. "No, I have to get to the station. Have Megan call if she regains her memory." Inhaling one last lungful of coffee-scented air, he turned to leave.

Rose's scuffling footfalls sounded behind him.

"Gordon, wait a minute, please."

He pivoted and gave her a patient smile. "Yes?"

She came closer, cleaned her glasses and gave him the once-over. Self-consciously, he rubbed his hand over his unshaven jaw. She made a tsk-tsk sound.

"Why are you here so early? You wouldn't show up unannounced at six-thirty in the morning simply to check on Megan. And to look at you, you haven't been sleeping. What's going on?"

Damn, she could read him like his mother. Better, maybe.

"I've been working a case since early this morning. And if you'll excuse me, I've got a meeting at seven."

"Should we be worried?" she asked. "Is this about Megan's accident?"

"No, not at all." What the hell. Better to hear it from him instead of the gossip mongers. "There was an ... incident at Vintage Duds."

"Incident?" Sam said. "What kind?"

"It might be a homicide." Might be? Talk about sugarcoating. "That's what my meeting's about, so I need to go."

"Was it Betty?" Rose asked, one hand to her mouth.

He nodded. "Yes. I'm sorry."

She blanched. "Her family. They know?"

"We called her sister. She'll make the arrangements."

"Can we help? She has no family here, but maybe a memorial service?"

Gordon put his hands on Rose's shoulders. "That's very kind, Rose."

"You'll tell me how I can help?"

"Promise. I've got to go."

Sam walked him to the SUV. "There is something you're not saying."

"Police business, Sam."

"I understand. But I'm thinking you would tell Rose to keep the doors locked, except you're afraid it would upset her. On the other hand, if I insist, she'll simply call me a worry wart. But the doors will be locked."

"You're a wise man, Sam."

Gordon tossed his ball cap onto a hook inside his office door, shrugged off his jacket and draped it over the back of his chair. Cinnamon wafted to his nostrils. His stomach rumbled. His mouth watered. He followed the aroma to the break room where several uniformed county deputies were stuffing their faces with cinnamon buns.

"Sorry we don't have donuts," Gordon said, insinuating himself between them and grabbing one for himself. "Nothing but fresh-baked cinnamon buns. Us being the poor country bumpkin police force and all."

One deputy wiped his mouth with the back of his hand, then licked his fingers. "If this is your normal fare, let me know when you have an opening, and I'm putting in for a transfer."

"No, this is a special service. Only happens when we get a homicide. At the current rate, you might tell your grandson to apply for the job." He poured coffee into his mug, raised it in salute. "Briefing in five, officers," he said, and went off in search of Laurie.

Irv approached. "Chief, do you want me to stay? I know I screwed up, but it won't happen again."

Damn straight. Irv had taken Gordon's initial instructions too literally. He'd told Irv that Vicky was in charge of dealing with Mrs. Bedford's whining, and Irv had extrapolated that to mean he shouldn't bother Gordon with any calls regarding Betty.

In retrospect, Gordon admitted he might have sounded irked when he'd talked to Irv after Betty's second call out. Still, the man should have known the difference between a homicide and a fear of ghosts. But, bottom line, Betty had been dead for a while before Vicky found her, and getting called out at oh two hundred instead of oh four-seventeen wouldn't have mattered.

Irv looked humble to the point of it being embarrassing.

"Sure," Gordon said. "We can use all the help we can get. Connie's working Dispatch, but she can use an assistant."

"I won't let you down." Irv spun on his heel and marched toward Connie's desk.

Gordon found Laurie with Solomon in the multi-purpose room, pushing desks together, forming one long table down the center. The white board was set up at the far end of the tables, creating the top of a T. Solomon had taped an eight-by-ten blowup of one of the crime scene shots.

Detective Tyler Colfax, the deputy who'd shown up at the scene to help work the case meandered into the room and leaned against the far wall, apparently content to let Gordon's staff handle setting thing up. Gordon nodded in his direction.

Colfax lifted a cup of coffee in response. Mid-forties. Average height, beginnings of a paunch, but his relaxed stance was deceptively casual. Steel-blue eyes grabbed every detail. Soft-spoken, but people did what he said, no questions asked, Gordon knew, after working with him earlier.

Members of the Mapleton force, most munching on cinnamon buns, filtered into the room. Nothing like a grisly murder to bring out the curiosity in everyone. He figured most of the off-duty staff was here volunteering to "help," although there wasn't a hell of a lot they could do. Consensus was, the asshole who killed Betty was long gone, but until the evidence was analyzed, they had no idea who they were looking for.

And what does the Mapleton PD have to analyze evidence with, even if we find it?

However, leaving stones unturned wasn't good police procedure, so he and the deputies would be knocking on doors, hoping for a lead. Didn't need any fancy equipment for that.

His crew and half a dozen deputies strolled into the room, finding seats around the table, dragging in chairs, or standing against the wall. Gordon strode to the white board.

"Thanks for coming," he began. "A few details to get out of the way. I'm Police Chief Gordon Hepler." He glanced around the room, making eye contact with the deputies. "We're working as a team with the Sheriff's Office on this one. Detective Tyler Colfax will be helping me head up the investigation."

He paused, half-expecting some reaction from Colfax,

but the man only gave a perfunctory nod of his head. *Nothing wrong with collaboration, is there, Dix? Doesn't make me less of a cop.*

Gordon regrouped and pointed to the picture. "The victim, Betty Bedford, was discovered at oh two-twenty-eight by Officer McDermott." He gestured toward Vicky, and she raised her hand.

He went on. "I had personal contact with Mrs. Bedford from twenty-three-hundred to approximately twenty-three-forty, so we know she was alive then. At that time, there were no signs of unusual activity at her place of business."

He picked up a black marker and began a time line across the lower portion of the board. At appropriate intervals, he drew vertical lines representing the times he'd mentioned.

"The victim had requested extra surveillance, being concerned about intruders, so special attention was paid to her store."

There was a brief undercurrent of murmuring from his officers, who were well aware of Betty Bedford's eccentricities. He shot them the look he usually reserved for the mayor, and they quieted.

"Officer McDermott's reports indicate no other merchants were in the surrounding shops, although Finnegan's, which shares the rear parking lot with Vintage Duds as well as eight other establishments, was open, and there might have been some witnesses."

"You think the suspect could have been in the bar?" a deputy asked.

"Anything is possible. We're a small town. On a weeknight, it's likely the patrons were regulars, so a stranger might be remembered. I want you to work in teams of two. One Mapleton, one deputy. Deputies will drive. Their cars have computers, and I'll expect your reports immediately. Nobody goes anywhere without backup. Check in with Connie in Dispatch. She'll assign sectors. Canvass the neighboring shops, in case we missed a merchant working late."

Vicky bristled. He shook his head.

"Officer McDermott had her routine patrols, plus I'd asked her to do extra surveillance of a residence on the north side. It's possible someone was in and out while she was performing the rest of her assigned duties."

"Maybe our suspect was hiding in one of the stores," a deputy said. "Would have had lights off, nobody would notice."

"True," Gordon said. "When you're doing your interviews, have the merchants check for evidence they had an uninvited guest."

"Drugs?" another deputy asked. "People go all kinds of crazy if they're high or need a fix."

Gordon considered it. "Other than a little weed, we've never had a serious drug problem, and I can't imagine Betty Bedford being involved. But it's an avenue to explore. Thanks."

He paused, trying to think of anything else he missed.

When he couldn't, he said, "Questions?" He waited out a short silence. "Ladies and gentlemen. We've got a bad guy to catch."

~ ~ ~ ~ ~

Justin sat in the waiting room of Doctor Evans' office, checking his watch against the clock on the wall for the umpteenth time. He picked up the tattered copy of *National Geographic* and tried to concentrate on an article about radio tracking whales when what he wanted to be doing was searching. But when Opa had asked him to drive, he couldn't think of a reason to refuse.

Finally, Opa, Oma, and Megan came through the door. From their smiles, he assumed they'd had good news. Hoping to avoid a protracted chat session with the receptionist, he rose, immediately heading toward the door. "Ready?"

"Megan's fine," Oma said. "No after-effects, except a sore wrist."

Typical, he thought, to put Megan's welfare first. "And what about you?"

"Nothing serious," Oma said.

He stopped, holding the door open, his pulse jumping. "But there was something?"

"He's changing my blood pressure medication," she said. "What I was taking lowered it too far, and that's why I got dizzy."

"And passed out," Opa added. "Maybe more than once. We need to stop at the pharmacy and get the new prescription filled."

Relieved, Justin said, "Of course. Megan, did he give you any different pain pills?"

"No, he recommended over the counter stuff." She held up her wrist. Yesterday's thick support had been replaced by a thin elastic sleeve. "It's much better."

Now, if he could figure out a way to keep everyone out of the house for an hour or two. Instead, Oma came up with half a dozen other essential errands, which Justin figured were primarily to catch up on what had happened at Vintage Duds.

Megan yawned. "I could use a cup of coffee. I'll walk over to Daily Bread. You can meet me there."

"I'll go with you," Justin said. "I could use a cup myself."

"I'll go with Rose," Opa said. "An hour?"

"Sounds good," Justin said. Could he skip the coffee, get home and have time to do a little poking around? Not enough. He resigned himself to another late-night excursion, after everyone had gone to bed. Maybe he'd have decaf now, and crash for an hour when they got home.

He followed Megan to a booth near the rear of the diner. Angie zeroed in on them, carafe and mugs in hand. "How's the memory?" she asked.

Megan glanced around, as if she were afraid someone

might be listening. "Same."

"Heard the news?" Angie said. "About Betty Bedford?"

"Yes," Justin said. "Kind of hard to avoid it."

Angie checked the room, then nudged Megan over and sat beside her. "Yeah, but did you hear how she died? All the details? I was there. It was awful."

"You were there?" Megan's jaw dropped. "You saw it?"

"Not exactly *there*, as in inside the store, but I heard about it when I came in to start the baking. So I brought over an urn of coffee."

"Being the good Samaritan," Justin said. Angie hadn't changed one bit. Always had to be in the thick of things.

"Nothing wrong with that," Angie said without looking at him. "The cops appreciate a good cup of coffee while they're working, and I figured they'd be there awhile." She twisted on the bench so she was facing Megan. "It was awful. Her throat was cut. I think I'm getting a burglar alarm. Or a big, loud dog."

"I'd go with the alarm," Justin said. "Don't have to walk or feed it."

Angie rolled her eyes. "Whatever."

Still dismissing him, as if he didn't exist, Justin thought.

"God, that's terrible. No wonder Sam made a fuss about locking all the doors," Megan said.

"Yeah, well they called in some county deputies, and the crime scene folks—they're not as cute as the ones on television—and they're all over town asking questions."

"Maybe that's why Gordon stopped by so early this morning," Megan said. Justin detected a hint of relief in her expression.

"He questioned *you*?" Angie said. From across the diner, someone lifted his coffee cup, and she slid out of the booth. Focused on Megan, she waved an "in a minute" gesture in the man's general direction. "Why would he think you knew anything?"

Megan chewed her lip. "I didn't talk to him. Sam said he

wanted to know if my memory came back. God, I can't believe it. A murder in Mapleton."

"Ronnie at the gas station said the cops were asking about drugs," Angie said. "But Betty Bedford doesn't— didn't—seem to be the drug dealing sort."

After Angie left to handle coffee refills, Megan silently nursed her coffee for several minutes. When she spoke, he had to lean forward to hear. Her scent, her only adornment, surrounded him. She wore no makeup, undoubtedly because she couldn't apply it left-handed. Even so, he didn't think makeup would have concealed the deep shadows under her eyes, or the worry lines between her eyebrows. Her lips were pinched together, as if she were keeping a secret trapped behind them.

She cast a furtive glance around the room, then studied the contents of her mug. "Gordon would be busy investigating the murder, wouldn't he? Even if there were county deputies, it would be his top priority, right?"

"I'd think so." He matched his tone to hers.

Another look around the room. "So why would he take time out to drop by Rose and Sam's unless he thought there was a connection?" When she lifted her mug, it shook in her hand.

Justin took the mug from her hand and set it down before she spilled coffee all over the table. He gave her what he hoped was a reassuring grin. "He wanted some *apfel kuchen*?"

She glared. "I'm serious."

He lifted his hands in apology. "My bad. But Gordon would have mentioned it, wouldn't he?"

"I guess." Her eyes went saucer-wide. "You can't believe he thinks Rose and Sam are involved? That he came by to search for clues? All hush-hush."

"That's totally ridiculous."

She picked up her spoon, then put it down. Repeated the motions with her fork. Then her knife. "Justin, I've got to tell you something. But you can't tell anyone."

His heart hammered. What did she know? "I won't."

She scanned the room again. He started to check, but she stopped him with a sharply whispered, "Don't turn around."

"Megan, you're being paranoid. Whoever killed Mrs. Bedford is long gone. Why would a killer hang around a small town where he'd stand out as a stranger?"

"Unless he's hiding in plain sight. Or ... or, I don't know. But I don't want to talk here. Let's go somewhere more private."

Justin left payment for the coffee on the table. He guided Megan toward the door, his hand at the small of her back. He felt her trembling. He threaded his arm around her waist, and she leaned into him.

Her cell chimed. She pulled it out, squinted at the display, and her eyes widened. "Sam texts?"

He chuckled. "I showed him how. He and Oma were always saying they hated the way cell phones interrupted everything. Texting seemed less intrusive, although he complained about the tiny keyboard. I didn't think he'd actually use it. What did he say?"

"That they're done, and they'll meet us at the car." Just then, Oma's voice carried from down the block. "Justin! Megan! We're finished." An array of bags hung from Opa's hands.

"Guess we'll talk later," Justin said. Megan moved away, but laced her fingers with his. Her vise-like grip telegraphed her fear.

The brief ride home was unusually quiet. The distressing news of the murder seemed to muffle any need for idle conversation. Justin pulled into the garage, hitting the remote to close the door behind them. Opa fumbled in his pocket for the key to the mud room.

Justin grabbed the bags and followed him inside. "Where do you want these?"

"Put them on the kitchen table for now," Oma said,

slipping out of her coat and sliding it onto a hanger.

Justin, contemplating Megan's fear, didn't realize his grandfather had stopped in the middle of the doorway to the kitchen, and collided with him. He stepped back, waiting for Opa to move forward.

"*Mein Gott!*" Opa said.

Then it hit Justin. The crawling sensation up the nape of his neck. The sense of disturbance. The faint odor of tobacco. Someone had been here. Or was here, waiting.

"Oma, Opa. Megan," he said in a whisper. "Get in the car."

"But I need to put some things in the refrigerator." Oma tugged at the bags Justin held, tried to push him out of her way.

Then she screamed.

Chapter Ten

Gordon shoved his notebook into his pocket. Another "Sorry, didn't see anything," interview. Some of Finnegan's regulars had offered descriptions of suspicious characters. Three strangers in the bar last night. Ten different descriptions. Tall, short, black, white. Maybe Hispanic, maybe Asian. Young, old. Fat, thin. He rubbed his eyes.

Every lead, however flimsy, had to be followed. So far, they'd had no luck. He started to think maybe there were ghosts involved after all. He got into his car, ready to tackle the next interview.

His phone rang. "Hepler."

"Tyler Colfax. Can we meet? I have some interesting information on your accident victim."

Detective Colfax's words took a detour on the way to Gordon's brain. Accident? What happened to Betty Bedford was no accident. Slowly, his thought processes found the right path. "The traffic accident yesterday? Karl Franklin? Thought that went to state patrol."

"It's ours now. Your office?"

"On my way." Shell casings. They'd been looking for shell casings, Patterson had said. Had they found some? Or evidence that it wasn't a routine accident? Why else would the Sheriff's Office have it? Was he dealing with a second homicide? And could it be related to Betty Bedford? He remembered the papers Franklin carried. Were Megan and the Kretzers in serious danger? Had he dropped the ball when he assumed the threat had died with Franklin?

He'd checked the Florida DMV records and hadn't come up with anything useful. Plenty of Franklins, although none of the pictures resembled his Karl Franklin. And they didn't even all have pictures. If the original license had been issued before they computerized the photos, the computer search came up blank on that count, because they just mailed stickers as renewals if a person's record was clean. Damn, he felt useless.

Was getting him behind a desk really why Dix pushed him into the chief's job?

Gordon snapped his phone shut and tossed it into a cup holder. He did a quick three-point turn and pointed his SUV toward the station, flipping on the light bar as he turned the corner.

He pulled into the rear lot, his tires kicking up gravel as he aimed for the station's rear entrance, glad nobody had taken his slot. In his office, Gordon found Colfax sitting at *his* desk, using *his* computer. He stopped in the doorway, cleared his throat. "Hello?"

The detective turned when Gordon entered, evidently taking in Gordon's frown. "Don't worry. I'm using your terminal to access the county system. Your secrets are safe."

Gordon kept walking. "I'll be right with you. First chance I've had to hit the head all day."

When he returned, Colfax had moved to the visitor chair. An open file folder sat on the desk. Gordon sank into his own chair and leaned back. "There's got to be a basic design flaw in cop work. You survive on coffee, but there are no bathroom breaks when you're working a case."

"Super-economy-sized bladder ought to be one of the job requirements."

"I hear you. What do you have?"

"Less than we should have. CSP ran the plate on the car. Gave us a blue Camry, but it's not registered to a Karl Franklin."

The tiredness brought on by lack of sleep and tedious interviews vanished. He leaned forward. "Go on."

Colfax leafed through the papers in the folder and pulled one out. "Car belongs to a Tomo Yamaguchi. Sixty-two years old. Lives in Fort Lauderdale. Is alive and well, and had no idea his plate was stolen. He and his wife were driving cross country. The plate could have been lifted at any one of countless stops. He's an amateur photographer, she's a free-lance writer. They're trying to put together some sort of off-the-beaten-path travel book."

"Maybe you can connect Franklin to one of their stops."

"We're working it. But they've been on the road six weeks. They've taken innumerable detours, stopped at scenic overlooks, schlocky tourist attractions, roadside rest stops, hole-in-the-wall eateries. They probably parked their car in a hundred different places."

"Did Franklin put his own plate on their car? Or steal theirs?"

"Swapped 'em. That's probably why the Yamaguchis didn't notice. Both cars had the standard issue Florida plates. Can't say many people actually pay attention to them. You put it on, forget about it. They'd probably notice if it was gone, but it doesn't surprise me that they wouldn't notice a different one."

"So, who is he?"

"The switched plate belongs to a rental car. Picked up in Des Moines two days ago."

"Des Moines? You said it had Florida plates."

"It did. I checked with the rental company. The rental originated in Orlando. Heavy tourist town, lots of vehicles needed. Things slow down, they don't need as many, they let some go. Figure they'll get them back when the tourist season picks up. The company has designated cars it uses for out of state and one-way trips. This was definitely booked as one-way out of Orlando."

Gordon started scribbling notes. "So Franklin didn't start

his trip in Orlando?"

Colfax shook his head. "No. We verified the guy who drove it from Orlando to Des Moines wasn't Franklin. College kid, flew to Orlando for Spring break, had a change of plans and ended up driving home. No connection to Franklin, no record. Clean."

"So why does Franklin swap out his plate?"

"You tell me."

Gordon felt like he was being tested. He let his brain grind the facts. "Could be he was trying to avoid the cops. Maybe he committed some crime while driving the rental, so he decides to switch plates. But what are the odds of finding another car the same make and model as his rental with Florida plates?"

Colfax seemed to have dropped the inquisitor demeanor. He crossed his hands behind his head. "Maybe not that high. Camry's are common enough. But it still feels opportunistic to me. Maybe he was paranoid. Or a nutcase."

"True. I think it's safe to say the guy acted on a whim. He's doing something shady, sees the car and figures switching plates will create another layer between him and whoever might be looking."

Colfax narrowed his eyes. "Franklin had a Mapleton address with him, for Rose and Sam Kretzer. And pictures of someone from San Diego. Megan Wyatt. Works for a company called"—Colfax thumbed through the pages.

"Peerless Event Planners," Gordon said.

"You know her?"

Gordon nodded. "Rose and Sam Kretzer were her guardians. They raised her when her parents died. Since she was five."

"You saw the papers in Franklin's effects." It wasn't a question.

"Megan swears she never knew anyone named Karl Franklin. Neither did the Kretzers, although I thought he was from Florida, not Des Moines. Damn, I never saw his driver's license, and made a rookie assumption. But they didn't recognize the name."

"You might have mentioned the connection," Colfax said.

Gordon kept his gaze steady. "I thought I'd do a little checking first. I know how busy you guys are. I'd have passed on any relevant information. Then everything hit the fan with this homicide, and since Franklin was dead, I guess it slipped onto the back burner."

"You spoke with Miss Wyatt? We haven't been able to reach her yet."

Gordon nodded. "She arrived yesterday."

"She's here?"

Gordon scratched his stubble. "I guess we might as well lay this all out." Gordon brought Colfax up to speed. When he got to the part about Megan's incident and short-term memory loss, Colfax interrupted.

"You find out who did it?"

"We don't even know there *was* a someone. She was the kind of kid who always had to be the best, to prove she was as tough as the guys. She might have been trying to catch up to Justin, but the altitude got her. If she took a tumble on the path out by the pond, she could be feigning the memory loss to save face."

Colfax's gaze bored through him. "What do *you* think?"

"I saw her last night. She said everything was still foggy. Her biggest concern was for the Kretzers."

"Do we agree that Franklin was coming to Mapleton, and that it's connected to the Kretzers and Megan Wyatt?"

"Yes," Gordon said. New worries snaked through his gut. "But Franklin's dead." It was Gordon's turn to stare down Colfax. "Was it an accidental death? The trooper mentioned shell casings."

Colfax consulted the file. "Looked like a bullet hole in the rear window, but hasn't been confirmed. Nothing was recovered from the vicinity of the crash. The lab's working on the car to see if they can find a link to a second party being involved. That stretch of the road has its share of accidents."

"Lots of questions," Gordon said. "Not many answers."

"Not yet. But we'll find them."

"I'd ordered surveillance on the Kretzer house last night. I guess I should reinstate it."

"Might be smart. Until we find those answers."

Laurie tapped on the door, then walked in. "Chief, you need to get to the Kretzers'."

~ ~ ~ ~ ~

Standing in the garage, Megan wrapped her arms around Rose's trembling body. "We can't go inside, Rose. Not until the police get here."

"But the ice cream. It'll melt all over the floor."

"Oma, we can buy more ice cream, and I'll clean the floor," Justin said. "Maybe even put in a new one. Someone might be in there. The police said to stay out."

Rose shuddered. "We locked the doors, yes. Sam?"

"Yes, I checked," Sam said.

"So how did they get in?" Oma asked.

Opa took Oma's hands in his. "That's for the police to figure out. They might have broken a lock, or a window. Right now, we need to leave. We don't want to mess any evidence."

"Exactly, Oma. Like on television."

"Where will we go?" Rose asked. Megan's heart ached at the plaintive tone. She'd never known Rose to be helpless. She'd always been strong, always made Megan find her own inner strength.

"What about Selma's house?" Sam said. "It's two blocks away."

"We can't go in the house to call her. What if she's not home? Or busy?" Rose said.

Sam came over and rested his hands on Rose's shoulders. "We have a spare key, remember?"

"True." Rose ducked her head. "But I hate to impose."

"Rose, don't be ridiculous. If Selma came to you, you'd invite her in, no questions asked," Sam said.

"I guess so. But I don't like hiding."

"You do what you need to survive," Sam said.

His tone prickled the hairs on Megan's neck. She'd never heard him sound so bitter.

"Let's go." Megan opened the passenger door of the car and gently nudged Rose inside.

"What? We can't walk a couple of blocks?" she said.

"Rose, be quiet," Sam said. Another new tone. Sharp, authoritative. He'd used a milder version on Megan growing up, and it had demanded immediate compliance. This one had her snapping to attention.

Rose's eyes widened, but she settled into her seat and fastened her seatbelt. Sam slid behind the wheel. Megan climbed in back with Justin. He seemed as surprised as she was at Rose and Sam's reactions.

Minutes later, they pulled into the driveway of Selma's white clapboard cottage. Megan hopped out of the car and trotted up the stoop. She pulled open the screen door and rapped the brass knocker, remembering how many times she'd gone through these same motions as a child. The siding needed a fresh coat of paint, and the concrete stoop was pitted and stained. It seemed smaller. Like Rose had when she'd given her that first hug yesterday.

"Who's there?" Selma's voice sounded smaller, too.

"It's Megan. Megan Wyatt, and Rose and Sam. And Justin. Can we come in?"

A lock snicked, and the door opened an inch. From behind her, Megan heard car doors open and close. In front of her, Selma peered through the thick lenses of her glasses. Her brown eyes hadn't lost any of their sparkle. "Megan Wyatt. All grown up. My heavens, child, come in." The door opened wider. "I thought you might be that reporter from the *Weekly*. He's after me to talk about the Holocaust. I haven't decided if I trust him to write what I say. But come in, come in."

Megan stepped aside so Rose and Sam could precede her into the house. Justin waited for her to enter. Once they were inside, Selma closed and locked the door. "Terrible thing, Betty getting killed. In her own shop. We never used to lock doors. The world is changing."

Sam's face clouded. "Maybe not so much," he said under his breath. If Megan hadn't been standing so close, she wouldn't have heard.

Justin leaned down and kissed Selma's cheek. "Hi, Selma. We won't bother you long. Only until the police check out Oma and Opa's house."

Selma's mouth dropped. "Police? What happened?"

Megan escorted Rose to the overstuffed chintz sofa. "You sit, Rose. You're probably not adjusted to the different blood pressure medication yet. You're shaking."

"Someone was in my house," Rose said. "That's not right."

"No, it's not," Selma said. "But the police will catch whoever did it. I'll put on some coffee while we wait."

"I'll call the police station, let Gordon know where we are," Megan said. She stood, surprised to find her knees wobbly.

After letting Gordon's assistant know where to find them, Megan helped Selma with the coffee, a ritual much like the one Rose performed for guests, and had been doing as long as Megan could remember.

"Terrible, terrible thing," Selma muttered under her breath as she measured grounds into the coffeemaker. "There are cookies in the jar. Store-bought, I'm afraid. Some pound cake is in the bread box."

Megan didn't bother to argue. Although Selma was soft and round where Rose was thin and wiry, the two shared the same mindset. Food equaled comfort.

Even if Megan didn't think she could eat, seeing the coffee and sweets arranged on the large coffee table in Selma's living room brought the reassuring memories of so many Sunday late-afternoon *Kaffeeklatsches*. Rose, Sam, and Selma seemed to settle into an uneasy silence broken by the chink of cup against saucer, or the clink of metal against china as they stirred their coffee.

Justin set his cup aside and paced, casting furtive glances toward the door, as if it might make Gordon appear. He jammed his hands into the pockets of his jeans. Catching Megan's gaze, he said, "I need some air."

"Should you go outside?" Sam asked.

"What difference does it make?" Justin said. "Our car is out there. If someone is looking, they'll know where we are. Besides, if they wanted one of us, why toss the house? Why be so obvious? Why not sit and wait?" The tension seemed to roll off him in waves.

"Go in the backyard," Selma said. "It's private."

Justin barged toward the kitchen. The back door slammed shut.

"I could use some air too." Megan wiped her mouth and carried her cup and plate to the kitchen. From the window over the sink, she saw Justin pacing circles in Selma's lawn. She let herself out and matched Justin's stride. A faint scent of roses wafted on the afternoon breeze.

After three trips around the yard, Justin's pace slowed.

"Guess I'm getting acclimated," Megan said. "I kept up."

He led her into the wooden gazebo in the center of the yard. They sank onto the wooden bench that circled the inside of the ivy-covered lattice structure. Running his hand over the slats, he said, "Could use some maintenance."

"We're not out here to talk about fixing Selma's gazebo, although she'd be thrilled. There's something wrong, isn't there? It's obvious enough you're upset."

"I keep thinking, what would have happened if we'd been home? You heard what they said about the lady in the dress shop. Her throat was cut. That's not an easy way to kill someone. I keep seeing"—he dug the heels of his hands into his eyes.

"You think both crimes are connected, don't you?"

"Geez, Megan. Nothing ever happens in Mapleton. And now, in less than two days, there's a murder. And a break-in? Two break-ins, because it sounded to me like Mrs. What's Her Name surprised a burglar. Only he didn't run, which would seem to be the normal reaction."

Her heart played battering ram against her ribcage. She struggled to breathe. Was she a target? Those pictures from the dead man. Was there a connection? But he was dead. It couldn't be a coincidence that someone had tried to mug her. How many other people might be looking for her? A cold, clammy sweat filmed her body.

Chapter Eleven

For the second time in far too few hours, Gordon stood in a doorway and inspected a disaster area. All he could think was, thank God no one had been home. Unlike lives, things could be replaced.

"Pictures, Solomon," he said. "Everything. Six ways from Sunday."

Solomon raised the camera to his eye and started snapping. "Looks kind of like my kids' bedroom after a temper tantrum. You think our guy had an objective, or was just plain ornery?"

"Maybe a little of both. Maybe he couldn't find what he wanted and got mad."

"Not your run-of-the-mill thief," Gordon said. "Television and stereo are still here."

Solomon clicked off more pictures. "Old models. Everyone wants a flat screen. The TV's probably twenty years old. And who uses video tapes anymore? It's all DVD. At least he didn't leave any of those dandy bodily function surprise packages."

"There is that high note. We'll have to ask the Kretzers if anything's missing."

"Want me to dust for prints?"

Gordon thought about Rose, the consummate housekeeper, returning to find not only the chaos, but also the black mess of fingerprint powder all over her house. He clenched his jaw. "Do it. There might be some matches with what the CSR team got at Vintage Duds. Might help narrow it down."

"I heard one of the techs grumbling about how many prints they'd have to run."

"Hell, it was a retail store. Ever watch a woman shop? Picking things up, touching everything?" His cell rang. Again. "Hepler."

"Chief, Megan Wyatt called," Laurie said. "They're at Selma Goldberg's on Woodlawn. You need the address?"

"No, I know the house. Send a deputy over to the Kretzers' to help Solomon."

"On it. How's it look?" Laurie said.

"Not good, but there doesn't seem to be much breakage. Mostly a mess. How are things holding up on your end?"

"Phone's are ringing off the hook."

"You need any help?"

"Irv is on it. He's good at polite and evasive. The Denver papers are calling. And their local television station. They're probably going to send a crew."

"And you're going to tell them?"

"No comment."

He thought for a minute, checked his watch. "I can talk to them at five-thirty. Let Colfax know." That way, nothing would be plastered all over the local early news shows. And nothing would hit the papers until tomorrow, although with half the news being on the internet these days, he didn't know whether they'd update their websites as soon as he finished. Wouldn't matter. He wasn't going to tell them much. "Let Buzz know, too. Reserve a seat up front for him."

"On it."

A damn press conference. He cringed. Maybe he could work an information officer into the budget. Wouldn't necessarily have to be a sworn officer. Might be smarter that way. Gordon figured he'd have to exercise considerable restraint to keep from shooting a reporter. He switched his phone to vibrate and stuck it in its clip.

"Hey, Chief?" Solomon called in from the kitchen. "You think I need to leave all this?"

Gordon walked over. The contents of the freezer sat in the middle of the floor. Canisters of flour, sugar, rice had been emptied. Even Rose's cookie jar was tipped onto the counter, gingersnaps spilling from its mouth.

Near the mud room, a sticky puddle of melted ice cream dripped from one of Rose's mesh shopping bags, mixing with some tomatoes, grapes, and spinach into an unappetizing sundae.

"You shoot it?"

"Yes," Solomon said.

"I'll take care of it. You finish documenting the rest of the house. Find the point of entry."

"Will do."

This was one part of the mess Rose didn't have to see. Gordon went to the mud room, found a broom, reevaluated the damages and changed his mind. In the garage, he found a snow shovel hanging on a wall. With it, he scooped everything into plastic trash bags he discovered under the sink. Then he used the broom. After that, he wet a paper towel, wiped up the ice cream residue, and threw everything away.

When he finished, he told Solomon backup was en route, and took off on foot for Selma Goldberg's. Anyone passing by would see the normal, peaceful streets of residential Mapleton. The days were growing longer, aspens were leafing up, and flowers brought colorful borders to many of the walkways from street to stoops. Gordon ground his back teeth. Whoever had brought ugliness to his town would pay.

He made his way up the steps to Selma's door. She opened it before he had a chance to knock. "Come in, Chief Hepler."

He stepped inside, took his cap off. "Since when are you so formal?"

"You're the police chief now. An important man. And

you're here on official business."

"You can still call me Gordon." He drew the line at Gordie, which she'd called him when he was in her second grade class.

"Rose and Sam are inside."

His heart did a quick hop. "Megan and Justin?"

"They're out in the yard. Said they needed some air."

He exhaled. "I'll talk to Rose and Sam first."

Sam stood as Gordon walked over.

"Sit," Gordon said. Both Rose and Sam seemed years older than when he'd seen them last. Sam's eyes had a steely coldness to them. Anger burned. "I know you're both upset. But let's be thankful you weren't home, that nothing happened to you."

He asked his questions as gently as he could. Neither was aware of anyone wanting anything they owned. Other than Sam's book collection, which was of more sentimental than monetary value, and the usual household collection of some silver pieces and basic jewelry, they didn't have much worth stealing. Then again, that was a totally subjective opinion. People had killed for the price of a cheeseburger.

"I'm going to need you to look around. But I don't want you staying there tonight. Is there someplace you can go?"

"They can stay here," Selma said. "I have plenty of room."

Rose and Sam exchanged uneasy glances.

"It's for the best," Gordon said. "And I'll have a car patrolling both your houses all night."

"Is that necessary?" Sam said. "Are we in danger?"

"I strongly doubt it. It's a precaution. And maybe a deterrent." He stood. "I'd like to talk to Justin and Megan for a minute, then I'll go to the house with you."

Gordon strode across the lawn toward the gazebo where Justin and Megan were tangled in an embrace. Her face was buried in his chest. Justin nuzzled her hair, tinged gold with the late-afternoon sun, and his hand moved up and down her back. Gordon slowed, about to announce his presence, when muffled sobs told him he wasn't interrupting a romantic interlude.

He trotted the last few feet and took the steps in a single bound. "Is there a problem?"

Justin pulled his face away from her hair long enough to say, "Scared," then murmured more sounds of comfort.

Gordon sat on Megan's other side. "Megan. It's Gordon. Did you remember what happened to you? Is that why you're afraid?"

When she didn't respond, Gordon put his hands on her shoulders and eased her away from Justin. "Megan, it's important. Talk to me. You're safe here."

She shook her head wildly and her sobs intensified.

"She won't say anything," Justin said. "She's been crying for about five minutes."

"What triggered it?" Gordon took over Justin's role of comforter as Megan buried her face in his chest now. He couldn't remember seeing Megan cry. Ever. She'd shaken off injuries, both physical and emotional, with a defiant toss of her braids. He wasn't sure she was even aware he'd taken her from Justin.

Justin frowned. "We were talking about how we thought the break-ins at my grandparents' house and the dress shop were related, and she went all white and clammy, then said someone wanted to kill her. Then she fell apart."

Gordon's skin prickled. "She say who threatened her?"

"No. But I'm guessing it pertains to what happened to her yesterday. Doesn't take a deerstalker cap and magnifying glass to deduce that."

"No shit, Sherlock," Gordon muttered.

He pried Megan loose and took her chin in his hands. "Megan. You're okay. Rose and Sam are okay. I'm not going to let anyone hurt you, or them. But we have to talk."

She squinted. Blinked. As if she was trying to see into some dark passageway. Which maybe she was.

Megan stared at Justin, then at him. Her vision cleared. "I

don't know why I went off the deep end like that."

"Someone threatened you. It's understandable," Gordon said.

"It's not me I'm worried about."

"Nothing is going to happen to Rose and Sam. I promise."

"Don't make promises you can't keep," she said. "But I know you mean you'll do your best."

"Me and the entire Mapleton Police Department, and a multitude of County Deputy Sheriffs. Rose and Sam will stay here tonight. Will you?" He included Justin with his gaze.

"I can probably stay with Angie," Megan said.

"I'm not afraid to sleep at my grandparents' house," Justin said.

"Nobody's going to stay at their place until it's released as a crime scene." Gordon stood. "Speaking of which. I want to take Rose and Sam to look things over."

"Was it bad?" Megan asked. "Justin shooed us all out of the house before I could see."

"I'm not going to lie. It's not good," Gordon said. Which was why he was going to handle this part of the investigation personally.

"I'm coming, too," Megan said. "They'll need support."

Justin stood. "I'm with you."

"It's not necessary," Gordon said.

"I'm going," Justin said. The rigidness of his expression, the sharpness of his tone, gave Gordon the feeling his insistence on being included had to do with more than moral support for his grandparents.

~ ~ ~ ~ ~

Justin hung back as they entered his grandparents' house. Rose clung to Sam. As a unit, they trudged into the living room. Rose's hands flew to her mouth. *"Mein Gott, mein Gott, mein Gott."* There were two other cops there. One, Justin recognized as the officer who'd shown up after Megan's accident. Solomon, he thought. The other wore a deputy sheriff's uniform. Gordon had mentioned getting help with the homicide. That the deputy was here reinforced Justin's conviction that the two cases had to be connected.

But were they connected to *him*?

The three cops conferred outside the front door before Solomon and the deputy departed, indicating they were off to follow whatever orders they'd been given. Justin's attention was focused on his grandmother, who stood in the center of the room, a dazed expression on her face.

"I know this is difficult," Gordon said, shoving Justin's focus to the immediate crisis. "I'm going to ask you to see if anything was taken."

"Let me help," Justin said. "Oma, you can sit on the sofa while I organize everything."

Megan picked up his unspoken signal and guided his grandmother to the couch. "Would you like me to get you something? Tea, water?"

"You think I should sit here drinking tea while you go through the mess some *ganef,* some *mamzer* made of my house?" Oma snapped.

Whoa. Oma swearing? Justin noticed the puzzled expression on Gordon's face. "Thief. Bastard," he translated.

The cop's eyebrows lifted. Apparently Oma's epithets surprised him, too. Justin cut a glance to his grandfather, who stood soldier-straight, fists clenched, lips pressed into a thin line.

"Not a thief," Opa said. He swept his arm around the room. "The television, the stereo—he didn't take those."

"But how did he get in?" Oma asked. She turned to face the cop. "We locked up tight."

Megan's hands shot to her mouth. "My window."

"Appears so," the cop said.

"I'm so sorry," Megan said. "It sticks, and it's so hard to open if you close it all the way. It was only open a couple of inches, honest. I ... I didn't think."

"I should have fixed it," Justin said. "Replaced the whole thing. All the upstairs windows."

"It wasn't anyone's fault," the cop said. "If he wanted to get in, a closed window wouldn't have stopped him."

Justin closed his eyes, took a breath, then opened them and studied the room more carefully, trying to ignore the innumerable black smudges of fingerprint powder. The television on the floor instead of in the entertainment center. Same for the CD player. The discs were heaped on the floor, but still in their cases. "He moved everything."

"We're assuming he was looking for something," Gordon said. "The question is, did he find it?"

"Is the whole house like this?" Megan asked.

The grim expression on Gordon's face twisted Justin's gut. He suppressed the urge to add a few colorful expletives of his own to Oma's outburst. His vocabulary had certainly expanded since he'd been working at the vocational school. Keeping his irritation in check, he asked, "Can I go upstairs? I'm familiar enough with my room."

"Go ahead," Gordon said. "We might be done faster that way."

Justin fished in his pocket for his phone as he ran up the stairs. He ignored the clothes blanketing the floor of his bedroom and crossed to the window. He shoved it open and leaned against the sill, where he knew he had the best cell reception. He scrolled through his contact list until he found the number he needed. He mashed the call button. After four interminable rings, he heard the annoyingly calm voice of his nemesis. "You have it?"

"No, I don't have it, you son of a bitch, and it's not Sunday."

"I know what day it is, but I have no idea what you're talking about."

"Tell me you didn't send someone to ransack my grandparents' house."

"I didn't send someone to ransack your grandparents'

house. Why would I do that when I have you there, acting with what is undoubtedly the epitome of discretion?"

Justin took a calming breath. A breath anyway. He was miles from calm. But the initial fury had ebbed, and he realized that there was no reason for this man to be involved with whatever happened at that dress shop. "Of course. But someone did break in here, and the house is a disaster area."

"That is not reassuring," the man said. "Because now we won't be able to ascertain whether the package is in the hands of someone else, or if it remains to be found."

"On the bright side," Justin said, "I don't need to use stealth to look around."

"You will keep me apprised, of course."

"Of course." Justin slammed the phone closed.

Justin gritted his teeth and put the mattress on the box spring, grateful the thief hadn't cut it apart in his search. Maybe it was obvious enough that it was intact, that nothing could have been stuffed inside. He had, however pulled off all the covers.

Justin sat on the edge of the mattress, trying to think. The two break-ins were related, no doubt, but why would a murder at a used clothing store have anything to do with his problem? Because he wasn't thinking. Because he'd seen the shock and horror on his grandparents' faces and had to yell at someone.

He crossed through the bathroom, noting little disturbance there aside from the inevitable fingerprint powder, and went into Megan's room. Her bed had been dismantled as well. Fingerprint powder was heaviest at the window. He moved closer, looking to see if there were any other clues, like a muddy footprint. As if.

She hadn't finished unpacking, and her suitcase was lying open on the box spring, surrounded by its contents. The books were in total disarray. Her dolls and stuffed animals, their cheerful innocence as they appeared oblivious to the wreckage, sent another wave of helpless frustration through his gut. He left them to their glass-eyed stares and headed for the master bedroom.

The door stood open. Justin approached with trepidation, as if he expected to find the burglar in the room. He almost wished he would, so he could knock the crap out of whoever did this. His real dread, he realized, was having to see his grandmother's face when she saw the mess.

Well, she wouldn't see it. He strode into the room and started hanging up the clothes. Most of them were on their hangers, as if the intruder had simply tossed them out of the way. Piles of sweaters were on their closet floor. As if they, too, were in the way. Only the fingerprint powder made the bedroom a crime scene instead of a fraternity boy's room.

Pondering that, he sensed someone's approach and spun around. The cop. "Did they find something?" Justin asked. "Or not find something, I guess is more accurate."

"Not yet." Gordon picked up a sweater, folded it and set it neatly on the shelf. "How about up here?"

"Nothing I've noticed."

Gordon didn't respond. He stood in the closet, his gaze sweeping the room beyond, then freezing on Justin, who stopped, holding an armload of his grandfather's trousers.

Cops. "So? You have any ideas you'd be willing to share?" Justin said.

Gordon picked up another sweater. "Whatever he wanted, it wasn't too small."

Justin surveyed the room again. His eye caught his grandmother's maple jewelry chest with all its tiny drawers. He pulled one open. Twelve pairs of earrings sat neatly in their individual compartments. "I agree. He didn't touch this, apparently. It would have been easy enough to pocket the contents."

Gordon nodded. "That's our working hypothesis."

"But we can't stay here tonight."

"Afraid not. I'll try to rush it, but we have to verify we've done a complete inspection."

Dealing with the kinds of kids he taught, Justin had enough experience with cops to recognize pure cop mode when he saw it, sweater-folding notwithstanding. He was pretty good at reading facial expressions and body language. His students had learned lying didn't work with him. But Gordon's expression was—expressionless.

"It's more than the mess, isn't it? You think he might come back," Justin said.

"If he didn't get what he wanted, that's a possibility."

"Or maybe murder was part of his intent? The mess-making was a diversion? Or he enjoys it?"

"Letting anyone stay here is a risk I'm not willing to take."

"But whoever did this might track down my grandparents. Is having them at Selma's house all that safe? Even with a cop outside? You can't cover every door, every window."

For the first time, Justin caught a flash of concern in Gordon's eyes. The cop immediately schooled his features to neutral. "If I could, I'd have them go to Denver. Hell, I'd send them to Paris. But the odds say that it's a *thing*, not them, our guy wants. That Mrs. Bedford was in the wrong place at the wrong time."

Justin felt the power of Gordon's gaze once again. "You think it could be someone else? Not my grandparents." He couldn't suppress the chill snaking through him. "You think Megan or I might be a target?"

"I doubt it's Megan," Gordon said. "Her arrival was completely unexpected."

"Me?" Justin swallowed. "You think I might be on this guy's hit list? Why?"

Gordon put away the last sweater and speared Justin with his gaze. "I was hoping you could tell me."

Chapter Twelve

Gordon waited, watching. Given the circumstances, the man's reactions and behaviors to this point had been consistent with a caring grandson. He'd looked totally shocked when Gordon suggested he might be in line to be murdered.

Even though Gordon felt the odds were slim, it was an avenue worth pursuing, if only to learn more about Justin Nadell. Because expected behavior or not, Gordon's cop radar said the man was hiding something.

"I don't know what you're talking about," Justin said. "Why would someone want to kill me? I admit I've pissed off more than a few juvenile misfits, but I don't think any of them would have the brains—or the resources—to do anything like this. They're not murderers."

"These misfits, as you politely call them, are your students?"

Justin's eyes narrowed. "Of course. You think I hang with that crowd socially? Look, Mister Chief of Police. Believe it or not, we're on the same side here. You try to catch the bad guys. I try to keep them from becoming bad guys. Or worse guys, since we don't meet a lot of the cream of society where I work."

"If we're so alike in our professions, you understand I have to eliminate every possibility."

Justin clawed his hands through his hair and sank onto the bed. "I guess. If this were the only crime, I could see you trying to connect me. But since the dress shop—" he paused, apparently searching for the right term.

"Incident," Gordon supplied.

"Right. Incident. That's sanitized enough. Since the *incident* came first, I don't see it."

"I'll accept that. So, we have two crimes, apparently related, although one includes a homicide. Ignoring the homicide for the moment. Do you have any idea what our suspect might be looking for?"

"How would I know what some creep wanted? My guess would have been valuables, but that doesn't seem to be the case. And I've been here less than two weeks. It's not like I'd notice any obscure missing whatever."

Gordon had to agree. If anything had been taken, it hadn't been in plain sight, or there wouldn't have been a need for the search.

Justin turned away and continued putting the room in order. "And if it's all the same to you, I'd rather not leave this mess here for my grandmother to see. Unless you think it's vital that she go through it the way it is, she shouldn't have to deal with it. What's downstairs is bad enough, but to know someone was pawing through her personal things? She should be spared that."

Gordon thought of Rose's face when she'd seen the living room. "I agree."

Justin seemed to accept the temporary truce. He bundled the sheets and piled them by the door. "Give me a hand?" He gestured to the mattress laying half off the box spring. The two of them repositioned the king sized mattress where it belonged.

Justin cast a curious glance his way. "Come to think of it, why are you here instead of one of your underlings? Why is the Chief of Police on clean-up detail? Shouldn't you be solving a murder?" The curiosity in Justin's eyes shifted. His gaze shot a challenge like darts at a dartboard.

So much for a truce. "Maybe I am," Gordon said.

"You suspect me? Of killing someone? I've gone from

potential victim to suspect?"

"No, I don't think you killed anyone."

"So, why are you here? Did the hot-shot homicide detective decide you weren't good enough to work on the murder, so he sent you to take care of some penny-ante crook?"

Gordon ignored the taunts. Something had set Justin off. And maybe that something hid a lead. Something he could follow.

He wandered past the open bureau drawers, leaving Justin with his grandmother's intimate garments. The night table drawers were open, their contents dumped onto the floor. "Guy must have been in a hurry. How long were you gone?"

Justin appeared to be replaying his timetable. "My grandmother's appointment was at eleven. She wanted to stop at the church to see about a memorial service for Mrs. Bedford. I'd say we left here about ten."

Pure Rose. Although the Kretzers were Jewish, Megan's parents weren't. Rose and Sam had respected the Wyatts' wishes and raised Megan in her faith, although they also included her in their own. She'd ended up embracing both religions. Small wonder, considering the double holiday celebrations, and the foods that accompanied them. The social connections Rose had made through the church hadn't been severed, even after Megan left Mapleton.

Justin continued. "Doctor Evans was running behind schedule, and by the time we got out of there, it was nearly one. My grandmother had errands to run. My grandfather went with her. Megan and I went for coffee. I'd say it was between two-thirty and three when we got home."

"No way for anyone to know when you'd be home, then."

"No, other than the doctor's appointment, everything was spontaneous."

Gordon's cell vibrated at his waist. "Hepler."

"Chief, I think you should get here," Laurie said. "The

vultures are descending."

Damn. The press conference. "On my way." After disconnecting, he scooped what he assumed belonged in the night table drawer and set it on the bed. "I've got to go. If anything seems the slightest bit out of line—anything—call 911 and have them put you through to the Mapleton dispatcher."

Gordon slipped into his office via the rear entrance. Damn, where had the time gone? He buzzed Laurie. "Is Detective Colfax around?"

"He's on his way. I called him right after I called you."

Good to see she had her priorities in order. "Thanks. Send him in as soon as he gets here."

He needed a prepared statement. This was a far cry from the usual Mapleton media interview, which usually entailed meeting Buzz at Daily Bread for coffee and a sandwich. There was a strong possibility this might be picked up by the networks. Newspapers were bad enough. His palms sweated at the thought of making a fool out of himself on national television. Press conferences. Media vultures. What a waste of time.

He closed his eyes, picturing Dix and his father sitting in some eternal cop bar, laughing, lifting their boilermakers, peering down at him. He felt like a rookie with his training partner putting him through the wringer.

You accepted the job. Suck it up.

As he organized his thoughts and jotted notes, it occurred to him that this might be putting things into a clearer perspective, and might actually help him move the investigation forward. While he worked, something niggled at the back of his mind. Something he'd made a mental note to ask, and then forgotten.

He rubbed his neck. His brain was more like the midway at the carnival, and his stomach felt like he was riding a Tilt-a-Whirl inside a fun house. It would come to him eventually.

Gordon looked up when Colfax strode into the room and flopped into a visitor's chair. He carried two cups of coffee and set one on the desk. Gordon nodded his thanks.

"You want me to handle the media?" Colfax asked. "I've worked with some of them before. No offense, but you look a little green around the gills."

Tempting as it was, Gordon wasn't going to let his own insecurities keep him from doing his job. "No, I've got it."

"How are you going to spin it?" Colfax asked.

"I thought I'd tell the truth."

Colfax grinned. "A novel approach." He sipped his coffee before going on. "It's not what you say, it's what you don't say. My advice, for what it's worth. Stick to the facts. Keep it short. And you're under no obligation to answer their questions. Better yet, no matter what they ask, give them what you want them to have."

Gordon laid out his talking points. "You have anything to add?"

Colfax arranged his features into a perfect "impassive yet concerned" expression and cleared his throat. "Ladies and gentlemen. I know you understand that we cannot talk about an ongoing investigation. Be assured that the Mapleton Police Department and the County Sheriff's Office are cooperating and working diligently to apprehend whoever is responsible for this travesty." He grinned again. "You'll notice I gave you top billing."

"I thought I'd read a statement, then turn it over to questions. For both of us."

"Not a problem." Colfax's grin disappeared. "When you answer, it's good to let a little outrage show."

Damn, but the man apparently enjoyed this stuff. "How do you stand it? Having all those people screaming questions and wanting dirt, not facts?"

"Come with me," Colfax said and walked out of the room.

Curious, Gordon followed him down the hall to their briefing room. Colfax stepped toward the white board and stood a respectful distance away, as if it were a shrine. "I do it for her," he said, indicating the photos of Mrs. Bedford. "All the crap, all the misquotes, all the interruptions at home when you're trying to have a life. They all fade away when you get the assholes who do stuff like this. And sometimes, it's a lead you get because someone saw you on the news or read an article in the paper." Colfax rested his hand on Gordon's shoulder briefly, giving a hint of a squeeze before backing out of the room.

Gordon lingered, staring at the white board for several long, heart-wrenching moments before tackling his statement. He lifted his gaze.

Just watch. I'm going to nail this.

~ ~ ~ ~ ~

Megan's talk with Justin would have to wait. Gordon had appeared, told them he was sending another officer to supervise locking up, then thundered out of the house, obviously upset. What had he and Justin talked about upstairs?

"You know," Rose said, sweeping her arm across the room. "Maybe we should give some of it to charity. To people who need it. We hardly use half of it. The house is too crowded."

Her tone was less than convincing.

"I think that's a wonderful idea," Megan said.

Rose sank to the floor and burst into tears. "These were my things." She looked at Sam, who hurried to her side and draped his arm over her. "*Our* things. Our memories. We should have the right to crowded memories, don't you think?"

Seconds later, Justin appeared in the room, panic on his face. "What happened? Are you all right?"

"She's fine," Sam said.

"Someone comes into my home and tosses everything

around and you say I'm *fine*? Betty Bedford is dead, and you say I'm *fine*?" Rose wiped tears from her cheeks. "I'm not *fine*. I'm angry."

"We weren't here," Sam said. "That's the important thing. We're around to enjoy these memories, crowded or not."

"Sam's right," Megan said. "We should be thankful nobody got hurt."

Justin helped Rose to the sofa. "You're leaving," he said. "You, Opa and Megan. And not to Selma's. Nowhere in Mapleton. Where will it be? Denver? The Springs? You're going to a nice hotel. You'll sit by the pool, you'll dance, you'll get a new hairdo. New clothes."

"Ridiculous," Sam said. "No crook chases us out of our house."

"He's not chasing you out," Megan said. "Remember, the police said we can't stay here yet. Not until they're done doing whatever they have to do. And I think Justin's got a great idea. When's the last time you treated yourselves to some special time together?"

"She's right, Oma. You always talk about blessings in disguise. Why not take advantage of the forced vacation. You know. When life gives you a lemon, make lemonade."

Megan watched Sam take a deep breath and nod to Justin with a hint of paternal pride. "The boy is a smart one, Rose."

"Only if he comes, too. Or maybe he and Meggie should go home. Come back another time. If it's not safe for us, it's not safe for him," Rose said.

"I'm not leaving," Megan said, almost in unison with Justin's protest.

"Then it's settled," Justin said.

Sam smiled at Rose. "Where would you like to go? Consider it an anniversary celebration."

"Sam, our anniversary isn't for six months."

"So, it's a very early anniversary celebration." Sam

brushed his thumb down Rose's cheek and kissed away the tears. "Besides, you'll go crazy at Selma's. The small bed with the lumpy mattress. You won't sleep a wink."

Justin pulled out his phone. "Where do you want to stay? I'll make reservations."

Rose peeked up at Sam. "You remember that hotel in Denver? Where we—" Good grief, Rose's cheeks turned a color that matched her name.

Sam took Rose's hand and brought it to his lips. Megan could feel the heat in that simple gesture. "I do," he said.

This was going to be some lemonade. Megan smiled at Justin, whose relieved expression spoke volumes.

"But it's so expensive," Rose said. "A plain motel would do."

Megan caught Justin's questioning glance, accompanied by a surreptitious rubbing of fingers against his thumb in a "money" gesture, pointing to her, then himself. She smiled and nodded in understanding.

Justin shook his head. "Don't worry about the cost, Oma."

"Consider it a gift from me and Justin," Megan said. What better use for some of her savings. Give Rose and Sam a good time and protect them. A two-fer.

While Justin made the arrangements, Megan went upstairs to pack. Seeing the mess, she could understand Rose's feeling of violation. She peeked into Justin's room, which looked almost as bad.

She walked down the hall to Rose and Sam's room. Their clothes hung in the closet, and with the exception of the fingerprint powder, the room passed for normal. Normal if you didn't know what a neat-freak Rose was.

That must have been what Justin and Gordon were doing. How could she have believed Angie for half a second? No way Justin was at the root of those premonitions of hers. A chill ran over Megan's neck and shoulders, trickling down her spine. Angie *had* said she thought something bad was going to happen. Could her vision have been right for a change?

She dismissed the thought. Coincidences happened. This was one of those times when the odds were in Angie's favor.

Rose's footfalls shuffled down the hall. Megan forced a smile before she turned to greet her. Rose paused at the doorway, as if she was afraid to enter.

"It's not bad in here," Megan said. "Maybe they didn't have time for your room."

Rose, hands folded across her chest, gazed around the room, and then at Megan. Megan could feel Rose sucking the lies from her words.

"If you say so," Rose said. From her tone, Megan knew Rose was playing along, making it easier to cope with the reality.

"I'll help you put a few things into an overnight bag. I agree with Justin. It's a perfect excuse to buy some new clothes."

"If you say so," Rose said again, even more despondent sounding.

A dagger pierced Megan's heart. She drew Rose against her chest and encircled her with her arms. If anything, Rose felt even smaller and more frail than she had when Megan arrived. "Come on. You and Sam are going to have a great time. You're not going to let whoever did this spoil your life. This is a crack in the sidewalk. You'll jump over it and keep on going."

Megan's heart warmed at Rose's smile. "I seem to remember saying that to you."

Megan kissed her on the cheek. "Hundreds of times. I know you're strong enough to get beyond this. And it'll be fun. Shopping together, like when I was a kid."

"You're right, sweetie." Rose strode to the dresser and yanked open a drawer. She hardly looked inside as she tossed some underwear and a nightgown onto the bed. "Simply because I can't stay here doesn't mean I'm a sniveling coward."

"Way to go," Megan said. She found the small overnight bag, open, on the floor in the closet. "And why don't you grab some things for Sam? I'll go pack my bag."

Maybe, once Rose and Sam were settled in for the night, she could snag some private time with Justin and tell him what she knew.

Chapter Thirteen

Gordon printed a dozen copies of his statement for the press conference, then kicked the font size up before printing his own. Last thing he needed was to lose his place and stumble. He rapped the pages on his desk, fanned them so they'd be less likely to stick together, and slipped them into a file folder. He picked up the phone and called for Laurie.

Her shoes clicked along the floor. Heels. Not her usual footwear. She'd upped her makeup, and wore a gray skirt with a deep blue blouse under a tailored jacket instead of her normal trousers and pullover.

He extended the papers. "I'm putting you in charge of distributing the statements if you think you can handle it."

"Of course I can." She beamed as she took the stack.

What was it with people and the media? Did everyone else yearn to be part of the news? He didn't release his grip on the papers. "Repeat after me. *I'm sorry, but I'm not a sworn police officer. You'll have to direct your questions to someone in an official capacity.*"

She gave him a quizzical look, as if she thought he was joking.

"I'm serious, Laurie. Whatever you say will be taken out of context and twisted until you won't recognize a single letter of the alphabet in what you said. I need to know you're going to stick to the script."

Her expression grew solemn. "You can count on me."

"I am." He let go of the pages.

"Um, Chief?"

"Yes?"

Her quizzical expression returned. "I know it's not my business, but are you going to wear that for the press conference?"

He peered down at the jeans, sweatshirt and lightweight hiking boots he'd grabbed when the call came in early this morning. "Think a uniform might make me look like I know what I'm talking about?"

"Couldn't hurt," she said. She crossed to the small closet and fetched the black garments, still in the plastic bag from the dry-cleaners.

"Thanks. You're a lifesaver."

She grinned. "As long as I didn't have to iron it."

After he changed, he took off for a much-needed trip to the men's room. Washing his hands, he stopped to study the man in the mirror. No question. His nerves and lack of sleep were screaming loud and clear. He splashed water on his face, finger-combed his hair, and looked again. Straightened his tie. Not a whole lot better.

Damn, he was a cop, not a television personality. What difference did it make what he looked like?

He went to his office, put some drops in his eyes, and picked up the folder. Colfax met him in the hallway, and they walked toward the lobby of the municipal building together in silence. Gordon pulled the door open. Beyond was a familiar space. The smell of floor wax and air freshener. The muted sounds of people milling around, waiting for their number to be called at the driver's license office, or for someone to finish in court.

Since he'd become Chief with his own office, Gordon rarely used the main entrance. Was the lobby more crowded than usual? Was everyone waiting to see him make a fool of himself? He wiped his palm on his trousers.

Throwing up was *not* an option.

"Nothing to worry about," Colfax said.

"I look that bad?"

Colfax grinned and slapped him on the shoulder. "Your statement's golden. Break a leg." He pushed against one of the double doors that led outside where the vultures waited, holding it open so Gordon could pass through first.

Gordon attempted to mimic the expression Colfax had demonstrated earlier. With a death grip on his file folder, he marched outside. A lectern crowded with microphones sat in the center of the wide brick stoop. He nodded to the mayor, and took his place behind the lectern, setting his folder against the narrow wooden lip. He sensed Colfax taking a position behind and to his right.

Halfway down the stairs, his officers had erected stanchions, as if this were a red-carpet event. One officer stood at either end, keeping the media at bay. Laurie stood alongside one, holding a large envelope, and flashed him a two-fingered salute. The stanchions were her idea, he'd bet. He nodded at her smiling face.

No smiling faces on the other side of the barrier. Cameras with their annoying flashes. Reporters with microphones, people shouldering video cameras. More microphones on booms, poised like oversized furry cater-pillars.

Below that, people. Must be half the town. Along the steps, across the sidewalk, and into the grass of the square. Mobile news vans, their masts extended, parked on the street. His stomach lurched.

What on God's earth? Denver? Colorado Springs? Networks, not local? CNN? What the hell were all these people doing in Mapleton? Must be a *really* slow news day.

From the edge of the crowd, he caught one more smiling face. Angie. She flashed a "thumbs up."

"Thank you all for coming." He opened the folder, took a breath. "I'm Gordon Hepler, Chief of Police here in Mapleton." He half-turned toward Colfax. "Detective Tyler Colfax of the Sheriff's Office and I are working together. We'll answer your questions after my statement. If you would like a copy, they will be available after the conference."

Two paragraphs in, the queasiness left, and he got to the end without mishap. Feeling more assured, he invited Colfax to join him. "Questions?"

Questions flew at him so thick and fast he almost ducked. Keeping the outrage Colfax had mentioned down to a mere hint took some doing. Gangs? Neo-Nazis? Drug cartel? Russian Mafia? Where was this crap coming from?

And then he saw Buzz, standing front and center, his Canon around his neck, mini-recorder extended, and a satisfied smirk on his face. His doing. Gordon would bet his next three paychecks on that one. Anything for a story. The man would pay.

Colfax dodged and denied. Gordon admired the deft way the man repeated the same information regardless of the question shouted at him. "We have found nothing to lead us to believe this was anything other than a senseless, tragic killing. We offer our sympathy to the family of the victim."

With most of his anger in check, Gordon leaned into the lectern. "Thank you, ladies and gentlemen." He pivoted and made his way to his office and slammed the door hard enough to rattle the windows.

Colfax came in behind him, closing the door in a more gentlemanly fashion. "What the hell happened out there?"

"Damn local reporter. We've got a weekly paper, but Buzz has delusions of working for the big city rags. Or television. Latest was a book deal. Always digging for his next big story. Doesn't matter. My guess is he called every damn contact he knows and leaked little bits of total nonsense to get them all here."

"You tell him not to talk to anyone?"

Gordon tried to remember his words to Buzz. "Crap. I told him not to *print* anything. Leave it to Buzz to take me literally."

"You handled yourself well," Colfax said. "I'm thinking

your reporter's alienated a lot of his precious contacts."

Gordon felt a little better. "So you don't think I should go over to his place and shoot him?"

Colfax laughed. "Not yet. I'm going to have to think about it. Whatever I decide now isn't going to be rational. Meanwhile, he's not going to get more than a 'No comment' from anyone on the force."

"The big players aren't going to take kindly to his stunt either."

Gordon thought for a moment. "Assuming—and this time I think it's reasonable to do so—that Buzz is responsible for that barrage of questions, do you think there's a germ of truth in there? Gangs? Neo-Nazis? Drugs? Russian Mafia?"

Colfax rubbed his lower lip. "For the most part, sane, rational people don't do what we're dealing with. Maybe it is connected to something Buzz hinted at. Whether he was just throwing a handful of spaghetti against the wall to see if anything stuck? That's an entirely different ballgame."

"What's next?"

Colfax held up a finger, then unclipped his cell phone and brought it to his ear. He listened, his eyebrows lifting. He thanked the caller and snapped the phone shut. "Got any aspirin?"

Ah, so the man wasn't invulnerable. Gordon fished a bottle from his desk and tossed it to Colfax. He tipped two into his hand and swallowed them. "We've got three crimes to solve."

"Three?"

"Yeah. I got a call. Forensics determined Karl Franklin didn't die in the car accident."

~ ~ ~ ~ ~

Justin handed out the key cards. "Oma, Opa, you're in twelve fifty-two. Megan, you're in ten twenty-eight."

"And you?" Oma asked.

"I'm in ten twenty-five."

Megan looked at him as if she'd expected adjoining rooms. Was she relieved? Disappointed? But if he wanted to follow his plan, he needed to be far enough away so she wouldn't notice, yet near enough to get to her if anything went wrong. He gave her a "that's what was available" shrug.

"We couldn't all be together?" Oma asked.

Justin smiled. "I think you'll like your accommodations. The bellman is delivering our bags." He'd requested a luxury suite for his grandparents, and figured if their bags were already in there, they might not put up a fuss about the extravagance. Too bad if they did. He and Megan had agreed they deserved some pampering.

"Like we couldn't carry those tiny cases?" Opa said.

"I thought we'd unwind in the lounge with a drink," Justin said. "This way, it saves a trip up and back."

"But this is such a fancy place," Oma said. "And I'm not dressed for it."

"This is Denver, not New York," Megan said. "We could all use a little relaxation."

Justin put his hands on his grandmother's shoulders and turned her toward the lounge tucked in a quiet corner of the lobby.

"Well, my special flower?" Opa said. He crooked his elbow, and winged his eyebrows. "Shall we go?"

Oma gazed up at Opa. She took his arm. "Maybe one drink."

Opa rested his hand atop hers, and they strolled across the lobby.

"They look so good together, don't they?" Megan whispered.

Justin almost offered his arm to Megan. "Yes, they do. It's hard to imagine them young and courting, but they've still got that spark."

"They always have. They need to put everything aside, and this place should do it. You did good." She stood on tiptoe and brushed her lips across his cheek.

He had a fleeting regret about her room being across the hall.

A short time later, settled into a grouping of chairs around a fireplace, they sipped the champagne Justin had insisted on over his grandparents' protests. He relaxed for the first time in days.

"To new beginnings," he said, lifting his flute. The crystal sang as they touched glasses.

He fortified himself with another gulp of champagne before he asked the next question. "I was thinking about going to Europe over summer vacation, and learning about my roots. Go see where you were born, where you lived, places that were special to you. What do you think?"

His grandparents exchanged uneasy glances. Oma's eyes widened. Opa's lips tightened.

He ignored Megan's not-so-subtle head-shake. He'd been working in the dark long enough, and time was running out. And there could be another player in the game, who'd upped the stakes.

"I ... you never talk about your pasts," Justin said. "It's my heritage. You never tell us stories about when you were kids. You must have happy memories too."

"That was a long time ago," Opa said at last. "Sometimes the past is best left in the past."

Megan jumped up. "More champagne?" She went to the chiller and topped off everyone's glasses. "Maybe we should have dinner. Justin, why don't you see if there's a table in the restaurant."

Subject effectively changed. "I made reservations for Oma and Opa for seven-thirty. There's time for them to freshen up." He gave Megan a pointed stare. "We can grab dinner on our own. After all, this is supposed to be their celebration."

"No, you should join us," Oma said. "A family evening."

"Not tonight," Justin said. "This is your night. You two

have a good time."

"Justin's right," Megan said. "Make this a private occasion. We'll fend for ourselves. But don't overdo it." She grinned. "Remember, Rose, we're going shopping tomorrow."

Oma didn't respond. She and Opa were exchanging a gaze that sent heat through Justin. And a newfound determination to protect them. He cut a glance toward Megan. She lifted her eyebrows and fanned herself with a cocktail napkin. "I could use a bit of freshening up myself," she said.

"We can meet for breakfast," Oma said.

"Um ... actually, I ordered you the anniversary package. Breakfast in bed is included. Call Room Service and let them know when you'd like it delivered," Justin said.

"So much, so much. Too much," she said. But her eyes telegraphed her pleasure.

He got up and hugged her. "I love you. We haven't seen enough of each other over the years. Have fun." Sam stood, and Justin clutched him in an embrace. "You, too, Opa."

The four of them strolled to the elevator, Oma on Opa's arm once again. In the elevator, backs straight, his grandparents faced the doors and watched the floor display above. But despite their formal posture, their fingers were interlaced.

When the elevator stopped at ten, Justin kissed each of them on the cheek. Megan did too, and then he and Megan stepped out, the doors closed, and the elevator continued its journey.

"They're so *cute*," Megan said. "I meant it, Justin. You did good."

"I hope Oma doesn't pitch a fit when she sees the roses and chocolate covered strawberries."

"You ordered them, too?"

"Part of the anniversary package."

"You're going to make someone one hell of a catch, you know that. Who'd have thought you had a romantic streak?"

They reached her door, and she took the key card from her purse. Her hazel eyes bored through him like two power drill bits. "Your room or mine?" she asked. "We could order in."

Her smile was less than seductive.

"Your call," he said.

She inserted her key card and pushed the door open. The king-sized bed dominated the room, but there was a small table with two upholstered chairs by the window. Megan's suitcase sat on the folding stand in a small alcove.

The phone rang. Megan jumped. "Who knows we're here?"

"My money says it's Oma."

Megan rushed to the desk and picked up the handset. "Hello?" She turned and leaned her bottom against the desk and smiled. "Hi, Rose. Everything's great." A pause. "Yes, my bag is here." Another pause. "Justin? He's here."

He stepped to the phone. "Hi, Oma. How's your room?" To his surprise, Sam's voice came out of the receiver. "The room is wonderful. Everything is wonderful. Your grandmother says thank you for your generosity, and that we're going to have a marvelous time. Isn't that right, Rose?"

Justin heard sniffling in the background. "Is there a problem?"

Sam lowered his voice. "She thinks you're going too far, and I told her to shut up and simply say thank you."

"I understand. It's not often she's willing to accept being on the receiving end."

"Oh, she's going to be receiving tonight. Thanks again, and we'll see you tomorrow." There was a brief silence, and then an even softer voice that hardly sounded like his grandfather. "Don't call us, we'll call you." And the line disconnected.

He stood there, the receiver dangling from his fingertips.

"What?" Megan asked. "Is something wrong?"

He set the handset in its cradle. "No. Oma turned on the waterworks, but she's happy." He sank onto the chair. "I think they're ... you think they ... ?" He covered his eyes. "I don't even want to think about it. But Opa said not to disturb them. They'll call *us* tomorrow morning."

Megan's mouth dropped.

"Yeah," Justin said.

They sat in silence for several moments, Justin willing his mind away from the idea his grandparents could be ... hell, he couldn't imagine his *parents* ...

Megan was the first to speak. "Speaking of phone calls, should we tell Gordon where we are?"

Yeah, he could think of phone calls. And break-ins, and gruesome murders. Why were those easier to deal with than ... no, he was *not* going there. "He's got our cell numbers, doesn't he?"

Megan thought for a minute. "I called him from mine, so he'll have it."

"Even if he doesn't, he's a cop. He'll find them. The fewer people who know where we are, the better."

Her eyes did that saucer thing again. "Do you think Rose called anyone? Selma to cancel their staying with her?"

"I told them not to tell anyone where we are. Opa said he'd make sure she understands."

There was another protracted silence. This time Justin broke it. "We need to figure out what's going on. I know you remember what happened to you. Talk to me."

Chapter Fourteen

"Karl Franklin is *alive*? You're shittin' me." Gordon studied Colfax's expression. Dead serious. "That's impossible."

Colfax laughed. "No, he's dead."

"Cut to the chase, man. What's the story?"

Colfax rubbed his temples, as if trying to rush the aspirin to their target. "The accident was staged. And Franklin was killed. Two independent occurrences."

Gordon reached for the aspirin bottle. He grabbed two bottles of water from his file cabinet, washed down two tablets and passed the second water bottle to Colfax. Taking out his notepad and a pen, he said, "Let me have it."

"Franklin was killed about a mile down the road. Body stuffed into the trunk of the car. Then he was tossed out, and the car was rear-ended off the road, into the tree."

"Did you ever confirm the bullet hole in the window?"

"Found a thirty-eight shell lodged behind the radio."

"But Franklin wasn't shot." Gordon pushed away from his desk and went to the window, staring into the parking lot. The media had gone, leaving the gravel-covered expanse almost empty. He watched the red-orange disk of the sun dip below the mountains. "My guys screw it up?"

"No," Colfax said. "I saw the pictures from the scene. It appeared to be a typical car accident, and your medics confirmed the guy was dead. The car was smashed. Anyone would assume the guy had been thrown from the car. No reason for your medics to check the trunk."

"One of my officers was on scene. Good cop."

"Don't kick yourself. There are three accidents a month, minimum, along that stretch of highway, and since the guy was dead, CSP approved the transport. Probably wanted to keep the road clear."

"So what clued them in?"

"Tow truck driver. Saw a bloody sheet of plastic in the trunk and called us."

Gordon considered that for a moment. "Premeditated, then, if the killer had the plastic on hand."

"Makes sense, but it's still an assumption. Franklin might be someone who liked to keep his trunk clean. Or the rental company put it there. And it could have come from either Franklin's rental or the killer's car."

"Sounds like you're listening for zebras, not horses. My money's still on premeditation."

Colfax nodded. "Agreed, but we have to keep every option open."

"What about cause of death?" Gordon asked.

"Multiple blows to the head."

"That's what it looked like from the pictures. But you said the guy was killed a mile away from the accident site."

"So we've got to figure out who else was there. You said you had a witness. Megan Wyatt."

"She saw the car pull off the road, the driver get out, walk into the woods. Assumed he was taking a leak."

"That appears to be where Franklin was killed. I've called for the techs to give it another once over."

"You think Megan's part of this? I've known her most of her life. She's not the killer sort."

"Which is?" Colfax said.

Touché. There was no killer type. Under the right circumstances, anyone could kill. But Megan? "Point taken. But there's no way she killed Franklin. I saw her face when I showed her the pictures. Nobody can go that white on cue."

"She seems to be at the heart of things. Sees the victim,

her name and pictures are in his possession. She gets herself snatched—or claims she does—and then the house where she's staying is broken into. Her room is the point of entry. And this happens shortly after another venue has a similar break in. And a homicide. I want to talk to her."

"I'll call her." That niggling, unreachable thought crystallized. Gordon gave himself a mental head-slap. "Shit."

"What?"

"There's another connection."

"Which is?"

"Sam Kretzer. He had a bookstore where Vintage Duds is now."

Colfax swigged some water. "And you're just getting around to telling me?"

Gordon lifted his hands in a gesture of submission. "I didn't think of it. I had one of those nagging tickles, but this is the first time I've had a chance to consider the bigger picture. I was dealing with the who and wasn't thinking about the where."

"The homicide victim from the clothing store. What's her relationship to the Kretzers?"

"None," Gordon said. "Sam retired about five years ago, I think it was. Sold his bookstore to some guy from Fort Collins. The guy lasted a year, year-and-a-half. Gave up, and eventually sold the place to Betty Bedford, who turned it into Vintage Duds."

"Where can we find the bookstore owner?"

Gordon shook his head. "Don't know."

"You don't remember the owner's name?"

Colfax seemed to think Gordon should have this information at his fingertips. He didn't mention that it all happened when he and Cynthia were splitting up, and his attention wasn't always a hundred per cent on the job.

"He didn't live here. Probably part of the reason it failed. Small town, you need a more personal touch. He hired clerks, but there was a lot of turnover. I was a patrol cop then.

Worked nights, so the store was usually closed."

He'd worked nights whenever possible simply to avoid Cynthia and the constant bickering. Of course, she hated that he worked nights, so that merely fueled the fire. He shook off the memories. His relationship failure wasn't relevant.

"Too bad," Colfax said.

"What's too bad?"

"You've got a whole bunch more suspects to investigate. If the former bookstore is the connection, you'll need to find the owner, and any of his employees who might have a motive. Meanwhile, I need the Wyatt woman's number."

"I can handle her. And the Kretzers."

"No. First, when Ms. Wyatt witnessed Karl Franklin getting out of his car, she did it in my territory. And I'm getting the feeling you're too close to the Kretzers."

"Are you saying I can't be objective?"

Colfax locked eyes. "Can you? From what I hear, they're virtual parents or grandparents to half the town. You included."

"Their involvement," Gordon said, not breaking eye contact, "happened in *my* territory." Technically, Mapleton was part of the county, so Colfax did have jurisdiction and could do what he damn pleased. "I'll talk to them tomorrow." Gordon waited.

Colfax held the stare for several heartbeats. "Then let's talk about how someone found Franklin where they did, why they killed him, and why they didn't leave him there."

~ ~ ~ ~ ~

With Justin's words, every one of Megan's aches and pains draped over her like a giant net. She searched her purse for her pain pills. Staring at the cautions on the label, she dropped the vial into her purse and found the ibuprofen instead. Falling into a dead sleep would be welcome, but wasn't going to solve any of her problems. She fumbled with the cap, and Justin appeared at her side.

"Let me," he said. He took the small bottle from her hands and wrestled with the childproof top. "How many?"

"One."

Justin popped out a tablet and set it in her unbandaged hand. "I'll get you some water."

He grabbed a tumbler from the table and disappeared into the bathroom. Should she trust him? Her nerves jangled.

All the vibes from Justin said he cared about Rose and Sam as much as she did. And always had. No matter how badly she'd tormented him when they were kids, he'd never retaliated. She got that scary feeling she got when she used to swing over the lake. She'd never liked the sensation of falling, but if you didn't let go of the rope, you'd swing back and crash into the tree.

Time to let go.

Justin returned with a glass of water. Megan swallowed the pill and gathered her courage. "The guy who grabbed me said he'd hurt Rose and Sam. I didn't get a good look at him, so it seemed safer to pretend I didn't remember."

"God, Megan, what happened?" Justin rested his hands on her shoulders. Concern filled his eyes.

Tempting as it was to bury herself in his strength, she pulled away and sat in one of the chairs. Justin sat on the bed, facing her, forearms on his thighs, hands between his legs. "Tell me, Megan."

She trailed her fingers through her hair. "I was ticked off that you were right about me being light-headed, but I was shaky, so I lay down on the bench. I thought I heard a deer, so I sat up—too fast, I guess, because things were swimming. And then someone grabbed me."

Justin's fists clenched, but otherwise he didn't move. "Go on."

"He had one hand over my mouth and nose, and he grabbed me with his other one. I tried to get away, but he was too strong." She chewed on her lip. "And, like you said, I wasn't adjusted to the altitude. I remember being dizzy. I didn't want to pass out, so I stopped struggling and started thinking."

"Smart move."

"Yeah, except what I was thinking was mostly what he might do to me, which didn't help."

"Have you told the cops?"

She shook her head. "I didn't want to take a chance at first. And everything got so crazy after the murder and the break in, there wasn't the time or opportunity."

"How did you get away?"

"He was dragging me into the woods. I was cooperating, and he loosened his grip." Her memory sharpened. "I finally calmed down enough to think. I stomped on his foot and kicked him in the knee as hard as I could. And then I ran like hell."

"He didn't follow you?"

"I guess I slowed him down. And I know that area. Remember that big rock grouping off the trail? The one by the oak tree? My favorite hiding place?" Her face flamed as she remembered teasing Justin about not being able to fit through one of the narrow passages.

"I remember," he said quietly.

"I got there and hid. Fear must counteract altitude, because I think I broke my best track record. And if you don't know exactly where to get off the path, it's hard to find."

"I remember that, too."

"Oh, God, Justin. We were so mean to you, weren't we? Playing hide and seek when we all knew every nook and cranny in the neighborhood, and thinking it was so cool that you couldn't find us."

"Hey, I'm not eight anymore. I'm over it."

Was he? There was bitterness in his voice, hurt in his eyes.

"No wonder you never wanted to play with us," she whispered.

"I said I'm over it. What's important is trying to figure out what happened to you. And why. Would you recognize the guy if you saw him?"

She thought for a minute. "I don't think so. I got a general impression of his size. Bigger than me, but nothing unusually tall or fat or skinny. I remember cigarette smoke on his breath, in his clothes."

"You're doing great, Megan. What did he say to you?"

She brought the memory forward, out of the mental cave she'd buried it in. A tremor rippled through her, and she shivered. Justin took her hand.

"He told me not to tell," she said. "His threats sounded so—anyway, I believed him when he said he'd know if I talked to anyone."

"Megan, you have to trust us."

"Us?"

"Me. The cops."

She knew he was right, but the fear wouldn't go away. She closed her eyes, as if she could pretend it wasn't real. "He said he'd kill me," she whispered. "But not until he killed everyone I loved."

Justin's grip tightened. His eyes popped open wide. "Why?"

"Don't you think I've been trying to figure that out? If I knew, I'd have told someone. But everything was so jumbled, and then the break-in, and Rose and Sam—"

"I know. I understand. Concentrate. What else did he say?"

"I told you. I was scared. I could barely breathe, let alone think. I was trying to get away. Nothing made sense." She wrested free of Justin's grasp and stood.

"Megan, relax." Gently, he gathered her to him. "Slow down. Sit. Take a breath. Clear your mind. Think. What else did he say?"

She sank beside him on the bed. "Mostly he was yelling. I know I was. That's when he smacked me, told me to shut up.

She tried to filter the memories, picking out the relevant ones. "Meal ticket. He called me a meal ticket."

Justin was silent. His fingers dug into her arm.

"What?" she asked, tugging her arm away. She twisted to face him. "Do you know what he meant?"

He released her, then got up and paced the room. "Let me think."

She watched him for a moment. Images and memories swirled, coming into crisp focus. She gasped. "Oh my God. It's all connected, isn't it?"

"What do you know about my grandparents' past? Their family?"

"Not much. They were always exactly like they were downstairs. 'The past is the past.' They never talked about it."

His phone rang. From the frown when he checked the display, Megan figured it wasn't someone he was happy to hear from. Instead of answering, however, he stuck the phone on his belt.

"Call room service," he said. "This might take awhile."

Chapter Fifteen

Gordon plowed his fingers through his hair. "You're the guy with the resources," he said to Colfax. "What do *you* think? You think whoever killed Franklin and staged the accident killed Betty Bedford and ransacked the Kretzers' place."

"Don't forget the Wyatt mugging."

"Crap. We're going to need a lot more whiteboards."

"But on the bright side, if they're all connected, we're looking for one guy. Maybe he has a partner, but we figure this out, we've solved them all. That's gotta be better than trying to solve five unrelated crimes."

"Why don't I feel better?"

Colfax laughed. "Maybe food will help. There's not a hell of a lot we can do other than speculate until we get the forensics reports. Any dinner recommendations? I'd like to grab a bite before I hit the road."

Gordon checked his watch. "Daily Bread's the best option. Otherwise, it's bar food at Finnegan's."

"Daily Bread it is."

After checking that everything was under control, the two men strolled toward the diner.

"Not a lot going on," Colfax said. "Sidewalks roll up at sundown?"

Gordon glanced around the square. A lone man picked up the litter from the press conference. Not the usual complement of joggers, or moms with strollers. No dog-walkers or kids playing catch. Empty sidewalks, a few parked cars. "There's usually more action. My guess is everyone's home behind locked doors."

"Probably wise."

Gordon pushed open the door to Daily Bread. Aside from the lingering jangle of the door chimes, the place was silent. And empty. He checked his watch. Not quite seven. "Hello?" he called.

Ozzie's face materialized from behind the counter. He set a newspaper aside. "Evenin', Chief. Detective. What can I get you? Got some good 'que."

"Where is everyone?" Gordon asked. If Mapleton had a gossip central, this was it. He understood the vacant streets, but hadn't expected an empty diner.

"Doin' takeout, mostly," Ozzie said. "Can't blame them, not with a killer on the loose. Figured I could handle things myself for one night. Talked Angie into going home early."

"Bet that took some doing," Gordon said.

"Oh, she'll be down here, before dawn cracks, to do the baking," Ozzie said. "But she worked late last night and had a long day today. I think she was too tired to fight."

Angie lived in a small apartment above the diner. Gordon wondered if she considered that short distance too far removed from Daily Bread, her dream. His gaze rose to the ceiling, as if he could see upstairs and check on her.

"She going to bake those cinnamon buns?" Colfax asked. "I'll definitely be here for breakfast. But for now, can I get a sandwich to go? You mentioned barbeque."

"Pulled pork," Ozzie said. "Want some slaw? Pickle? I could cook up a batch of fries if you'd like."

"Don't go to the trouble. Just the sandwich."

"Chief?" Ozzie said.

"Same, but I'll take the pickle."

"Have a seat," Ozzie said. "Be with you in a minute."

Ozzie disappeared into the kitchen, and Gordon pulled out a chair and sat at a central table. Colfax joined him.

"So," Colfax said. "This Angie. She the cute blonde I saw in here earlier?"

Gordon nodded, an unfamiliar feeling rising in his gut. "Yeah. Why?"

"She attached?"

Gordon's immediate visceral reaction surprised him. Good Lord, he was responding like a territorial dog. Why? He'd never taken any action with Angie. Or anyone else, really, not since Cynthia left him. So why were his hackles up? Colfax seemed like a nice enough guy. True, he seemed a bit old for Angie, but that was her call, not his.

The door chimed, interrupting his thoughts. He twisted toward the door. Three men, dressed in cargo pants and multi-pocketed vests, cameras slung around their necks, entered. They took in their surroundings, hesitating when they saw Gordon and Colfax. Two fell back half a step. The third, apparently the leader, pulled off his ball cap, revealing a receding hairline, his remaining hair in a short buzz cut.

"Is there a problem?" the man asked, surveying the empty room.

It dawned on Gordon that he was in uniform, and Colfax had his badge around his neck. "No, we're waiting on dinner." He approached the group. "Your first time in Mapleton?"

The leader nodded. "We came up from the Springs. We've been out shooting wildlife since sunrise." Apparently realizing his words might be misinterpreted by his audience, he touched the Nikon around his neck. He pulled a business card from one of the pockets on his vest and handed it to Gordon. "Taking pictures. I teach photography." He glanced at the counter. "Are they still serving? Could use some food."

Gordon pocketed the card. "You came to the right place. You staying long?"

"No, we're heading out after dinner."

"Come again," Gordon said. "We've got some nice little B&B's so you wouldn't have to drive so far." He put on his best public relations smile and returned to his seat.

"My take is they're what they say," he said to Colfax.

"Who'd he say he was?"

"J. P. Pauley." Gordon handed him the photographer's card. Colfax pulled out his cell phone, punched some buttons and stared at the screen.

"You calling him?" Gordon asked. "He's here."

"Nope. Google is my friend."

Gordon wondered if the town council would approve smart phones for the department. Probably not, given that until recently they'd had pagers. He could hear the mayor saying something about how the officers would use them for playing games.

"Yep. Guy's website matches the card, and he runs photography field trips, like he says." Colfax passed the phone across the table.

Gordon took a quick peek at the screen. "Shame we can never take people at face value."

"There are two kinds of people in the world," Colfax said. "Cops and everyone else. Comes with the territory."

Ozzie appeared with a plastic bag and a plate of food. He smiled at the newcomers. "Be right with you." He set the plate in front of Gordon and handed the bag to Colfax. "Careful. Coffee's in there too."

Colfax rose and reached for his wallet. "On me," he said to Gordon. "I've got to get going. I'll be back by eight tomorrow morning."

Ozzie waved his hand. "No, no. On the house."

"Can't do that," Gordon said. "You know the rules."

"I insist," Ozzie said. "My contribution to the next police fundraiser, if you're going to be pigheaded."

Colfax crossed to the register and slipped a bill on the counter. He picked up the bag. "Thanks for dinner, then. Consider this your tip."

Ozzie frowned, but opened the register and put the bill inside. "Thank you. And in case nobody's spread the word, you tell your people that there's coffee out back all night."

"I know they'll appreciate it." Colfax nodded to Gordon and strode out of the diner, already opening the bag and sniffing the contents. Gordon felt a twinge of relief. Apparently Ozzie's pulled pork trumped Angie.

Ozzie disappeared to take care of the photographers. They sat at the counter, and Gordon moved to a rear booth with a cup of coffee. He motioned Ozzie over.

"Tell me, Ozzie. You been in here all day?"

"Yes. Since six this morning." With a quick glance at his other customers, he took a seat across from Gordon. "One busy day, I'll tell you, until your big television show. I was thinking I should have a big screen on the wall, like Mick Finnegan. Folks high-tailed it his way if they weren't at the square." He winked. "Angie said you were *cool*."

Gordon let the comment slide. "So, what can you tell me?"

"You mean, like suspicious strangers? Hiding behind newspapers? Passing off secret messages?"

"The good ones are smart enough not to look suspicious. But I don't think we're dealing with a Mapleton resident."

"Well now." Ozzie scratched his chin. "Early mornings, most of the crowd is local. The tourists stay at the Bed and Breakfasts, and the motel chains serve breakfast nowadays. But we get some business from folks on their way someplace else." He tilted his head toward the men at the counter.

"I don't think our guy had a kid with him. One male, probably late forties or older. Maybe two. Possibly a smoker. My guess is that it's someone new." He thought about the timeline. The guy could have stopped here before he killed Franklin, or after. Or both. Or before killing Betty Bedford, or breaking into the Kretzers'. Or not at all. "Could have been anytime from yesterday morning on."

Ozzie did another chin scratch. "Yesterday morning, I was out front awhile." He closed his eyes for a minute. "Two eggs, over easy, no bacon or sausage. Hash browns, whole wheat toast with honey. That might be your man. Smelled like cigarettes. Seemed anxious. Saw him head to the restrooms."

The three photographers swiveled and mimed writing a check. Ozzie left to handle their bill.

"What about them?" Gordon asked when Ozzie returned. "They been here before?"

Ozzie shook his head. "Can't say I've seen them." He waited for the men to leave, then flipped the switch to turn off the lighted "Open" sign in the window and ambled to the table. "Then again, it could have been the corned beef sandwich, extra mustard, pickle, slaw, and potato salad instead of chips. Another smoker. He hung around. Like he was killing time. Didn't look like a fisherman or a photographer."

"Thanks. That might help. Anyone else? Any unusual behavior?"

Ozzie's brow furrowed. "Think that's it. Everyone else was the usual crowd. Yolanda from the salon, she was trying to get Buzz to do an interview. Ask me, she's too cheap to pay for an ad. And a couple of the morning power-walking group, figuring they'd walked off one of Angie's cinnamon buns." He shook his head. "Nope. Nothing out of the ordinary."

"You have credit card receipts?" Gordon asked. A long shot, but they caught most crooks because they were stupid. "Everything for the last three days."

"No problem, Chief. You want 'em now?"

"If you don't mind."

While Ozzie collected the paperwork, Gordon ran through the possibilities. Someone had killed Franklin. It seemed logical to assume there was a prearranged meet.

Megan had driven by shortly before that happened. Maybe she'd remember another car on the road. He grabbed a napkin from the dispenser and started making notes. Angie might remember the customers. She interacted with them more than Ozzie did.

He cast his glance to the ceiling again. Was she asleep?

151

Should he disturb her? She was normally at work before five a.m., and he doubted she'd taken her normal mid-day break given all that was going on.

As if in answer, a door slammed above, followed by a quiet thudding of footfalls. Angie appeared from the rest-room alcove, breathless, barefoot, and clad in a plaid flannel robe. "Gordon. I heard you talking. I think someone's been in my apartment."

~ ~ ~ ~ ~

Justin stood at the window and watched ribbons of red and white light move along the distant highway. People rushing to and from destinations, while he felt as if he were stuck with a flat and out of gas at the same time.

He thought of his grandparents, their faces as they gazed at each other over a glass of champagne, and knew it was time to put the metaphorical car in gear and get on the road.

Megan set down the phone. "Twenty to thirty minutes," she said. "I've been in hotels all over, and room service always says 'twenty to thirty minutes.'"

He heard the forced lightness in her tone, which didn't match the worry in her eyes. She moved to the window, staring into the distance for a few heartbeats. Then, in typical Megan fashion, she switched gears.

"So, the guy who grabbed me is the same one who broke into Rose and Sam's, and Vintage Duds, and killed Mrs. Bedford. And you think he wants to kill me, or Rose, or Sam, or all three of us? Or are you included, too?"

He left the window and flopped into one of the easy chairs. "You ever heard of Heinrich Kaestner?"

The abrupt change of subject didn't faze her. She shook her head. "Doesn't ring a bell. Should I?"

"I don't know. Wait here."

"Where are you going?"

"Down to my room. I'll be back in a minute."

"Better hurry." She gave a poor imitation of a jaunty smile. "Just your luck, dinner will be early and you'll be stuck with cold chicken."

"Five minutes, tops. Promise."

"Should there be a secret knock?" she asked, a little more cocky Megan in her tone.

"How about you look through the peephole?"

As soon as he left, he heard the deadbolt snick home, and the security lock flipped in place. In his room, a twin to Megan's, but with two double beds instead of the king, he found his suitcase on the luggage rack. He dumped everything onto the bed, then punched the voicemail on his cell while he folded back the lining at the bottom of the case.

"I've got nothing for you," the message said. "Tick, tick, tick." Hearing the voice tied Justin's stomach in knots. He pressed the code to delete the message. Drawing a shaky breath, he found the papers where he'd hidden them. He debated a quick shower, but he'd seen the fear in Megan's eyes. How she hadn't wanted him to leave her alone, but wouldn't admit it.

Would she want him to spend the night in her room? Or would she prefer to stay with him? He looked at the beds again. Didn't matter. He had other places to be, other things to do.

He snagged the complimentary bottles of water from the night table. Giving himself a silent pep talk, he went to Megan's room. "It's me," he said, tapping on the door. He had half a mind to step out of peephole range, or cover it with his thumb, but now was definitely not the time for payback. He wasn't eight anymore, he reminded himself.

The locks released, and Megan opened the door. She'd washed her face, and he got a subtle whiff of her perfume. There was an air of confidence surrounding her as well. As if she'd taken some sort of action.

He noticed her cell phone on the desk next to her purse. He thought she'd agreed not to call anyone.

Slow down. Don't jump to conclusions. She might have received a call, not made one.

"Everything all right?" he asked.

She nodded. "Rose and Sam called. They wanted to let us know they're getting the royal treatment in the restaurant, and to thank us again. I haven't heard Rose sound so happy in such a long time. For herself, you know what I mean. Not for someone else." She picked up her cell and eyed the display. "Damn, I forgot to pack the charger."

"Oma called on your cell?"

"Yes. Is that a problem? She said she didn't want to go find a hotel house phone." Megan sucked in a breath. "You think someone's tracking our phones?"

He shook his head. "No, I strongly doubt that. The cops can do it, and the phone company records will show where the phone is, but it's not as easy as it is on television."

She took one of the water bottles from him and tapped it against his. "One last time. You done good. But we've got more important things to talk about now, don't we?"

"That we do." He extended the printouts he'd brought with him. "Have you heard anything about this?"

She took them, unfolding them as she walked to the bed. She flipped on the bedside light and studied the first page. Sinking onto the bed, she stared at him with an expression somewhere between blank and puzzled. "Who's Henry Carpenter?"

"How's your German?" he asked.

"Rusty," she said. "I picked up enough to get the gist of what Rose and Sam were talking about, but I never spoke it. Why are you asking?"

"Kaestner can be translated as a joiner, or furniture maker," he said.

"Or Carpenter," she said, the connection clear on her face. "And the Americanized version of Heinrich is Henry. So you think Heinrich Kaestner and Henry Carpenter are the same person. Why is that important?"

A knock on the door, followed by "Room Service" cut off his response.

"Wow," Megan said. "Eighteen minutes. Points for the kitchen."

They agreed to postpone further discussion of the Heinrich-Henry question until after their meal. "No need to spoil your digestion with unhappy thoughts," Oma had always said. Justin eyed his plate. Not a lot of happy going on.

Judging from the way Megan twirled her pasta Alfredo, her wrist seemed well on the way to recovery. Nothing wrong with her appetite, either. He washed down a mouthful of over-broiled chicken with a glass of water and poked at his steamed green beans.

"Rose would pitch a fit if she saw that meal," Megan said. She set down her fork and wiped her mouth. "Can I ask you a personal question?"

"Go ahead. As long as I reserve the right not to answer."

She gestured to his plate. "It's obvious your ... eating habits ... have changed. So have you. When? Why?"

"Second year of college. I got sick of being Jumbo Justin," he said. "Not that anyone called me that anymore, but that's how I saw myself."

"Oh, God, I'm sorry. Kids are so cruel."

"I never blamed anyone. You know Oma. Fat-and-healthy is one word to her. If you don't eat her food, you don't love her."

"Yeah, I definitely can relate," Megan said.

"Same went for my mom. Don't get the wrong idea. I had a decent childhood, but my folks were always busy. So I ate for comfort, because I thought food would make me happy. Seeing me eat certainly made *them* happy." He tackled a few lettuce leaves from his salad. "And, I wasn't blessed with your metabolism. I got mine from my father. If I ate like that—" he used his fork to point to her plate— "I'd be Jumbo Justin again. I separated food from happiness, started eating healthy and working out, and felt a lot better. But it's a constant struggle, and being in Mapleton doesn't help."

"Dieting is definitely a lost cause where Rose is concerned." Megan moved her pasta plate to the side and put a slice of chocolate cake in front of her. "Want to share?" she said, eyeing his half-eaten chicken breast. "Maybe the hotel has a fitness center and you can work it off."

"No, thanks," he said.

She forked up a mouthful of cake, and he was flooded with the desire to savor a chocolate-flavored kiss.

"You sure?" she said. "It's really good."

"I have no doubt. But I don't have the time to work it off—not on top of everything else I've been eating since I got here."

"I do a few miles on the treadmill, maybe three times a week," she said around another mouthful of cake.

"Running's not my first choice, but I can do it anywhere, so I carry running shoes when I travel."

"So what is your routine of choice?"

"I swim," he said.

Her cake-laden fork stopped halfway to her mouth. "Swim? But—you never—"

He felt heat rise to his neck. "Which is why I took it up. I had to prove something to myself. That I could get past it."

"Past what?"

"Being scared to death of the water. You couldn't tell?"

She ducked her head. "I thought it was because you didn't want to be seen in a bathing suit."

"I could have handled that. No, it happened a few years before that, when my family went on vacation to California and went to the beach. I'd never seen so much water. I started playing with some other kids, building drip castles, dodging the waves."

"Sounds like a good experience."

"Oh, it was. I knew I wasn't supposed to go out past my knees, but I wanted to stay with the other kids. At the time, the surf wasn't all that high and I was jumping the breakers with everyone else. I was totally unaware of the currents, that I was slowly drifting down the beach.

"I ended up nowhere near where my parents were sunbathing, and in the surfer section. A huge wave knocked me down, pulled me under. I didn't know which way was up. I panicked. I tried to shout, but choked on a mouthful of salt water. I didn't remember anything until I was on the beach, throwing up half the ocean. I didn't have my glasses. I was totally disoriented. Couldn't find my parents, or even tell the lifeguards where they were." He shrugged. "It kind of put me off water sports."

"You could have told me," Megan said. "I'd have understood."

He shook his head. "You say that now, with an adult's hindsight. When you were six, it would have been one more thing to tease me about. I didn't need 'scaredy-cat' added to the epithets you already had for me."

Her face turned pink. "You're probably right. But, as Rose and Sam say, 'The past is the past.' Are you happy now? I mean, except for the fact that someone might be bent on killing us."

Chapter Sixteen

Gordon rushed to Angie's side, gripped her by the shoulders, and thrust her toward Ozzie. "Behind the counter. Down. Both of you."

Ozzie wrapped his massive arm around Angie and dragged her behind the counter.

Following the rule he'd established at their briefing, Gordon radioed Dispatch for backup. "Roll a unit to cover the entrance to Angie Mead's apartment. Two officers. One in back, the other in the diner with me."

"On it, Chief," Connie said. Seconds later, she was on the line. "Solomon and a deputy will be there in three."

"Roger."

Gordon unsnapped his holster, his hand resting on the butt of his Glock. Taking a cleansing breath, he stood flat against the wall in the alcove and flipped the switch to illuminate the inner stairwell leading up to Angie's apartment. No sounds came from above.

"Angie. Did you sense anyone was in there with you?" You'd think with all her *feelings,* if she had company, she'd have been aware of it on some psychic level.

"No," she said in a shaky voice. "But it's not like I routinely check under the bed or behind the couch."

"What about smells? Perfume? Aftershave? Cigarette smoke?"

"No."

"What made you think someone had been there?" So

help him, if she said one word about ghosts, he'd whack her.

She emerged from behind the counter, Ozzie close beside her. "There must have been signs that registered on a subconscious level, but I didn't want to stick around and check them out. Not when I heard you down here. I figured you could do that."

He apparently failed to keep the skepticism out of his expression, because she crossed her arms across her chest. "Come on. Don't tell me you've never had the feeling some-one's watching you? Or you're thinking about someone, and they call on the phone right that minute?" She caught Gordon in a steely stare. "Or the way you can tell when someone's hiding something when you question them? You don't think about how you know, you get that ... feeling."

He wasn't going to debate that now. Cops learned to read body language and facial expressions, see red flags waving. Angie could believe in her forms of communication. He preferred things he could point to. "I suppose," he said. Meanwhile, he needed more information.

"Ozzie," he said. "You happen to notice anyone head for the restrooms and not come back?" The rear entrance to Angie's apartment was through a small storage room next to the restrooms, clearly marked "Employees Only."

"Can't say that I did."

"Angie, anyone else have a key to your place?" Gordon asked.

"Not really."

"What's that supposed to mean?"

"I leave a spare key down here, on a hook in the kitchen. Donna goes up sometimes on her breaks. Especially now. Her son and his wife are staying with her with the new grandbaby, and she needs a nap more than lunch. But she always tells me. And she puts the key back."

Ozzie cleared his throat. "I found it by the register yesterday. Not the first time Donna's forgotten. I took care of it."

Angie's eyes widened.

"Is it there now?" Gordon asked.

Angie went to check. The front door chimes rang. Solomon appeared. "What do we have?"

"Angie thinks someone might have been in her apartment. Given the recent events, I think it warrants checking out. The deputy in position in the alley?"

"Yep. Nobody's going to get by him."

Angie returned. "Key's where it should be."

"Okay. Tell me. What am I going to see up there when I open the door? What's the layout?"

"There's a small landing at the top of the stairs, then about three steps to my door. There's a braided throw rug inside the door, a coat tree immediately to your right. Straight ahead is the living area. Back and to the right, there's a small kitchenette separated by a low counter. The outside entry door is at the end of the kitchen. It was locked. The bedroom and bath are to the left."

Gordon nodded to Solomon. "Let's do it."

"I'll go up first."

"No. I will." He stared at Solomon, who backed down. Gordon wasn't going to lead from the rear. Besides, he told himself, there was nothing up there except whatever Angie's overactive imagination had created. And their guy used a knife. Gordon had a gun. Which he unholstered and held at the ready.

His heart hammered as he approached the narrow staircase, keeping his eye fixed on the door above. Well, he'd been grumbling about not doing enough street work. Here he was, about to clear an apartment. Of what? Killer, ghost, or nothing at all?

"We're sitting ducks here," he said to Solomon. "Let's rush it. I'll go left, you go right."

"Gotcha." Solomon said.

"Police!" Gordon shouted. He thrust the door open. "Drop your weapon. Hands where I can see them."

Weapons raised, they burst into the room.

Gordon scanned the space, which seemed empty at first glance. He moved quickly to the bedroom, doing a quick check for unwanted guests. That room, as well as the closet and bathroom, were as deserted as the living area. "Clear!"

Solomon returned from the kitchen. "Clear in there, too. The back door's deadbolted from the inside."

Gordon re-holstered his weapon. "You and your deputy partner can resume your duties. I'll interview Angie."

Solomon's mouth curved up in a grin. "Roger, Chief."

Gordon scowled. "Take the kitchen stairs down and let me know if you see anything, *Officer Solomon*."

Solomon flipped a snappy salute.

"Go." He waited for Solomon to leave, then threw the deadbolt. Taking time to peruse the small living quarters more closely, he absorbed the evidence of Angie's presence. Family photos. Framed prize ribbons from the County Fair. Bookshelves filled with cookbooks. More on the small round table by her bed.

He heard a soft mewing sound. A black-and-white cat perched on the windowsill above her bed. The sash window was partially open. Gordon crossed the room, noting the rumpled bed. Impulsively, he touched the sheets. Warm, exuding Angie's scent.

The cat mewed louder, then scampered past him, over-turning the candlestick lamp on the bedside table. "Hi, there, fella. Are you the cause of Angie's worries?" Gordon said. "Playing with things you shouldn't be touching."

Funny, he'd never heard Angie mention a cat. The cat evaded his attempt to pick it up, so he left it and trotted downstairs to the diner. Ozzie and Angie popped up from behind the counter. Ozzie's arm was still holding Angie in a protective embrace. His other hand gripped his pistol.

"All clear," Gordon said. "Ozzie, you can close up and go home. I'll escort Angie upstairs, and she can show me what's out of place."

"Sounds good. Chief, I've got those receipts here." He plopped a manila envelope onto the counter.

"Thanks," Gordon said.

"You going to be okay, Angie?" Ozzie said.

"I'll be fine." Her bare toe traced a circle on the floor. "I might even have been dreaming. You know, one of those half-awake, half-asleep dreams where you're doing normal stuff, and you think you're awake. Not like a nightmare or that crazy kind where you show up at school for a test and you're naked."

Gordon shoved that image aside. "Let's go upstairs."

"I'll set up the coffee service and be on my way," Ozzie said. He lumbered into the kitchen.

"I feel kind of stupid," Angie said. "The more I think about it, the more I think it was probably a dream after all."

"Either that or your cat," he said.

She spun around and looked at him like he'd grown another head. "What cat? I don't have a cat."

~ ~ ~ ~ ~

Megan forked up the last bite of her cake, then scraped the plate clean of the fudge icing. "So, you didn't answer my question. Are you happy?"

"I like my life, yes. So, overall, I'm happy. With the exceptions you noted."

She sighed. "I guess we should get back to murder and mayhem."

Justin carried the tray and set it in the hall, then went into the bathroom. She retrieved the printouts he'd brought, and spread them on the table. What was the connection to her? Or Rose and Sam?

"I don't get it," she said when he joined her. She waved the printouts she'd been reading. "How is all this connected? You've got Heinrich Kaestner, who is believed to be a Nazi war criminal. And Henry Carpenter, who's dying of cancer in some nursing home in Arizona. You think they're the same guy?"

"I'm not the one who thinks so—I'm merely repeating what's in those articles."

She squinted at the pictures. "These are lousy repro-ductions. I can see some resemblance, I suppose, since you told me about it. But in this picture, Kaestner is decades younger than Carpenter. If his identity is important, can't they test his DNA?"

"They didn't exactly do DNA testing during World War II," Justin said. "There wouldn't be anything to match it to."

Duh. "So, for argument's sake, Henry Carpenter is Heinrich Kaestner. That makes Carpenter a Nazi war criminal. He's going to die soon anyway, probably before they can bring him to trial, assuming the trip doesn't kill him first. I didn't know you felt so strongly about making them pay their dues."

"I don't. I mean, until recently I've never given it any in-depth thought. Do I think they should be punished? Yes. Do I think people should be dragged from their deathbeds to stand trial? I don't know."

Megan waved the pages. "Even if these two people are the same man, and based on these pictures, I'm not con-vinced they are, what does wanting to deport a dying old man have to do with me being mugged, or Betty Bedford being killed?"

"Probably nothing," he said. "But think about it. There's another connection."

Her heart did a rendition of Riverdance in her chest. A chill slithered through her. "Rose. Sam. They never talk about it, but yeah, they come from Germany. You think one of them knew this Kaestner guy?"

Justin bolted to his feet. "Megan, I need your help here." He paced to the door and back, yanking at his hair. "I can't ... I won't have them hurt." His voice was a soft whisper, but there was no masking the determined vehemence behind it.

As if she wouldn't sacrifice everything for them. "Of course. What do you need?"

"I don't want them to know. Promise me, this stays between the two of us."

She got up from her seat and studied him. For the first time, she recognized the strain in his face, strain he'd been carrying since she arrived. It wasn't because Rose had passed out, or their house had been ransacked. This went deeper.

"Justin. Slow down. Take a breath." She blocked his path and trapped him in an embrace when he collided with her. She leaned into his chest, his heartbeat pounding in her ears. "You've got to tell me what's going on so I can help."

He blew out a sigh, warm against her hair.

"We're in this together." She raised her face to his, stared into his worry-filled eyes. Without thinking, she grazed her lips against his. Heat flamed her cheeks. She pulled away. "Sorry."

He smiled. "Don't be." Some of the worry left his eyes.

"I might have some information for you, too," she confessed, remembering the notes Gordon had shown her. Back to dead bodies.

"You go first," he said.

"You remember the car accident I didn't exactly witness?"

"The one the cop mentioned?"

"Yes. The dead guy had some papers in his car." She explained how they might connect her, Rose, and Sam to the dead man.

Justin went board-stiff. "And you didn't bother to mention it?"

"The man was dead. And then everything went crazy. It didn't seem important anymore. Nobody'd heard of Karl Franklin. You said you didn't know him."

"I don't. But someone sent him after you. And my grandparents."

"We don't have proof. Gordon's job is to figure out

exactly who he was, and why he had those pictures." Justin clawed at his hair again. She reached for his hands and gently pulled them away. "Keep that up and you won't have any hair left. Now it's your turn. Why is this guy—" she tapped the picture of Kaestner— "so important?"

"First, tell me. What do you know about Opa's family? Did he ever tell you anything else—about his parents, brothers, sisters, aunts, uncles?"

"Only that everyone died in the war. That's all he ever says. He never mentioned brothers or sisters. Did you ask your mom? Maybe they told her stories."

"If they did, she's as close-mouthed about it as my grandparents. It's as if life for Oma and Opa didn't start until they hit the States."

Megan thought for a minute, trying to sort through her memories. "I know they didn't grow up in the same city. They didn't meet until she was at UCLA, and Sam worked in a nearby bookstore. They met, fell in love, got married and moved to Mapleton. That's all they'd say."

"Yeah, that much I know," Justin said.

"I have a feeling Sam was lucky to get out of Germany, and that he might have been caught up in some of the persecution, but he won't talk about it. And Rose follows his lead. The most I've ever heard her say was that she was very lucky. And since anything else seemed painful, I never pressed. When there were stories about the Holocaust on the news, Sam would storm out of the room, cursing in German."

"You should have heard him last week. The local paper had an article discussing whether or not the Holocaust actually happened. He was livid." He rubbed his forehead. "But he has all those books on World War II. That might be a way to bring the conversation around to what we need to know. They shut me down when I tried to broach it over drinks."

Megan tried to rerun that conversation. "You mean when you said you wanted to go to Europe?"

"Yes."

"And I jumped in and changed the subject because it seemed to upset them. If I'd known, I'd have helped."

"Not your fault. I didn't confide in you, so you had no way of knowing I had an ulterior motive in asking."

"And I'm assuming that motive is related to why you showed up in Mapleton."

"You're right. What about you?"

So he'd thought the same things about her. "Angie called. Said she had one of her feelings about Rose and Sam. And I realized how I'd let time slide by, so I came."

"Maybe we should get Angie to figure this out," Justin said with a wry grin.

"Wouldn't that be nice? Seriously, tell me why you're here. What made you think Rose and Sam are connected to your Nazi war criminal?"

He didn't answer immediately. His gaze wandered from her to the papers, to the ceiling, and just about every other point in the room before he sucked in a deep breath, released it, and said, "I have it on reasonable authority that he's Sam's older brother."

Chapter Seventeen

Gordon took the lead as he and Angie ascended the staircase. His leather-soled dress uniform shoes thudded on the wooden risers. Behind him, her bare feet made no sound. Tempted as he was to take her hand, he settled for enjoying her scent.

"I definitely saw a cat in your apartment," he said. "Black and white. He was sitting on your bedroom windowsill."

"Not my cat," Angie said. "No pets. Avoids problems with the Health Inspectors."

At the open door, Gordon paused. "Don't touch anything. Walk through, tell me what you see that's out of place."

He crossed the threshold, stopping on the braided rug inside the door. Gordon sensed Angie tensing behind him. He moved inside, indicating she should enter.

"Your bedroom window was open," he said. "Is that normal?"

"Yes," she said. "I sleep with it open if the weather is good. I'm on the second floor. I never felt unsafe." She strode to the bedroom and approached the window, arms across her chest. "Do you think someone came in that way?"

He peered outside. A narrow brick ledge ran underneath the window and along the wall of the building. Not wide enough for easy human access, although he supposed it was possible. However, given the nearby trees, it would be an effortless journey for a nimble cat. He played his flashlight's beam over the ledge. No footprints of the human variety, but some smudges could pass for feline.

"I think your cat burglar was an actual cat," he said. "Probably left the way he came, after I scared him. Did you notice signs of someone using your window to get in and out when you came home? Evidence on the bed?"

"No. I was tired, but I think I'd have noticed that."

"Bathroom window?"

"Too small," she said, but she went to the doorway and peeked. "It's closed, and all my shampoos and stuff are still on the windowsill."

"He left a total mess in the other two places. But it's worth a look around." He forced the next words out. "Let me know if you sense anything...unusual."

She snorted, and he knew he hadn't disguised his cynicism. Too bad. He couldn't arrest one of her *feelings*.

Eyes closed, she stood in the center of her bedroom. After a moment she brushed her fingers through her hair. "I feel so stupid. It was probably Donna taking a break on the couch. With all that's happened, I'm overly sensitive, I guess."

Whether it was true or not, she believed someone might have violated her personal space, and he couldn't dismiss her emotional response. He took her hand, turned her so she faced him, and grasped her other one as well.

Her voice had quavered. Probably not noticeable to someone who didn't know her. He knew she was thinking ahead, wondering if she would have to lock herself into her apartment every night. He snickered. This was Angie. She'd shake off the aftereffects of her *feeling*, and life would go on. Windows wide open, he'd bet.

Her eyes blazed. "This is *my* space." Gone was that hint of a tremor. Yep, Angie was back.

However, this second he didn't care how the damn cat had gotten in, out, or what else might be out of place.

Her scent enticed him. Citrusy, and maybe a hint of cinnamon, as if her bakery specialty had become a part of her. Maybe she smelled like cinnamon all over. He'd like to test that theory.

She squeezed his hands. Her eyes widened, then closed. Her head swayed from side to side.

"Angie?" he said. "What's wrong?"

"I'm ... I'm getting one of my ... feelings. Oh, God, this one's incredibly strong. Hold me."

He gripped her biceps. "What? What do you see?" Christ, did she *really* see stuff?

Her voice grew distant, dreamy. "I see ... a man. Dressed all in black. He's tall. Strong. He has a gun! Wait, no, he has two guns." She panted short, rapid breaths. "No, not two. Just one. He wants something."

Her voice grew quiet. He could barely hear her. He strained to make out her words. "From me," she whispered. "I can sense it."

"What, Angie?" Gordon cupped her face. "Tell me. Can you see him? Do you recognize him? What does he want?"

She opened her eyes. Her lips parted. "Come closer."

He leaned in. She flung her arms around his neck. "Closer." She pulled him lower, until her breath fanned his face. "He wants ... wants to..."

And then her lips were against his. He realized he'd been duped, but he didn't give a damn.

"Angie." It took two tries to utter her name. "This is ... are you ... sure?"

She gazed at him, lips swollen, eyes glistening. But twinkling. "Sure about what? That you're the man in black I saw? Are you doubting my gift?"

He understood what she meant by gift, and it had little to do with her infamous premonitions.

"You don't think this is too ... fast? It's not even our first date."

She burst out laughing. "Chief, we've had breakfast, lunch, or dinner together at least four times a week for the past year. I think we're past the first date stage."

"Close the damn door. And lock it."

She stood about six inches from him, her body heat

reaching him like the sun on a July afternoon. She tugged on his tie. It came off in her hand. She dangled it in front of him, her head tilted, a smile playing about her lips.

"I missed that one," she said. "Didn't picture you for a clip-on kind of guy."

"Bad guys can't choke you that way."

"Ah, a practical, sensible man. Are you practical and sensible in other ways?"

"Bedroom. Bed," he said.

"You have too many clothes on." She reached for the buttons on his shirt. "Get rid of them."

"You giving orders?" he asked.

"Yes. You got a problem with that, Chief?"

~ ~ ~ ~ ~

Justin couldn't detect anything but shock on Megan's face. If she had any knowledge of Kaestner-Carptenter, she was one hell of an actress.

She sat, rigid in her chair. "Sam's brother? A Nazi? A war criminal? How can that be?"

"That's what I'm trying to figure out."

"You haven't told Rose and Sam, have you? My God, it would probably kill them. He has no love for the Nazis. I know he donated to the Simon Wiesenthal Center regularly."

"And now you see my dilemma. I've been trying to get what I need without involving my grandparents, but things are getting out of hand."

"You think some neo-Nazi is after them? But why kill Mrs. Bedford? Nobody would mistake her for Rose."

"I think Mrs. Bedford was in the wrong place at the wrong time." Justin wiped his hands on his jeans. He was going to have to start at the beginning, tell Megan everything. And maybe she'd have some ideas, some hidden memories that might surface and give him what he needed.

"About three weeks ago," he said, "I got a call from

someone claiming to be a long-lost cousin, through Opa's side of the family. He had quite a tale to tell."

Megan's eye's popped wide. "Cousin? Tell me."

"Eventually. I have other plans for tonight."

He caught the way her eyes cut to the bed, then to him, frowning. "Like what?"

He gazed at the bed as well, wondering if her thoughts were aligned with his. No, he told himself. Her frown said otherwise. Tempting as it was to pursue it, he had a mission to attend to. Besides, she was practically a sister to him. At least, that's what he kept trying to convince the part of his anatomy that kept regarding her as a woman.

She sat, waiting for his response. And it didn't seem to be about the bed. He snapped to the task at hand. "Like going to Oma's house and doing a thorough search."

"For what?"

"Some kind of journal, or diary. Heinrich was supposed to have written it while he served in one of the camps."

"You think the guy who broke in is looking for them, too."

"That makes the most sense, don't you think?"

She chewed her lip. "It fits the facts. But what about Karl Franklin? How does he tie in? He didn't have anything on him about Vintage Duds or Betty Bedford."

"I don't have a clue about who he was." He hesitated.

"What? You're thinking something. I can tell. I'm in this, too."

And she was. More than he was, perhaps. Unable to sit, he paced to the door and back. "Do you think it was a coincidence that Franklin got into that car accident when he did?"

Her mouth gaped. "You think someone killed him?"

"What do you think?" He sat on the bed across from her. Took her hands in his. Waited.

"Oh, God. You think whoever killed Franklin is the same guy who caught me." She jerked her hands away and this time, she did the pacing. "He might have killed me. If I hadn't gotten away ... Oh, God."

"I don't think he meant to kill you, Megan. I think he meant to use you to make Opa talk. To tell him about the journal, or whatever it is."

She spun around. "But you said Sam didn't have it."

"I don't know."

"What do you mean?" Her voice rose half an octave. "How can you be looking for a journal that might not be there?"

"Slow down, Megan. What am I supposed to do? We both assume my grandparents don't know about Heinrich Kaestner. The whole reason I'm trying to keep this quiet is to avoid them finding out they might be related to a Nazi war criminal. You think I should ask them? What do I say? 'Hey, did you know your big brother might be alive? Except there's this one little thing. He represents everything you hate.'" He scrubbed his hands over his face. "We don't even know that Opa *had* a brother."

She clutched fists of her hair. "Oh, damn. This is hard."

"Trust me, if I thought they knew anything about Kaestner-Carpenter, I'd have said something. But if they don't, I didn't want to be the bearer of that kind of news."

"I see your point. But if they don't know about this journal, why can't we stick with the way things have been? What nobody knows can't hurt them."

"But someone else knows. This cousin swears he's not responsible for the break-ins."

"What did this Kaestner do, anyway?" Megan asked.

"According to what I could find on the net, he worked in one of the camps. He had the power of life or death over the prisoners. Details were sketchy."

"You don't have positive proof it's Sam's brother."

"Catch 22. The proof should be in the journal."

"So, let's go find it."

"I'll go. Someone should be here with Oma and Opa."

"But two of us could cut the search time in half. Besides, they told us they didn't want to be disturbed." She paused. "You don't think someone's going to come after us here, do you?"

"No, nobody should know where we are." But telling Megan what he thought would either scare her or raise her stubborn streak, and he didn't particularly want to contend with either.

"Then I'm coming."

"No, you're not."

"I'm not a kid you can order around. Give me one good reason why I shouldn't help you."

"Because I'm afraid the guy who killed Mrs. Bedford might show up and hurt you." The words escaped before he had a chance to engage his brain.

Megan didn't back down. If anything, she grew more defiant. Hands on her hips, she leaned forward, eyes blazing. "It's my call, Justin. If I'm in danger, *I* get to decide. Not you. If you're that worried, we could call Gordon. Didn't he say he was putting extra patrols on the house? How did you plan to get in without being noticed? They'll probably arrest you for breaking into a crime scene."

He hated to admit she could be right. And hadn't Gordon said he didn't think they'd be collecting any more evidence? That he'd kept the crime scene tape up to convince his grandparents not to stay there?

"No telling how long it will take," he said. "Unless I find it relatively soon, I might not make it by breakfast."

"After breakfast should work," she said. "Rose and Sam said not to bother them, remember?"

"They're early risers. They could be finished and ready to meet us by eight. You could keep them occupied."

"So, we're on the road by six. That gives us lots of time."

"Megan, no. It's better with one of us here. Plus, I know where I've already looked." And he knew, no matter what she said, if they were both there, he'd be worrying about her.

By now, they stood nose to nose. She was talking, but he wasn't processing.

He grabbed her by the shoulders, not knowing whether he should shake her or kiss her. Her widened eyes tipped the scales. Almost without thinking, he shoved his mouth against hers. Her lips parted in surprise.

What the hell. All his frustration poured into the kiss. Instead of shoving him away, she joined him. Willingly. Tenderly. Eagerly. After savoring the moment, he pulled away. "Write a note telling Oma and Opa we decided to go out, we might be late, so they shouldn't worry. Tell them to call our cell phones if they need to reach us. You can slip it under their door. I'll go grab a few things and meet you by the car."

She stood there, cheeks flushed, eyes bright. She put her fingertips to her lips. Smiled. "In your dreams. I do that, and you'll be gone before I get downstairs. We go together or not at all."

Chapter Eighteen

Megan saw the guilt flash across Justin's face and knew he'd have bailed on her. She pressed her fingertips against her eyelids, trying to ease the exhaustion behind them. She pushed her heady reaction to his kiss aside, and concentrated on what Justin had said. The more she thought about his plan, the less she liked it.

"We should stay here," she said. "Both of us. Going to Mapleton will create more problems than it solves. We need to talk to Gordon first. He's a cop. He knows how to keep things confidential. And we can do better searching in broad daylight, not skulking around like burglars."

"Fine," he said. "I'm going to bed. I'll meet you for breakfast at six-thirty."

"Justin, wait."

He turned. "What now? I've already said I'll go along with your plan. You need to figure out how we're going to keep my grandparents out of the house. You know Oma is going to want to rush in and clean from top to bottom. Twice."

She debated with herself, reluctantly seeing the logic in Justin's plan. "You said we have until Sunday. What happens then?"

He shoved his hands in his pockets and trudged to her side. "The cousin sends somebody to confront Oma and Opa."

A chill ran through her. "Worse than what's already happened?"

"He swears he knows nothing about that."

The pieces fell into place. "That means ... there's someone else. Your cousin wants the journal, but so does someone else, and your cousin didn't send him."

"That's how I see it." He rubbed his belly, as if he was in pain. She could believe it. Her Alfredo sauce and chocolate cake weren't sitting all that well either.

"So why is it so important to him to find this journal thing?"

"He said his career would come to a screeching halt if he was connected to a war criminal."

"Why? Aren't people smart enough to know you can't blame someone for what his grandfather did?"

"He doesn't think so. There's very little he's willing to tell me other than he needs top government security clearance, and if he's related to a Nazi, he's not going to get it."

Her brain was running in circles. "So, didn't you check him out? Google him? Justin, I can't help unless you tell me everything."

"I told you what I know. Someone says he's a long-lost cousin, that Sam had a brother, and the brother, according to the cousin, is a Nazi war criminal. Without the journal, we have nothing but his word."

She spun at a tap on the door. She exchanged a questioning glance with Justin. He shrugged. She pushed past him and checked the peephole.

"Just a minute," she called. She turned to Justin. "It's Rose and Sam." Quickly, she finger-combed her hair. "We are *not* going to spoil their evening. Happy thoughts."

She repeated that to herself under her breath, then released the locks and opened the door.

"We saw the light," Rose said. "Oh, good. Justin, you're here, too. We won't keep you, but we wanted to tell you everything was wonderful."

"Delicious," Sam said. "There, Rose, we told them. Let's go upstairs."

"One minute more," Rose said.

"Come in," Megan said. She took Rose's hand and tugged her inside. She closed the door behind them. Rose glanced at her, then Justin, then Sam. "Are we ... interrupting?"

Not what you think. "No, Justin and I had room service for dinner, and we've been catching up."

"I'm glad," Rose said. "You weren't close when you were growing up."

"They *have* grown up," Sam said.

"Of course they have." Rose flapped her hand in a dismissive gesture. "The other reason we stopped by—we saw some brochures about tours." She handed one to Megan. "Museums, art galleries. It's been a long time since we've been in the city, and we signed up. Would you like to join us? The concierge said there were openings."

Megan exchanged a glance with Justin. Sometimes the stars aligned in your favor. "No, you two go. Have fun. I ... um ... got a call. From the office. There are a couple of things I have to straighten out. I can take advantage of the hotel Internet. Justin?"

"I'll think I'll pass," he said. "I'm not the art gallery sort. Maybe I'll check out some flooring samples for your kitchen."

"You do too much," Sam said.

"I enjoy it. It's a change from what I do at work."

"Oh, but we were going to go shopping," Rose said to Megan. "The tour will take up most of the day, and I know I'll be too tired when we get back."

"Don't worry about it. We can always shop another time."

"Rose. Let's go," Sam said. "It's late." He took her by the shoulders, turned her around, and marched her to the door. "We'll get together for dinner tomorrow."

Rose reached up and slapped his hand. "Relax. The night is young."

Megan managed to control her fit of laughter until they'd left.

"I *so* don't want that picture in my head," Justin said before he, too, burst out laughing.

It had to beat the pictures that had been forming before they'd arrived. Megan wiped tears from her eyes. "They've just handed us tomorrow. You said six-thirty for breakfast?"

"Yes. I'll pick you up here."

"Justin, there's one more thing." Megan braced herself for Justin's reaction.

"What?"

"Give me your car keys."

"What? Where do you need to go?"

"Nowhere. And neither do you."

"Oh, so you think I'd sneak out without you?"

"In a heartbeat."

"And why should I trust *you*?"

~ ~ ~ ~ ~

Gordon jerked awake to the incessant klaxon of what sounded like a red alert for an enemy attack on a starship. As abruptly, the noise ceased, and a gentle kiss landed on his forehead.

"I have to get to work. Go back to sleep."

Angie's voice. Her touch. Her bed. Awareness returned. Gordon caught a shadowy glimpse of Angie's bare backside as she padded into the bathroom.

The shower ran. Yawning, he debated joining her, then checked the time. Four-thirty. In the fricking *morning*? How long did it take to get dressed and walk down a flight of stairs? His mind cleared some more. She'd warned him about the alarm before they finally called it a night and went to sleep. She had to bake.

He flung back the covers and set about picking up the scattered foil packets. Heat rose to his neck as he recalled his fumbling attempts with the first one. Hell, their entire first encounter was a series of awkward moments. He'd been with

Cynthia for three years; she'd been on the pill. As for sex, they'd fallen into their own predictable rhythm.

Angie had said she understood. With a new partner, there was always that initial clumsiness, and he'd admitted he hadn't had much practice since the divorce. He smiled, remembering the fun they'd had practicing. Fun had been missing from his sex life far too long. Even with Cynthia.

The shower turned off. The curtain scraped against the metal rod. Seconds later, the door opened, and a towel-encased Angie stepped into the bedroom. She shook her wet hair, then gave him an appraising glance.

She grinned. "Looks like my cinnamon roll dough isn't the only thing rising this morning."

"I'd better go," he said. "I've got to get home, change, and check the night reports before Detective Colfax show up."

"So soon? There's time between kneading and rising. The dough," she added with a grin. "I can come back. With coffee. Unless you want to help."

He slipped into the closet behind her and tugged at the towel where she'd tucked it together above her breasts. Squeezing them gently, he said, "This is the only kneading I want to do. How long?"

"Long enough. That is, if you're as good as you were last night." She let the towel fall to the floor, turned, and gave him a parting kiss that would carry him well past breakfast. "See you later."

"Count on it." He took his turn in the bathroom. From downstairs, the aroma of coffee wafted up, along with cinnamon and yeast. He pulled on his briefs, then sat on the couch to watch the early morning news. Nothing about the Mapleton murder, thank goodness. He drifted off to thoughts of Angie.

The next thing he knew, a coffee-flavored kiss woke him. "Mmm." He blinked his eyes open, not sure if he was still dreaming. He stared into her blue eyes. She held a condom in one hand, a mug of coffee in the other. "Which first?"

Afterward, he reached for the coffee. Cold, but the caffeine worked. While Angie redressed, he straightened the couch cushions. Finding a well-read paperback romance novel, he sat and thumbed through it, wondering if Angie'd been inspired by its prose.

She came out, smiling. "Whatcha got?"

He handed her the book. "Found it in the couch."

She checked the cover, then frowned. "Not mine. I'll bet it's one of Donna's. I'll give it to her." She kissed him on the forehead. "Gotta run."

He checked the time. Five-thirty. The café didn't open until six. "Is Ozzie in?"

She sniffed. "Bacon's going. Yep."

So much for tiptoeing out through the café. "I'll go out the back way. But lock up. And unless you want that cat coming back, close the window."

"Roger, Chief."

He drove home on autopilot, changed into street clothes and got to the station in time to grab a cup of coffee and review the night reports.

"Chief?" Laurie snagged him when he passed her desk, handing him a manila envelope. "This is for you."

He glanced inside the envelope. The credit card receipts from Daily Bread. Which, he recalled, he'd left on the counter where Ozzie had put them before he'd gone upstairs with Angie. "Thanks. I've got work to do."

"Gotcha, Chief."

He closed his office door, which hardly increased the odds that he wouldn't be disturbed. With the caffeine working its way into his system, Gordon lifted the pile of reports from his "In" box and read as he sipped.

As expected, there'd been more call outs to check on strange noises, but with the increased manpower, they'd had excellent response times, and minds quickly put to rest. He was almost through the stack when Laurie informed him Colfax was here.

"Send him in," he said.

Seconds later the door burst open. "Morning. Quiet night."

Gordon kept his eyes down, skimming the final three reports while he banished the thoughts of his not-so-quiet night from his brain. He tapped the stack of papers into alignment and set them in the tray for filing. "Seems that way."

"Good for the citizens, not so good for us," Colfax said.

Gordon lifted his gaze. "What do you mean?"

"We had great street coverage. Anybody tried anything, we'd have caught him, and we'd be done." He jerked his head toward the doorway. "I'm starved. How about we get breakfast? Think the blonde's on duty?"

"Suppose," Gordon muttered.

Colfax seemed oblivious to Gordon's reaction. "Great. I've been craving one of those cinnamon buns."

"I'll send Laurie for them," Gordon said. "We can have a working breakfast here. What you say at Daily Bread is common knowledge in about seven minutes. With Angie, maybe three."

Colfax tipped his wrist and checked his watch. "Forensics is supposed to have their preliminary reports in by nine. Plenty of time for breakfast without shop talk. Nothing that involves any open cases, anyway."

As if two cops could avoid shop talk. Half the time, other cops were the only people they *could* talk to. They understood the job.

"Actually," Gordon said, "I've got a stack of credit card charges from the diner that I want to check."

"You think our guy was at the diner? And was stupid enough to pay with a credit card?"

"We catch 'em because they're dumb. An outside chance we might pick up a lead. Ozzie said he remembers a couple of customers who might fit the bill."

"Think the waitress might remember?"

Gordon could tell Colfax wasn't going to give up on seeing Angie. "She might." He picked up the envelope. "Let's go."

Daily Bread was jammed. Nobody minded being out in daylight hours. Or the urge to gossip overpowered any fears. Angie, carrying an armload of meals, turned when the door opened, and smiled. "Empty booth in back," she called.

They wove through the tables and settled in. Colfax frowned when Gordon took the seat facing the door, but didn't object.

Gordon didn't know whether he was glad or disappointed when Donna, instead of Angie, approached with coffee. Gordon flipped the mug on his table right side up, and Donna filled it. Colfax did the same.

"Busy this morning," Gordon said.

"That it is. I came in early to help out."

"How's the newest grandbaby? What is this one? Number six?" Gordon asked.

Donna pulled a pencil from behind her ear. "Eight." She stifled a yawn. "And worse than his daddy when it comes to being a night owl."

After they'd placed their orders, Gordon tipped the contents of the envelope onto the table. Ozzie had clipped each day's receipts together. Gordon found the ones for the day in question and divided the slips into two stacks. He pushed one across the table, then pulled out his notebook and read the notes he'd transcribed yesterday.

"We're looking for a receipt for two eggs, over easy, with hash browns and wheat toast, and one for a corned beef sandwich, extra mustard, pickle, cole slaw, and potato salad instead of chips."

"Be nice if they had the actual order forms the waitress turns in to the kitchen."

"Customers keep those," Gordon said. "Otherwise, our job would be too easy."

"Can't have that," Colfax muttered. He pulled a pair of

readers from his pocket. "Damn, these receipts might as well be in code."

The abbreviations were definitely cryptic. "When things quiet down, we'll get someone to decipher it."

"We're cops," Colfax said. "We don't have to wait, you know." He craned his neck, scanning the space, apparently searching for Angie.

"First, let's see if we can figure it out on our own." Gordon gave a wry grin. "You're a detective, after all. How many abbreviations for eggs or toast can there be?" He leafed through several slips. "See. This one says '2ESSU'. That's probably two eggs, sunny side up."

Colfax growled, but went to work. "I suppose I should be glad it's not a Waffle House. They still use diner lingo."

By the time Donna returned with their food, Colfax had winnowed out seven possibles. "Let me," Gordon said. He set four of the receipts aside. "These are all local folks. Highly unlikely they'd be our guy." He copied the information from the other three into his notebook and tapped his own stack. "I've got two."

"Don't suppose either of them matches mine."

Gordon laughed. "Only in the movies."

"Then we have five names to search. Maybe the waitress remembers some of them." Before Gordon could reply, Colfax had snatched the slips, swung out of the booth, and waylaid Angie. His back was to Gordon, and his height blocked any view of her. Gordon waited, wondering if Colfax was being pure cop, or if he was turning on the charm. And why was it knotting his shorts? What concern was it of his if Colfax was flirting with Angie. If last night hadn't meant anything to Angie, they'd move on. They were consenting adults.

Angie followed Colfax to the booth. "Hi, Chief." The smile she gave him didn't seem any different from the one she flashed to every customer at the diner. "Detective Colfax says you have some questions." She glanced around, seeming more like she was checking for suspicious-looking eavesdroppers than making sure the customers were satisfied. "It's about the murder, isn't it? And the break-in at the Kretzers'," she whispered.

"Miss Mead has assured me of her discretion," Colfax said.

"We want to know if you can describe any of these customers. Give us your general impression."

Angie examined the credit card slips, setting each down on the table. "This guy was young," she said about the first. "Kept telling me about all the great birds he spotted." She tapped the next. "Didn't wait on this guy—not my code." She moved on. "Now this guy—he was a real piece of work. Sent his eggs back because the yolks weren't the way he wanted them. Cut the crusts off his toast. I think he bathed in cheap aftershave."

"Clothes? Height? General appearance?" Colfax said.

"Average height, I'd guess. Shabby cords, knit cap, so I couldn't see his hair. Kept looking at his cell phone."

Gordon picked up the piece of paper. "Will Johnson. The name rings a bell. I'll check it out."

Receipt number four belonged to a flirt, and the last to a twinkly-eyed man Angie put in his eighties, on his way to Boulder to see his new great-granddaughter.

"Does that help?" she asked.

"Yep," Gordon said. "And if anyone asks, we were talking about the Fourth of July picnic menu."

Her eyes sparkled. "I know how to keep a secret," she said.

Colfax's phone rang before that went any further. The detective listened, nodded, and snapped it shut. "Thank you, Miss Mead. We'll be on our way." After Angie resumed her duties, Colfax gave him a long, hard stare. "Why didn't you say something?"

"About what?"

"You and Angie. Man, it's written all over your face."

"What?"

"Don't tell me this is new? Last night?" He clapped Gordon on the shoulder. "Don't worry, man. I don't poach." Colfax strode toward the door.

Great. Angie'd kept her mouth shut, and he'd obviously telegraphed to a virtual stranger that he'd spent the night with her. Thankfully, Gillman and Reynolds weren't in to collect on their bet. Gordon dropped some bills on the table, stuffed the slips into the envelope, and hurried after Colfax.

Chapter Nineteen

Justin awoke, disoriented. Light filtered in from under the door and the edges of the window. Unfamiliar shapes appeared as shadowed silhouettes. Sounds of breathing, not his own, permeated the quiet. Slowly, the world reassembled. *Hotel room.* Memories slipped into place.

When Megan had insisted they stay together, he'd played along as she tried to decide how best to share her bed when he refused to sleep on the floor—or in the bathtub. She'd been arranging the spare blankets and pillows into a makeshift bundling board when he took pity on her and admitted his room had two beds.

He'd gotten thwacked with a pillow for that one, but the look on her face had been worth it. He eased out from under the covers. He stood, yawned, and stretched, twisting the kinks out of his back.

"Morning," Megan mumbled. Her eyes blinked. "Time is it?"

"Six-fifteen. You mind if I shower first? You can grab some more sleep."

"'Kay." She punched her pillow into submission.

He crossed the room, passing her bed to get to the bathroom.

"You've filled out nicely," she said. Her half-lidded eyes were pointedly directed below his waist, to the cotton boxers he'd slept in.

"It's morning," he muttered, stomping to the bathroom

and closing the door.

When he'd finished, he found Megan sitting cross-legged on her bed, watching television. She glanced away from the set. "Nothing on the news. You don't think they've caught the guy yet, do you?"

"Don't know. Would your cop friend call if they had?"

"I'd think so."

"We should get moving. Your turn." He cocked his head toward the bathroom. "Unless you want to use the one in your own room."

"I can handle it," she said, flouncing across the room.

Shortly before nine, they pulled into Mapleton. Justin parked in front of the municipal building. After spending the better part of the drive arguing about how much to tell the police, they'd agreed it made the most sense to let the authorities know they were going to be in the house, and leave the rest unsaid.

"Remember," Justin said. "Tell him, don't ask him. Don't give him an excuse to think about it, or say we can't be there."

She scrunched her face in exasperation. "You've said that three times. I know how to handle people. It's part of my job."

She was halfway up the steps before he got out of the car. "Wait up," he called. He trotted to her side. "We're in this together, remember."

"I know. I'm just antsy to find out if he's caught the guy."

Justin pulled on the brass handle of the massive wooden door. Probably original to the building. Megan sidled past him, striding across the lobby toward one of the doors at the rear. Inside the Police Department office, she wasted no time, nodding to the clerk at the front desk as she swished by.

"She's here to see Chief Hepler," Justin said, shrugging. He walked in the direction Megan had gone, finding her standing by a desk, talking with a middle-aged woman.

"He's in a meeting," the woman said, "but I'll let him

know you're here."

"Thanks. We'll wait." He glanced around and took a seat in one of the chairs against the wall. Reluctantly, Megan joined him.

"Relax," he said. "He's a busy man, and we don't have an appointment."

"I didn't think you needed appointments to talk to cops. What if it was an emergency?"

"Then they'd send a regular cop out. Your friend is the Chief of Police."

"I know, I know. It's ... "

"You're anxious. Nervous. It's understandable." Inside, he felt exactly the way she did. It was Thursday already. He suppressed the urge to check his watch, knowing it was only a few minutes later than the last time he'd done so. His mental clock was ticking away the minutes until Sunday.

Gordon appeared, an underlying weariness in his features. He gave Megan a welcoming smile, nodded at him. "What's going on? Laurie said you needed to talk to me. Have you found something?"

Megan popped to her feet. "No, we've been in Denver. Rose and Sam are still there. Did you find him?" Her hands wagged, punctuating her words. So like his grandmother. Justin couldn't help but smile.

Gordon smiled, too. "Why don't you two come into my office? We can talk there."

A man stood when they entered. His piercing blue eyes lingered on Megan before he spoke. "Detective Tyler Colfax, Sheriff's Office. I've been wanting to meet you."

Why? Justin's neck hairs prickled. Because he was a cop, and Megan was involved in an investigation, he told himself. Realizing he'd instinctively stepped closer to Megan, he held back when she moved forward to take Colfax's outstretched hand.

"I'm Megan Wyatt. Why did you want to talk to me? Have you found the killer?"

Colfax sat, gesturing for Megan to take the chair next to his. Gordon went to his desk. Justin positioned himself behind Megan, resting his hands on the back of her chair. Gordon opened a file folder, searched through it, and extracted a piece of paper, which he laid in front of Megan.

"Does this man look familiar?"

Justin leaned in, his pulse quickening in anticipation. Megan picked up the paper and moved it back and forth, as if trying to see it from different angles. It appeared to be a reproduction of a driver's license photo, enlarged and grainy. His fingers brushed against Megan's shoulder, and he felt her trembling. Was this the man? He rested his hand on her shoulder and squeezed gently.

"I ... um ... " She squinted at the picture. "I never got a good look at his face. And this isn't a very good picture."

"It's also five years old," Gordon said.

"What's his name?" Megan asked.

"Willard Johnson," the detective said.

"Maybe if I saw him in person," Megan said. "Do you have him in custody? Have you figured out if he's connected to Karl Franklin?"

"Afraid not," Gordon said. "We're going to talk to him and find out."

Justin straightened. "Then we should let you go. We wanted to let you know we'll be at my grandparents' house until mid-afternoon, while they're in Denver. There are some things I need to do before we head back."

The two cops did some sort of silent communication thing. The detective scratched his chin and turned to Justin. "There's nothing more we can get from the scene. But call if there's the slightest sign of trouble."

"You've got the direct number to Dispatch?" Gordon said. "We're likely to be out and about."

"Yes, we're set," Justin said.

"You'll be in Denver again tonight?" Gordon said.

Justin nodded. "Easier on my grandparents."

"Agreed," Gordon said. "Tell them we're doing everything we can."

"They know that," Megan said.

Justin said, "Thanks." He nodded at the detective, then put his hand on Megan's back and guided her to the door. He waited until they were in the lobby before speaking. "That detective wanted to put the moves on you, in case you didn't notice."

"I did. I'm a big girl." She grinned and punched his biceps. "And you realize that if you noticed him, he noticed you being the territorial dog. But thanks. You were cute."

Rapid footfalls approached from behind. "Miss Wyatt. Please wait. I have one more question."

Justin turned. Detective Colfax bore down on them like a charging bull.

"I thought his name was Colfax, not Columbo," Justin muttered. He maneuvered Megan so she was half behind him. "What can we do for you, Detective?"

~ ~ ~ ~ ~

Gordon dialed Flo and Lyla Richardsons' B&B. The sisters had retired to the outskirts of Mapleton about ten years ago and found that turning their home into a rustic B&B that catered to the "commune with nature" crowd suited them. Since they'd come of age during the Summer of Love in the sixties, Gordon wondered if they bothered screening their guests.

Flo answered, sounding a bit out of breath.

"Flo, it's Gordon Hepler, Mapleton Police. Do you have a minute?"

"Is this related to the murder?"

Gordon groaned inwardly at what now was part of every conversation he entered. "No, this is a routine follow-up to a report one of my officers filed. About one of your guests."

A pause. "What are you asking?" He heard the wariness

in her tone.

"Is a Willard Johnson staying with you?"

Another pause. Before he had to remind her he could get access to all her records, she responded. "Yes, he's been here since Monday night."

"So he's still there?"

"Yes. Is there a problem?"

"No, not at all. Like I said, I'm dotting Is and crossing Ts. Is he likely to be there awhile? I can ask him a few questions and wrap this up."

"He's stuck to his room most of the time. I imagine he'll be here another hour or two."

"I'll be out in twenty minutes."

And another pause. "You'll be...discreet? I don't like the idea of a murder being associated with our establishment."

"My department and the County Sheriffs are dealing with the murder. Which leaves all the routine stuff to me." As a rookie, he'd learned to stretch the truth, if not outright lie. In the background, he heard Lyla calling Flo's name. "I'll let you attend to your guests. And I'd appreciate it if you'd not mention my visit to Mr. Johnson."

The queen of pauses. "Fair enough."

Gordon had a hunch he ought to get out there before she changed her mind. He told Laurie to let Colfax know what he was doing, and drove out to the B&B. To look at the Richardson sisters, one would never guess they'd made their money on Madison Avenue.

When they'd retired, they'd exchanged power suits for granny gowns, and now looked like well-aged hippies. Which, judging from some of the photos in their B&B, they were. They served homemade granola and whole-grain waffles along with omelets made from the eggs provided by the chickens in the coop out back. In season, their herb and vegetable gardens rounded out their fare.

He found Lyla tending the flowers surrounding the hand-painted sign at the top of the curving roadway to the

B&B. She glanced up as he made the turn, and stood, brushing her hands on the legs of her denim overalls. She flipped the long braid of salt-and-pepper hair. "Good morning, Chief Hepler. Flo said you had some questions for Mr. Johnson."

"I do. Is there anything you've noticed about him that seems out of character for one of your typical guests?"

Her lips flattened. "We respect our guests' privacy."

"Of course. But in your kind of place, I imagine your guests share their plans and adventures around the breakfast table as part of normal conversation. I wondered if you knew why Mr. Johnson chose to come to Mapleton. Is he a photographer? Hunter? Fisherman? Artist? Hiker?"

"I don't know," she said. "He keeps to himself. Breakfast is included, but we don't require our guests eat it. Today was his first breakfast with us, and he didn't talk much."

"Where's he from?"

She frowned. "Utah. Ogden, as I recall."

"You don't know where he goes during the day?"

"No. I suggest you ask him. Assuming he wants to talk to you, of course."

Definitely picking up the 'toe the line' vibes. He smiled, lifted his palms. "Of course. Actually, there's a possibility he was witness to a traffic accident, and I wanted to ask him about it. Where can I find him?"

She gestured behind her with her trowel. "He should be at the house."

Gordon had no doubt Flo and Lyla knew how their guests spent their days. But he understood both their reluctance to share that information with a cop, and their obligations to the privacy of their guests.

He wound up the narrow wooded lane to the dirt-packed parking area near the front of the Richardsons' house. More flowers, and another painted sign. He adjusted his jacket so both his gun and badge were obscured. As Flo had said, having a cop show up when the town was abuzz with a murder wouldn't be good for business.

The front door stood open behind a screen door. He jangled a bell suspended on the outer wall beside the jamb. Flo was there within seconds, wiping her hands on a dish towel.

She gave a token nod of greeting as she opened the screen door. "You made excellent time. Mr. Johnson is upstairs. Iris room. To the left."

Gordon climbed the stairs, inhaling the aroma of this morning's breakfast and the fresh coffee he knew was always available to guests. Given neither sister had offered any, he knew he'd been switched from friendly acquaintance to intruding cop.

He wandered down the hall, seeing the ceramic doorplates with different flowers painted on them. Glad he could recognize an iris, he knocked. "Mr. Johnson?"

Feet scuffled to the door. "Yes?" a gravelly voice said.

"Mr. Johnson, my name is Gordon Hepler. I'd like to talk to you for a few minutes, please."

The door opened a couple of inches. A gnarled, liver-spotted hand kept it from opening further.

"May I come in?" Gordon asked. "Or would you rather go downstairs?"

There was a hesitation, as if the man were weighing all the possible outcomes with a mind working at molasses-in-January speed. "Who'd you say you were? Don't know anyone named Helper."

"It's Hepler, Mr. Johnson, and I'm with the Mapleton Police Department. I have a few routine questions." Until he could see the man's face, Gordon wouldn't give him more than that.

The door swung open on silent hinges. "Inside's good enough, I guess."

According to Johnson's driver's license, he was fifty-eight. The man standing in front of him looked more like seventy—an old seventy. He thought of the Kretzers, who *were* in their seventies but seemed decades younger than Johnson. He couldn't imagine this man wrangling Betty Bedford into submission and taping her to a chair, much less slitting her throat. The man wore black pants and turtleneck, both too large for his frame, as if he'd lost a lot of weight too fast. His hands shook, and his skin carried a gray tinge beneath matching stubble. If he had accosted Megan, she shouldn't have had any trouble getting away.

He hoped Colfax might dig more memories out of her. Meanwhile, he reminded himself not to jump to conclusions. The man might have drugged Betty Bedford, or he might have had a partner.

Gordon stepped into the room, the scent of air freshener more cloying than refreshing. Didn't seem to fit the Richardson image. As Gordon moved closer to Johnson, he caught the cigarette smoke. The man had probably been sneaking smokes in his room and spraying the cheap floral aroma to cover it.

"Hope you don't mind if I sit," Johnson said. "Haven't been myself lately."

"Go ahead." Gordon waited until Johnson lowered himself gingerly into an easy chair. "What brings you to Mapleton?"

Johnson licked his lips. His gaze darted around the room, not lighting anywhere. "Heard this was a good place to relax. Clean mountain air, away from the rat race. Homemade food, no chemicals. Thought it might help."

"You mind telling me what's wrong?"

Johnson wheezeed. "Cancer. Third time it's recurred. You know what they say. Third time's the charm."

His resigned matter-of-factness said he'd come to peace with it. Gordon steeled himself and went on with his questions.

"You have friends, relatives around here?"

More eye darting. "No, no, I found this place on the internet."

"You were at Daily Bread for breakfast on Tuesday. Why didn't you eat here, if the food's what attracted you?"

Johnson stared at the floor. "Couldn't sleep. Left early, before breakfast. Meant to get back in time, but I didn't."

"What time did you leave?"

He shrugged. "Shortly before daybreak, I guess. Don't wear a watch no more. Drove around, watched the sunrise. Maybe dozed off. Got hungry, so I stopped at that restaurant in town. No crime in that."

"You're right." He changed tactics. "Actually, we're more interested in finding someone who might have seen an accident on the road, about half an hour outside of town. Did you notice a blue Toyota Camry while you were driving around?"

"Can't say that I did."

"After breakfast. Did you come straight here after you ate, or did you drive around some more?"

Johnson's head lifted, and he met Gordon's gaze. "I don't have to tell you nothing. Not unless you arrest me, and then I get a lawyer." He folded his arms across his chest. "So, I'd say we're done."

Chapter Twenty

Megan felt Justin tense as Detective Colfax closed in on them. She prodded Justin in the ribs with her elbow. "Down, boy," she whispered. She turned her attention to the detective. "Yes?"

"Should we go to the office?" he asked. "It might be more comfortable."

"Here's fine," she said. "What do you need to know?"

"First, we're trying to locate the man who bought Sam Kretzer's bookstore. Do you know him, or where we can find him?"

She shook her head. "That happened years after I'd left Mapleton. I understood it didn't work out for him, but I had no involvement."

"What about you?" he asked Justin, acknowledging his presence for the first time. "You have any information?"

"No." Justin gripped Megan's elbow, and she resisted the urge to slam it into his ribs this time. "We do have a lot to do, so if you'll excuse us?"

"There is one more question," Colfax said. "Why don't we sit?" He started toward the cluster of wooden benches in the center of the lobby.

Megan looked at Justin, who seemed ready to drag her out of the building to get her away from Detective Colfax. "Justin, you can go on ahead. Maybe the detective will give me a lift when I've answered his questions."

"Like hell," Justin said through clenched teeth. "Make it

quick."

She chose a seat across from the detective. "What can I tell you?"

"We're trying to connect the dots." He pulled out a notebook. Leafing through the pages, he said, "You told Chief Hepler someone grabbed you while you were waiting for Mr. Nadell to get back from his jog, but that you didn't remember the details. We're hoping your memory has returned and you can help point us to the man."

"Because you think he might be the same one who killed Mrs. Bedford and broke into Rose and Sam's house," she said.

He studied his notes before meeting her eyes. At least he didn't give her one of those, "My, the little lady has a brain" looks. "It's a logical conclusion."

"Exactly. It's the same one Justin and I reached."

"So, what can you tell us?" Detective Colfax said.

"I did remember what happened, which is that a man grabbed me, I managed to escape and hide. But I have nothing in the way of description other than average. And he smokes."

"Was he smoking? If he threw his cigarette butt away we can get his DNA."

"No, I smelled it on his clothes."

"When you got away. Did you hurt him? If he sought medical attention, we might find him. We'd know to look for someone with an injury."

"He might have a slight limp," she said. "I kicked him in the knee pretty good. It hurt him enough so I had time to get out of sight before he could come after me."

The detective made a note. "Right or left knee?"

Megan laughed. "I have no idea."

"Stop, think about it. How was he holding you?" He stood. "Show me. Your senses have the memory, it's a matter of calling it up."

Megan could almost hear Justin growl when she complied. She shot him a dirty look and stood. The sooner she got rid of Detective Colfax, the sooner they could get on with their search. And before Justin broke a tooth from clenching his jaw. "Let's do it."

With the detective playing the role of her assailant, she demonstrated the way he'd grabbed her. The memories the detective had mentioned surfaced, and she shivered.

"You're doing fine. Start with height. I'm five-eleven. Did he feel taller or shorter than I am?"

"Shorter," she said without thinking. "He wasn't short, but he wasn't as tall as you. He wasn't as big, either. He seemed ... thinner."

She felt the detective suck in his belly. Justin coughed and averted his gaze.

"I stomped on his foot." Megan raised her foot to demonstrate.

"Wait," Detective Colfax said. "What did his shoes feel like? Sneakers? Boots? Hard, soft? Concentrate on the way things felt. Use all your senses."

Intrigued by the detective's directive, Megan stopped mid-stomp to retrieve the memory. She let her mind replay that afternoon's events. "Sneakers," she said. "I can see them. Not narrow, like running shoes. More sturdy, like cross-trainers. Or walking shoes."

"Color?" he asked.

"Black. Dusty. Scuffed." She switched her gaze to Justin, who'd lost his alpha dog attitude and was listening intently.

The detective went on. "Look higher. Can you see the bottom of his pants? Cuffs? Color? Fabric? Close your eyes if it helps."

She did, and the picture formed behind her lids. "Black, too. Not dress slacks. They didn't hang that way. Stiffer, like denim, or hiking pants."

"Excellent. Think some more. Move higher. What else can you see?"

She tried, but the images wouldn't come. "Nothing. I was looking down."

"What about feeling?" He secured her the way the man had. "Where he touched you. Was he wearing a sweater? Something knit? Or slick, like a nylon parka?"

"Smooth," she said. "I remember trying to grab it, to get away, but I couldn't get a grip."

"His hands. You say he had one across your mouth. What did it feel like?"

She shuddered. "Smelly. Like cigarettes."

"Could you see his sleeve? The color of his jacket?"

"Black. He was all in black. I remember, because at first I thought it was a deer. I'd been half-asleep. I had this flash that a black deer was really unusual, and then he was all over me."

"Excellent, Miss Wyatt. Now, replay your escape, please."

She demonstrated her stomp and kick. "We were both struggling, so I can't be sure which knee I caught." Their reenactment proved it could have been either.

"You've given us some valuable information. We're probably looking for someone around five-nine, about one-fifty, wearing scuffed black sneakers, black pants, and a black parka."

"And a black knit watch cap," Megan blurted out. "I remember that."

"What did he say? Pretend it's a recording. Play it back."

She caught Justin's eye. Should she tell the detective? The quick bob of his head said yes. They needed this guy caught, and the cops had the resources.

"He said he'd kill everyone I loved, and then kill me," she said. The words came easier this time. "He called me his meal ticket."

"Do you know who he was referring to?"

"It had to be Rose and Sam. They're the only family I have. And it's the only thing that makes sense."

"Last question. Who knew you'd be here?"

"In Mapleton? Angie Mead from Daily Bread. Back home? My boss, my team—probably anyone at the office could find me."

"Thanks." He made more notes, then handed her his card. "Thanks for your help. Call if you remember anything else."

"We have the number," Justin said. "For the police here."

"Keep it anyway," the detective said to Megan. "It's a joint effort. We've got more resources. Why don't you give me your numbers, in case I need to get in touch."

"Chief Hepler should be able to reach us," Justin said.

"It would save a step," Colfax said.

Megan found a business card and handed it to the detective. "My cell number's on there."

Justin seemed reluctant, but he pulled out a card. "Got a pen?" Megan handed him one, and he wrote on his card, then extended it to the detective. "Cell's on the back," Justin said.

"Thank you," Detective Colfax said.

"If we're finished, we have to get to the house," Megan said.

"One more thing." The detective smiled.

She felt Justin's exasperation rubbing off on her. She put his card in her purse and snapped it shut. "Yes?"

"Be careful." The detective's phone rang, and he checked the display. He lifted it, saying, "One minute" to the caller. He gave her a stern look. "If bad guys did what we expected, we'd know where to be so we could stop them before they did it. Don't lose my phone number. I'm going to be around the station, and Chief Hepler's off working other aspects of the case."

"We'll be in touch, detective," Justin said. He had her elbow again, and he turned her to the door.

Outside, Megan glanced around the square. There seemed to be a large number of people wearing black.

Megan kept her eyes on the side mirror as they drove, acutely aware of every other vehicle on the road. "Should we take a circuitous route? In case we picked up a tail?"

~ ~ ~ ~ ~

All the way to his office, Gordon's cop senses were launching flares, telling him there was more to Willard Johnson than a man dealing with his own mortality. But he shoved them away, to be dealt with later, after taking care of the more urgent need to find Betty Bedford's killer, Megan's assailant, and the Kretzers' intruder. He couldn't get his head around Willard Johnson being their man.

Once again, Colfax had made himself at home at Gordon's computer. "How are we doing?" Gordon asked.

Colfax smirked. "We? I'm doing fine."

"Enlighten me."

Colfax leaned back, interlacing his fingers behind his head. "Thanks to my excellent interrogation techniques, Megan Wyatt was able to remember more details about her assailant."

"Did you need the rubber hose? Or were the bright lights enough?"

Colfax chuckled. He relinquished Gordon's chair. "Actually, we did a little reenactment. A few steps short of hypnosis, but we've got a better picture of the man."

Gordon's attitude did a quick U-turn. "That's great. Any ID?"

"Unfortunately, she's described the most generic suspect possible. But she did say she smelled cigarette smoke on the guy. According to the reports, your man Solomon found a couple of cigarette butts in the clearing."

Gordon shook his head. "He found the two kids who were there. They admitted to smoking them."

"They have anything to add?" Colfax asked.

"No," Gordon said. "They snuck out for a smoke and some necking. Solomon reminded them of the "No Smoking" sign and the fire danger, and left it at that. What else did Megan tell you?"

After Colfax filled him in on the details, Gordon relayed

what he'd found out about Johnson.

"The guy's generic enough to match Megan's description, but I can't buy him as our guy, especially if Megan said he managed to subdue her. Johnson probably couldn't pin a butterfly. There's something hinky about him, though. You get a report from forensics?"

"They're supposed to be emailing everything. I asked them to copy you. I haven't seen it come through yet."

"Maybe it will by the time I get some coffee. Want a cup?"

Colfax shook his head.

"Then can you pull any strings and get an investigative subpoena for Willard Johnson's cell phone records? He might not be good for our guy, but he could have a partner."

"I'll see what I can do." Colfax flipped open his cell.

Gordon stopped at Laurie's desk on his way back from the break room. She glanced at his mug, then hit him with a questioning look.

He checked the wall clock. Nearly ten. "Nope. Station coffee today. All I have time for. What do you have for me?"

She handed him a few message slips. "Dispatch is where the real action is. These are your everyday non-crime crises."

"If there's another budget meeting, shoot me now."

"No, but the bigwigs want updates."

"Which they'll get when we have something to update. Who else?"

"Your SUV is overdue for its maintenance check. And a couple of people who insisted on speaking to you. I tried to grill them, but they weren't cooperative."

"Probably more damn telemarketers or charity fundraisers. Don't worry about it." He started for his office, then turned. "Can you get Solomon for me? I'd like to see him."

"On it."

Colfax had his cell phone to his ear when Gordon got back. Gordon slipped behind the desk and scanned the messages Laurie had given him. He stuck the reminder about his vehicle maintenance in his "In" box. He should take care of it before the mayor dragged it out as one more example of dereliction of duty. Later. He leafed through the rest. Tempted to rip them in half and toss them in the trash, he tossed them intact in a drawer instead.

How telemarketers got his office number never ceased to amaze him, but several calls a week slid under all the normal precautions. He'd deal with these the way he'd dealt with all the others. A firm reminder of the law. The fact that he was Chief of Police usually shut them up fast.

Colfax snapped his phone closed. "Ball's rolling on the subpoena."

"Sounds good." Gordon opened his email program. "And we've got some of those reports." While he waited for the pages to come off the printer, he looked more carefully at the attachments. "We've got a preliminary report from the M.E. I thought we'd feed the Vintage Duds case into ViCAP's database. See if there are any others that match. I've asked one of my officers to come in. I'd like him to handle it."

"He ever done one?"

"No, but he's one of my best men, and I'd like him to expand his horizons. He did the crime scene photos, so he's had a good look at the scene. That, together with what your techs and M.E. provide, should give him plenty of data. I thought you could supervise."

"*You* ever done one?" Colfax said.

Gordon bristled. Was Colfax implying that Gordon didn't have the chops? Just because they didn't see much violent crime and didn't have dedicated detectives didn't mean they didn't know their jobs. "As a matter of fact, yes, I've kept my education up to date. All my staff has. But since this is a joint operation, and you're a homicide detective, I thought it appropriate to keep you in the loop."

"Untwist your knickers, Hepler. I'll check his work before he submits it, and I'll be happy to offer advice. *If* he asks."

"Solomon's man enough to ask."

"Ask what, Chief?" Solomon walked into the room, nodding to Colfax. "Sorry, Detective. I didn't know you were in here. Laurie told me the Chief wanted to see me. Should I come back later?"

"No, come in," Gordon said. "I've been explaining to Detective Colfax how up to date we are, even in this tiny backwater of a town."

Solomon took a step backward, a guarded expression on his face, as if he was aware he was stepping into a pissing contest and didn't want to get sprayed.

"What do you know about ViCAP?" Colfax asked.

Solomon winged his eyebrows at Gordon.

"Answer the man, Officer Solomon. Do Mapleton proud."

Solomon drew himself to his full height and thrust his shoulders back. "Sir, ViCAP is a nationwide data information center designed to collect, collate, and analyze crimes of violence. Sir."

Colfax burst out laughing. "At ease, Officer Solomon. Let's get cracking." To Gordon, he said, "Is there another computer we can use? The form's about twenty-five pages long. It'll take awhile."

"War room," Gordon said.

Solomon looked over his shoulder, rolling his eyes, as Colfax snagged the printouts and ushered him out. Gordon gave his officer a quick, discrete salute. And a wink.

He took a moment to relish both his coffee and the quiet before printing another set of reports. While the printer hummed, Gordon thought about what Colfax had told him. Megan's assailant had been clad in black. Johnson was wearing black. Megan thought she kicked the man hard enough so he might be limping. Johnson had shuffled across the room, as if in pain.

Talk about jumping to conclusions. But maybe … . He picked up the phone and called the Richardsons' B&B. "One question," he said to Lyla when she answered. "Did Mr. Johnson have any visitors?"

Another annoying Richardson pause.

"I'm not asking you to identify anyone. But we're trying to clear a police investigation. If Mr. Johnson is involved in any way, it could be bad publicity for your business. And before you duck the question, I know darn well nobody gets into your place without a key, and you run a tight ship."

"Let me check with Flo," she said.

"I'm asking you."

"What I mean is, I don't recall any of our guests having visitors this week. But it's possible someone came while I was out. In order to answer your question properly, I need to ask my sister. Or, if you'd prefer to ask her yourself, I'll have her call you. It's her turn to shop. As a matter of fact, you might run into her in town."

"Thank you." He hung up and rested his forehead in his palms, debating whether he should intercept Flo. She'd probably evade the question as well as her sister had.

He swiveled his chair and pulled the reports from the printer. Unlike the Richardsons, they were straightforward.

Colfax and Solomon would be focusing on all things related to the incident at Vintage Duds. He sifted through the pages searching for the car accident. As long as they were working under the assumption everything was related, it shouldn't matter that the scene was technically out of his jurisdiction. Two scenes, actually. The place of death, and the staged accident. And maybe some more background on who the hell Karl Franklin was.

Chapter Twenty-one

"You've been watching too many cop shows," Justin said. "How many routes to the house are there in this town?"

Then again, they were doing exactly what anyone would have expected by returning to the house. No need to follow them at all. Just wait. But he checked his rearview mirror more often than usual.

Crap. Now Megan had him imagining phantom attackers behind every tree.

Megan had her eyes fixed on the mirror. "It can't hurt to be careful. Like Detective Colfax said."

"There's careful and there's paranoid. The cops were doing surveillance on the house last night, according to Gordon. They would have noticed someone poking around, or lurking in the bushes."

"That assumes someone was watching at the right time. Think about how easy it would be for someone to park a few blocks away, approach on foot, then duck into the acreage behind the house to hide. They could be there now."

"Megan, we're going to go inside, lock the doors, and look for the journal. If anyone's been following us, they know we were at the police station. They'd assume we've got the cops on alert."

"I hope we find it fast. This is *not* what I expected I'd be doing when I decided to visit Rose and Sam."

"It's not playing out the way I'd hoped, either."

"Did you ever wonder if Rose and Sam know about

Heinrich Kaestner? That maybe they're trying to protect us—well, *you*, I guess, since I'm not a blood relation—from knowing there's a really ugly skeleton hanging from the family tree."

He almost hit the brakes as the question sank in. Protect *him*? And his parents. "No. I never did. I've been working under the assumption that I can keep them from finding out about that particular skeleton. Nice mixing of clichés, there, by the way."

She scratched her nose. "I don't suppose it makes a big difference who knows what at this point. We can't exactly say, 'By the way, if you're trying to hide the Nazi in the closet, don't bother, because we already know.'"

"I agree, we need to keep up the deception a little longer." He turned down Maple and hit the remote for the garage door as soon as they were within range. He wheeled the car in and hit the remote again, and the door growled shut behind them.

Megan slotted the key into the mud room door and hesitated. "This feels creepy. Like we're trespassing."

Justin slid his hand along hers, grasping the key. "We told the cops we're going to be here. They didn't say we shouldn't."

"I guess. But we didn't tell Rose and Sam we were coming. We lied to them. I guess that's what's bothering me. All the deception, even though I know why we're doing it. And then there's that 'someone might be trying to kill us' factor, too."

Justin twisted the key and pushed the door open. "If you want to go somewhere and wait, I can do this myself."

She gave a brisk shake to her curls. "Just because it feels creepy doesn't mean I'm not doing it."

Holding Megan's hand, he stepped inside. "I'll take my grandparents' room, and you can start in yours. I've already done mine. After that, I think Opa's study would be the next best bet."

"What about the attic? Or the crawl space over the garage? The tool shed? What if he buried it in the yard somewhere? There are a couple of acres."

Justin rubbed his eyes. "God, I hope it doesn't come to that."

He went to the kitchen for a glass of water and caught the blinking light on the answering machine. He pressed the play button. There was a throat-clearing sound, then a male voice.

"Mr. and Mrs. Kretzer, this is Buzz Turner from the *Mapleton Weekly*. I'm aware you've had some trouble, but that's not why I'm calling. First, I want to apologize if my Holocaust article offended you. I'd like to come by and talk to you about it, get your take, let you present your side. Will you please call me?"

Justin exhaled the breath he'd been holding as the man left his phone number.

"Should we erase it?" Megan asked. "Rose and Sam probably don't want to be bothered."

"That's up to them." He drained his glass. "Let's get to work."

They stepped into the living room, where most of the mess had been organized. He stood in the center of the room, wondering if what they were seeking was buried somewhere in the pile of things Oma had decreed would be donated to charity.

"It's hard enough for me to imagine Sam destroying a book, no matter what it said. But a journal—that's different, I suppose. Do you have any idea what it looks like?"

He shook his head. "For all I know, it could be loose pages, hidden anywhere."

"But if they hid it, they have to know about it, right?"

"That's what I thought, but—"

"But if it's disguised as something else, they might not know it's here. Or if someone else hid it. What did that guy say?"

"That he'd been informed the journal was in Sam's possession."

She pursed her lips, a mannerism he was finding distracting. He fought the urge to kiss her again.

"Someone could have come for a visit, and stuck it anywhere without them knowing." Her eyes sparkled. "What if ... what if it's a book inside a book? You know, one of those hollowed out books. Or ... or a regular book's dust cover over the secret journal. Or ... or maybe someone got in while they were out, and planted it. You know, like inside a pocket, or the lining of an old coat."

"I hadn't thought of that." Justin eyed the pile of clothes. A longer-than-long shot, but they should probably check. "Let's do the rest of the upstairs first."

"Maybe whoever broke in did some of our work for us. Because if it *was* in any of those places, like taped underneath a piece of furniture, don't you think he'd have found it already?"

"That's what scares me the most," Justin said. "That we *don't* find it, but we don't know why. Whether it doesn't exist, whether Opa got rid of it, whether it's in the hands of someone who plans to use it to—I don't know what. Blackmail comes to mind."

"Or Rose got rid of it, or hid it from Sam, because she thinks she's protecting him." She blew out a sigh. "Too many possibilities. Let's find the damn thing."

Justin started up the stairs. "Agreed."

He started with the bookshelf in his grandparents' room. One day while his grandparents were out, he'd given the books a quick once-over, but hadn't thought to check for switched dust jackets. Part of him wanted the journal to be out in the open. That would mean his grandparents knew about Heinrich, and Justin could simply ask them to comply with his cousin's wishes. Or leave the decision up to them, so he could remove himself from the plan.

Three hours later, he and Megan had eliminated every

nook and cranny they could think of upstairs and regrouped in the living room.

They sat beside the pile of clothes, shaking and feeling each one for any telltale rustling, or unusual weight. They'd collected an assortment of receipts and theater ticket stubs, a few dollars in change, some old peppermint candies, but nothing remotely resembling what they sought.

"It's not here," Megan said. "We'd have found it. We're going to have to ask them. Maybe we should go back to Denver."

Justin folded the last of the discarded clothing. "Shit!"

"What?"

"Vintage Duds. I mean, before it was a used clothing store, it was another bookstore."

Megan's jaw dropped. "Why didn't I remember that? You mean the journal might be there?"

"It's as good a possibility as any."

"But Sam sold out. And then the other owner sold it, too. So any books are long gone."

"But we don't know where they went. If Opa sold all his books to the new owner, or if he sold them to collectors, or donated them to libraries. And what if—" Megan's bullet-train thought processes were rubbing off on him. "What if the killer hid the book in some secret place in the store when it belonged to Opa. Maybe he wasn't sure what to do with it at the time, but he wanted it handy. Someplace nobody would notice, even if they moved everything out."

Megan hopped on his train. "And he came to find it? Only Betty Bedford was in the store watching for ghosts?"

"Why not? He starts asking questions, he thinks she knows about the journal. She refuses to answer—"

"Because she doesn't know what he's talking about, and he gets mad and he kills her because she's seen his face and she can identify him."

"Whoa. I think you're getting into cop show territory again." Despite the gravity of their situation, Justin couldn't help but smile at Megan's eagerness. But he went dead serious as he followed her line of thought. Even if Megan was being melodramatic, Betty Bedford was dead, murdered in a horrendous way, and if the killer *had* done it because she'd seen him, then Megan might still be a target. The killer might think Megan could identify him.

Justin rose, rubbing his sweaty palms along his jeans. "Wait here one minute." He rushed to Opa's study and yanked open a file cabinet drawer. He walked his fingers through the file folder tabs until he found the one he needed. He copied the name and address onto a slip of paper, put everything away and went to the living room, where Megan was organizing clothes into neat piles.

"Let's go." He grabbed Megan's wrists and tugged her to a standing position.

"Where?" Megan asked.

"To the police station."

~ ~ ~ ~ ~

Gordon slipped his eye drops into the drawer, remembering the message slips Laurie had given him earlier. Computer printouts and reading on-screen reports were no easier on the eyes than the lousy handwriting of some of his officers. This would be a good time to return those phone calls.

An alert from his email program had him closing the drawer instead. Thanks to Colfax's string-pulling, he now had the cell phone records from Willard Johnson's phone. He printed out the file and rubbed his eyes.

At the sound of a gentle knock at the rear entrance to his office, he turned. Was Colfax back already? What was the point of a surveillance camera outside if the monitor was somewhere else? He fanned the blinds at the window and saw the Daily Bread van in the lot. He shoved the paperwork into a folder before unlocking the door. Angie stood there, two large bags in her hands.

"Hi, Chief. I brought some lunch."

He stepped aside, taking the bags and setting them on his desk. "All this for me?" The aroma of fried chicken had his mouth watering and his stomach rumbling.

She grinned. "You wish. No, it's to share. We know how hard you're all working to catch Betty's killer."

"You shouldn't do this. You keep it up, the guys are going to expect it."

"We prefer to think of it as a gesture of support for those who protect and serve."

Gordon reached for the bags. "Noted and duly appreciated. I'll take these to the break room and let Connie know so she can alert the duty officers."

"Wait," Angie said, intercepting his hand. She opened one of the bags and extracted a smaller one. "This one's yours. You did some extra protecting and serving." She set the bag aside and slid her hands along his jaw. He bent down, and she brushed a kiss against his lips. "I have to go help with service. See you tonight?"

She left him standing there, with what had to be a stupid, dazed expression on his face and a warmth below his belt. Jerked back to reality when he heard her van start, he quickly locked the door and picked up the bags. With a deep breath, he shifted brains and went to deliver lunch.

At his desk, he attacked the fried chicken and his printouts. His cop sense tingled when he saw the frequent repeats of several numbers, both in and out of Johnson's cell. He zeroed in on the one with the most appearances and set about tracing the owner. While he jumped through the requisite hoops, he noticed what else Angie had packed in his lunch. A jumbo sugar cookie, frosted in white, with a chocolate heart piped in the center. A heart he'd never seen on any cookies in the pastry counter.

He was mulling his reaction when the door opened and Colfax breezed in. Gordon wolfed down the cookie, then wondered why he hadn't wanted Colfax to see it. It's not like the man knew what cookies were or weren't sold at Daily Bread. He washed down the cookie with some too-cold coffee and wiped his hands.

"So, while you've been here stuffing your gut, some of us cops have been working," Colfax said.

"Try that one again when you don't smell like fried chicken," Gordon said.

Colfax grinned and plunked himself down in the chair. "Busted."

"And, for the record," Gordon continued, "I've got a strong lead on a connection to Willard Johnson."

"Great. Who is it?"

"According to this—" Gordon handed the spreadsheet to Colfax. "The highlighted calls, all forty-six of them, were either incoming or outgoing to one Albert Norton Stein."

"Albert N. Stein? You're kidding."

"People do have unusual names. Maybe his parents thought he'd grow up and be a genius."

Colfax rolled his eyes. "Have you run him?"

"Address is somewhere in the sticks beyond Steamboat. Three hours, give or take. Certainly doable. I'm trying to get the cell carrier to pin down the location of the phones for the last few days. Still waiting on that."

Colfax nodded his approval. "Yeah, if the guy was nowhere near here, it's not likely he killed Franklin."

"Or, there's a third player in the mix. You have a response from ViCAP?"

"This quick? You jest. Frankly, I'm not optimistic. Hell, half the cases we input haven't given us squat. But it was worth a shot. If nothing else, we've added to the database."

"So what are you doing?"

"Going on with what we have, which are reports from the CSR techs and the M.E. The autopsy showed the victim was hit on the head."

"Can you match whatever hit her on the head?"

"Yes," Colfax said. "For all the good it did."

"Why?"

"Because it was something found in the store—some kind of doohickey that goes up the butt of a manikin. No prints. And not the cause of death. Probably used it to subdue her."

Knowing Betty Bedford, that made perfect sense. "So our guy wore gloves, but was opportunistic. What about the knife? You think he brought it with him? Or the duct tape, for that matter?"

"I talked to the employees. Blue-haired church ladies, not happy about the blood. They promised to search the back areas, where it was just a mess, not a bloody mess. Mrs. Bedford kept knives in the kitchenette, and duct tape in the inevitable junk drawer. Our techs didn't find any bloody knives, but if the suspect took it with him, we wouldn't know. The employees are going to see if one's missing. Likewise with the duct tape."

"Maybe we'll get lucky."

Colfax flicked a crumb from his jacket, wiped it, and frowned at the grease stain he'd created. "Damn. This'll have to go to the cleaners now." He fixed his eyes on Gordon. "Oh, and your man. Solomon. He's got the chops."

Gordon refused to acknowledge the comment. "We've got work to do."

Chapter Twenty-two

Megan stood as Gordon approached. From his expression, he wasn't happy about being interrupted for a second time today. "Megan. Justin. What do you need?"

"I'm sorry," Megan said. "Should we come back later?"

Justin jumped to his feet. "Actually, Chief Hepler, it's important that we speak to you now. Alone, if possible."

Gordon's gaze moved from Justin to hers and back again. His lips flattened. "This way." He spun and walked away. Megan grabbed her purse and hustled after him, Justin behind her. Gordon opened the door to his office, where Detective Colfax was marking pieces of paper with a yellow highlighter.

"Give us a minute." Gordon said.

The detective looked up, first at them, then at Gordon. Without bothering to question Gordon's directive, he stuck the papers in a folder and stood. "I'll be in the war room."

"Sit," Gordon said. He moved more papers aside. His expression shifted, as if he'd realized that she and Justin wouldn't have barged in unless it was related to the case. "Have you found something?" he said.

"Not exactly," Megan said. "But there's some information we think you should have."

"I'm listening."

"Please," Justin said. "I withheld it to protect my grandparents, and we'd appreciate it if you don't say anything unless it's absolutely necessary. I didn't think it was relevant to the case.

"Withheld what?" Gordon said.

Megan took a breath. "We think whoever is behind all these crimes is looking for an old journal. As of now, I don't think you need to know more than someone apparently wants it badly enough to kill for it."

"And you're certain the journal exists?" Gordon asked.

"Not one hundred per cent positive." Justin said. "But even if it doesn't, the break-ins indicate that someone else thinks it does."

"Which is why we're here," Megan said. "Because we think the guy who bought Sam's store has it. And he probably doesn't know someone wants it. And that whoever wants it might kill him, although we think he didn't intend to kill Mrs. Bedford, but she'd seen him, so she could identify him."

Gordon's lips twitched. "Good to know you've confirmed what we figured out from the evidence."

"Oh," Megan said, knowing her cheeks were bright pink. "Of course. So, do you think the killer is on his way to Fort Collins to find the guy Sam sold his store to? And what if the guy doesn't even know he has the journal, and then the killer gets mad and kills him too?"

Gordon narrowed his gaze. "You said you didn't know him."

"We don't, but Justin—"

"I have his name and address," Justin said, handing him a slip of paper. "I found it in my grandfather's files. I can't promise it's current."

Gordon took the slip, and copied the information onto his tablet. "Thanks." He flashed her a quick smile. The kind she used on clients when they tried to tell her how to do her job. "We'd probably have figured this one out, too, but you saved a few searches."

"So, I take it you haven't found him yet. It's not like I think you can't do your job, but if our theory is correct about why he killed Mrs. Bedford, and if it's the same man who grabbed me, and if he thinks I can identify him—"

Justin grabbed her thigh and squeezed. Hard. She slid her glance to him, and she could tell he was trying not to laugh. Gordon had pretty much the same expression.

"Hey," she said, mollified. "This isn't exactly the sort of thing I'm used to."

Gordon immediately put on a cop face. "I understand. And we're doing everything we can to keep everyone safe. You were smart to go to Denver. But it might help if you tell me why you have to keep the journal's existence away from Rose and Sam. Or what it looks like, what it says, so we'll be able to identify it."

She turned to Justin. He squeezed her hand. "Can I have your word that until it's absolutely necessary, you won't tell anyone?" he said to Gordon.

Gordon's cop face went into uber-cop mode. "If you understand that the definition of 'absolutely necessary' is mine."

"We don't know what the journal looks like," Megan said. "Mostly, it's Rose and Sam we're concerned about."

"Go on," Gordon said.

With a nod, she deferred to Justin, afraid she'd already sounded like enough of a ditz. Probably because deep down inside—well, not so deep—there was this fear that someone might be looking for her with killing in mind. The cool, calm, professional demeanor she wore like an expensive suit when dealing with clients had moved into thrift shop territory.

"The gist of it is," Justin said, "it's possible my grandfather had a brother." He paused, as if the next words pained him more than they would pain Rose and Sam.

Gordon's face showed compassion now, tuning in to Justin's obvious discomfort. "And there's a reason you can't ask him?" Gordon said.

"You tell me," Justin said. "Maybe I'm being too overprotective here. You and Megan have probably spent more time with my grandparents than I have. But somehow, telling them my grandfather's brother might be a Nazi war criminal is something I don't want to contend with."

~ ~ ~ ~ ~

Aware he was gaping, Gordon snapped his mouth shut. "A Nazi? Sam's brother? Sam has a brother?"

"You see my point?" Justin asked.

Gordon let it grind around in his head. "I do. But I also think Rose and Sam are two very strong people. If this journal could put them in danger, why not tell them? They might be able to help." Justin's gaze kept darting to Megan. Even a rookie would know he was hiding something.

"Justin, we have resources you can't tap," Gordon said. "If you'll tell me the whole story, I might be able to do more for you."

Justin shared one more lingering, pained glance with Megan. Her eyes held nothing but confusion. Justin rose. "I know. We're just not ready yet."

Gordon looked to Megan for help. He couldn't do his job if he only had part of the story. She shook her head. "If you find the bookstore guy, and he does have the journal, will you please let us know first?"

That he could agree to. Whether he'd turn the journal over to her and Justin was a question he'd answer should the need arise. He tried another tack. "What's this supposed brother's name? Let me see what I can find in our databases."

Megan and Justin locked eyes again. Justin nodded. "Heinrich Kaestner." Megan spelled it for him. "Or Henry Carpenter."

"You talking one or two people here?"

"One," Justin said. "We think. One's the Americanized version."

"Older or younger than Sam?" Gordon asked.

"Older," Megan said. "We're not sure he's alive." To Justin, she said, "We should give him your papers. He does have more resources. And he's promised to keep things quiet."

Justin stood, staring out the window. "They're in the car. I'll go get them."

With Justin gone, Megan seemed reluctant to do more than stare at her hands, which she kept clasped in her lap.

"I'm on your side, Megan. Rose and Sam were always special to me. Remember that time I broke my leg? I was nine."

"Vaguely." She twisted her hands. "I hadn't been living with them long then. A lot of those first two years are fuzzy."

"Well, Rose brought cookies over almost every day. And she'd bring books, read to me, trying to keep my mind off not being able to play ball with the other kids. And she insisted I kept up with my schoolwork."

Her gaze finally lifted. Her cheeks darkened. "I used to resent the way she took care of everyone. I wanted her to myself." She uttered a forced laugh. "Although since I was always out playing, I don't know why. In denial that my parents were gone, I suppose."

He leaned forward. "Promise you won't tell anyone?"

Her eyes widened. "Of course."

"I couldn't read. Not worth a damn, anyway. Hated school. Rose made me see the magic in stories, in books. Without her, I might have been one of those kids who ends up in a school like Justin's. Trust me, I wouldn't want to hurt Rose or Sam."

Before Gordon had to deal with where this conversation was going, which was way too far down a dark and rocky memory lane, Justin strode into the office and handed him an envelope, then turned to Megan.

"Did you forget to lock the car?" Justin asked.

"You've got the remote." Megan said. "Was it unlocked?"

"I remember locking it. I heard the beep," Justin said. "It's a reflex. Like putting on a seat belt. You do it without thinking."

"What happened? Did someone break into your car?" Gordon asked.

"I don't know. The door was unlocked."

"Which door?"

"Um ... backseat, passenger side," Justin said.

"Wait here. One minute." Gordon hurried to the supply cabinet and got an evidence kit and one of the point and shoot cameras they kept there, then went to fetch Megan and Justin.

"Where did you park?" he asked.

"Out back," Justin said.

"This way's faster." Gordon unlocked his back door. "Which is your car?"

Megan pointed to Sam's blue Impala. Gordon judged the position of the car against the surveillance cameras. Not the best angle, but there was a slim chance they'd caught someone breaking in. He approached the car, motioning Justin and Megan to stay behind him. After snapping pictures, he pulled on a pair of gloves from the kit and went to the door Justin had indicated, then walked around the car checking the other locks.

"I think someone popped the lock on this door. Did you have any valuables, anything tempting on the backseat?"

"Nothing," Justin said with a headshake.

"Did you notice anything missing?" Gordon asked. "Anything out of place?"

Again, Justin shook his head.

"What about when you were here earlier?" Gordon asked.

"We parked on the street."

No surveillance cameras, then. "And when you were at Rose and Sam's?"

"In the garage," Justin said. "Do you think the killer was looking for the journal?"

Gordon got out his fingerprint kit and went to work on the rear door and handle. They hadn't found prints anywhere else, but it was another step he had to take, just in case. "I'd say no, because based on the other two scenes, he'd have ripped the interior apart."

"So maybe it wasn't the killer?" Megan said.

"I'm going to assume someone got into the car," Gordon said. "Beyond that, the possibilities as to why, when, and where are up for grabs. Our suspect might have been scared away before he got past popping the lock."

"What if he planted something?" Megan said. "A bug. Or a bomb? Shouldn't you call the bomb squad, or the dogs, or whoever finds stuff like this?"

Gordon stifled a laugh, then rethought it. Remote, but it was definitely a T-crossing, I-dotting issue. "Why don't you go inside?" he said. "Give me your keys. I'll only be a few minutes."

They left, and he called Colfax. "Come out to the back lot. Bring a flashlight. And an undercarriage mirror."

While he waited for Colfax, Gordon printed the outside of the car. Nothing on the rear door area, but he went ahead and checked the rest of the exterior. He already had elimination prints from the Kretzers and Justin and Megan. The valets at the hotel probably would account for the rest.

"Whatcha' got?" Colfax said.

Gordon took the flashlight and used the mirror to check for surprise packages. "Nothing, I hope. But there's a question of an unlocked door, and given it's one more connection to the Kretzers, we should investigate."

"One door?"

"Yes. Rear passenger side. Everything in the car looks normal. Do me a favor. Go inside, check the surveillance videos. If our guy was trying to break in, maybe he'll show up."

Colfax scanned the area for the camera, caught it. He walked around the Impala, evaluating the line of sight between the camera and the vehicle. "Not likely."

"But we have to check. I'm going to bag what's in the car

and we'll go over it with Megan and Justin. See if we can figure out what someone might have wanted."

"Any recent history of kids breaking into cars here?"

Gordon lifted his eyebrows. "Most of our kids are smart enough not to break into a car in the PD parking lot."

"On a dare, maybe? Initiation? Rite of passage?"

"If so, this would be the first."

"I'll see what they've got."

Gordon gathered what was in the car. A map, some receipts, the valet ticket from the hotel. Two empty water bottles. And a sweater, probably Rose's.

He brought everything to his office, where Megan and Justin waited, and spread everything on the desk. "This is what I found. Anything added? Missing?"

The two of them verified that the sweater belonged to Rose, and that the water bottles were theirs. They examined the assorted papers.

"I can't think of anything else that should be here," Megan said. "What does it mean?"

Justin paled. "It means we need to get to Denver right away."

Chapter Twenty-three

Engulfed by a sense of urgency, Justin grabbed Megan by the wrist and jerked her to her feet. He reached for the envelope on Gordon's desk. "I need these back."

"Two minutes to make copies," Gordon said. "What's the rush to get to Denver?"

"My question, too," Megan said. "Rose and Sam are on a tour, perfectly safe."

"I'm counting on it," Justin said. He collected all the bits of paper from Gordon's desk, and handed Megan Oma's sweater. "If someone broke into the car, they didn't have to take a thing. The valet parking stub told him exactly where we are."

Gordon nodded and snatched the envelope. "Two minutes." He left the office, closing the door behind him.

Megan took Justin's hands. Hers were frigid in his. "Do you think that's what happened?" she asked.

He expelled a slow breath, trying to relax. "We've agreed it's not likely the journal is in the house. So, there's no reason to stay here, and I'll feel a lot better when I see my grandparents are safe. Since we have to go back anyway, I say the sooner the better."

"Do you think we should change hotels? Maybe even leave Denver? Find some out-of-the-way motel?"

Thank God she had a head on her shoulders and could think clearly. All he could see was Oma and Opa being dragged off at knifepoint when they got to their hotel room.

Not likely, but tell that to his stomach and the adrenaline pumping through his bloodstream. Megan's eyes, worried as they were, showed strength as well. And trust. He squeezed her hands, trying to set up some sort of conduit between them. Her strength when he needed it. She seemed to understand, because she smiled.

"We're a team," she said.

"And a damn good one." He pulled her into a quick embrace, which untied some of the knots in his belly. He released her when he heard someone approaching.

The door opened, and Gordon crossed the room, opening the rear door for them. He handed Justin the envelope and a business card. "That's my direct line. Cell's on the back. Keep me informed."

"Same goes," Justin said. "We're at the Frontier. And you have our cell numbers, don't you?"

"Yes."

"Speaking of cell phones," Megan said. "We have to make a quick stop at the house. I forgot my charger."

Some of the tension returned, pecking away at his insides like a flock of pigeons. He knew he'd carry it until he saw his grandparents, so he shoved it aside. "Let's hurry."

At his grandparents' house, while Megan retrieved the charger, Justin confirmed that everything looked exactly as it had when they'd left.

"Should we take my rental?" Megan asked once they were ready. "Maybe the killer won't recognize it."

"Why not? Keys?"

Megan fished through her purse and tossed him the car keys. He got behind the wheel and took a calming breath. "Last chance. Did we forget anything?"

"I don't think so. I thought about grabbing more clothes for everyone, but we can manage with what we have."

He didn't draw an easy breath until they were on the Interstate. Even then, his heart thumped and his mind raced. Should he call his cousin? Should he tell his grandparents?

Gordon had brought an outside perspective to things. His grandparents *were* strong. It was one thing to want to spare them pain or humiliation. It was a whole different thing if sparing them put their lives at risk.

Megan seemed as lost in thought as he was. "Should we call them?" she asked. "Rose and Sam?"

"Not now. You know Oma. She'll pick up that we're worried, and then she'll worry."

"You're probably right," she said. He glanced her way and could almost see the gears turning in her head as she angled toward him. "Gordon cares about them. He's got more than his cop responsibility going. He said Rose is part of the reason he became a cop in the first place. If she hadn't encouraged him, he might have ended up in a school like yours."

At this point, Justin didn't give a damn about the details. That the cop felt beholden to his grandmother was good enough for him.

He pressed the accelerator, trying to keep the car between clusters of traffic. Easier to see if someone was following. And how would he know? He was on the Interstate, along with dozens, if not hundreds of other cars, heading for a major city. He moved to the right lane, as if he might be preparing to exit, and kept an eye on the rearview. Behind him, cars were changing lanes, seemingly at random. Some would be exiting, others would be trying to get around slower traffic. He debated actually exiting, driving around on surface streets to see if anyone followed.

He ditched that idea. All it would do was waste time. His goal was to get to his grandparents fast, and he was going to adhere to the straight line between two points theory.

"What time is their tour supposed to be over?" he asked.

"I don't know. Rose said, 'Most of the day,' and at the time, we were hoping they'd be occupied as long as possible. But I bet they'll hit their room for a nap before they go anywhere else."

He checked the dash clock. Near as he could figure, the earliest they'd get to the hotel would be three-thirty. Would they arrive first? He nudged the accelerator again. Another check of the mirror, but this time for cops.

~ ~ ~ ~ ~

By now, Gordon had grown accustomed to Colfax's knockless entries. When the detective swept into the room this time, Gordon noted his place in the copies of Justin's printouts. "You have something?"

"Surveillance videos don't show anyone approaching the Impala," Colfax said. He flopped into a chair. "What are you working on? The cell-phone caller? Albert Einstein?"

"It's going to take a lot more probable cause to get his cell phone company to release the information we want. You mind running him through the databases? I'm trying to get up to speed with what might be a missing link."

"Which is?"

Gordon caught the hint of *You're keeping me out of the loop* in Colfax's expression. He set the papers aside. "Probably nothing. If it pans out, I'll let you know."

Colfax shot him a glare. "I'll see what I can find out about Mr. Stein."

Gordon went back to the printouts, wondering what Justin hadn't told him. Carpenter was an old man, riddled with cancer, in a nursing home.

What was in the mysterious journal? Proof positive that Kaestner was Carpenter? And Sam's brother? And what did Justin intend to do with the journal if he found it? Destroy it?

He debated that for a moment. If Kaestner truly was a Nazi war criminal, should he, a man in his nineties and dying of cancer, be deported?

Gordon tried not to let his personal feelings play into it. He was a cop, and he'd sworn to uphold the law. All of them, not only the ones he approved of. Hell, for all he knew, the man might be dead already. The articles Justin had given him were over a year old.

It's all in the details. Gordon plugged both names into search engines while he mused.

Whether Sam had a Nazi brother who was dead rather than alive didn't seem to matter to Justin. He was more concerned with protecting his grandparents.

But didn't everyone have black sheep in their families? Gordon knew his great grandfather's brother had been a bootlegger during Prohibition, when half the population either made or indulged in bathtub gin. But then again, in Germany during the war, your typical run-of-the-mill, everyday Nazis weren't considered evil criminals. If you could ignore the six million people they exterminated, he supposed. But did the average Joe, or whatever the German equivalent was, even know what horrors were being perpetrated?

The phone interrupted his ponderings. "Yes, Laurie?"

"Chief, I hate to bother you, but this caller insists on talking to you. Do you think you might take the call, so she doesn't keep calling me every fifteen minutes? Please?"

Gordon opened his drawer and found the message slips he'd stashed there. "Is she one of the calls you gave me earlier?"

"Yes, but she doesn't want to give her name."

Might as well get rid of her, especially if she was bugging Laurie. "Put her through." He wondered what kind of a deal she was going to offer him. Insurance? Land? Or was she pushing a pet charity?

"Police Chief Hepler," he said in his most officious tone.

"Sir, this is Esther Pomeroy. From Vintage Duds. I need to speak to you. Privately. That other policeman was here, but he's not one of us, you know. I trust you."

"One of us?" he said. Colfax was a cop, just like he was. He couldn't think of what he might have in common with Esther Pomeroy. He couldn't even draw up a mental image of the woman.

"You know, from Mapleton," she said. "When he talked to us before, he didn't seem to care. Not the way I know you do. Betty, bless her soul, always said what a kind man you were."

"Thank you." He picked up a pen. "So, what is it you want to tell me? I assure you, this conversation will remain private." Until it interfered with his job.

"No, not over the phone. Please come to the store. Come around back, and I'll let you in."

"I'll be right there." He hung up, found a folder for the Kaestner printouts, and put them in his pending file.

He hoofed it to Vintage Duds, enjoying the spring breeze and warm afternoon sunshine. He cut between two buildings to the alley, then knocked on the door to Vintage Duds. When it opened, the smell of death hit him first. Next, he took in the stately, broad-shouldered woman who opened it. This was not the "blue-haired church lady" he'd pictured from Colfax's report. He showed his badge and ID wallet. "I'm Gordon Hepler. I'm looking for Esther Pomeroy."

"Yes, yes. Please come in."

The voice matched the one on the phone, even if the woman standing in front of him didn't fit his expectation. She was a few inches shorter than he was, her gray hair braided and piled on top of her head. Blue plastic-framed cat's-eye glasses hung from a beaded chain around her neck. She wore faded gray flannel trousers, baggy at the knees, and a red floral-print smock. Scuffed sneakers adorned her feet.

She led him to the office and closed the door. "I found this. It had fallen in between some file folders in Betty's desk. I shouldn't have opened it. I know the laws about tampering with the mail, but I wasn't paying attention. I promised Betty's sister I'd go through her papers, in case there was an insurance policy or other important documents her sister may need. I didn't notice it wasn't addressed to Betty, so I opened it." She handed him a standard number ten envelope, addressed to Sam in a handwritten scrawl.

Reflexively, he took it by the corner. "An honest mistake. We don't arrest people for accidentally opening someone else's mail." Nobody was that anal about turning herself in after opening a letter not addressed to her. "So, why did you call?"

"The questions that other policeman asked. All about how someone might have been searching for something, and then I heard what happened at the Kretzers', and I thought you should know."

"You touched it?" he asked.

"Yes, of course. As I said, at first, I didn't realize it wasn't meant for Betty." She was obviously chagrined at having possibly destroyed evidence. "It could be nothing, but I thought someone official should see it. I don't read German, but I recognized a few words. She twisted the chain holding her glasses. "'Police', and 'NSDAP,' which I know is German for what we call Nazis."

Gordon cleared his throat. Judging from the thickness of the envelope, this was no journal. A few pieces of paper, perhaps, but there might be a clue or directions to the journal. "Thank you, Ms. Pomeroy. Was there anything else you found that belonged to Mr. Kretzer?"

"Not in here," she said. "And there was nothing in the front. I've been working here since six months after Betty opened the store, and I'm quite familiar with the stock." She heaved a sigh. "So much of the merchandise was ruined. I don't know what to do. Most of what we sell is taken on consignment. It's going to be a nightmare matching every-thing, tracking down the owners, and coming to some kind of settlement."

"What will happen to the store?" he asked.

"I don't know. Betty never spoke of it. Who would have thought something like this would happen?" Her eyes glistened. "She had her quirks, but she was a warm-hearted woman, and far too young to die. Especially like that."

This was taking on the atmosphere of a death

notification, one of Gordon's least favorite duties. "She certainly was," he said. "And maybe there's a chance that this letter will give us a clue to the killer's identity. Thank you for calling me."

"I … I guess I should finish going through the files for Betty's sister."

"Then I'll leave you to your work. I can let myself out. Call if you find anything else. I'll arrange to have your calls put straight through."

"Thank you. I feel better now."

She might feel better, but Gordon wasn't sure he did. First, he didn't read German, so if he wanted to know what the letter said, he'd have to bring someone else into the loop. He assumed Sam could read it, but he'd promised Megan and Justin he wouldn't tell the Kretzers anything without checking with them first. And he didn't want anything left untranslated.

Maybe Megan or Justin read German. Megan would have heard it growing up, and Justin's parents would have as well. Or did Rose and Sam speak Yiddish? Mapleton's Jewish population had its roots in immigrants not only from Germany, but also from Poland and Russia.

The envelope was probably a lost cause as far as prints went, but the pages might give them something. Or touch DNA, although Satan would be in a snowball fight long before they got results for a low-priority case like this one.

Stop overthinking. Call Megan and Justin.

He went to his office, grateful to find it empty. He gloved up and scrutinized the envelope. The postmark was faded and blurred, as if it hadn't gone through the machine properly. He got out his magnifying glass and could decipher a few numbers from the ZIP Code. The first was either an eight or a three, the last were a two and a five. Or was it a six? The ones in between were totally illegible. Maybe the lab folks could enhance it.

Carefully, he removed the letter. Four pages. Not the

same handwriting as the envelope. The date on the first was five years ago. So, this wasn't World War II vintage. In case there was any doubt, the paper confirmed it. Off-white stationery, neither brittle nor discolored with age. He scanned the pages. The spidery writing style would have been hard to read even if it had been in English. The writing was irregular, as if the person who penned the letter did so with a trembling hand. At the end of the last page, he recognized the word *Bruder* above the signature, which was large and clear. "Heinrich."

Chapter Twenty-four

Slow-moving traffic ensnared them on the approach to the hotel. Megan glared at the gridlock, as if her gaze would slice through the cars, zapping them into nothingness.

Everything will be fine. Everything will be fine. If she repeated it enough, maybe she'd believe it. And why shouldn't it be fine? She smoothed out the tour brochure and studied it. Again. Looked at her watch. Again. One city tour was due at two, one at three, and the last at four. They'd already missed the first two, and if traffic didn't let up, they'd miss the arrival of the last one.

The tour brochure had been in Megan's purse, not in the car, and there were over a dozen tours listed. Nobody could know where Rose and Sam were. Nobody could have hijacked their bus and absconded with them. And the hotel wouldn't give out a guest's room number. They wouldn't even say it out loud when they handed you the key cards. Rose and Sam wouldn't open the door without checking the peephole, would they?

"Is there a faster way to the hotel?" she asked Justin. "A side road?"

"We're almost there. Besides, I don't know any shortcuts."

"Look! Over there. Isn't that a tour bus?" She pointed off to the right, where a large shuttle van was pulling into a hotel's *porte cochere*.

"Megan, we don't know which tour company they're

with, and even if we did, there are probably half a dozen tour busses in this area. We'll get there. Worrying about it isn't going to speed things up."

How could he sound so calm? She took her eyes off the traffic and cut her gaze to Justin, noticing the white-knuckle grip on the wheel and the little muscle twitching in his jaw. Maybe he was better at hiding his emotional state. Then she recalled his anxious pacing in the hotel room. She'd calmed *him* down.

"You know, I have this theory," she said. "There's a finite amount of panic allotted for any situation, and we're sharing the load for this one. It seems that when I'm ready to freak, you're steady, and when you're coming apart, I've got it together. Or else we're both halfway nuts."

"Come apart? Me? No way. I'm a guy. We don't come apart. Not allowed. Can't risk losing any man points. We all come with special internal settings that keep everything tight."

She managed a smile. "See, you're doing it now. I'm scared to death, and you're teasing me out of it."

"Bet we're there before you can count to a hundred," Justin said.

"You remember Rose's game?"

Justin grinned. "Of course. Mom used it too."

"Did she use it for going to the doctor? Getting shots?"

"It did provide the necessary distraction."

"It probably helped that I used to lose count and had to keep starting over."

Justin reached over and patted her thigh. "And the magic is still there. We made it."

Megan was ready to jump out, but Justin didn't pull into the valet parking lane.

"Where are you going?" she asked.

"If we have to leave in a hurry, I don't want to wait for a valet."

The words "leave in a hurry" didn't ramp down her

worry meter. "You could drop me off at the entrance, and meet me upstairs."

Justin didn't stop. "No, we stick together." He drove around to the hotel's self-parking area.

She scanned the lot for empty slots. "There's one. And it's close to the rear entrance."

Justin went past the spot, then spun the wheel and backed in. All the better to leave in a hurry. She drummed her fingers on the armrest, waiting for the car to stop. As soon as it did, she grabbed her purse, popped out, and slammed the door. "Don't forget to lock it," she called over her shoulder. She listened for the chirp of the remote, then walked faster.

"Megan, wait for me. Together, remember?"

"Right. Together. That's probably better for the worry-sharing."

"I think proximity helps," Justin said, moving closer. He took her hand. "Physical contact seems to enhance the effect."

She had to agree. The tension level eased. Not for long. The anticipation grew with each step toward their goal. By the time they'd crossed the lobby, she practically dragged him toward the elevator, where a car awaited passengers, door open. Inside, she mashed the button for twelve, tapping her foot until the doors closed and the car began its ascent. From her purse, her cell chirped. She fumbled through her bag, finding the phone resting on the bottom.

"Who's calling?" Justin asked.

Megan checked the display. "The 'last chance to recharge your battery' fairy. Remind me to plug it in as soon as we check on Rose and Sam." She powered off the phone and dropped it in her purse.

"They're all right, aren't they?" she said, more to convince herself than anything else.

"I'm sure," Justin said. "Probably having a nap after all that sightseeing."

The elevator dinged, the doors slid open, and Megan

marched down the hall, her pace slowing as she approached the door. She hesitated before knocking. "I hate to wake them."

"If so, we'll apologize for disturbing them. You're the one who insisted we rush up."

"I guess I can be impulsive."

She thought she saw Justin's lips curve upward before he fisted his hand and lifted it toward the door.

"Wait." She grabbed his hand before he knocked. "What if they're ... you know ... *not* sleeping?"

"Geez, I thought I'd finally shaken that picture out of my head. I guess then we'll *really* apologize for disturbing them."

"I'm sure that's not the case," she said. "I mean, it sounded like last night would be ... and it's awfully soon after, considering ... if they even—"

Justin shut her up with a glare and rapped on the door. "Oma, it's us."

Megan pressed her ear to the door, hearing nothing but silence. She knocked. "Rose? Sam?" Still no response.

"We could go to my room and call," Justin said. His color deepened. "They might not ... you know ... want to come to the door."

"Call their cell," Megan demanded. "There's no point in all this speculation. I'm getting a stomach ache."

She leaned over, trying to see the display on Justin's phone as he scrolled through contacts. "Don't you have them on speed dial?"

He scowled. "I didn't even know they had cell phones until I got here. And if you hadn't forgotten your charger, we could be using *your* phone to find their number, because they called *you*, remember?"

Megan fished her phone from her purse and pushed the power button. Nothing. "It's dead. Sorry."

"Got it," Justin said. He lifted the phone to his ear.

She watched, trying to read the expression on his face. He shook his head. "Voice mail." After a pause, he said, "Hi,

Oma. It's Justin. Please call when you get this message. We're okay, but we'd like talk to you as soon as possible."

"Tell her how to hit call back," Megan said. "And not to call me instead, because my phone's dead."

He rolled his eyes. "There should be a prompt telling them how to return the call when the message is over." He snapped the phone shut. "I know they have my number. I programmed it for them myself."

"Try Sam," she insisted.

He did, with the same result.

She pounded on their door, taking her frustrations out on the wood. "Rose? Sam?" All she got for her efforts was a set of sore knuckles. She turned and leaned against the door, fighting panic. When there was no response, she conceded the battle. Panic emerged victorious.

~ ~ ~ ~ ~

Gordon copied the letter and envelope, then placed the originals into a paper evidence bag before adding it to his pending folder. He punched Megan's number into his cell phone. Before she answered, Colfax burst into the office.

"Got something," he said.

Gordon hit the end button. "What?"

"We can put Will Johnson and Al Stein together—or their phones, anyway. They were both in the same place at the same time."

"You got the cell tower data?"

"Yep. Took a little tap dancing, but you can call me Fred Astaire."

"Excellent. Shall we go pay another visit to Mr. Johnson?"

"Sounds like a plan." Colfax grabbed his jacket from the hook. "I'll drive."

Gordon tugged his off his chair. "We going to play good cop, bad cop?" he said as they drove.

"Only if I get to be good cop," Colfax said.

Gordon frowned. "That won't work. I live here. I prefer the locals think of me as someone they can trust."

Colfax laughed. "I figured you'd say that. You can be Officer Friendly, then. I think I have a nice length of rubber hose in the trunk."

Gordon huffed. Colfax might be a damn good detective, but his sense of humor was wearing thin. He was also grinning like the proverbial canary-eating cat. "What else should I know before we start talking to Johnson?" Gordon asked.

"You didn't ask where those phones were," Colfax said.

"So, tell me."

"We put it not far from the faked car accident. We can't pinpoint the exact location, but it's within half a mile."

Gordon's heart rate kicked up. "Time?"

"Maybe an hour before. We don't have precise time of death, or time of the crash."

"They wouldn't be talking on the phone to each other if they were both in the same place. I can see them hooking up, verifying where the other one was, especially if they were off the road."

"Sounds reasonable," Colfax said.

"Maybe one arranged a meet with Karl Franklin, lured him off the road, and the other did the killing. Given the state of Johnson's health, he'd probably be the arranger, not the killer."

"Agreed." Colfax turned down the lane to the B&B.

"What do you know about the good Mr. Stein?" Gordon asked.

"Not a lot. Mechanic. Works for a garage in Steamboat. No arrests or warrants."

"Thought all your fancy databases and big-city contacts would know what he ate for breakfast."

"Not quite. I couldn't tell if he had his eggs scrambled or poached."

Gordon shook his head in exasperation.

"Seriously," Colfax went on. "He's living in a big house,

with three vehicles, and pays all his bills in full. Lives higher than expected from a garage mechanic's salary, but we'll need more cause to dig any deeper."

After convincing the Richardson sisters not to announce their presence, Gordon and Colfax strode past the women's disapproving frowns and went upstairs to the Iris Room.

Gordon gave the door a sharp rap, then moved out of the doorway. "Mr. Johnson. This is Police Chief Hepler and Detective Colfax. We'd like a minute of your time, please."

"Definitely Officer Friendly," Colfax muttered.

After some shuffling sounds, the door opened. Willard Johnson blinked, rubbed his eyes, and ran his fingers through sleep-tangled hair. "You come to arrest me?"

"No, sir. It's like I said. We have a few questions."

"Unless you want us to arrest you," Colfax said. "You done anything we should arrest you for?"

"No, no. Come in. I was asleep. Takes a while for my brain to kick in."

Colfax marched into the room and went straight for the bedside table, where he lifted a pill vial from several lined up in a neat row beside a stack of paperbacks. Squinting at the label, he held it at arm's length. "Potent stuff. You take a lot of this?"

Johnson swiveled his head toward Colfax, then gave Gordon a bewildered look. "I have prescriptions for those. What's this about?"

Colfax set down the pill vial, picked up one of the paperbacks, and clumped across the room, a scowl on his face.

"Relax, Mr. Johnson." Gordon smiled. "May I call you Will?"

"Um ... yeah, why not."

"Will, why don't you sit down? Get comfortable." Johnson took the only chair in the room, so Gordon sat on the bed, assuming a relaxed posture. Colfax stood in the doorway, thumping his knuckles against the book.

"You met with a Mr. Stein on Tuesday. Can you tell us what you did?" Gordon said.

"I ... I don't know what you're talking about."

"Cut the dumb act," Colfax said. "We know you were together."

"But ... but nobody could have seen us," Johnson said. "He said so."

"We don't need witnesses," Colfax said. "We have proof. What was it? Drug deal? Or maybe a lover's meeting? Interesting reading material." He tossed the book to Gordon.

Gordon started to set the book on the bed when the cover caught his eye. His cop radar bleeped like Angie's alarm clock.

"What are you talking about?" Johnson said.

Gordon lost some of his Officer Friendly expression when he addressed Johnson. He strode to the night table and examined the books more closely. "The drugs may be legal, but we can arrest you for breaking and entering."

"Hey, wait. I didn't break in anywhere. What are you talking about? Nothing illegal about reading romance. You can buy those at any bookstore. Old, sick man like me, I enjoy a little fantasy."

"What would you say if I told you we found another book like this one in the apartment above Daily Bread?" Gordon asked.

Guilt flashed like a neon sign from Johnson's expression. He mopped his brow with a sleeve. "I told you, I'm sick. All the drugs, treatments. I had to lie down, just for a few minutes. Get out of the bright lights. Saw the waitress come back from the storeroom and set the key down. I took the key, went in, saw the stairs. And the door at the top wasn't locked. I didn't touch anything, I swear. Just took a quick lie-down on the couch. I put the key by the register where I found it."

Gordon and Colfax did a quick non-verbal consult, Colfax's slight head bob indicating Gordon should take the lead.

"We'll see what the woman who lives there has to say. For now, you were waiting for Mr. Stein, weren't you?"

Johnson nodded. "I live in Utah. They're ... conservative, you know."

"Cut to the chase," Colfax snapped. "What does that have to do with your business with Mr. Stein?"

For Gordon, everything clicked into place. "Stein's your supplier, isn't he?" he said. "The Richardons let you use this address?"

Johnson bowed his head. "It's all legal."

"Medical marijuana," Gordon said.

"Yes. Stein's my official caregiver. Like I said, it's all legal. Bad enough I have to travel this far, and the amounts I can get are controlled. Lyla and Flo understand. But they don't want me smoking in the house. And even though it's legal, they don't like the exchange happening here."

"So, you were meeting Stein and getting your drug fix," Colfax said.

Johnson's head snapped up. "Hey, you try living with the pain and the nausea sometime."

"And you didn't run into anybody?" Colfax went on. "Just the two of you, doing your thing out in the woods?"

"Woods? What woods? We were at a scenic overlook. I got in his car, got my stuff, and left. There weren't any other cars around."

"Stein happen to mention seeing more ... patients?" Colfax asked. "Maybe a Karl Franklin?"

Johnson shook his head. "Never heard of him. Stein and I didn't talk. It was a business transaction, plain and simple. It sucks that it has to go down like this. The marijuana works, but I'll be dead and buried long before Utah legalizes it, even under controlled conditions."

Gordon took a long, hard look at Johnson, and another one at Colfax. He stood and offered Johnson his hand. "Thank you for your cooperation, Mr. Johnson. Good luck."

Johnson's bewildered expression returned, but with a layer of gratitude mixed in. "Um ... you're welcome."

Gordon closed the door behind them. The silence filled the staircase like a winter snowstorm as he and Colfax walked down. Flo and Lyla sat in the living room. Flo was knitting, Lyla reading a magazine. Both women stopped at their approach.

"How many?" Gordon asked.

Flo set her magazine aside. "In the past two years, maybe six. They deserve some comfort."

"Would you have a Karl Franklin among them?" Colfax asked.

"No," Flo said. "We merely allow them to use this address. We don't grow or distribute, Chief Hepler."

Gordon nodded. "If you do, make certain all your paperwork's in order."

Colfax didn't utter a word until he pulled into the parking lot behind the station. "Guess we can scratch Johnson off our list of suspects. You want to do anything about his using Angie's place for a nap?"

"I'll let her know to be more careful with the key." Relieved that he wasn't going to get into a debate about marijuana for medical purposes, Gordon unlocked his office door. Colfax entered and made himself at home.

"I suppose it's possible that Franklin showed up during the deal and started raising a ruckus."

"Makes no sense," Gordon said. "It's legal—or close enough, as far as I'm concerned in this case. Why kill someone? And how could that tie in with Betty Bedford or the Kretzers?"

"Damned if I know. What I do know is that we eliminated two suspects, so we need a whole new guy. I'll verify Stein's who Johnson says he is. And I'll see what's up with our background check on Franklin. It should have come through already."

And Gordon needed to call Megan and Justin. "You do

that. I've got a couple of loose ends to tie up." He tossed his hands in the air. "Budget crap," he said, hoping Colfax couldn't read the lie.

"Ah, it's good *not* to be the Chief. I'll see you tomorrow."

After Colfax left, Gordon tried calling Megan again. Straight to voicemail. He stared at the unfamiliar script on the copy of the letter he'd made. He hadn't learned to read German in the last hour. He picked up the phone and called the Frontier Hotel in Denver. "This is Gordon Hepler, Mapleton Chief of Police," he announced to the receptionist. "I have a confidential fax for one of your guests. Justin Nadell."

The clerk promised to watch for the fax and ensure it got to Justin.

"Thanks." He typed a quick cover sheet and headed for the fax machine.

Chapter Twenty-five

Justin wrapped his arm around Megan's shoulders. "Deep breath. Let's think."

"Think? I hope your brain is working better than mine, which is caught in an instant replay of someone hurting them. Where could they be?"

Justin knew he had a lot of those same pictures in his head. "We can't jump to conclusions. We have to stay calm." He wasn't all that convinced either, but speaking rationally helped clear his mind. "We'll check with the concierge. They must have tour records. We'll check the lounge, the restaurant. Maybe they're having a nosh. If we can't find them, I'll see if I can get hotel security to let us into their room."

"Good. That's a plan. Action. I can get behind that."

Her smile had him almost believing it. He tried not to think of what *could* happen. There was no guarantee that whoever had broken into the car was connected to Betty Bedford or his grandparents.

He kept Megan close during the elevator ride. Her theory about sharing the stress seemed to be spot on. When the elevator chimed and the doors slid open at the lobby, he squeezed Megan's hand. "We're going to be concerned, but calm. Rational."

"Speak for yourself," she muttered.

"Megan—"

"I know, I know. Calm. Rational. But try telling that to my

stomach. I hope I don't barf all over the concierge."

He glanced around, spotted a small alcove with a house phone and bench. Hands on her shoulders, he steered her into it. He tucked a finger under her chin and lifted her face. "We are two people, justifiably concerned about our relatives. We are going to ask for help. We are not going to make demands, or do anything else that would create an antagonistic situation."

She closed her eyes and exhaled a shaky breath. "I know. I do this kind of troubleshooting for a living, for God's sake. I spend half my time putting out fires."

"You don't troubleshoot for people you love, though. Pretend it's another meeting fire you have to put out."

She nodded, and flashed a quick, tentative smile. "I can do this."

"*We* can do this." He leaned down and threaded his fingers through her hair, tilting his mouth to hers. The kiss was explosive, as bright and fleeting as a bolt of lightning.

They separated, and Megan's eyes met his. "That seemed to work," she said. "Even more than holding hands. Let's go." Back straight, head high, she marched toward the concierge desk.

He strode after her. Once this was over, he was going to have to explore the Megan attraction thing. It might not hold up when stress left the equation, but it would be worth finding out.

Who was he kidding? Once this was over, he'd be back at work, and Megan would be back planning her events.

He scanned the lobby, hoping to see a stream of people who looked liked they'd been sightseeing all day. No streams. Only a harried set of parents trying to keep their offspring in tow.

After a fruitless inspection of the lounge, restaurant and gift shop, he headed toward the concierge's desk.

"What about the spa?" Megan asked.

"I can't see them splurging, but the concierge can check

that for us."

"Okay. I can do this." Megan fluffed her hair and smiled, first at him, then at the woman behind the concierge desk.

"Hi," Megan said. "I hope you can help us."

From her tone, Megan had pulled everything together. Definitely calm, confident. Rational. Justin let her talk.

"Yes?" The woman looked up, a perfect hospitality industry smile on her face.

"Our grandparents," Megan continued. "They're here celebrating their anniversary, and took a city tour this morning. We didn't think to check with them about which tour, but they should be back. We checked, and they're not in their room. Can you help?" She glanced in Justin's direction. "They're in their seventies, and they get confused sometimes."

He managed a worried frown instead of a snigger at the thought of Oma and Opa being as feeble as Megan had painted them.

"Oh, of course. I certainly understand. If they purchased their tickets here, we'll have a record. What are their names?"

"Kretzer," Justin said. "Rose and Sam."

The woman opened a drawer and set a receipt book on her desk. She leafed through a few pages. "Yes, here they are. It was a Medallion tour. The bus left here at nine-thirty. It was due in at two. If you'd like, I can call to verify."

"Please," Megan said. Justin heard the strain creeping into her voice.

They waited while the woman made the call. "Thank you," she said, and hung up the phone. "The tour picked up six people from the hotel this morning, and we had six tickets sold. They don't track names, but it's reasonable to assume your grandparents were on the bus. It got back at two-fifteen, and six people got off."

Megan asked the concierge to check spa reservations.

She called, then set down the phone and flashed a

sympathetic smile. "Sorry. Nothing for either a Rose or a Sam Kretzer."

"Thank you," Justin said. "We'll check around." He took Megan's hand and found an empty seating area. He got out his phone and tried both numbers again. Voice mail.

"We told them to keep their phones on, didn't we?" Megan said.

"I don't remember what we said, other than they should have fun and not worry about us. If they got in at two-fifteen, they could be anywhere."

"What now? Hotel security?"

"Let's try a house phone first. Maybe they *are* asleep, or turned off their cells."

"Go ahead, say it. You're thinking it loud enough. *Or they forgot to charge them.*"

"If that's the reason they're not answering, I'll be happy."

"Okay, you go find a house phone. I need a bathroom break. I'll meet you at the front desk."

He watched her walk away, not leaving until she disappeared into a hallway marked "Restrooms." As he headed toward the front desk, it was as if the cartoon light bulb lit up over his head. Maybe his grandparents had left a message for him. He quickened his pace.

"I need to know if Sam and Rose Kretzer are still registered," Justin said to the clerk. "And if I have any messages. Justin Nadell. Or Megan Wyatt." He gave her their room numbers.

He waited impatiently while the clerk checked her computer, verified that his grandparents hadn't checked out, then disappeared into a back room. She returned with a large envelope and handed it to him. He thanked her and worked the seal free. Before he could check the contents, Megan rushed to his side.

"Did you find them? What's that?" Megan snatched the envelope from his hand. "Let me see."

~ ~ ~ ~ ~

Once Colfax had gone, Gordon tried Megan again. His call went straight to voice mail. If Justin had received the fax, he should have called. He rummaged through his desk, checked his notes, searching for Justin's number. He knew he had it somewhere. He scrolled through his cell's contacts and call logs, with no luck. Damn.

Gordon did a quick regroup. Solomon had shown up after Megan had been accosted, and Justin had given a statement. His number should be on the report. He picked up the phone and called Laurie. Moments later, she came in and dropped the report on his desk.

"Thanks," he said. "Everything under control out there?" One of Laurie's greatest assets was her ability to keep a buffer between him and the annoying minutiae of the job, but sometimes she left him a little too far out of the loop.

"Considering this is the biggest crime wave I can remember in Mapleton, yes."

"Deputies getting along with our guys? No turf wars?"

"Thanks to Angie's generosity, there's no trash talk. The deputies don't want to be cut off."

The way to inter-departmental peace, like almost everything else, was through the stomach. But if it meant inter-departmental cooperation, he was all for it. He saw the fatigue behind her cheery attitude and checked his watch. "If you want to cut out early, feel free to leave. You've had a long couple of days."

"There's about an hour left. I don't mind staying."

"Go. Get some rest. Or whatever you do to unwind."

She smiled. "Thanks. I will. And I called Lou at the garage. He's expecting you. If you leave now, you'll get there before he closes." She left, closing the door behind her.

He rubbed his eyes. It had been a long couple of days for him, too. He'd drop his car off at the garage, call Justin, then see if Angie's invitation was still open. An interval of detaching his brain from the rest of his body might help him see things with a refreshed perspective.

Solomon's report was as detailed as Gordon expected. He found Justin's cell phone number and plugged it into his cell.

Before he left, he poked his head into the squad room. "Anything I need to know about?"

Heads swiveled at his words. "We've got it covered," Vicky said.

"Carry on," he said. He grabbed his jacket and headed for Lou's garage. Routine vehicle maintenance wasn't high on Gordon's priority list, but it would make one less thing for the mayor to whine about.

"Hey, Chief. Been expecting you." Lou wiped a greasy hand on a slightly less greasy rag. "But I won't get to it until tomorrow, so if you need her tonight, you can bring her back in the morning."

"Nah, keep it."

"Shouldn't take long. One job ahead of you, and I'm waiting on a bumper for the next, and it ain't gonna get here for a while, so I should have yours done by noontime. You need a lift anywhere now?"

"No. I'll walk to the station, pick up a ride there."

"You're the boss." Lou guffawed. "Boss. Chief. Get it?"

"Yeah. Good one, Lou. Key's in the ignition. And make sure the paperwork's in order. The city fathers love tormenting me about paperwork."

"Been maintaining the fleet since before you were born, Chief. I know the drill."

"I know you do." He retrieved his jacket from the SUV. "Call me when it's ready."

"Will do."

Gordon turned to walk away.

"Chief?"

"Yes?"

Lou scuffed his feet and fussed with his rag. "You're

doing a good job. From what I've seen, Dix would be proud of you. The council knows it, too."

"Be better if we catch the creep. But thanks for the endorsement."

More foot scuffing and rag fussing. "My money says the mayor ain't gonna be reelected. The town folks know he's in it for himself."

"We'll see." Gordon lingered as Lou got behind the wheel of the SUV, wondering once again why he'd promised Dix he'd serve as Chief.

Because Dix saved your father's life, idiot. Not to mention the mayor's choice was a brown-nosing suck-up who didn't have an independent thought in his brain.

He shook it off. Why he'd accepted the job didn't matter. He had, and what mattered was doing it well. Lost in thought, he meandered across the lot as Lou parked his SUV alongside the open garage bay, where one car was up on the lift, and another sat in the second space, its hood gaping open like a shark out for the kill.

He turned his thoughts away from the job and dialed Daily Bread. "Hey, Ozzie. It's Gordon Hepler. Is Angie around? I've got a couple of questions for her about last night."

"Hang on."

While he waited, Gordon heard the sounds of a busy diner. Guess the citizens were over their initial panic. Said a lot for their trust in the police department, and he felt a brief surge of satisfaction.

"Hey, Chief, what's up?"

Her voice brought the memories of the previous night. He glanced around, checking to see if any passersby were within earshot. "How about we get together and you can see for yourself."

"What time?"

"You name it. I'll be in my office." He'd tell her about Willard Johnson's visit in person.

"Things are crazy here. Let me call you back."

"Wait. Use my cell." He gave her his number and drifted the rest of the way to the office on a warm glow.

Glad to find his office empty for a change, he shifted to cop mode and dug through the mountain of paper that had accumulated in the last few days, trying to get a feel for the big picture. The more he read, the more the picture resembled a Jackson Pollock. The one connection they'd been able to make, tying Willard Johnson to his marijuana supplier, had been a dead-end.

Time for a different perspective. He carried the mountain down the hall to the war room and stared at the white board. Dix's voice echoed in his ears.

Things happen for a reason. As a cop, it's your job to find it. Don't worry about whether it makes sense. People are nuts.

He heaved out a sigh and started organizing paper. With the mountain now divided into more manageable foothills, he started climbing. Thank goodness these were all computer printouts. Less handwriting to decipher. As he read, his father's voice replaced Dix's.

Find the beginning. Then start there.

He glanced at the board again. Where *was* the beginning? Were they dealing with a single case? Did it matter? Karl Franklin's accident was at the earliest end of the timeline. Who was he? Colfax had said he was waiting on the background check. Had it come in? Gordon started to hunt for it. This time Dix and his father spoke in unison.

Teamwork is essential, but if you want something done right, do it yourself. And then Dix would wink and add, *Just don't let anyone think you're checking up on them when you do.*

Given the demands of proving anything in court nowadays, triple-checking didn't carry the stigma of distrust, not on his watch. He preferred to think of it as fresh eyes, not duplication of effort. He went to the computer and entered what information he had about Franklin into a search engine. Mapleton might not have the budget for all the programs the county cops could access, but they weren't totally without resources. Results came back within minutes.

Whatever he'd expected to find, it wasn't that Franklin had been a private investigator.

Gordon felt that thrill-of-the-hunt tingle as he studied the screens of data. Franklin had moved around a lot. He'd lived in seven states, had held PI licenses in five over the last thirty-three years. Nevada, Washington, Pennsylvania, Virginia, and Arizona, although all had lapsed. His current residence was in Urbandale, Illinois. Same address for the past three years. Sixty-five years old. Drove a 1997 Ford Probe. No criminal record, no outstanding warrants. Collecting Social Security. No other income, or not the kind one reported.

Gordon started making notes. The man was a retired PI, not visibly well-off. Gordon moved on. The man had a permit for a .38 Smith and Wesson revolver. That rang a bell. They'd found a bullet in the radio of his rental car, and a revolver explained the lack of shell casings. He snorted. Some of the crap that came out of the radio these days had him wanting to shoot it, too.

No, the bullet had entered through the rear windshield. Had whoever killed him tried to shoot him first? Had the techs recovered the gun? Still too many questions.

He pulled the accident reports as well as the follow-up search. Cold, dry facts. It was like handing someone a dictionary and saying, "There's a great book in here. All you have to do is put the words in order."

Colfax had left copies of everything. Evidence logs, crime scene contamination sheets, plus the reports from forensics, which weren't many, due to backlog in the labs. He noted that they *had* found Franklin's Smith and Wesson. A revolver, one shot fired. And a cell phone. Both near a streambed about fifty yards from where they'd determined Franklin had been killed.

He called Colfax. "I've been digging into Franklin's

background and reviewing the crime scene evidence logs from the spot Franklin was killed. Any prints on the gun? Anything in the phone?"

"And a good evening to you, too," Colfax said. "Franklin wasn't a priority. The Bedford homicide is ahead of him. Why is it important?"

"Just a hunch. Were you aware Franklin was a retired PI?"

A pause. "No, I haven't seen the report."

"I fed him through our system, and that's what I got. I'm thinking he might have been working under the radar. If I knew who he'd been in touch with, it might give us some leads. Will you do some more of your Fred Astaire routine and get the phone records?"

"I'll go get the damn phone from Evidence and call you."

While he waited, Gordon pondered the Mapleton connection. Who would have hired a private investigator? Had Franklin known about the mysterious journal Justin and Megan had been looking for? It made more sense now, one more commonality that tied all three cases together.

Common denominators. Unlike the ones in math class, he actually enjoyed ferreting them out in police work.

His phone rang. "Hepler."

"Got it," Colfax said.

"Tell me whoever threw it into the stream was too stupid to wipe out the call log. And that the water didn't ruin it."

"Consider yourself told. Which is a good thing, because I've worn out my welcome with my cell phone company contacts, and I'd have to get subpoenas for all the numbers otherwise."

"So what do you have? Any Colorado numbers?"

"One. Incoming and outgoing calls over the last two weeks, including one shortly before we think Franklin was killed."

"Give it to me," Gordon said, reaching for a pen.

Colfax recited the number. "You recognize it?"

Gordon pulled out his own cell and scrolled his contact list. "Damn."

Chapter Twenty-six

Megan dug into the envelope, pulling out several sheets of paper. She scanned the first page. "It's a fax. From Gordon. Says it's confidential."

Positioning the page so Justin could see it, they strolled across the lobby to a seating area. She dropped onto a loveseat, and Justin sat alongside. She passed off the cover sheet and stared at the next page. Expecting the message to relate to finding whoever was after them, it took a few seconds for the text to register as handwriting, and in German at that. A letter of some sort.

She snatched the typewritten cover sheet from Justin, who sat, slack-jawed, hardly seeming to notice she'd removed the paper. Rather, he was staring at the German writing on the sheets she held, a puzzled expression on his face.

She handed off the letter and read the cover sheet.

Megan and Justin:
The following letter, addressed to Sam, was misfiled at Vintage Duds. I'm honoring your request for confidentiality before sending it off to be translated. I'll let you decide how you want me to handle it, but be advised that if it turns out to be evidence in the Bedford case, I'm going to have to follow procedure and turn it over to the county investigators.
G.

"Could this be what we've been searching for?" she asked, handing the cover sheet to Justin and reclaiming the other pages. "Four pages. It's not much of a journal. Did your cousin say how long it should be?"

Justin shook his head, still looking stunned.

"Earth to Justin." She waved her hand in front of his eyes.

He took the first of the German pages from her and stared at it for an endless moment. He handed it back and lowered his head to his hands. He'd gone three shades of pale.

"Are you all right?" she asked.

"Fine," he said, his voice flat and barely audible.

His obvious distress had the squadron of butterflies in her belly doing a darn good imitation of the Blue Angels. She took his hand, then snaked her arm around his waist. "No offense, but you don't look fine. You need some water? Or a drink?"

He stood, pulling her up with him. "I'm said I'm fine. But I don't know how to tell Opa."

"Tell him what? You can read it?"

"Maybe, with a couple of days and a dictionary. We spoke English at home. I've got two years of high school German. You were probably exposed to more German than I was."

"Rose and Sam spoke English around me. And most of what I picked up was Yiddish. Mapleton didn't offer German in school."

Justin's brow furrowed as he started reading the pages again. She itched to take them from him, but why? It wasn't like she could read them.

"Does it mention the journal?" she asked.

"I don't know. Like I said, I don't remember much, and handwriting isn't the same as a textbook."

"So what *do* you know?"

"It's from someone's brother, and says something about the camps. And death. And it's signed 'Heinrich', but Sam's name isn't in the letter. But there's a reference to Kaestner. And Carpenter."

"So there *is* a connection between them."

"That says that the stuff I Googled is likely accurate. The big question is, do I show it to Opa?"

"If it's not for him, he says, 'I don't know who this is,' and maybe he'll have ways to trace it to its rightful owner. I say we have to show him."

"You're right," he said. But he still looked shaken.

Something squeezed her heart. All those years she'd thought he was a pain in the neck. She'd been too shallow, too self-centered to see beyond his exterior and recognize the compassion inside. She thought he was in more anguish than Rose and Sam would be if the story turned out to be true.

Without a glance to see if anyone might be watching, she grasped his neck, pulled him lower, lifted her lips to his. His quiet groan was swallowed by their kiss.

"Megan." His voice was hoarse in her ears. "God, Megan." He broke the kiss, broke the body contact, but held her hands. "This isn't the time."

She sucked air. "I disagree. I feel a lot better now."

His gaze bored through her. "You can't tell me that was just another sharing the stress trick."

She lowered her eyes. "I could. But it would be a lie."

He jerked away and reached for his belt, unclipping his phone.

"What?" she asked.

He shook his head, a puzzled expression on his face as he stared at the display. "It's a text. From Opa."

She tried to grab the phone, to read it herself, but he spun away. "What does it say?" she asked.

"They're in Mapleton." He extended the phone.

She stared at the screen. *Rose not feeling well. Rented car. Back in Mapleton.* "Oh, God. She overdid it. Or her medication is wrong. We have to get back. Now."

"We will. Let's get our stuff."

She grabbed his hand and started dragging him toward the elevator. "Call them. Find out what happened."

Justin complied as the elevator doors opened, then shook his head. "Voice mail."

"So text them. Tell them to call, that we're on our way." She pulled him into the elevator, pressed ten and grabbed his phone, unable to wait. She punched in a message. Somehow, doing it herself gave her a feeling of control. Justin put his hand on her shoulder.

"Share the stress?"

She smiled.

"Are you trying the land line?" Justin asked. "Speed nine."

Damn. She should have thought of it. She got their machine. "Rose? Sam? It's Megan. Please call. Let us know you're okay." The doors opened on the tenth floor. Megan rushed out. "Meet you in my room as soon as you're packed."

A few minutes later, she opened the door to Justin. "Almost ready," she said. She did a quick check to make sure she hadn't forgotten anything, then zipped her bag shut. "Should we call, let the desk know we're leaving?"

"I'd rather leave it open. For all I know, we might end up back here."

Within minutes, they were on the road. Megan clutched Justin's phone, squeezing it as if that would force Sam to pick up. When it rolled to voicemail again, she shoved it into a cup holder. "They don't let you use cell phones in hospitals, do they? You think that's why he's not picking up?"

"Could be. But if it was major, Opa would have insisted on taking her to an emergency room here in Denver, not gone to Mapleton. They're probably trying not to worry us, the same way we were trying not to worry them."

"That's not quite the same," Megan said. "They don't know they have something to worry about." She gazed out the window, her foot subconsciously pressing on an imaginary gas pedal.

"We're almost there," Justin said. "We'll probably all have a good laugh when it's over."

He wasn't laughing now, though. His knuckles were white on the steering wheel, and that muscle in his jaw twitched. He met her gaze, and his features softened. He took one hand from its death grip on the wheel and rested it on her thigh. She covered his hand with hers and closed her eyes, trying to keep her thoughts focused there instead of on Rose.

The physical contact held her together until they left the highway and he needed both hands to navigate the mountain road.

Her emotions swirled.

Relief that they'd heard from Rose and Sam. Worry about why they'd left Denver. How they'd left Denver. Apprehension about showing them the letter. Fear that there was a killer on the loose and he might strike again.

Frustration that she hadn't been able to reach Gordon, compounded by the frustration that he hadn't responded to her messages, asking him to check up on Rose and Sam. At least not before they'd been sucked into that cell phone void.

And then there was the totally new one. Desire.

For Justin? But there it was, overwhelming the whirlpool of other emotions. A fling. That was what she needed, and Justin was safe. He'd go home to his job, she'd go home to hers, and they'd have some nice memories. She could still taste their kiss. Oh, yeah. The memories would be more than nice.

~ ~ ~ ~ ~

Gordon stared at the crime scene contamination sheets, the lists of every person who crossed the boundaries of a potential crime scene. He spread them on the table.

Common denominators.

Ridiculous, he thought. The man had every reason to be on all the lists. Jumping to conclusions didn't solve cases.

Neither did assuming anything. One of Dix's favorite reminders.

Don't assume. It just makes an ass out of you and me.

Every detail had to be checked. Even if there was a good reason for it to be there didn't mean it should be eliminated.

For now, the only person he was going to eliminate was himself. But he was damn well going to start checking with the name that not only appeared on all the logs, but also owned the phone number retrieved from Franklin's phone.

He punched in the call. Voice mail. Didn't *anyone* answer a phone anymore?

He took a mental step back. Think. Start at the beginning. He re-read the accident reports. The car had been rear-ended off the side of the road and into a tree.

Crap. He replayed what he'd seen at Lou's garage. He scrambled for his office, went through the old Rolodex, a leftover from Dix's days. Fingering through the cards, he found Lou's number.

"Lou. Gordon Hepler. You said you had a bumper repair. Whose?"

"Buzz Turner. Said he'd had a close encounter with a deer. Tried to fix it himself, he said, but decided a new one would be a smarter move. Although it's not so easy to get replacements for the older models. I told him I could probably fix the old one but—"

"Wait," Gordon said. "Do you have the original bumper?"

"I was getting to that. Nope. Buzz said he tossed it."

Little red flags waved. "Thanks. Do me a favor, though. Don't touch the vehicle. I'm going to get some crime scene guys out tomorrow."

"Crime scene?" Lou said. "Killin' a deer ain't a crime now, is it? Come to think of it, he never said he killed it, just hit it. A kill'd probably have done more damage."

"Lou, trust me. Lock everything up tight. I'll explain

later."

"Sure thing, Chief."

Buzz still wasn't answering his phone. Gordon called the hot line number for the paper. A recording. Swearing under his breath, he found the home phone for the editor. Buzz Turner was off doing interviews. No, he hadn't said where. Yes, it was common for him to turn off his phone. Didn't like interruptions, they interfered with the flow when he had someone talking.

All innocent enough, but the hair on Gordon's neck prickled. He could prove opportunity, with Buzz's name on every crime scene sheet. And means, since the murder weapons were already at Vintage Duds. But he had no motive. That Gordon knew of. Yet.

He plugged Buzz into his search engine and called Colfax. "I need your techs to come up here ASAP to examine a car. I might have found the vehicle that pushed Franklin's car off the road. And I want everything you can dig up on a Bradley Turner, aka Buzz. Including the way he eats his eggs."

"Your reporter? I know they're a pain in the ass—"

Gordon couldn't wait for Colfax to finish. "His car's in the shop. Says he hit a deer. He got rid of the old bumper, but I'll bet your guys can find enough trace to connect him to Franklin's accident."

"You're liking him for both murders? A reporter? Isn't that a stretch?"

"He was at every scene, and was quick to arrive."

"They always are. Scanners, Hell, that stuff's all over the internet. Anyone can listen in."

"Open your mind, Colfax. What if he committed the crimes? He'd be there."

"If he murdered the Bedford woman, he'd have been covered in blood. Plus, we figured our killer didn't come with the intent to kill. He used a murder weapon found on the scene."

"I know. But maybe he cleaned up. You've got a change of clothes in your vehicle, don't you? I do. And he's such a damn fixture around here, nobody would look at him twice. Hell, they'd go out of their way to avoid looking at him."

"Maybe," Colfax said after a prolonged pause. "The timeline work?"

Gordon checked. "He had time to go home, clean up and be back shortly after our first responder arrived."

"Like a firebug wanting to admire his handiwork."

"I think it's more likely he hoped to find what he was searching for."

"You figure that one out yet?"

Gordon hesitated. At this point, apprehending a killer, not to mention keeping the Kretzers and Megan and Justin safe, took priority. And he'd warned Justin and Megan that if the information was tied to his investigation, he wouldn't suppress it. "No, but the connection seems to be some kind of book, or papers."

"Must be pretty valuable."

"I guess we won't know that until we either find it or find him. I've got to hook up with Denver."

"Why Denver?" Colfax asked.

"The Kretzers, Justin Nadell, and Megan Wyatt are there. And there's a good chance Buzz knows it. Update me on my cell." He killed the connection before Colfax could get another word in.

Gordon hit the print icon on his computer. While the printer worked, he grabbed his Glock from the drawer and checked his extra magazine.

Chill. What are you going to do? Haul ass to Denver, go in shooting?

He slowed down to let his brain catch up with his gut. He had no proof Buzz had committed any crime. He took three deep breaths.

Call the hotel.

He identified himself, then drummed his fingers on the

desk while his call was put through to the Kretzers' room. When it rang over to the hotel's voicemail system, he drummed his fingers some more waiting to get connected to the operator again. This time, he asked for Megan.

Another voicemail. "What about Justin Nadell?" The same. His gut twisted. "I've got reason to be concerned about the well-being of the Kretzers," Gordon said to the woman on the phone. "Will you please send someone in your security department to their room? I'll hold."

"It might take a while," she said. "I can't tie up the line, but I'll be happy to call you back."

And if he agreed, who knew how long it would take, or if he'd ever be able to get her on the phone again. "Then please transfer me to security."

Gordon repeated his request, keeping his impatience and rising temper in check. Whoever screened calls for security sounded like a cop wannabe who got all his information from watching television and seemed to enjoy being in a position of power. Gordon waited out an interval of vanilla hold music while the man insisted on ringing the Kretzers' room.

When the man finally came on the line, Gordon tried to remain civil. "I know they didn't answer the phone. And I understand a guest's right to privacy. I'm asking someone to confirm they're not in need of medical attention. Better to err on the side of caution, don't you think, rather than generate the kind of negative publicity the hotel would get if there was a problem and you hadn't taken appropriate action? Or should I call the Denver police?"

Gordon set the phone on speaker and tried to concentrate on the paperwork in front of him. His cell interrupted.

"Got something on your reporter," Colfax said.

Chapter Twenty-seven

Justin pushed the compact as fast as he dared along the winding mountain road. Squinting, he lowered the visor against the setting sun.

Megan put the phone in the cup holder.

"Nothing yet?" he asked.

She shook her head. "Out of range. I can't decide whether cell phones make life easier or add more things to worry about. I can see why Rose and Sam resisted them. They're from the letter-writing school. We expect instant communication."

Justin sucked in a breath, then exhaled slowly. "Megan?"

She shifted, facing him. "Did you remember something else?" Her eyes reflected the worry he knew was obvious in his own.

"No." He ignored the heat rising to his neck, gathered what little courage he had left, and rested his hand on her thigh. "I wanted to say ... no matter how this turns out, and I'm sure everything will end up okay ... I'm glad you were here. It helped."

She lowered her gaze, but he caught the pink tinge rising to her cheeks. Her hand pressed against his. "Same goes."

Out with it, idiot. You'll be home in ten minutes, and you'll lose your captive audience.

Despite the fact they'd had an adult conversation at the hotel, he felt like he'd reverted to Jumbo Justin. He concentrated on the warmth of Megan's hand. She hadn't tried to remove his from her leg. That was a good thing, wasn't it? "You think ... after this is over ... that we could get together? If you ever have an event in my neck of the woods, or something?"

She flashed a mischievous grin. "What if I don't want to wait for an event? I've still got plenty of unused vacation time coming. I'd love to visit. You know, catch up. See what we've missed out on all these years." Her tongue circled her lips. Her eyes twinkled.

His breath caught. "Any time."

She removed her hand and angled herself away. But she'd squeezed his hand before removing hers, and a faint smile danced on her mouth.

He dared not break the comfortable silence for fear he'd say something stupid. Talking to women wasn't part of his daily repertoire, and although he was ninety percent certain he'd read her correctly, he wasn't going to blow it by making assumptions.

The road straightened as they approached Mapleton's city limits. Megan thrust her shoulders back and faced him again, a determined look on her face. "Where should we start? House, clinic, or the police station?"

His phone signaled an incoming message. At last. He eased his grip on the wheel, feeling some of the tension leave. He was definitely hooked into the instant communication lifestyle. Megan picked up his cell. "Another text from Sam," she said. "Nothing wrong with Rose. They're at the house, waiting for us."

"Thank God."

Megan twisted in her seat to face him. "I wish I could undo all the times I forgot to call when I was a kid. No cell phones, but I thought it was babyish to have to check in when I got to a friend's house after school, or was going to be a few minutes late. I feel so guilty about all the worry I must have caused them."

Justin laughed. "If instilling guilt was an Olympic event,

my grandparents would have taken the gold every year. And my mom would have nailed the silver."

"I should call Gordon and tell him to ignore the other messages."

Justin turned onto Maple. "Might as well wait until we get home." It took all his control not to floor it for the final few blocks. A sense of homecoming washed over him as he pulled into the driveway. Except for a few fluttering remnants, the crime scene tape was gone. Had the police removed it, or had Oma yanked it down? He could see her doing just that. Probably had a fight with Opa about cleaning the house, too. He smiled. Opa could hold his own, especially if Oma's best interest was at stake.

Megan dashed up the walkway and skipped up the porch steps ahead of him. He lengthened his stride and joined her by the door. Before he inserted his key, the door swung open.

"Come in, come in," a man in neatly pressed khakis and a blue sport coat said. "You must be Megan and Justin. I'm Buzz Turner, with the *Mapleton Weekly.*"

The voice from the answering machine. Had Oma and Opa agreed to talk to him?

The man continued, smiling as if he were hosting a get-together. "I'm so glad you made it. Your grandparents and I have been having a fascinating chat." He waved them in, slipping back to let them pass.

Megan stepped inside. Justin took her hand, slowing her down. Genetic hard-wiring surfacing perhaps, but he wanted her close. The man's smile gave him the creeps. There was something annoying about his over-friendly demeanor. Then again, there was something annoying about reporters, period.

The living room looked exactly as it had when Justin and Megan had left. "Where are my grandparents?" he asked.

"Waiting upstairs," Turner said, still smiling. "They had something interesting to show me."

Megan shot him a wide-eyed look. He knew she was

thinking exactly what he was. The journal? Had his grand-parents known about it, where it was, all these years? If so, why were they sharing it with this reporter? Wondering if he'd put himself through hell for nothing, Justin massaged the nape of his neck and let Megan lead him up the staircase, Turner close behind.

"How is Rose?" Megan asked over her shoulder. "The first message said she hadn't been feeling well."

"She's fine," Turner said. His cheerfulness had switched to more of a grunt. Hackles raised on the back of Justin's neck, but before he could process his unease, Turner shoved them through the open door into Oma and Opa's bedroom. The door slammed. Turner barreled past them. "I think we should all chat."

Blood pounded in Justin's ears. Turner stood at the bedside, a knife pressed to Oma's throat. She and Opa were sitting against the headboard, their ankles and wrists bound with tape. Another strip covered their mouths. A purple bruise stood out against the pale skin of Oma's cheek. Justin dashed forward.

"Very noble, but you don't want to do that," the man said.

Justin froze, fists clenched, breathing as if he'd run twice around the pond.

Megan gasped. "You're him. The man in the park. How dare you hit her."

"Shut up," Turner said. "No noise. No moving. Not if you want her to live."

Justin raised his hands. "We're not going to do anything." He shifted his gaze to Megan. "Right, Megan? We can discuss this like calm, rational adults."

As if a man holding a knife to his grandmother, a man who'd probably killed another defenseless woman, was anything remotely approaching calm and rational.

"Cell phones," Turner snapped. "On the floor. Now."

"The battery's dead," Megan said.

"Do what I say."

She dropped her phone onto the carpet. Justin tossed his beside it.

"And your purse," Turner said.

Justin could feel Megan's anger as she threw her purse to the floor beside the phones. Turner took a roll of duct tape from the night table and tossed it toward Megan.

"You, Justin. Have a seat." Turner gestured toward the floor. "Legs out in front of you. Hands behind your back."

Justin followed the man's directions, his eyes fixed on his grandparents. Oma's head was tilted away from the knife. Opa's fists clenched beneath his taped wrists. His expression was one of pure fury, one Justin had never seen from him. One he'd never thought his grandfather capable of.

"You, Megan. Tape his wrists and ankles. And no cute stuff. I'm going to check."

Megan hesitated. Turner jerked his arm. Oma's cry was muffled by the tape. "Next time she'll shed blood," Turner said.

"Do it, Megan," Justin said. He leaned forward so she could tape his wrists. When she ripped the tape, the sound ripped his heart. Buzz Turner had killed once. Justin's mind whirled, trying to formulate a plan. "Cooperate. Don't make him angry. We'll get out of this."

She knelt by his side and wound the sturdy gray tape around his ankles.

"More," Turner said. "And tighter."

When she opened her mouth, Justin shook his head. "It's okay," he said, then lowered his voice to a whisper. "Think of where he has that knife. Don't do anything foolish. You can't get to him before he hurts her."

Her head turned toward the bed for several heartbeats. Oma and Opa's eyes shot warnings in her direction. She puffed a sigh and continued taping.

"Done," she announced.

"Go sit over there." Turner pointed to a spot along the

adjacent wall. "Tape your ankles in front of you."

When Megan finished, Turner approached her, brandishing the knife. One of Oma's cooking knives, it appeared. All Justin could think about was how angry she'd be, because that was her favorite knife, and he knew she'd never use it again.

He realized he'd assumed Oma would have the opportunity to cook again. Good. Positive thoughts.

"Hands behind you," Turner said to Megan. He grabbed the tape, then used it to restrain her wrists. Next, he checked Justin's bonds, running another layer of tape over Megan's handiwork. Apparently satisfied, Turner strolled to the bed and waved the knife. "The rule is simple. You promise not to scream, and I'll take the tape off. Understand?"

Opa nodded. Turner ripped the tape from his mouth. A trickle of blood dripped from the corner. Turner reached for the tape covering Oma's mouth.

"Please," Opa said. "Don't hurt her."

Turner shrugged. "She's a nice enough old lady." He eased the tape away and crumpled it. Oma licked her lips. Justin held his breath, praying she wouldn't say anything foolish. Turner paused, as if waiting for an excuse to inflict more damage, then perched on the bed beside her. He rested his elbows on his thighs, the knife displayed prominently in his hand.

"Now that we're all together," Turner said, "it's time to talk."

~ ~ ~ ~ ~

Gordon narrowed his focus to Colfax's call. "What do you have?"

"Married twice, divorced same. Grounds were abuse, both mental and physical. He's hard up for money."

"And on the professional side?" Gordon added notes to his legal pad.

"Seems to be even more of a sleaze than your typical reporter. He was fired from two papers for getting too creative with his stories. He was free-lancing until he got his job with the *Weekly*."

"Too creative? What's that supposed to mean?"

"You gotta relax, Hepler, or the job will kill you. I mean creative, as in he'd create his own news. They never proved it, but rumor has it he *really* didn't let the truth get in the way of a story. He was suspected of planting evidence, feeding rumors, then breaking the story himself."

Gordon rolled that one around. "That fits with the damn press conference. But I can't buy him killing someone, and vandalizing the Kretzers' to break a story. Not unless he's a total sicko."

"You might not be far off. His second wife filed assault charges. The courts sent him to anger management classes about ten years ago."

"I've never seen that kind of behavior since he's been in Mapleton."

"Maybe the classes took. Stranger things have happened."

"Any way you can track down his counselor, find out what kind of a ... student he was?"

"I'll give it a shot. But it was a long time ago."

The background music stopped. "Officer Hepler?" came from the desk phone.

"Gotta get back to you, Colfax. No, wait. Hang on one sec." Gordon grabbed the receiver. "Hepler."

"Sir, we checked the Kretzers' room. There's nobody inside, and there's nothing out of the ordinary. Clothes in the closet, toiletries in the bath. No cause for alarm." The man delivered the words as if he were indulging the whim of an annoying child.

Gordon thanked him and went back to Colfax. "Anything in Turner's history that would give him a motive?"

"Nothing yet. It'll take a deeper background check. I'll let you know."

"I've got searches running on this end too. There's something I'm missing. It's there, dancing around in my head, but I can't get a handle on it yet."

"Happens all the time. It'll show up when you're doing something entirely different. You need me for anything, call."

"Keep your dancing shoes handy."

Think of something else, Colfax had said. Gordon scrolled through his missed call log. Two from Justin, one from Angie. They'd rolled to voicemail.

Work before pleasure. Instead of Justin, Megan's voice followed the robotic tones of the cell phone's message system.

"Gordon. We're on our way home. We got a message from Sam saying Rose wasn't feeling well and they were going home. We can't reach them. Could you please check? Maybe they're at the emergency clinic. Thanks."

The second was a repeat of the first, but with more urgency in her voice. The third was Angie. Listening to her voice made his chest ache. Work before pleasure. He groaned and called the clinic. No, the Kretzers hadn't been admitted. He tried Doc Evans next. He hadn't heard anything from them.

Gordon replayed Megan's message. Definitely said Mapleton, not Denver. Had they had an accident en route? Or had Rose been taken seriously ill? He called their house. Answering machine.

He left a message, then bit the bullet and returned Angie's call. "Something else came up. I'll be working late."

"You want me to bring dinner over?"

What the hell. A man had to eat. "Use the back door."

While he waited, he told Dispatch to order a patrol car to swing by the Kretzers' place, and he put wheels in motion to check for traffic accidents between Denver and Mapleton. He wandered to the war room and stared at the white board again. There were answers in there. Connections he hadn't seen yet.

He added Buzz Turner's name to the board. Was he the common denominator? Was everything connected? Karl Franklin's staged accident. Megan's aborted abduction. The break-in at the Kretzers'. The murder at Vintage Duds. And what about Justin's missing journal?

He found a notepad and drew a circle in the center, then added a series of spokes extending outward. He wrote Buzz's name in the circle. He added names he could connect to Buzz along the spokes, and jotted his notes.

Karl Franklin. Cell phone calls. At scene.

Betty Bedford. At scene.

If Buzz was responsible for the break-in at Vintage Duds, logic said he'd be the one behind the Kretzers' break-in as well. Which tied him to Rose and Sam. Or Justin. Or Megan.

Could Buzz be Megan's mystery man? She'd described him as average, and Turner fit that description—along with half the male population of Mapleton.

He wrote "JOURNAL" above the circle and underlined it. Was that the missing link? He added Heinrich Kaestner's name to the page and dug for the articles Justin had left. Henry Carpenter, if he was alive, was at a nursing home in Arizona. He looked up the number and dialed.

He was on hold with someone in records when Irv tapped on the door. "Sir, Solomon reported nothing unusual at the Kretzers' on a drive by. Did you want to talk to him? He's checking into a possible intruder on the other side of town. Given what's happened, I sent McDermott out as backup."

Gordon smiled at Irv's apologetic tone. "Have him call me on my cell once he's clear. Thanks."

"Oh, and Angie said you were expecting her. She's out front."

Shit. So much for being discreet. "Send her to my office. I'll be there as soon as I get off the phone." Which he hoped would be in this lifetime. Or before his dinner went cold.

The records clerk finally returned to the line, apologizing for the delay. "I thought the case was closed," she said. "It took awhile to find the records. But why are the Colorado police interested in an old man's death? The local medical examiner ruled it accidental."

Accidental. Not natural causes. Gordon resigned himself to a cold dinner. "Did you know Mr. Carpenter? How did he die?" He added a bit of good cop to his tone. "It might help with a case we're working on out here."

"I'm new," she said. "But I heard the rumors. That it was suicide."

"Why would you say that?"

She hesitated. "I think you need to talk to someone in administration for details. But they've already gone home for the day."

She sounded as if she was supposed to be home too. "I'll call tomorrow. Do you keep records of visitors? Or is there someone who worked there while Mr. Carpenter was alive I could talk to?"

"I'll have to check. Can I get back to you?"

Since Carpenter was dead, there didn't seem to be a lot he could do now. Tomorrow, he'd follow up with the local cops, see if he could get more answers. He gave her the number to his direct line and went in search of dinner.

"Busy day?" Angie smiled as he walked into his office. "Still hunting for whoever killed Betty Bedford?"

"Yes to both." He decided even a cold dinner wouldn't counteract the warmth of being in the same room with Angie.

"I was afraid you'd had another emergency when you weren't here to let me in."

"No, just working down the hall. I didn't think I'd be gone that long."

"Life of a cop," she said. "Always on the job."

"It's not usually like this. You probably put more hours in than I do. But I did find your intruder." He explained about Willard Johnson. Angie's eyes flashed momentarily, but she seemed to shake it off.

"A painless way to learn a lesson. No harm, no foul. But I'll talk to Donna about the key and being more diligent about locking up. Ready for some food?"

His rumbling stomach answered that question. Angie took containers from a large paper bag. "It's just salad and lasagna. But after you tie things up here, you could always stop by for … dessert."

He turned, making sure he'd closed the door behind him. He cradled her face, capturing her pale blue eyes with his gaze. "Maybe I need a sample." He grazed her lips with his. "Delicious. I'll save room."

His desk phone rang. Angie brushed his cheek with a fingertip. "I'll let myself out."

Gordon gave her a parting smile as he reached for the phone. "Hepler."

When the caller identified herself as someone from the nursing home in Arizona, he shoved his dinner aside in favor of his notepad.

"I remember Mr. Carpenter well," she said. "He was such a nice old man. I couldn't believe the rumors. That he was a Nazi. He grew up in Pittsburgh. And Carpenter is a common name. I figured it was one of those cases of mistaken identity."

"Did he have any family?"

"Not that I know of. He never mentioned anyone. He'd chat with other residents in the recreation areas, but no outside visitors. Not until shortly before he died."

"When was that?"

"Let me think. Nine months ago, give or take. I'd have to look up the exact date if you need it."

"That won't be necessary," Gordon said. "If I may ask, how do you think he died?"

Her voice grew quiet. "He was old and dying of cancer. In a lot of pain."

Gordon immediately wondered if Carpenter might have

had a little assistance leaving planet earth, and he made a note to check with the ME. "You said he had visitors before he died. Do you keep records?"

"I remember them," she said. "The first one, a Mr. Franklin, only came once, but Mr. Carpenter seemed more at peace after he left. The way people get when they're putting their lives in order. But not with the other man. He came several times. Mr. Carpenter was always agitated after those visits."

"You remember his name?" Gordon asked, pen poised.

"Mr. Turner," she said. "I remember having to ask him to leave the last time he visited, because Mr. Carpenter had a medical crisis."

"What kind?"

"He had trouble breathing, his blood pressure went way up. They took him to critical care for a while."

"So he didn't die at that time?"

"No, not until several weeks later."

"Was anyone with him?"

"Not that I know of. The morning nurse said he'd died in his sleep."

"So why was suicide considered?"

"He'd been depressed. That's all I know, and I've probably said too much. I have to go."

He'd just hung up when his cell phone rang.

"Chief, it's Vicky. I think you should get to the Kretzers'."

Dinner forgotten, he jerked up from his chair and grabbed his weapon.

Chapter Twenty-eight

Megan leaned away from the wall, trying to relieve the pressure on her wrists. Rose sat, tight-lipped on the bed, glowering at Buzz Turner. Silence filled the room like a heavy fog.

"I said, talk," Buzz said. He pounded his fist against his thigh. "Where is it?"

Sam spoke, his voice calm, but there was no mistaking the fury behind it. "I have told you, I know nothing about a letter, a book, or anyone named Henry Carpenter."

Megan shot a glance at Justin. He shook his head a fraction. Rose gasped. Megan snapped her head around. Buzz had the knife at Rose's throat again.

"Stop! Don't hurt her. We might have what you want," she said. Justin's nod confirmed her decision. "In my purse. A letter. It's not important enough to die for."

"I'm sorry, Opa," Justin said. "I wanted to spare you, but if I'd asked at the beginning, this might not have happened."

"You're speaking nonsense," Sam said. "Spare me from what?"

Buzz was digging through Megan's purse, his eyes gleaming when he found the folded papers. He snatched them out, opened them and read. He tossed one to the floor—Gordon's cover page, she assumed, then stared at the next sheet. Then the next, and the next. His fists clenched. He pounded his thigh again, still holding the knife. Megan wished he'd turn it around and stab himself. He threw the sheets of paper on the bed. "What is this gibberish? You read German, old man?"

"Without my glasses I can read nothing," Sam said.

"What about you?" Buzz asked Rose.

She shook her head.

"Damnation, where are they?" Buzz brandished the knife, then pounded his thigh again.

Megan sucked in a breath. *At least he's not hitting Rose.*

Sam straightened with as much dignity a man in his position could convey. His tone was firm. The one he'd used when she'd wanted a too-expensive toy, or later, when he wouldn't let her get a motorcycle. "If you hadn't been so eager to lure us from the hotel with your tale of Megan being captured again, we might have had time to collect our things. My glasses are in the pocket of my coat, which is in the closet of our room. Our hotel room. In Denver."

"And mine are on the night table," Rose said, her chin lifted in defiance. "Also in Denver."

"You've got to have a spare pair," Buzz said.

"I saw them," Megan said. "Downstairs, when we were cleaning up the mess."

"I don't think so," Rose said, then glared at Buzz. "I went through the mess *you* left."

"No, Rose, I saw them." When Rose turned to her, Megan shot her a pleading look. *Play along.* "They must have fallen out of the drawer on the end table by the couch."

"*Ach, ja,*" Sam said, seeming to understand. "You know how you're always misplacing them."

Rose clamped her mouth shut. Megan tried not to let her relief show.

"So, where are they now?" Buzz asked.

"I don't know," Justin said. "Could be they're in the end table. Or maybe there's a pair in Sam's study somewhere."

"Wait," Rose said. "I think maybe I had mine in the kitchen. When I was paying bills."

"Cut me loose and I'll help you," Megan said. She tried to

look as helpless as possible. Not a stretch. Her muscles were already starting to tighten. She knew he'd never release Justin.

Buzz scowled. "I assume you're kidding. You're staying right where you are. All of you. And if I hear a sound, it's back to the duct tape."

He left, taking the knife. Yeah, as if he'd leave it behind so they could cut themselves free.

"Are you okay?" she whispered. Buzz had taped Rose and Sam's hands, wrists crossed, in front of them, and Sam was already gnawing at his bonds.

"Trussed like turkeys in our own home?" Rose said. "That's hardly okay, but we'll think of something."

"Try to start a tear, Opa," Justin said. "You can't stretch the tape enough to get it over your hands."

Sam mumbled something unintelligible and kept working. Rose bounced to the edge of the bed and clawed her fingers on the night table drawer.

"What are you looking for?" Megan asked. "Your glasses?"

"Nail clippers," Rose said. "Mr. Turner shouldn't assume because we're old, we're helpless. Or stupid." She hissed. "But with my wrists crossed, it's hard to make my fingers work properly."

"Careful." Megan squirmed, trying to get to her feet, but with her hands behind her and her ankles taped, she couldn't get the leverage she needed to do more than roll to her side. She was afraid to work too hard, for fear Turner would hear her. "We have to be quiet. I think he's the man who killed Betty Bedford."

"I don't doubt it," Rose said. "And they say it gets easier to kill each time. We need to be careful we don't upset him. He seems rational until things don't go his way." She wriggled around, trying to get a better grip on the drawer pull. "*Scheisse.*"

"Shh," Justin said. "Did you hear something? A car out

front?"

She strained to listen. Yes, an engine's rumbling. Did she see lights through the narrow gap in the curtain?

Seconds later, Buzz swept into the room. He snatched the letter and shoved it into his pocket. He plucked Rose from the bed, clamping a hand over her mouth. He paused at the doorway and shot them a threatening scowl. "Not a word if you want to see her alive." He slammed the door behind him.

~ ~ ~ ~ ~

Gordon listened to Vicky McDermott's report as he wheeled out of the parking lot toward the Kretzers'.

"I ran the plates on the car in the driveway. It's Megan's rental. I checked the garage, and the Kretzers' car is there, too. The curtains are drawn, but there are lights on."

Which fit with Solomon's report that nothing looked amiss. "So why are you concerned?"

"I knocked on the door. No answer. And the tape is down. It feels ... wrong. That's when I called you."

From the determination in her tone, she was making up for her perceived guilt at missing the Bedford killer until it was too late. He wouldn't discount Vicky's unease. Cops became sensitized to things feeling "off." And, unlike Angie, they were right more often than not.

"Get Dispatch to roll another unit. And wait for me. Don't move without backup."

He had a flash of panic when his car wasn't in its slot, before he remembered it was at Lou's garage. Shit. He regrouped. Went inside, checked out a cruiser, let Irv know where he'd be.

On the drive over, he concentrated on a plan. A Well Being check wasn't out of the ordinary. Elderly residents not answering the door. But if their killer was inside, would that spook him? Would that exacerbate the problem? Was there a problem? Maybe they were all in bed. He pulled alongside

Vicky's cruiser. Worry etched her face. Rolling down his window, he twirled his finger, letting her know he was going to do a quick circle. There were a lot of hiding places in the wooded acreage behind the house. Visions of Rose and Sam Kretzer duct-taped to chairs, their throats sliced open, ran through his head. He knew Vicky'd been thinking the same thing since she called him.

He wound his way along the meandering street surrounding the tree-filled space. His heart rate accelerated when lights appeared in the darkness, making him cut his eyes away from the sudden brilliance. Car headlights? They moved, confirming his guess.

No way he could intercept the car from his position. He keyed his radio and alerted Vicky. "It should be coming your way. Follow it, run the plates. Let me know. I'm going to check the house."

"What about backup?" Vicky said.

"Get the plates, update Dispatch, and have them route backup to you. If that's our bad guy in the car, then he's not in the house."

"You shouldn't go in alone. What if it was only some kids making out in the woods? He could be in there."

A perfectly legitimate question, and until a few days ago, the most logical assumption. Now, Gordon went with his gut. "It's a chance I'm willing to take. Find out who's in that car. That's an order."

"You want me to pull it over?"

"Not without backup. If it's kids, let 'em get away with it this time, and get back here."

"Roger. But I haven't seen any vehicles yet."

Damn. Why had he assumed the driver would be stupid enough to drive out in front of the Kretzers'? Even kids would avoid driving past a marked cruiser.

"Vicky, get over to Maple and Third. Any car in this area's going to have to drive past there."

"What am I looking for?"

"No idea. All I could see was headlights. Run 'em all."

"On it."

By now, he'd circled the perimeter and hadn't seen anything suspicious. He killed the lights as he pulled his cruiser along the curb, stopping about twenty yards from the Kretzers' driveway.

He updated Dispatch and got out of the car. The front door was locked. He unsnapped his holster and worked his way to the rear. No open windows. No movement. No sounds.

The porch light illuminated the back door. The wide-open door.

He drew his weapon. "Police! Come out! Hands where I can see them!" His voice seemed to echo through the empty space. His own heartbeat pounded in his ears. He stood alongside the open doorway, controlling his breathing, visualizing the layout of the house. "Rose? Sam? Megan? Justin?"

"Gordon? Upstairs. He's got Rose!" Megan's voice.

He bolted for the stairs, then edged his way up, flattening himself against the wall. Gut feeling or not, there was no point in painting a bull's-eye on his chest if Buzz was lying in wait, threatening Megan to say what he told her.

"Where are you?" he called.

"Rose and Sam's bedroom." Justin's voice conveyed anger more than fear. "We're alone. But Buzz Turner took Rose."

"Hang on." Gordon cleared each room before entering the master suite. "One second." He did a check of the closet and bathroom before moving to Sam's side. Using his Leatherman, he slit the tape at Sam's wrists and ankles. "Sorry. Couldn't take any chances someone was still in here."

"Understood," Sam said. "Don't worry about us. You must find Rose. The man is crazy."

Gordon released Megan, then Justin. "We're working on it. Do you have any idea where he might have gone?"

"No," all three uttered in unison.

Sam swung his feet over the edge of the bed and wiped his jaw. "He said he would hurt her if we talked."

"That was to keep us quiet while he was downstairs searching," Megan said.

"For what?" Gordon asked. "Did he tell you?"

"Rose or Sam's reading glasses so they could read and translate the letter," Justin said.

"Not that he would have," Sam said. "You did an excellent job of sending him off to find the wild goose." He stood, and Megan rushed to his side to support him. "He obviously wasn't paying attention when he was ransacking the place, or he'd have found them himself."

"Where?" Megan asked.

Sam pointed to the dust cover surrounding the box spring. "One of Rose's sewing projects." He smiled. "That's my spare pair. They never leave this room."

Gordon stepped to where Sam pointed, finding a small quilted contraption with two pockets—one the size of a paperback, and a narrower one that held a pair of readers. Made from the same fabric and stitched to the cover itself, Gordon hadn't noticed it when he'd helped Justin replace the mattress.

"All I wanted was to get him out of the room," Megan said. "Good thing I didn't know about this, or I'd probably have told him. I was so afraid he'd hurt you."

"You don't give in to bullies," Sam said. His tone said he was talking about more than Buzz Turner's threats. "Please, go find Rose."

"Wait," Justin said to Gordon. "The letter. You have the original. Can we get a copy? There might be some leads in it."

"Good idea. I'll take care of it."

"I can go to the station and get it," Justin said. His expression told Gordon he was trying to make sure nobody else saw it before he turned it over to Sam.

"No need. I'm going to want someone here with you in case Buzz calls. They'll bring it." Gordon was already concerned that he hadn't heard from Vicky. "I'll make the copy personally. I need to get to the station and coordinate the search."

He went to the bed, where Sam sat, head down, fists clenched. Gordon set a hand on the man's shoulder. "I'll get her back. You have my word. Buzz Turner will pay."

Sam met his eyes, his expression grim. "I trust you." A tiny smirk flashed across his mouth. "Maybe you should be worried that Mr. Turner will need rescuing from Rose."

Gordon gave Sam's shoulder a gentle squeeze. "You may be right." He turned to Megan who approached him and gave him a quick hug. Justin hadn't moved from the floor. "You okay?"

Justin gazed past him to Sam. "Yeah. Fine."

Gordon went over and extended a hand, hoisting Justin to his feet.

Justin chafed his wrists. "Megan, stay here with Opa. I'll see Gordon out."

Gordon followed Justin downstairs. He paused at the front door. "We're going to catch Turner and bring your grandmother home."

"I know. It's the other part I'm having trouble dealing with. Telling Opa about everything."

"Don't underestimate him. I'll get that letter over right away." Gordon shook Justin's hand. "Lock up. Back door, too." Gordon strode toward the cruiser, keying the radio as he walked. "Vicky. Report."

"We're working on it. We had four cars come by. Three residents and one rental."

"Who's the rental?"

"We're waiting to hear from the company."

Had to be Turner. "Give Dispatch the details. Have them put out a lookout order on the rental. And on the secure channel."

Vicky might have wondered why he wasn't waiting to see who'd rented the car, but she didn't hesitate. And after she'd reported, Gordon got on the radio himself. "Irv, call in all available personnel. War room. Yesterday. And keep eyes open for Buzz Turner and Rose Kretzer."

"Yes, sir."

Gordon grabbed his cell and called Colfax.

Chapter Twenty-nine

Justin paced the living room. Megan fussed in the kitchen making some sort of herbal tea. Like drinking flowers, Justin thought, but it gave her something to do, and heaven only knew they didn't need any caffeine. Officer Solomon had arrived moments ago and was hooking a recording device to the phone in Opa's study.

Opa's footfalls on the stairs sent another cramp through Justin's stomach. Justin turned his head and forced a semblance of a smile as his grandfather entered the room, twirling his reading glasses. Slipping them on, he crossed the room and stood behind Justin.

"Most of the time," Opa said, "it's unwise to keep things bottled up." He massaged Justin's shoulders. Memories of nights when Opa had comforted him the same way un-clenched some of the knots in Justin's stomach, but brought a lump to his throat.

Opa gave a final squeeze, then a firm pat. "Whatever it is, we'll get through it." He sat in one of the easy chairs. Megan came in with a tray of three steaming teacups and a plate of ginger cookies and set it on the coffee table. Justin sat on the couch, and she sat at the other end. Nobody touched the tray.

Justin cleared his throat and met Opa's gaze. "Do you have a brother?"

Opa's eyes widened. He took off his glasses and let them dangle from his fingertips. "I did. He was many years older than I. But he died in the war. Along with my sister Hilde and my parents. I was young, and was smuggled out of the country. To Holland, where I spent a good number of years living with a most generous family."

"Why didn't you ever speak of them?" Megan asked. Justin could tell she was comparing Opa's situation to her own.

"In order to survive, nobody could know who my family really was," Opa said. "Those who took me in put their own lives on the line. When word came my birth family was dead, I moved on."

Justin handed Opa the letter Officer Solomon had given him. "This was found in Betty Bedford's files. Apparently it had been misfiled years ago."

Opa settled his glasses on his nose and perused the pages. His lips moved silently as his eyes scanned the words. "*Mein Gott.*" He paled. Stopped. Went back to the first page and read again, as if the words might have changed. Faster now, it seemed, as though he had been regaining proficiency in reading the language. Tears rolled down his cheeks.

He set down the last page, shaking his head. Flushed now, not pale.

Justin exchanged an uneasy glance with Megan. He could tell how hard it was for her not to rush to Opa's side. Avoiding his grandfather's eyes, Justin waited.

"*Mein Gott.*" Opa's voice rasped. He shook his head in a slow rhythm. "*Mein Gott.*"

Megan finally voiced the question Justin couldn't bear to ask. "What does it say? Is it from your brother?"

"*Ja, Ich glaube schon.* I believe so."

Even though he'd prepared himself for the inevitable, Justin felt sick.

"Will you read it to us?" Megan asked.

Justin shot her a frown. "If you don't want to, or aren't ready, we understand. You don't have to."

"*Nein. Ihr habt das Recht, die Wahrheit zu wissen.*" He paused, as if he realized he'd spoken in German. "You have the right to know." He took out a handkerchief, wiped his eyes and then his glasses and shook the pages. With a shaky breath, he began reading. Slowly at first, as he dealt with translating, but then faster. His voice was flat, as if he'd dealt with his emotional response on his first, private read.

My dearest brother,

I have only recently learned you, too, survived, and it has taken me so long to find you. I am dying now, and cannot rest without explaining.

I regret all the horrors our life thrust upon us, and hope you can find it in your heart to forgive—or to understand. You were away when the police came for us. For that, I thanked God. What I did from that day forward sickens me, yet I am not sure I was strong enough to be the man I wish I could have been. The instinct to survive is strong, stronger than conscience, I fear.

The cattle-car trip to the camp was only the beginning. At first it was not so bad, and I spoke with another young man, also named Heinrich. He was from Danzig, with a special travel permit. He was optimistic that he would be released at our destination. But it was not to be. Three people died before we got there, and Heinrich Kaestner was among them. We were not so different in general appearance, and I swapped his papers for mine, hoping I could use them to my advantage.

After two days, we arrived at the camp in the dark of night. Mother and Father were among those sent to the so-called "showers" almost immediately. I was young and healthy, so my life was spared, along with that of our sister. We were separated, and I could only hope Hilde wasn't sent to the showers or the oven. Every day, I tried to see her. Occasional glimpses would give me the strength to go on. I heard once that she was working as a typist, and prayed her work pleased her Nazi masters enough to keep Hilde alive another day. And I prayed that you had remained out of reach of the evildoers.

The overseers looked at my papers, but laughed when I said there was a mistake and I didn't belong. They said as long as my name was Kaestner, they had the perfect job for me. Thus, I toiled as a carpenter, learning enough of the craft and discovering a latent talent, so my labors were deemed worthwhile enough to keep me alive, although one never knew if each day would be one's last. I crafted some furniture—a desk, some shelves—for one of the officials, which were well-received. This blessing was a curse in disguise.

Survival depended on being invisible, and I strove not to call attention to myself. I was only moderately successful, as I was given the dubious honor of serving as the intermediary between prisoner and guard when my skills as a carpenter were no longer needed. While the "promotion" bought me some minor privileges, I was now faced with the resentment of my fellow prisoners, and their deference. I, you see, was often required to decide who would live and who would die.

One night, while escaping the stench of the barracks for some less-stifling air, I saw a guard bring a woman to an area not far away. It was Hilde. I listened to her screams as he raped her, but did nothing. To react would have meant my own death. I tried to rationalize my actions, telling myself that being raped was better than being killed, and Hilde would survive her assault. Several months later, I saw her once more, her belly rounded with the beginnings of a new life. I'm sure you know of the appalling health conditions at these places. The strain on Hilde was too great, and she weakened and was doomed to the gas chamber.

The shame of my inaction, of my cowardice, festers inside still today, along with everything else I did—or did not do—during those horrendous days.

Inside, something snapped. I denounced my heritage, my upbringing, and crossed the line. In my mind, I became one of "them," as if it would be easier to do evil deeds if I were one of the evildoers. For how much more evil can one be than deciding between another's life or death? And while I never forced myself upon a woman, I took many, in return for promises—often unkept—that their lives would be spared. For I had quotas to meet, and any slacking on my part would end my own life—and deny me some of the simplest "luxuries" of existence in that place, such as an occasional shower, or an extra ration of soup.

But in the depths of my soul, I knew I had to act. I was assigned to assist in scientific "experiments"—atrocities that at first caused me to become physically ill. I am ashamed to admit, I became hardened to the screams, the blood, the voiding from fear. I began to keep my own records of everything that happened at the camp. As it was my task to record collected data, I had access to pens and paper, and each night, I transcribed my notes, which I kept hidden. The risk was great, but it appeased my aching conscience.

The war finally ended, and when our camp was liberated, I made my way to Berlin, where I kept my secret hidden and married another survivor. The marriage couldn't handle the strain of our pasts, however, and I take the blame. I was plagued by nightmares, drank too heavily, and had trouble holding down any kind of job. After barely a year, we parted, and my wife took custody of our infant daughter, Ingrid. It was undoubtedly better for both of them.

I decided to leave my past behind—as much as I could—and I left Germany for the United States. I settled in a suburb of Pittsburgh, in a community with a varied ethnic mix, so I had ties to the old country, but new horizons. I had Americanized my name to Henry Carpenter, and I lived a modest life as a bookkeeper.

But I was an old man, and my health had deteriorated after the years in the camp. I found a nursing home that seemed adequate for my remaining years. One can never escape the past, however. Heinrich Kaestner was being hunted as a war criminal. And, at the same time, there were people saying the Holocaust had never happened. I knew that I needed to make my notes public. However, I didn't feel that my transcriptions would be safe from prying eyes, so, before I entered the home, I sent them to a man I could trust, telling him to release them only to someone bearing a special note from me. If he was to hear of my death before then, he could release them to the media. It was in a sealed package. If he ever opened it, I do not know.

But if you are reading this, it means that I have found you, and that the transcripts should be arriving shortly. I have confessed my sins to you, and it pains me to have you know that I, who shares your blood, was a cruel monster. If you choose to burn it without reading, I understand. If you choose to take this information with you to your grave, I also understand. But know that I have always loved you.

Your brother,
Heinrich

~ ~ ~ ~ ~

Gordon spread a map of the county on the tables in the war room. If Buzz was on the run, he couldn't have gotten far. Colfax had deputies setting up a checkpoint on the main route to the Interstate, although Buzz was probably too smart to try to head for the highway. No, he'd have some-place more isolated in mind. But there were countless possibilities, each more remote than the next.

Gordon thought of Karl Franklin, killed in one place, transported to another, and the car abandoned. Had Buzz already taken care of Rose? Was she in the trunk of a rented blue Ford Fusion, on her way to being dumped or buried somewhere?

Damn, all the forensics bells and whistles on the planet weren't going to find them. He was a small-town cop, and he needed to remember that. More often than not, simple legwork got the job done.

"Got anything?"

Gordon looked up at the sound of Colfax's voice. "Nothing new. I want to swap one of your deputies for my man at the Kretzers'. He's waiting for a call from Turner, but I've got a better use for his skills."

For once, Colfax didn't come back with a snappy retort. He got on the radio and ordered one of his men to report to the Kretzers'.

Ten endless minutes later, the room filled with somber-faced officers, their frustration and guilt that their previous mission to unearth Betty's killer had failed, almost palpable. Gordon skipped pleasantries or platitudes.

"Listen up, people. We've got a repeat of what we've done before, but things are more urgent. About thirty minutes ago, Bradley—Buzz—Turner took Rose Kretzer from her home. He's our most viable suspect for two murders. We *are* going to find them. The old-fashioned way. I want every door knocked on, every citizen, every visitor questioned. You've got flyers with the car information and pictures. Someone out there has seen something. Find them. Use the secure radio channel or your cell phones. You've got your assigned sectors. Go."

Other than chairs scraping across the floor and the sound of footfalls, the room was silent as the officers filed out.

"You look like crap," Colfax said. "Get out there. I'll coordinate from here."

"I'll be close," Gordon said. "I'll check Finnegan's and any other places still open. Hit more people than door-to-door. I've got Solomon on Turner's house and neighborhood."

"Alone?" Colfax's brow lifted.

"He knows what he's doing. He'll call for backup if he sees anything. We don't have the personnel to spare." Gordon hoped that was one decision he wouldn't regret. But they needed optimal coverage, and they needed it fast.

"I'll see if I can shake a few more deputies loose."

Gordon nodded his thanks and headed for Finnegan's. Heads turned and a hush blanketed the room when he entered the bar. Mick set down a glass he was drying and came out from behind the counter. Word got around fast.

"How can we help, Chief?" Mick wiped his hands on a towel tucked into his apron. "Coffee's on the house for any of your guys as long as we're open."

"I know they'll appreciate it. The county deputies are out too." Gordon surveyed the room, seeing primarily familiar faces. "Mind if I take a booth to interview everyone?"

"You can have my office."

"No, easier out here where I can keep an eye on things." He addressed the crowd. "Most everyone here knows Rose Kretzer, and that she's missing. Our best lead says she's with Buzz Turner. I'm going to ask each one of you to think about where we might find him. Any places he frequents, people he hangs out with. Maybe he's mentioned where he might go to get away from it all. I know it's an inconvenience, but I'm going to ask you all to stay until you've talked to me. Let's get started."

Gordon slid into a booth and set a notepad in front of him. Three men stood. Gordon gestured toward them. After exchanging glances, one stepped forward. Nick Upton. Retired, divorced, lived in the hills. Gordon picked up his pen. "Good evening, Nick. What can you tell me?"

The man hung his head, fumbled with his cap. "Probably nothing."

"Why don't you let me decide? You might have something helpful and not know it."

With the ice broken, more volunteers offered their thoughts, most of them related to opinions of Buzz's stories. As Gordon worked his way through the interviews, he relayed any possible leads to Colfax, who alerted the nearest officer. It was slow going.

Gordon rubbed his eyes and motioned the last patron forward, searching his memory for a name. The man was a relative newcomer. Worked out of town. Probably stopped for a drink on his way home and was now regretting it.

The man lowered himself across from Gordon. "Keith Valade."

"What can you tell me, Mr. Valade?"

"It's nothing. But you did want to talk to everyone."

"A whole lot of nothing can add up to something. Every detail can be important." He felt like a recording, but it seemed to relax people, get them talking. Now, if there was some magic way to get them to cut to the chase … . He smiled.

"I've lived here about six months. Early on, Mr. Turner tried to get friendly. I figured he was just being a good neighbor. We're kind of isolated. That's why we moved here. My wife and I love it in the mountains, away from people."

Gordon nudged the conversation back to Buzz Turner.

Keith pinched the bridge of his nose. "He invited me fishing. Took me to this out of the way spot. Said it was his secret place. I wondered if he was gay, trying to put the move on me, but he knew I was married. And he's so much older. I figured he was lonely, so I went a few more times."

"Did he have a cabin there?"

Keith shook his head. "No, it was strictly woods. But from the way he'd go on about how a person could come out there and totally disappear, that nobody knew about it but him, that it was the one place in the universe that sang to him—those were his words—I thought I should mention it. When we went, he told me I shouldn't tell anyone else about it, but I thought that was because of the fishing." Keith smiled. "We did get some awesome trout."

Gordon's cop radar blipped. Buzz's condo was empty, and the neighbors hadn't seen him this evening. "Could you give me directions?"

"Maybe. I wasn't driving, and wasn't familiar enough with the area to know all the turnoffs."

"Could you give me an approximation if I showed you a map?"

Keith seemed calmer, more confident. "I could try."

Gordon left a stack of business cards on the bar, telling everyone to call if they had any new information. "I want you to come with me to the station," he said to Keith.

Minutes later, Gordon had the map spread on his desk. Keith leaned over it, palms splayed, arms locked, brows knit in concentration. Finally, he lifted his hand and traced a dotted line representing an unpaved road about ten miles out of town. "I think this is where we turned off."

Trouble was, "think" wasn't a guarantee. And there were no fewer than eight other choices, assuming all the preliminary turns Keith had pointed out were correct. They'd need serious manpower to cover that expanse of territory, especially if there was no cabin, no structure, no logical place to conceal Rose, nowhere to keep her tucked away while Turner made whatever demands he had in mind.

Colfax pulled up a mapping program on the computer

and started zooming in. "Too many trees," he grumbled. "Be nice if the damn rental company installed LoJack on their vehicles."

"Wait!" Keith's voice reminded him they weren't alone. "Zoom out." Colfax did. "There. That rock formation. By the fork. I remember it. That's where we turned off."

"Enough for me. Get the GPS coordinates." Gordon turned to Keith. "Thank you. You can go home."

Keith stared at the monitor one last time. "I hope ... I hope it works out."

Gordon scribbled down the numbers Colfax read from the computer and grabbed his jacket.

"You're not going alone," Colfax said.

"No. You're driving. My SUV is in the shop."

"Who's minding the store?" Colfax asked.

"Getting to that." Gordon walked to Dispatch, Colfax dogging his heels. "Irv, get Solomon on the radio. Tell him we need Buster, and give him these coordinates." He read off the numbers Colfax had given him. "Get Connie in here to back you up. And tell the night duty officer to get to the station. He's got the con." He took a breath and met Colfax's gaze. "Anything else you think I've forgotten?"

"Nope. Let's boogie."

Chapter Thirty

Megan had to remind herself to breathe. Sam set the letter on the coffee table and stared into nothingness. She'd never seen him so—empty. Without thinking, she went to his side. Sitting beside him, she enfolded him in a gentle embrace. She tasted salt and realized she'd been crying.

"*Ich liebe dich.* I love you, Sam." The words barely made it past the thickness in her throat. How many times had she said that as he'd tucked her in as a child?

"*Ich liebe dich auch,*" he said, but his "I love you too" seemed automatic, a reflex formed by long-established ritual.

He pulled away, and she jerked back. But he stood and walked, robot-like, down the hall toward the powder room. When the door closed, she turned to Justin. "What should we do? We have to ask him about the journal. He's read the letter, so he knows it exists. If he has it, or knows where it is, maybe we can trade it for Rose."

Justin scooped his hands through his hair. "I'm trying to figure out how that reporter found out about it."

"It doesn't matter. We have to save Rose. If Sam knows where the journal is, that's our bargaining chip."

"I hate to hurt him. He's upset enough as it is."

"He's the one who always said how important it was to tell the truth."

"And the one who pretended his past didn't exist."

The doorbell interrupted. Her heart pounded. Officer Solomon appeared, gesturing to them to stay where they were. If he noticed their emotional state, he gave no indication. "That should be for me."

He checked the peephole, then swung the door open admitting a uniformed deputy. "This is Deputy Olivera. He's going to take over. If you get a phone call, use the extension in the study." The deputy came inside, and Officer Solomon trotted across the porch, his footfalls heavy on the wooden steps.

His abrupt departure sent a frisson down Megan's spine. Had they found Rose? Was she hurt? Sam strode into the room. Megan made a quick round of introductions and offered to make coffee for their new watchdog. Relieved when he declined, instead asking to be shown the study, she led him down the hall. He looked around, then checked the recording equipment. "Looks good. You can get back to your family."

"Did something happen? Is that why Officer Solomon left?"

"No, ma'am. Just switching assignments. They're doing some door-to-door, and he knows the area."

Although there had to be more, she retreated. Gordon knew what he was doing. Sam was her first concern.

In the living room, Sam sat in the center of the couch, Justin beside him. Sam motioned for her to join them. When she sat, he put his arms around them. Megan leaned into him, happy to take a moment of comfort. And how had things done a complete reversal? She and Justin had been worried about protecting Sam, yet he seemed to be taking care of them.

Justin spoke, dumping a dose of reality into the brief tranquility. "Opa, I can't imagine what you must feel, but there's more. Your brother's daughter, Ingrid. She married and had a son. He ... he got in touch with me a few weeks ago. About the journal. He demanded I get it for him. He said if I didn't ... "

"So you couldn't ask me?" Sam said. "All this—the visit, the remodeling—was so you could find some old book?"

Justin leaned forward, the heels of his hands pressed against his eyes. "I ... you'd never spoken of a brother." His voice quavered. "I didn't know how to tell you there was a possibility your brother had been a Nazi. And a war criminal. I ... I wanted to keep from hurting you and Oma."

"And now Rose is gone."

Megan jumped in. "Sam, we didn't know. We were both trying to find the journal and turn it over to this new cousin of Justin's." She paused. "I guess he'd be your nephew."

"Grand-nephew," Sam mumbled. "Family. *Mein Gott.*"

"And Justin's cousin swears he had nothing to do with Buzz Turner," she continued. "Apparently there are two people who want this journal. Do you know anything about it?"

"*Two* people wanting this secret book?" Sam convulsed into laughter so intense Megan was afraid he'd gone hysterical. She gripped his hands. Deputy Olivera rushed into the room.

~ ~ ~ ~ ~

Gordon breathed in the brisk night air, the scent of pine and earth wafting on the breeze. Buzz Turner's out of the way spot, assuming Keith Valade had been correct, was definitely remote. They'd been on dirt roads for the past five miles, and hadn't seen a sign of civilization. Cell service had disappeared half an hour ago. No radio contact with the station for the past fifteen minutes. Damn mountains. The GPS gave coordinates, but none of the local roads—if you could call them that—had been digitized for their system. He'd been staring at a red triangle on a white screen ever since the last turnoff.

"This is it," Colfax said, turning onto a side road.

Gordon's pulse accelerated at the sight of the large rock formation Valade had pointed out. Shadows danced in the headlights as the car navigated hairpin turns and bounced over the bumpy road.

"Crap," Colfax said. "Which way now?" He stopped the SUV. Ahead, the road forked in three directions. A department SUV sat on the shoulder, lights flashing. Colfax pulled alongside, and Solomon rolled down his window.

"Hey, Chief," Solomon said. "Where to?"

"Valade didn't mention hiking in." Gordon pointed to the left, the widest option. "We'll try that one. You try the other two. Maybe Buster will pick up a trail. Buzz's car has to be here somewhere."

Colfax aimed the SUV down the road. Images of Rose being bound and tortured filled Gordon's head. He shoved them away, concentrating on being a cop. A cop in the field, not behind a damn desk.

His heart pounded away the seconds. His radio crackled. At least they had car to car coverage. "Buster alerted," Solomon reported through the static. "Meet you at the fork."

Colfax swung the SUV around and backtracked to the fork and Solomon's SUV. The German shepherd sat at Solomon's feet, whining and quivering, impatiently awaiting the order to get to work.

"Let's do it," Gordon said. "Colfax, you wait here in case he tries to rabbit. Solomon, you sure this is the right road?"

Solomon displayed a sweater. "I borrowed this from the Kretzers'. We went about fifty yards down each possibility. This one got Buster excited." Solomon gestured to the right-most option.

Buster swerved toward Gordon, barking. Then the dog sat, cocking his head at his master. Gordon recognized the sweater as one he'd folded and put away. "I touched that. And Buzz probably did too."

Solomon praised Buster for finding Gordon, rubbing the dog's ruff. "Rose's scent should be the strongest, but finding Buzz would work, too." He gave him the sweater again. "Okay, Buster. Find."

The dog bounded off, nose in the air. In seconds, he'd

disappeared into the darkness, dragging Solomon behind. His flashlight illuminating the trail, his heart hammering, Gordon followed. This was being a cop. Not worrying about budget line items.

A frenzied barking brought Gordon to a halt. He swept the area with his light. Weapon drawn, Gordon rushed toward the sounds, the beam from his flashlight bouncing as he ran.

Buster sat, panting. Solomon stood in the middle of the narrow road, his weapon trained on Buzz, who knelt, one hand raised in surrender, one clutching his belly. Gordon pointed his light at the man. Sweat glistened on his face despite the chill. Fear showed in his eyes, which seemed trained on Buster.

"Don't move," Gordon said. "Or we'll release the dog." An empty threat, because Buster wasn't an attack dog. But Buzz wouldn't know that. He hoped.

"She tried to kill me. I'm hurt. You gotta help me," Buzz said, right before sinking to the ground.

Gordon and Solomon reached Buzz within seconds. Gordon crouched beside the man, his flashlight revealing a dark stain spreading at Buzz's midsection.

Solomon lifted Buzz's shirt. "Knifed."

Gordon called for Colfax. "Get in here. Call the medics. We've got an injured man to transport." Damn, he should have had rolled the medics from the start.

"On my way," Colfax said.

"I'll wait here," Gordon said to Solomon. "You go find Rose."

Solomon and Buster raced off. Gordon applied pressure to Buzz's wound. Where the hell was Rose? Had they fought? Was she lying somewhere, hanging on by a thread? As triage went, this sucked. He had an injured man, probably a killer, in hand. And his victim, somewhere in the great beyond, condition unknown.

He'd be happy to leave Buzz where he was until he

found Rose. But a cop couldn't let emotions rule. He didn't bury them completely, however, and snapped at the man lying beside him. "Wake up, you bastard. Where's Rose?"

Not even a groan.

Seconds ticked into eternity before headlights illuminated the trail. A car door slammed. He twisted his neck to see Colfax jogging toward him, a first aid kit thumping against his leg.

"Give me more light," Colfax said. His motions smooth and competent, he snapped open the medical kit and checked Buzz's wound. "Go. I'll keep an eye on him until the medics get here."

Trusting Colfax, Gordon rushed after Solomon and Buster. Hearing the dog's eager barking raised his hopes, and he headed down a side trail in the direction of the sound.

"Rose! Rose Kretzer! It's Gordon Hepler. You're safe. Where are you?" Buster dashed back and forth along the trail, darting into clumps of trees, in one direction, then the other.

"What's with him?" Gordon asked.

"Don't know," Solomon said. "He's definitely got a scent."

Buster bounded off, barking louder. Gordon followed Solomon and the dog down a side trail where Buster, sniffing and whining, circled Buzz's rental car. Both front doors were open.

Gordon rushed forward. "Rose?" The car was empty. Gordon's heart sank.

"Flat," Solomon said, pointing his light at the right front tire. But she was in here. He gave Buster the sweater again. "Find."

They continued on, both calling Rose's name. Had she escaped only to meet with some other disaster? Bears came to mind.

"Here." A quiet voice came from the trees to his left, well off the trail. He shone his light in that direction. Near a large fallen tree, a pile of leaves moved. A form emerged, like some forest monster, shedding leaves and detritus. And clutching a bloody knife.

"Rose!" Gordon said. "Are you all right?" He dashed toward her.

Solomon released Buster. "Let him reach her. It's good for him to succeed."

Gordon made a mental note to increase Buster's kibble ration no matter what budget items he had to cut. Hell, he'd throw in for some steak out of his own pocket. Gordon cradled Rose. Buster sat at their feet until Solomon called him back.

"Sam? Justin? Megan?" Rose asked.

"All fine."

"Mr. Turner? Alive?"

"Yes."

She sighed. "I'm sorry, but I don't seem able to walk very well." The knife slipped from her fingers.

"Get the knife," Gordon ordered Solomon. Carrying Rose like a rag doll, Gordon started toward the vehicles.

"I'm fine," Rose said.

"Of course you are. But it's against regulations to let an injured victim out of protective custody. Especially if she's also a witness."

Rose's quiet laugh was the nicest sound he'd heard all night.

When they got to the car, a cuffed Buzz sat in the backseat of Colfax's SUV. Colfax leaned against the front bumper. Apparently Buzz wasn't as bad off as Gordon feared. Rose hadn't been willing to talk about how she'd escaped. All she'd said was Buzz wanted some mysterious journal, and would go to any lengths to get it.

Colfax stepped forward and helped ease Rose into the front seat of Solomon's SUV. "Time to go home."

Gordon recognized the subtext. *Get rid of the woman, there's work to be done.* He smoothed Rose's hair and kissed her hand. "You're going to the emergency room. No arguments. And yes, I'll call Sam. I'll see you later."

She smiled, the way she had when he'd stumbled through a passage in a book when he was nine. He swelled with the same pride.

With Rose safe, Gordon turned his attention to Colfax. "Turner hasn't asked for a lawyer?"

"Not yet. Don't know why, but that's a gift horse I'm not playing dentist with. I told him I'd cancel the medics if he didn't tell us what he's been doing. I guess he's hurting enough to believe me."

Hell. Given the way Buzz operated, he was probably composing his next story, figuring out how to spin this one to his advantage. "You have a recorder?" Gordon asked Colfax.

Colfax tapped his pocket. "Does a bear shit in the woods?"

Gordon pulled open the back door of the SUV. After dealing with the formalities, he said, "It's over, Buzz. Time for you to do the talking. Why the hell did you do this?"

Buzz shrugged, then winced. "Money. Fame. Glory. Why else?"

"Why don't you start at the beginning, Buzz. Help us understand."

Another shrug, another wince. "With everyone who'd lived through World War II dying, I needed to write my book while there was time."

"The book you told me about. The Holocaust?"

"Yeah. I did a lot of research. I found this old guy who was going to get away with being a war criminal. Henry Carpenter, but his real name was Heinrich Kaestner. I was checking him out, and I found he'd kept records, then hired a PI to dig up his brother so he could clear his conscience."

"The PI's name?" Gordon asked.

"Karl Franklin. He tells me about this secret journal connected to this one-horse town in Colorado. Said the journal was full of war secrets, and worth a fortune. I did some digging. There were a lot of immigrant Jews in the town, so I moved here to do more research. All on the QT, of course. About a week ago, Franklin says he has more information for me, but insists on meeting in person to close the deal, and then he tries to up his price. We fought. He lost." Buzz scowled. "Bastard kicked off before he told me what the new information was."

"You never saw the envelope?" Gordon asked.

Buzz squinted in puzzlement. "What envelope?"

"Guess you're not the investigative reporter you think you are."

"Go on," Colfax urged. "Did Franklin say what was in the journal?"

"Not in so many words. He thought it might tell about all those treasures the Nazis stole, where they hid them. Or a list of war criminals. Either way, it would give me information for a great story. At the very least, I'd get a list of people who might be willing to pay to have their secrets kept out of print."

"Why Betty Bedford?" Gordon asked. "What did she have to do with all this?"

"That's the address where Franklin told me he mailed the journal. The biddy said she didn't know what I was talking about. She was getting noisy, so I had to shut her up. She said she'd turned everything over to the Kretzers, so I went to their place. But they came home before I could finish. Then, I figured it would be easier to deal with them directly, and if you hadn't shown up, they'd have told me where it was, and I'd have my book deal. Money. Fame. Glory. I've earned it." He crossed his arms across his chest and stared into nothingness.

The wail of sirens announced the medics were on their way. Gordon restrained himself from dragging Buzz out of the backseat of Colfax's SUV and leaving him for the medics to deal with. He stormed away, leaving Colfax to take charge.

How had someone as sick as Turner kept it hidden so well? Were his actions brushed aside as part of the annoying reporter perception? Hell, Gordon hadn't seen it, and he prided himself on having a first-rate bullshit meter. And what if Turner had seen the envelope? He'd have gone straight to Rose and Sam. Betty might still be alive. But Rose and Sam … He refused to follow that thought train.

Once the medics had ministered to Buzz and loaded him into the ambulance, Gordon threw himself into Colfax's passenger seat. "Get me out of here."

For once, the detective kept his trap shut.

Chapter Thirty-one

Nothing like putting away a bad guy to counteract sleep deprivation. Gordon relaxed his grip on the bouquet of flowers and knocked on the door. After a moment, Megan appeared.

"Hope it's not too late." He extended the flowers. "For Rose."

Megan motioned him in and took the flowers. "She'll love them. I'll put them in water. Everyone's upstairs."

Gordon collected his thoughts until Megan returned, and they went upstairs together. "How's she doing?" he asked.

"Typical Rose. Took a few stitches to close the gash in her arm, and she's got a strained ligament in her ankle. She's not complaining about the pain. More about how she's not allowed on her feet for a few days."

"I trust the three of you will be able to hold her down. If you need help, I can send a couple of cops over."

"As if she'd be afraid of them," Megan said. She stepped into the room and announced his arrival with a flourish of her hands, as if he was being presented at court, then set the vase of flowers on the dresser beside a bottle of brandy. Sam sat on the edge of the bed, Justin in a chair. Both swirled crystal snifters.

Gordon crossed to the bed and kissed Rose's forehead. "You scared us, you know. Should have known you could take care of yourself."

She'd been holding the bloody knife. How had she

explained Buzz's injuries to her family?

"I hid." She drilled him with a defiant stare that sent a chill through him. "Where I grew up, hiding from evil tyrants was a skill we learned at an early age. I had plenty of practice." Her face closed, and he didn't ask for more. There would be time for her official statement another day.

"I just wanted to check on you," Gordon said. "I should let you rest."

Sam's gaze shifted from Rose to him, saying he knew damn well that was only part of the reason for his visit. "Justin, get Gordon a drink. We might as well go over every-thing now. And then Rose will sleep." The last was delivered with an attempt at a stern look.

Gordon accepted a brandy from Justin. He sipped. Warm and smooth. He nodded his approval to Sam.

"You want to know of the mysterious journal," Sam said.

"We all do," Justin said, a touch of impatience in his tone. As if Gordon's arrival was Sam's signal to talk.

"You know where it is?" Gordon asked.

Sam took a slow sip of his brandy. "*Ja*. I saw it."

"You did?" Megan's voice was incredulous. "When? You knew?"

Sam gave her an indulgent smile. "Slow down, *Kinde*." He swirled his snifter again, staring into the amber depths. "Several years ago. I don't recall exactly. It was in a box of books, papers, other *tschotschkes* that Betty found while she was setting up her shop."

"But you read it?" Justin said. "And it didn't bother you?"

"Why would it?" Sam asked.

"But … your brother … what he did … " Justin grew pale. He took a huge swallow of brandy, then paced the room. "All this. Everything. It's all my fault. If I'd only come out and said something."

"*Ach, nein*. No, no." Sam started to get up.

Gordon motioned him to stay where he was. He trapped Justin and gripped his shoulders. "You can't blame yourself.

Things happen. We accept them and move on." How many times had his father and Dix said similar words to him? Would Justin accept them any more than Gordon had? In time.

"Listen to me," Sam said.

Justin jerked away.

"Justin, listen to your grandfather. And Gordon," Rose said.

Justin's jaw was clenched as he returned to his chair. "I shouldn't have been so secretive."

"Are you through?" Sam asked. When Justin nodded, Sam continued. "I saw the journal. Yes, reading it angered me. All thoughts of that time and its atrocities angered me. But there was nothing in the journal, nothing that would ever have led me to believe it was written by my brother. Whoever wrote it did not identify himself as such." Sam waved a gesture of dismissal. "I sent it to the Wiesenthal Center."

Silence descended over the room. Justin drained his snifter and set it on the dresser. "So, what are you going to do?"

"I am going to mourn the loss of my brother once more." He patted Rose's hand. "And then I am going to bed. I think we will all feel better in the morning after a good night's sleep. Then you, Justin, will call this cousin of yours and let me speak to a new-found member of the family. Perhaps we can meet for *Pesach Seder*."

Gordon shook Sam's hand, kissed Rose again and went downstairs. Megan and Justin saw him to the door. "Sam has it together," Gordon said. "Don't beat yourself up over it. Turner was crazy. He'd probably have done what he did even if you'd told him the journal wasn't here. He wouldn't have believed you."

"Yeah, maybe," Justin said.

"I think Sam has the right idea," Gordon said. "Get some sleep. It's been a stressful few days."

"No kidding," Megan said, but she was gazing at Justin.

The heated look they exchanged propelled Gordon's thoughts to Angie. He checked his watch. Not *that* late. "Good night."

He'd solved three crimes, put away the bad guy, and his staff could take care of the paperwork. Mapleton's citizens could rest easy tonight. With luck, so would he. He glanced upward.

How'd I do, guys?

Maybe it was good to be the Chief. Especially when you could still be a cop.

A Note From the Author

I hope you enjoyed reading this book. One thing readers can do to let an author know they've enjoyed a book is to pass the word along. If you're willing to let your friends know you think they might like the book, or tweet about it, or post it to your social media sites, that would be wonderful. Also, the best way to help readers find authors is to post a brief review. If you have a minute, I'd appreciate it if you'd go to the site where you bought this book, or any review site such as Goodreads, and let others know you liked it. And, to keep up with future works and to have access to exclusive content, I'd love it if you'd sign up for my newsletter.

Thanks!

Terry

Acknowledgments

When I first began writing, I thought I would write a mystery. According to my daughters, that book (and the 7 that followed) were actually romances. So, at long last, I've created a book that can be classified as a mystery—although hints of relationships continue to sneak in.

Deadly Secrets has its roots in my own roots. I want to thank everyone in my family—my own Oma, Opa, Nana and Gramps, and long-time family friend Curt (whose own experiences provided valued information for Heinrich's story), as well as Mom, Dad, and the countless cousins and all the family gatherings. There's a little of everyone in here. Traditions deserve to be preserved and shared, and our heritages should never be forgotten.

And for all the technical help, as always, Steve and Karla of Novel Alchemy provide critical eyes and advice. Mark Hussey, Lee Lofland, Josh Moulin: Thanks for answering my questions about radios and cell phones. Wally Lind and the rest of the wonderful helpers at Yahoo's crimescenewriter group—many thanks. Special thanks to L.J. Sellers who read the draft manuscript and gave it the green light. And of course, thanks to my wonderful editor, Brittiany Koren. Working with you is a pleasure, and the book is better for your suggestions.

And, as always, mistakes are my own, or I've stretched reality for the sake of the story. It IS fiction, after all.

Lastly, thanks to you, my readers, who give me the motivation to keep writing.

About the author

Terry Odell began writing by mistake, when her son mentioned a television show and she thought she'd be a good mom and watch it so they'd have common ground for discussions.

Little did she know she would enter the world of writing, first via fanfiction, then through Internet groups, and finally with groups with real, live partners. Her first publications were short stories, but she found more freedom in longer works and began what she thought was a mystery. Her daughters told her it was a romance so she began learning more about the genre and craft. She belongs to both the Romance Writers of America and Mystery Writers of America.

Now a multi-published, award winning author, Terry resides with her husband in the mountains of Colorado. You can find her online at:

Her website - terryodell.com

Her blog – Terry's Place

Facebook –AuthorTerryOdell

Twitter - @authorterryo

Join her newsletter – terryodell.com/newsletter

Booklover's Bench, where readers are winners

Made in the USA
Charleston, SC
15 September 2016